Mona's Secret Diaries
Book Two

Shadows of the Past: Turning Point

A G ELLIOTT

DEDICATION

This book is dedicated to my aunt Annie Stephens, one of my biggest fans, "I looked forward to Book Two," she had said. Unfortunately, she passed away one month before Book Two was published. I wanted to thank her again for supporting, inspiring, and encourage me on my journey to writing. I enjoyed our talks about the book and its many foods, characters, and drama that unfold. Thank you, Aunt Annie, for believing in me. I will never forget your love, strength, and support. I know you are still supporting me.

To Joan

Thank you for all your support and help. Much respect

Angela A. Elliot

Aug 13 2021

CONTENTS

About the Author

ACKNOWLEDGMENTS

To those who consistently follow their dreams, the journey is the story, keeping doing what you do until someone notices and joins you on your voyage. Live your dreams in beautiful colours.

ONE
The Wishing Well

Matthew Christian St. James, the heir to a wealthy Washington D.C family fortune, was returning home by coach wagon through Fairbanks after a family gathering of the reading of his father's Will.

It had been a beautiful Autumn evening, the final night of Fairbank's Annual Fall Harvest Festival. Hundreds of people gathered to enjoy the late festivities. Chatter was all around; young and old folks moved from one attraction to the next. Vendors, hawkers, and sideshow ringmasters shouted their enticing entertainment.

Beautiful Mabel Johnson joined the festivities, wearing a calf-length, floral three-tiered skirt dress and white ankle-wrap sandals. She cared less about mud on her white sandals at the end of the fair and more about meeting new friends from neighbouring towns.

With money to spend, Mabel was bent on having an enjoyable evening. She relished the music and the brightly lit stalls and booths as she moved in unison with happy folks.

Mabel decided on a Ferris wheel ride. People were queued up in pairs, awaiting their turn to get on board. She felt odd without a partner.

1

In the corner of one eye, she saw a handsome young man standing alongside her; tall, muscular, dark complexion, dark brown eyes, perfectly set teeth, and a broad smile. He was wearing a Felt hat, slightly tilted to one side; well laundered white cotton button-down shirt and dark-gray linen trousers tucked in his laced-up black boots. His eyes fixed on Mabel.

"May I share this ride with you?"

Mabel blushed.

"Sure," she said, thankful to be rescued from sitting alone on the Ferris wheel ride.

Matthew secured Mabel in her seat and sat next to her.

"I'm Matthew St. James," he said, his hand extended; "Nice to meet you."

Mabel hesitated; she had never had a male sat so close to her, except in church. Matthew's citrus cologne, the expensive kind sold in Mr. Beatly's store, was irresistible.

"My name is Mabel Johnson," she said.

The ride began to move.

"The Ferris wheel is my favorite ride, Mabel; I can see far and wide. Fairbanks is beautiful, so different from where I come." Matthew said.

"I love Fairbanks too; it is a beautiful place .... where do you come from?" she was curious "and what makes Fairbanks different?" Mabel probed.

"Washington, D.C, the capital of this great nation, is where I live ... a terrific place but not like Fairbanks. There are many more people, buildings, and cars, in Washington, D.C., yet it is gloomy. New York, where I was born, is even more gloomy." Matthew said.

"Is this your first visit here?" Mabel asked.

"Yes. I am passing through on the couch-wagon, which stops here to let off and pick up folks. I noticed the banners, streamers, and people—you live here?"

"Lived here all my life. Yes, I agree Fairbanks is a beautiful place."

Matthew turned and looked across the distance, "Those two mountain peaks are amazing; to think Fairbanks sits in the middle of all this beauty. You are fortunate to live in this place, Mabel" Matthew was overwhelmed.

Mabel was impressed with Matthew's open admiration of the surroundings. A kindred spirit between her and Matthew was beginning to develop. She shifted in her seat.

"I'm sorry if I am making you uncomfortable," Matthew said.

"I've never been this close to a boy, I mean—a man, before." Mabel was tongue-tied.

"Nothing to worry about with me, Mabel."

Mabel was unsure; after all, Matthew was a stranger in town. She laughed softly to suppress her nervousness. "Matthew, you could teach the men around here about respecting their women's feelings."

Matthew returned the laugh. "Lessons in 'How to Train Your Man Child." would be the topic." They laughed at the idea.

The ride ended.

"Mabel, if I may, I would like to spend more time with you at this fair—what would you like to do next?"

Mabel was forming trust in this stranger of whom she knew nothing.

"I would love to spend the rest of the evening with you, Matthew. Let's just walk, talk and get to know each other," Mabel said.

"As milady wishes," Matthew said.

Matthew extended an elbow; Mabel looped her arm in it, and they were off.

They participated in games, enjoyed more rides, food, cotton candies, candied apple, and fudge. Mabel noticed Matthew's gentle mannerisms.

They talked and enjoyed each other's company until the festival ended.

Matthew brushed a light kiss across Mabel's cheek during a leisurely walk. Her heart skipped several beats. She felt a shiver and her knees wobbled. She hoped Matthew did not notice.

"Goodnight, Ms. Mabel Johnson. I enjoyed your company at the festival," Matthew bowed.

"Good night Mr. Matthew St. James. I enjoyed sharing the festival with you too," Mabel said and followed his lead with a curtsy.

"I can hardly wait for tomorrow to spend more time with you, but I must go now." Matthew wanted to kiss Mabel one more time; he curbed his desire.

"Tomorrow is a few short hours away; I, too, look forward to seeing you," Mabel said.

Matthew headed into town to find an Inn for the night. He was sure sleep would not come.

Matthew extended his stay in Fairbanks.

He and Mabel were together every day for two weeks. Their friendship blossomed during long conversations, with kisses that became progressively passionate.

Matthew was prodded by Mrs. Cooker and Mrs. Nelson, the women who had been in charge of Mabel since her mother's sudden death, to tell them everything about himself.

Mrs. Cooker's son, Ned, who welcomed everyone to the family, looked at Matthew with narrowed eyes during his introduction to the family. Ned questioned Matthew relentlessly though he warmed up to him later. Ned was delighted that Matthew enjoyed his quirky jokes and stories about his adventures within the mountains of Fairbanks and Maple Lane.

Matthew quickly inserted himself into Mabel's family. He helped Ned and the other boys with the gardening and the reconstruction of a broken-down fence. In the process, he soiled his shoes and clothing.

"Matthew, you need to get some work clothing if you be coming around here, young man. This work will damage your good clothing." Mrs. Cooker called out.

Ned brought a change of clothing for Matthew.

"Thank you for making me feel at home in Fairbanks," Matthew said; sweat glistened on his brow.

Matthew's thoughts turned to his father; how he would have been proud to see him sling a sledgehammer. His father believed in hard work, just like Mabel's family.

Matthew would not regret his decision to extend his stay; his mother would understand. "I have found the woman of my dreams." He had said to himself. During a leisurely walk, Matthew told Mabel more about himself.

"I was born on April 10, 1915, to Sabastian and Sabrina St. James. I am my parents' only child. My father was a rich businessman who made his fortune in import, export, oil, and communications. He worked hard and always put family first. My mother stayed home. I studied business, economics, engineering, and history in school, and I graduated at the top of my class. My parents and I travel all over the country and to Europe. They wanted me to take over the family businesses, but my dad died of a heart attack a few months ago. We were devastated. Dad cared deeply about my mother. I loved, respected, and cherished my father," Matthew was visibly sad.

He continued.

"I attended the reading of my father's Will, looked after other family matters, and I was returning home when I observed the Festival in Fairbanks. I stopped, and here I am." An intriguing story in a nutshell.

"I am sorry you lost your father; I know what it's like to lose a parent. I lost my mother when I was five. I never knew my father. It is good that you had twenty-one years with both of your parents, though it still hurts. I was born May 17, 1921, to Monica Michelle Johnson right here in Fairbanks; I have never traveled beyond Fairbanks and

Maple Lane, but I always wondered what lies beyond our mountains" Mona lifted her gaze to the mountains.

"This countryside is beautiful." She stopped abruptly when Matthew excitedly interrupted.

"You have to tell me more about you." He said.

Mabel continued.

"I went to school here, top of my class; my wish is to have a food business and share my family's recipes. For over a hundred years, the recipes have been in my family, passed on by women to their daughters. I took time off from my work to attend the final day of the festival. All I wanted was to have fun for one night. I'm glad I did because here we are."

Mabel's story impressed Matthew.

Mabel felt like she and Matthew were of the same mindset, and it was possible to spend the rest of her life living out all her dreams and goals with someone like him.

Mrs. Cooker invited Matthew to stay for the night.

"Thank you, Ma'am; I would instead return to the Inn."

Each day Matthew showed up first in the morning and fell into the family routine. He was in the kitchen with Mabel, Mrs. Cooker, Jenny, Ned, or outside with Mr. Hedley and the other men hammering, sawing, digging, nailing, plowing, and doing whatever was required.

Matthew had secretly spoken to Mr. Beatly at the general store about purchasing an engagement ring for Mabel. However, he intended to ask for his mother's engagement ring to present to her.

He was planning a life together with Mabel in Fairbanks.

All this time, Mabel had been falling deeper in love with Matthew. She was charmed by the world about which he spoke and the places he and his parents had visited. She especially liked his stories about riding the riverboats across America and Europe, how his father had insisted they had taken as many trips as possible, and how they were treated like royalty everywhere they went. Mabel pictured rides on the riverboats like being on the "River Grand of Life" and where it could take her.

Matthew's time with Mabel during his two-week stop-over in Fairbanks was wonderful. He expressed his love for her in ways she never dreamed, and she reciprocated to his heart's content.

Unbeknownst to anyone, Matthew had asked Mrs. Cooker for Mabel's hand in marriage, and Mrs. Cooker had replied yes with a caveat that he should let no harm come to Mabel.

Mabel was sure that Matthew was her destiny.

Thomas Kimberley, a man with an eye for Mabel, lurked in the dark corners of Fairbanks and observed Matthew and Mabel's movements. He plotted evil actions with accomplices. He waxed envy and jealousy, and his drinking increased.

The night before Matthew's departure to Washington D.C., he said goodbye to Mabel and was returning to his room at the Inn in Maple Lane. He had promised Mabel he would return in one week to marry her. Both were excited about starting their life together.

A woman appeared out of the darkness.

"Excuse me, mister, can you spear some food change."

"Sure," he said, reaching into his jacket pocket. Suddenly, someone landed a skull-crushing blow at the back of his head, and all went dark.

The week that passed seemed like a lifetime to Mabel; she waited for her love to return to her, he did not return. Mabel's disappointment was deep; she could not be consoled.

Soon after, Mabel discovered she was expecting a baby, and nine months later, she welcomed Mona Amanda Johnson—the gift love left behind. Mabel grieved Matthew every day for the rest of her life. Although Mona was satisfied that her mother and father's story was true, the chasm in her heart widened.

Many years later, details surfaced in a letter to the Sheriff of Fairbanks about Matthew's mysterious disappearance.

TWO

Educating the Future with the Past

A cool breeze flowed through, gently lifting the curtains, and spreading the scent of Lilac and Orange in the house. Mona went to the kitchen for a lemonade drink, then to her room, put the money, envelopes on her bed, and brought out a cash box.

First, she organized all the paperwork for Ms. Henderson to do the bookkeeping and accounting, placed receipts in one pile, inventory list, purchases and sales, and a breakdown of expenses and supplies; she organized everything atop each other.

Then she examined the envelope containing Mr. Calvin Kimberley's money; reread it: *For Ms. Mona Johnson's Future.* She opened and counted the money, put it back in the envelope, into her cash box, and then back in the closet.

Mona was puzzled by the extravagant monetary gift from Mr. Kimberley but remembered her mama saying, "*Never kick a gift horse in the mouth,*" which meant, accept a gift gracefully.

Mona smiled when she remembered the sayings of Mrs. Cooker, Mrs. Nelson, and Mrs. Baker; she was glad for their insights.

Mrs. Cooker and Mrs. Nelson are of the same generation as Mrs. Baker. They spoke in riddles. If someone said, "Good morning, Mrs. Nelson, how are you today?"

She would answer, "I'm fine, thanks, Chile," or "My knees ache; I know it's gone rain." Those phrases would turn into an extreme conversation with her.

Unlike Mrs. Nelson, Mrs. Baker quoted bible passages: *the meek shall inherit the earth,* and *by the sweat of your brow, you will eat bread.*

Mona put on her favorite forest green dress dotted with tiny white flowers and white lace at the collar, sleeves, and hem. Her Mama had bought that dress just weeks before she died, and she had worn it only once. She tied forest green ribbons in her hair, looked at her image in the mirror, and smiled with satisfaction.

She placed crates with her painting supplies on the bed, set aside her workbooks, put two small canvases on her bed, and cataloged the contents in the containers, just as her mama taught her. Mona looked at the pile and marveled that Mr. and Mrs. Beatly had faith in her ability to be a great painter one day. She would not disappoint the Beatlys. She would become the famous painter they want her to be. First, she would start studying her books.

She liked that Mr. Beatly bought every color paint available on the market; a large bottle of cleaner for the brushes and cloth to clean them. He had also purchased a sizeable roll-up canvas paintbrush carrier.

Mr. Beatly had thought of everything Mona needed to be a painter. She was overwhelmed; she began to cry. She wished her mama were by her side to see how well she was doing.

There was a knock; the door slowly opened; Jake poked his head in and said, "Mona, are you alright?" he was concerned because he heard Mona whimpering, and he knew Mona rarely cried.

Mona straightened up, wiped her tears, and said, "I'm fine, Jake. Does Aunt Kelly or Mrs. Cooker need me?" her voice still strained from the crying spell. Jake never wanted to see Mona cry.

"Just checking to see if you were still coming to play; Uncle Ned is gone back to town—I like your pretty dress," he said, coming closer to look at the painting stuff.

"Mr. Beatly gave me all of this to help get my painting off the ground," Mona said, with renewed pride pointing to all her painting stuff.

Jake moved closer to look at everything, "Wow, Mona, this is such a fantastic gift. Can I paint with you sometimes, please? Do the paints and brushes fit in the case?" He was excited.

Mona was happy to have something she could share; "Come, look at everything, Jake," she said.

She opened the case and unrolled the paintbrushes and paints; Jake looked at the colors and paintbrushes the same way he looked at his meal, with love and affection.

"I will ask Ms. Henderson to let me use these instruction books as part of my reading requirement so I can learn faster. Mr. Beatly said he wants to be my Patron of the Arts, and he will Sponsor me." She said. Jake looked in the painting case and shook his head.

"Mona, these are the best. Mr. and Mrs. Beatly must care about you," he said, sounding like an expert in the field.

Mona was impressed. She never suspected he knew painting.

"Jake, how come you know so much about painting?"

"Before we came here, our neighbor Mr. Crump used to sit in his backyard and paint. He taught me about painting; he gave me books and supplies of my own. When we ran away from dad, I forgot about them. He was kind to my family and me. Mr. Crump had a carrying case like yours...." Jake paused; the memory of his past was painful.

Mona sensed his pain, "Teach me what you learned from Mr. Crump and use my supplies to paint your work." Mona felt good about sharing her stuff with Jake.

"Thanks, Mona, I don't know much, but I'll do my best," he said. "We will learn together," she said.

Jake realized that learning alongside Mona would fulfill his dream of becoming a painter.

Ned had been considering an approach to ask Jenny for her hand in marriage. George and Sarah had already made their wedding plans; Mona is happy about all of it.

Jenny thought about Ned for what seemed like the hundredth time, and each time she shivered. She concluded that this must be what Mabel meant when she told her about the thrills of love before she died.

She puttered around the kitchen with Ned in her thoughts as she made sure everything was ready for the late lunch and dinner crowd.

Mr. Hedley had built a small nook with a daybed for needed rest during the day. Jenny had been napping on the daybed; a slow kiss on the lips awakened her. Ned had come for a nap; his temperature began to rise; he embraced Jenny, she sighed. The wait had become unbearable. Ned walked away; it was not yet time.

.

THREE

Borrowed, Blue and Black

Ned startled poor Mr. Beatly when he burst into his store.

"Sorry I frightened you, Mr. Beatly; I'm here to purchase an engagement ring for my future wife," he was smiling.

"So, you finally decide to ask beautiful Jenny to marry you," Mr. Beatly said, pulling out his book of rings.

"These here are about fifty dollars, these about one hundred, these about two hundred, and these are about three hundred, and I have more expensive ones in another book," Mr. Beatly said.

"I'll like this one, Mr. Beatly; purple is Jenny's favorite color; it's beautiful."

"You have sharp eyes, Ned; this is an Amethyst, it is a beautiful stone; the tiny diamonds around it make it unique. It is priced at three hundred dollars, but for you, it is one hundred and fifty dollars; the discount is our wedding gift for you and Ms. Jenny. Ned, I also have a beautiful necklace, bracelet, and earring set that matches the ring; would you like to see the set?"

Ned looked at the set. "How much, Mr. Beatly?" Ned asked - excitedly.

"Four hundred and fifty dollars; I will let you have it for three."

"That's a deal, Mr. Beatly; I'll take everything,"

12

Mr. Beatly gestured. "Ned, Mrs. Beatly, and I planned to have our thirtieth wedding anniversary dinner at Mr. Spillman's Bar. Would you ask your mama to make our anniversary cake and prepare a special dinner for Mrs. Beatly, our son, and me? Your mama's roast beef, Cornish hens, and mashed potatoes are delicious. How much will that cost?"

"No charge, Mr. Beatly; it will be our gift to you and Mrs. Beatly." Ned exited Mr. Beatly's shop with a skip in his step.

Mr. Beatly opened his ring book and ordered a ring that typifies thirty years of marriage to his wonderful wife.

Ned listened to his heart. He would ask Jenny to marry him.

The following weeks kept everyone busy with weddings, a wedding anniversary, and the new restaurant and bakery chaos. Mona loved every moment of the excitement.

Ned was rounding the corner on his way to the Bar when he saw Calvin Kimberley rushing into the hospital where his son Thomas Kimberley lay dying.

Calvin quietly stepped into the hospital room, not wanting to talk with anyone except his son. He sat next to him, hand in hand. He realized this was the most time he had spent with his son over a lifetime, and he felt ashamed. It seemed like Calvin's whole life had passed by while he had lived in a haze at the bottom of the bottle.

"I'm sorry, Thomas, I'm so sorry," he said over, over again in his smallest voice. He began to pray aloud.

Calvin had been praying a lot. He could not help but pray because prayer was the only thing that soothed his savaged soul. He recognized his mess; he had destroyed many people's lives, including his own, and prayers helped him talk out his pain, hurt, sorrow, and shame without compromising or burdening anyone.

He had been searching for forgiveness and redemption, not salvation. He did not believe he could be saved or should be. He wanted to make amends for the things he could change and forgive himself for the things he could not change.

Calvin looked at Thomas; he had become paler; his chest had stopped moving. He panicked and screamed, "Dr. Taylor, Thomas stopped breathing." Nurse Terry and Dr. Taylor raced into the room.

Dr. Taylor began chest compressions and mouth to mouth. Nurse Terry reached for the oxygen mask. They furiously worked on Thomas, but after twenty minutes, they stopped. Dr. Taylor shook his head. Nurse Terry shed a tear.

"I'm sorry, Calvin, he's gone; we tried everything we could." Dr. Taylor said. Calvin Kimberley stood motionless.

"Can I stay with him a while, Dr. Taylor" was all Calvin Kimberley could muster as he looked down at his son, who, a moment earlier, had been breathing, though labored.

"Calvin, you can stay as long as you wish," Dr. Taylor said.

Calvin's thoughts flashed back to Thomas as a baby, a two-year-old, a ten-year-old, a fifteen-year-old, a twenty-one-year-old, and the man he became. Thomas Kimberley was born into family chaos and had returned to his maker; in the presence of his dysfunctional father, who never knew his son or even cared about him. Calvin sobbed, knowing he had abandoned his son. He could cry no more; he kissed his son, squeezed his hand, and left his bedside.

Mrs. Cooker woke up, startled. She thought she had heard someone calling her name; she looked around the room, then at the door, confident that someone had been calling her. But she was awakened from a terrible dream in which she was running, and someone was calling out to her though she did not know whom. She suspected the buried secrets rose from the grave to haunt her. Her ghosts had been chasing and calling after her in her dream. The dread she felt told her that things were coming to a head.

She saw her image in the mirror in her room; she looked old. She sighed. It was time to come to terms with her demons.

FOUR

The Cleansing Joy of Tears and Confession

Ned came through the back door in a rush.

"Mama, mama Thomas died, Thomas died, mama" he had tears in his eyes as everyone looked on, stunned.

"What did you say, Ned? When? Francine asked; she sat down, she started crying too.

"I went to see George at the hospital before I came back here, he told me. He said Mr. Calvin was in bad shape, crying like a baby, over his son Thomas. George said he was anxious about Mr. Calvin because he stayed three hours after Thomas died just talking to him, apologizing, everything. George said it was sad to listen. Mr. Calvin accepted George's condolences, said it was nice knowing him, but he wasn't all there when he said it," Ned was hysterical; he was pacing as he spoke.

"Okay, Ned, let's go see Calvin Kimberley right now; make sure he's okay; we'll pick up Mrs. Baker on the way." Mrs. Cooker grabbed her purse.

"Mrs. Cooker, do you want me to help today?" Mona asked.

"No, Mona, stay and finish your lessons.

Ned helped his mama and Kelly onto the wagon.

15

Ned lashed the horses to quicken their pace; he was concerned about Calvin just as much as his mama.

Ned saw Thomas and his father Calvin through the lens of his Mama—as good souls. He remembered a happy childhood; when Calvin and Thomas were frequent visitors to his house, but something terrible must have happened along the way to cause the two men to change. He never enquired from his mama; he realized that she carried many people's burdens and secrets. He was worried for her.

He understood the enormous responsibility his mama carried around with her every day of other people's sins and secrets, and he marveled at her strength.

Mrs. Cooker was in deep thought that brought her to tears. Tears for Thomas, Mabel, Calvin, and Monica, Mona, and especially herself; she felt responsible for all that happened because of the secrets she kept for them.

She looked over at her son; he never asked too many questions. She recognized his thoughtful face; he might have questions she did not want to answer. Another time, perhaps. Mrs. Cooker's thoughts turned to Mona; what would Mona wish to know. Mrs. Cooker tried to silence her mind.

Kelly sat in the back of the wagon. She thought there must be a story behind the death of Mabel that involved Thomas Kimberley. Mrs. Cooker's body language, her constant hesitation, and avoidance were signs that there are more questions than answers.

Would the true story about Thomas Kimberley surface? Was Mrs. Cooker ready to tell all? Was Mona the key to the mystery? Kelly had pondered these questions over the years; she was convinced the linchpin was yet to be exposed. But her mama told her to "let sleeping dogs lie; let them rest in peace," so she let go of her thoughts about the Kimberleys.

Ned abruptly stopped in front of Mrs. Baker's house.

Mrs. Baker was sitting on her porch, waiting for them to arrive.

Ned helped her into the front of the wagon.

"Ma Baker, I am going to see Calvin; I was hoping to see Thomas before he died. George told Ned, Thomas is gone," Mrs. Cooker lamented.

"Francine, please give Calvin my condolence; Thomas was kind to me before all that drinking took over his life. That family has had some troubles over these years; the fathers' sins still haunt these boys' lives, very sad".

"Beverly, now is the time to pray for that man; I feel like I've spent all of the past twenty years praying for him; he's in God's hand now…." Mrs. Cooker stopped herself from saying more.

"I understand, Francine; it must be a great burden to carry" Mrs. Baker and Mrs. Cooker became silent.

Ned whipped the horses one more time; he was mindful that it was not the time to start falling apart.

He looked at his mother, saw how troubled she was; he worried about her general health, especially now that she was about to have love in her life again.

He had heard from others about Calvin's father, Thomas's grandfather; the man did not leave lasting feelings during his encounters with townspeople. Because of him, the entire Kimberley family was swept with the same brush. Ned had experienced the kindness and generosity shown to him by Calvin and his son Thomas over the years. He believed Calvin and Thomas were better men because his mother helped to make them better. The reason that these two Kimberley men showed up on his mother's doorsteps many years ago was yet to unfold.

Ned was not sure what to expect when they arrive at Calvin Kimberley's house.

Calvin sat in the darkened living room with twenty boxes of files that contained the sorted history of his and his family's life; he knew it was messy. They weighed heavily on him, but the past haunting memories engulfed his mind, leaving little room for any other thought. He took another long drink from the newly opened rum bottle; he had much to catch up on; he had only one drink.

It was early evening; he was expecting Mrs. Cooker.

He opened all the windows to let out ghosts and let in life and fresh air. A warm breeze warded off the chill that hung in the room.

His hope now lay in the last of his heirs. Unbeknownst to her, Mona Johnson was the last of the Kimberley line. His heart skipped a beat when he remembered the compassionate hug, she had given him; he was grateful for the compliment. Mona was not afraid of him like the other children in town; he did not fault them.

He contemplated whether he should sell his mining business and other assets; Mona would be financially secure for the rest of her life. His assets were millions at the last assessment. He knew money could not change the past or bring Mona's mother and grandmother back, but he would sure as hell try and make Mona's future comfortable. He took another swig from the bottle; he did not want to be too drunk when Mrs. Cooker came.

The truth was that Mrs. Cooker could always see through his facades over the years and dug the fact out of him with not much effort. She was like a pin to a bubble; the bubble always lost, no matter how big it became.

Francine Cooker was the only woman, other than Calvin's mother, his wife, and Mrs. Chambers, who looked out for him since he came into the world via Francine's hands; All these women had a hand in his outcome after his mama had died.

Calvin sighed and picked up the bucket and mop.

He finished mopping the floor. He had learned domestic skills, limited as they were when he visited Mrs. Cooker's house.

Calvin remembered, Mrs. Cooker used to say boys and girls should do the same chores before playtime, and she taught everyone the same necessary survival skills of washing, cooking, and cleaning.

Later, when he became an adult with his son Thomas, they visited Mrs. Cooker's home, where Thomas found acceptance among the other children.

Calvin smiled when he remembered when his son Thomas would disappear and ended up at Mrs. Cooker's house. His grandfather, old Mr. Kimberley, never liked the idea and raged against Calvin to allow Thomas to hang out at Mrs. Cooker's home where Mabel Johnson lived.

Thomas would say, "I don't understand why I can't go to Mrs. Cooker's; all the children do, you can't make me stop," which always earned him a smack from his grandfather.

Mortimer Kimberley would spitefully say, "Like father like son," and walked away, fuming.

Calvin laughed when he remembered that Thomas came home with blueberry or raspberry or strawberry stains on his mouth and clothing after visiting Mrs. Cooker.

"I love going to Mrs. Cooker's," Thomas would say and ignore his grandfather's warnings about the Johnson women, whom he despised, especially Mabel.

Calvin often remarked to Thomas, "I loved going to Mrs. Cooker's when I was a child; your grandpa is just an angry, bitter man, an old goat."

They might have been happy men if there were not so many secrets that kept the facts about their intertwined lives buried for so long. Calvin was responsible for the lies and deception that resulted after Mabel's birth and Monica's death, all to the detriment of Mabel and Thomas; it was as if destiny replayed the same cruel joke on their family again; he felt sick.

He looked over at his father's gun case, a beautiful piece of woodwork carved into dragons, warlocks, ghouls, and demons. He was in love with the craftsmanship of his father's gun case. He admired it more than the antique, modern guns displayed inside of it. He surveyed the guns to decide which one he would use on himself when the time came. It was appropriate to use one of his father's cherished guns. When he was a child, he feared those guns, mainly when his father was drunk and sat with one in his lap, looking mean, angry, hateful.

Calvin heard a wagon in the distance and knew Mrs. Cooker was approaching. He concluded she heard about Thomas's death. He smiled at Mrs. Cooker's remarkable capacity to love and forgive him; he felt he did not deserve her kindness but was grateful for it.
He had wealth, yet all that he had did not insulate him from loneliness.

He went to the door; opened it wide; there was nothing he would hide from Mrs. Cooker; she probably knew more of his family's secrets than are in the files anyway. It was time for him to release her from his family's burdens, dirty deeds, deals, and all the secrets she has kept; he finally saw how unfair it was to her. He could tell it was wearing on her. The last time he saw her at Spillman's, he was sure the money given to Mona troubled her; now that Thomas was gone, she was probably even more terrified of what he would do.

Calvin did not want to hurt her or Mona; he just wanted to be able to do the right thing finally. He had tried to cleanse his soul over the past two weeks, mulling over all his sins, shames, secrets, demons. Cried tears of pain and joy; he had pleaded guilty.

The wagon came into view as it started up the road to the main house; he was happy to see them; he waited.

Mrs. Cooker saw Calvin waiting at the front of his house. She noticed how he braced himself against the door, and even at a distance, she could tell he had been drinking; who could blame him this time. She faulted herself for many of the things that had happened to the people she loved, including Calvin and Thomas; she had hoped they would be respected.

Ned pulled up in front of Calvin Kimberley's house and helped his mama down; they greeted Calvin at the door.

"Mr. Kimberley, I am sorry to hear about Thomas," Ned said; then he turned to his mama, "I will come back for you later."

Mrs. Cooker entered the house; Calvin closed the door behind her and invited her into the living room. She looked around, thankful that he had taken the time to clean up before her visit; she inhaled the fresh scent of pine. She noticed the boxes of files and said, "Calvin, are you packing," she sat on the closest sofa.

"Just some paperwork I had to retrieve from ex-lawyer Michael McIntyre. I fired him. I reported him to Sheriff and asked him to start an investigation regarding his theft from my estate. He is on the run with Leila Landers. The man stole one hundred thousand dollars from my family's estate and the townspeople. I want every penny back; every penny or both should go to jail."

Calvin sat opposite Mrs. Cooker.

"Would you like lemonade or something else to drink?"

"Michael and Leila stole from you; I can't believe it," Mrs. Cooker said, settling her rump in the sofa.

"I thought I could trust him with my family's money, and he thought I wouldn't discover the theft because I was always drunk and never really cared about money."

"I will have Lemonade, thank you, Calvin," Mr. Cooker said, staring at the boxes. She knew the contents told terrible stories of Calvin's family's dark secrets. She signed.

In her gut, she knew there must be several mentions of her late mama in them. Calvin's father and grandfather had called upon her and her mama to keep some deep dark secrets. Especially secrets involving the women they injured and the children they fathered.

It began with Grandfather Milton (the devil) and his son Mortimer. She did not want to read the filth within the pages of the contents in those boxes; she hoped Calvin would burn them.

"I'm sorry about Thomas; life is fragile, isn't it, Calvin? I know that you do not care about my option, but you should burn those boxes with the contents. You do not need to see any of what is on these pages. You need to leave the past in the past. The past of you and your family is painful. Why punish yourself anymore."

She took a sip of lemonade and shook her head up and down.

"Very nice," she said, recognizing the smooth taste, the same recipe as she had taught Calvin when he was a child.

Calvin smiled.

"Thank you, Mrs. Cooker, for taking care of Thomas and me; without you, our life would have been devoid of joy, love, affection, and kindness. I remember when Thomas came home with pie stains on his face and clothing and how Dad would fume. I never forbade Thomas to visit you; maybe I should have; because he grew close to Mabel."

Calvin moved towards the boxes. He lifted one lid.

"My family's whole life history lay within these boxes; over fifty years of records, carefully maintained by the McIntyre family under the watchful eye of my good friend the lawyer, Michael McIntyre. He held the secret about what happened with Samantha, and me, how she blackmailed me regarding the truth about Mertel's birth, and my punishment was a lifetime of payments to him, which I did not approve. Michael smiled with me every time he saw me, generously indulged my drinking, and supported my recklessness with new ways to avoid any responsibilities. However, I still cannot blame him, Francine. I had my hands in everything, too," he said, looking into the box he had opened.

"Calvin, we all have a price to pay for every decision made in life, whether we start out thinking we are doing a good or we know we are doing a bad. Sometimes a good thing becomes a bad thing; life is like that. I have thought about some decisions I made fifty, twenty, ten, five, two years, a month ago, a week, or a day ago. I have second-guessed you and Thomas for more than thirty years. I feel at fault, but

I cannot explain why; I know you understand what I'm saying; Princess, Monica, Mabel, and now Mona, you, your son Thomas, and your dad are the big secret," Francine said, becoming emotional.

"Francine, none of this is your fault—none of it. You were trying to protect us from the ugly truth. The truth is in all these boxes. They speak for themselves; I am sure I have a few boxes dedicated to just me, Calvin James Kimberley. I am responsible for Thomas, Mabel, and Monica; I allowed Mertel and Sam to be in Mabel's life far too long until Mabel became unhappy. I should have stood up, a long time ago. God! I hated my father, Calvin said, and started to cry like a small, wounded child.

Mrs. Cooker wrapped Calvin in her arms; she cried with him because she also needed to purge herself of some of the guilt and pain she also felt. Calvin wiped his tears, blew his nose.

"Calvin, it's time to let go of all that pain, forgive yourself and others, even Michael. I must do the same, or I would go mad. I could be walking on the sidewalks of this town, naked and crazy like old Mr. Finlay, poor soul. Nothing in those boxes will change anything that happened; they only bring more pain." Mrs. Cooker said.

"Francine, I wanted to correct some of the mistakes I made—do the right thing—I updated my Will. Mona changed my life; she touched my soul without knowing it. I wanted to live again, for myself, for Thomas, and Mona. The money I gave her is just the beginning; you and Mona are beneficiaries of my estate now that Thomas is gone. He leaned back on the sofa; "in the end, Mona owns everything."

He looked exhausted.

"You did that for me? Mrs. Cooker was stunned.

"Yes, Francine, you and Mona are the sole beneficiaries of the Kimberley estate. Little Mona's assets are about ten million dollars. You will have a million dollars to your name," he said casually.

"This is unbelievable," she said, reaching for another mouthful of lemonade to relieve her parched throat.

"It is signed and sealed. You have done so much for me, my son Thomas, Monica, Mabel, Mona, my mom, and even my dad. I would never forget your kindness. I remember how you stood up to my father when he battered my mother; how she was happy when you came to visit; she trusted you, so did my dad though he would not admit it; my dad knew you would make everything okay again.

My mother said you would take care of me, and she made me promise to take care of you in your later years. I have kept my promise to my momma; thank you for loving and taking care of me. Without you, Francine, I would be alone, probably taken my life". Calvin looked at the gun case to emphasize his point.

Francine wiped away tears from her eyes—again.

"Thank you, Calvin, for considering Mona; I will shield her from the cruel truth of her birthright, for as she matures, she will have questions about her inheritances."

"I hope she would forgive me; I love her; always have."

Calvin's father had become abusive to his mother even when he was still unborn. She protected Calvin with her life and nearly killed his father with a kitchen knife during a brutal beating.

The records would show that when Dr. Morgan came on the scene to attend to Calvin's father's wounds, Calvin's mama had a swollen eye, still holding the bloody knife and screaming. And Mrs. Cooker assisted while Dr. Morgan delivered Calvin during the chaos.

"Calvin, you came out kicking, screaming, and making a big ole fuss." Mrs. Cooker laughed. "The next day, when your father saw you, he cried and begged forgiveness from your mother, and she forgave him. Your father tried to be a better man after that night; he grew to love your mother—she was a good woman, but when you were four, she suddenly passed away, then he became a full-time drunk."

Mrs. Cooker reached for her glass of lemonade and finished it.

"On your mother's deathbed, I promised her I would look out for you, and that's what I've done. Your mama loved you, Calvin". She walked to the window and looked out.

"Your father was a good man—in his youth; then your grandfather slowly changed him into someone else; I watched the whole thing."

"Mrs. Cooker, I don't remember much, though, as a child, I often saw my father holding my mother's photograph and crying. He never told me why. Calvin wiped a tear.

Then he said, "Francine, I'm sure none of that is in these boxes. Should I read more of what is in these files? I want to know, then again; I do not. I know that a lot of ugly things are in there; more than fifty years of family secrets."

"There is much that is not in these boxes, Calvin, but what's in those boxes should be burned because I'm sure that snake oil of a salesman lawyer Michael McIntyre Sr., was a vile man who would have added more dirt to those files to have something extra over your family. I knew that Mertel was not your child. Her mother swore me to secrecy at Mertel's birth. She again swore me to secrecy on her deathbed; so did Michael McIntyre Sr. Mortimer did not want his precious son to be the center of that whole nasty affair with Samantha. When she accused you, Michael Sr. quickly came up with a plan to silence her with a payment package. Calvin, I am so sorry that I never said anything; living with everyone's secrets always puts you in a conflict with the dead and the dying. It was painful to watch how Mertel manipulated everyone, including you, Thomas, and Mabel. I should have said something." she signed heavily.

"Calvin, give me some of what you were drinking when I arrived earlier and dilute it with lemonade," she said, giving him her classic Mrs. Cooker smile.

Calvin smiled and poured him and her a fresh drink.

She toasted, "To life, new beginnings and forgiveness," they clicked glasses and drank.

Calvin Kimberley looked closer at Mrs. Cooker; he observed how much she had aged. She had been the mother he knew; she had guided him, encouraged, and supported him, especially during the worst of times; he was privileged to have had her in his life. Then he noticed her ring finger.

"Francine, are you getting married?"

"Yes, Herman Headley proposed to me. The man is clearly out of his mind," Francine chuckled.

"Out of his mind in love, I would say. That is beautiful, Francine—he will be Mr. Cooker; number four, Calvin said, taking another drink.

"It's all happened quickly; the wedding is in two weeks; Your grandchild, Mona, is helping with the wedding arrangement," Francine said, laughing. "Mona is very loving and compassionate, yet she stands up for herself when necessary; she is her mama's child," Mrs. Cooker concluded.

Francine Cooker lamented the secrets she kept about deaths and destruction in the Kimberley family, beginning with Mona's great-grandmother, Princess Johnson, her mother's grandmother. She was surprised Calvin knew about Mona's great-grandmother's story.

Mrs. Cooker choked up about Thomas and Mabel and the circumstances of Mertel's mother, Samantha. She begged Calvin to forgive her for not telling him Monica was his sister and about Mertel's mother.

"I've sinned; if I had known Monica was my sister, I would have still done what I did; I could not help myself. Every man loved her, even Spillman and Gilmore." Calvin confessed.

"I am happy. Now Mona is in excellent hands—your hands," he continued. He poured himself another drink.

"Calvin, all things come to an end," Mrs. Cooker said.

FIVE

All Things Come to an End Good and Bad

Mertel walked through the house with a bit of trepidation at the possibility of vacating it someday. She and Sam had taken up residence since her sister Mabel died. She believed the townspeople had forgotten her wicked deeds, so she went about her business quietly.

Pastor Michael Amberton crossed her mind; he had touched her innocence. Bitter feelings welled up. After his wife died, he moved with his son to a new town, leaving his sorted history behind. Mertel wondered if he was still preaching the good ole gospel or had abandoned the cloth that he had so hypocritically worn with pride. She did not care one way or another; she wanted his wall of lies to come crumbling down on his head; she would be satisfied to see him publicly shamed and humiliated.

Mertel remembered how Thomas Kimberley had been whining and complaining to her about Matthew St. James's bold attempt to steal Mabel's heart. So, she plotted to destroy Mabel and Thomas; he had forbidden her, and if she could not have Thomas, no woman would, especially not Mabel.

Thomas had said he wanted Matthew gone for good, although he never said he wanted him dead. Mertel was only interested in taking away everything that made Mabel happy. She planned to befriend

Mabel as a beloved sister, and she and Sam would find a way to be rid of her and Mona. She would blame Sam for everything.

Sam was lying in bed. He was likely pretending to be asleep to avoid any contact with her. She would walk into Fairbanks to get food.

Mertel stepped out into the sunshine. It felt good against her skin. Her thoughts were on Mabel's only love and Mona's father, Matthew St. James, whom she had lured to his death under the guise of needing help. The poor fool was a gentleman; he had no idea what was coming when Sam clobbered him over the head, stole his money, and ran away.

When Mertel reached Spillman's Bar, she placed an order for a whiskey and a meal of roast beef, fried chicken, and mashed potatoes. She was happy not to share the meal with Sam.

She ate her meal slowly, deliberately enjoying every bite; she wanted it to last if possible. She was planning Sam's downfall.

Sam rolled over, stretched out, and opened his eyes; he had heard when Mertel left the house. He knew that she would have a meal at Mr. Spillman's, and she had no plans to bring him food.

Sam realized their time together was coming to an end; he knew about the wicked things Mertel had done, and he would expose her secrets to save himself. He wanted to get out of the relationship before she had a chance to blame him for more of her cunning plots. He was not sure when he got so deep into her plotting and planning. And he never signed up for murder, yet he had committed one for her. He knew she would make him go to prison. He had to save himself.

Sam first became involved in Mertel's lies and schemes when she convinced him to help her go after Calvin Kimberley, supposedly Mertel's father, the richest man in town.

It should not have lasted as long as it did; he hoped she would have been able to ply some good money out of her scheme and be done. But, days passed, and Mertel's lies and deceptions continued, and Sam became wrapped up in all of it.

Everything was fine until the murder of Matthew St. James, Mona's father; Sam still does not know why Matthew had to die, but what Mertel wanted Mertel got, back in those days, and he had grown to love her. Now, he was ready to escape with his life or what remained of it; he was worth nothing to Mertel; he was disposable, like everything else to her.

Sam thought about Mabel; she was a wonderful woman; she would have made a great, loving wife. He had quietly fallen in love with her over those years, just observing her from a safe distance, not to bring her discomfort; he wanted to help her in her business, but Mertel had insisted against it.

He pulled out a small suitcase, retrieved his dirty clothing, which had been on the floor, and packed. He reached into his secret hiding place for his stash of money and took all the cash Mertel had stashed away for herself, not caring that he was leaving her penniless. He had lost interest in Mertel Fletcher; her fall was coming, and he did not want to be anywhere in her vicinity when it happened. He needed to start running.

Sadness welled up inside Sam when he remembered the familiar smell of food coming out of the small kitchen and the chatter and laughter from Mabel, Mrs. Cooker, Jenny, Ned, and little Mona.

He remembered fondly a family filled with love, joy, happiness, and caring for each other, which was missing from his home when he grew up. He had longed for the love a real family brought to one's life; he wanted that.

To protect himself from Mertel's lies and accusations, Sam wrote down everything he knew Mertel had done, including her sworn promise to make him rich beyond his wildest dreams from Calvin Kimberley's fortune. He finished the letter, with the words **Sheriff Gilmore** in large print written at the top. He tucked the letter neatly into his pocket. Sam looked around the home for the last time; he felt free as he locked the door behind him, a weight removed. He walked out into the sunshine and started on his way, carefully avoided Spillman's Bar, where Mertel was eating. He slipped the letter under Mr. Hedley's door as he passed by; he knew it was sure to get to the Sheriff. He would disappear just as he had entered Mertel's life.

Meanwhile, at Spillman's Bar, Mertel was in deep thought. She felt justified in her destruction of five people's lives—Calvin, whom she hated, Mabel, whom she was jealous of, Thomas whom she loved but could not have, Matthew, whom she never met but, because he loved Mabel, he had to die, and little Mona, who humiliated her. She smiled because she was still not finished with them, especially Francine Cooker, the old windbag who knew too much for her good with her self-righteous looks of condemnation; she would find a way to hurt her. Mertel never thought for a moment that she should be digging a grave for herself while she plotted to bury others. Sam, the only person that could hurt her, lay in bed waiting for her return; he had too much to lose to even think about destroying her; Sam loved his freedom, and she would not let him go free.

Mertel had heard whisperings about a falling out with Calvin Kimberley and his lawyer Michael McIntyre who was on the run for theft, with his secretary Leila; the news had just broken.

She heard Thomas Kimberley died; she smiled.

Mertel knew about her biological connection with Michel McIntyre, whom she had decided to embrace. Even if it were out of guilt, he would take care of her to reclaim what Calvin and her mom had stolen—Mertel, his biological child. Now he was on the run thanks to Calvin; if nothing else, she knew that they shared one thing; their hate for the Kimberley's and their desire to destroy them all. She would find him; they had much to catch up on, father and daughter.

She finished her drink, ordered more sandwiches and pot pies for later, and left the Bar for Mr. Beatly's store. She would purchase a mixture to poison Sam slowly and be rid of him; Sam's usefulness had come to an end. He would suddenly turn up dead with a confession note in his pocket; she had been planning it for many months when she realized that he was in love with Mabel. She could tell when she caught him watching her with longing eyes. Damn you, Mabel Johnson, she screamed in her head; you have taken every man's love I wanted, including Sam's. She was seething mad.

Mertel entered Mr. Beatly's shop to purchase rat poison; he seemed surprised that Mabel's home had been infested with rats when none had ever been there in all the years he had known Mabel. He sold her anyway, not thinking anything else of it; he just wanted her to leave his business place because she gave off such bad energy. She paid him, smiled delightfully, mumbling to herself that this should do fine to get rid of both large and small rodents; she walked out satisfied with her purchase. Mr. Beatly watched as she left; he did not believe rats had infested the house in such a short time.

Mertel's heart was racing as she walked home. When she reached the house and opened the door, she immediately knew something was wrong. She went into the bedroom. Sam was gone; his small suitcase and dirty clothing were gone. She wondered what else Sam had taken before he left.

She noticed a note, scribbled in Sam's handwriting on the kitchen table:

Good luck Mertel, I think you should get out of town before the Sheriff gets here, do not try and find me. Sam.

"You bastard," Martel was enraged.

She sat on a chair, too stunned to move; Sam had betrayed her. How could he? She squeezed the rat poison tween her fingers until it dribbled down to her wrist.

SIX

Fighting the Headwinds and Monsters on the Sea of life

Jenny busied herself as the time came closer to the re-opening of dinner service at Spillman's; it was the rebirth of Mabel's dream; she wanted to be sure everything went smoothly.

She was worried about Mr. Calvin Kimberley; his life seemed so sad. She had heard bits and pieces over the years about his family; she felt more secrets were in that family's history and not good ones either. Still, no one was permitted to say anything wrong about Calvin Kimberley around Mrs. Cooker or Ned. It was like they forgave him just because of the family he came from; they saw goodness in him that they never forgot. She was sorry to learn that his son Thomas had died but angry to know he had been responsible for Mabel's death—accident or not. There were so many secrets. She left it alone; she realized Mrs. Cooker; had a special love for Calvin and Thomas Kimberley.

Jenny was deep in thoughts when Kelly came to check if everything was in place and ready for the opening at Mr. Spellman's—small baskets of chips and candles were put on tables—to make the Bar more family-friendly and classy.

Mr. Spillman had heard about Thomas Kimberley's death. He was shocked. He said a prayer for the child, the young man, and the grown man. He was familiar with the back story about Thomas and Calvin Kimberley. Thomas was his godson.

Meanwhile, Mertel was packing her clothing in a suitcase; she was getting ready to leave town. She lamented that none of Mabel's clothing was of her size. Her secret stash was nowhere. She looked out the window and saw when Mr. Headley put an envelope in his pocket.

Herman Hedley was a decent man. He noticed an envelope shoved partially under his front door, addressed to Sheriff Gilmore, with *Urgent* written in big letters at the corner. He hurriedly unhitched the wagon and drove off.

Could the letter be from Sam? No point in speculating. She smeared grease on everything in the house and started a fire with the old kitchen stove. She would be long gone, and the house would be in flames. She inhaled the smell of burning wood and smiled.

Mertel would be remembered as the woman who burned her sister Mabel's house to the ground and fled on the same path Sam took.

Mrs. Nelson had been sitting quietly beside the big tree in her backyard. She observed Sam creeping away from Mabel's house; he disappeared into the woods carrying a small suitcase.

She took another swig from the whiskey bottle.

She saw how quickly Mr. Hedley's wagon took off; she had never seen him in such haste.

She saw Mertel tiptoeing off in the same path that Sam took.

She saw smoke. Mabel's home is engulfed in flames. She was grateful there was not a wind to carry the ambers to Mr. Hedley's and her home. She knew Mertel intended to burn everything in sight, including nearby homes.

The flames rose into the evening skies, lighting up the property. The smell of burning wood filled the air. She watched Mabel's old home burn to the ground, too late to save.

Mrs. Nelson said a prayer. The burning down of the house was the beginning of a dreaded story.

Sheriff Gilmore had just sat down to finally have a bite of the sandwich he had bought earlier; he took several bites and washed it down with the stale coffee from the pot in the small kitchen. His office door suddenly flew open.

Mr. Hedley dashed in; he seemed out of breath, a little distressed; his eyes were darting around.

Sheriff Gabriel took his last bite of the sandwich. He sighed deeply. Thomas's sudden death was on his mind.

Sheriff Gabriel greeted Mr. Hedley with a handshake and guided him to the closest chair.

"Mr. Hedley, what an unexpected pleasure to see you, sir. How can I help you?" the Sheriff said, sitting behind his desk. He respected Mr. Hedley, a man who gave generously to everyone without thinking twice.

Mr. Hedley reached into his jacket pocket and pulled out the envelope addressed to Sheriff Gilmore.

"Gabriel, I found this envelope lodged under my door. I don't know who put it there; it is addressed to you," he said.

Gabriel took the envelope and turned it over very carefully. He did not want to disturb fingerprints as instructed in the police information package he had received from the big-city department with more money and equipment than he did. Still, he liked the idea of looking professional. He reached for his letter opener and slowly opened the envelope. He read the letter to the shocking scandalous, appalling, unbelievable, and disturbing end.

Mr. Hedley sat at the edge of his seat—waiting to hear Gabriel speak.

"What is it, Gabriel?" he asked anxiously.

"It's from Sam; it says that he and Mertel had killed Mabel's fiancée, Mona's father; Mertel plotted against Mabel using Thomas, and how Mertel had a role in Thomas, Mabel's death, how she cheated her and planned to kill Mona. It also talked about Calvin being fooled by her. Mertel wanted to take over Mabel's business, steal all her money, and how she had been plotting against Mabel for over ten years because she was in love with Thomas. Still, Thomas never loved her; he just wanted the sex.

Mr. Headley was devastated.

"Let's go pay Mertel a visit, shall we," Sheriff Gilmore said, getting up from his desk, reaching for his hat, and putting the letter in his pocket. They left the office together in his car, leaving Herman's wagon hitched up at the station.

They approached a block of homes and came to a screeching halt in front of Mabel's house, which was in flames.

Sheriff Gilmore watched helplessly as Mabel's house burned. The town's volunteer firefighters arrived barely on time to save the other homes on the block from the fire.

"Nelly, have you seen Sam or Mertel; today?" he asked Mrs. Nelson. "Gabriel, I saw Sam sneaking off with a small suitcase about four hours ago; Mertel followed the same path about an hour or so ago with her suitcase—they went toward the river and woods," she pointed. "They kept looking behind them as if worried someone would see them. I watched them leave; they did not see me. I have been sitting at that table in the back beside that big ole tree all day. They are long gone, Gabriel, running like thieves in the night," Mrs. Nelson reported.

Gabriel looked in the direction Mrs. Nelson pointed; he would send cables to the other police departments in other towns and cities to be on the lookout for Sam and Mertel. He drove Mr. Headley back to the station house to retrieve his wagon.

Ned was shocked about Mertel and Sam's sudden flight into the woods, and Mertel had burned down Mabel's home. He informed Sheriff Gabriel that Mrs. Cooker was visiting with Calvin Kimberley.

A short time after, Sheriff Gabriel stood at Calvin Kimberley's door. "Come in, Gabriel. Did they catch Michael and Leila? He asked, stepping aside for the Sheriff to enter.

"No, Calvin, this is not about them. I am here to see you and Mrs. Cooker about something new that I just found out. And since I am here, I wanted to give you my condolence about Thomas. I'm so sorry," he said, taking off his hat as he entered the house.

Calvin walked Sheriff Gilmore into the living room where Mrs. Cooker had been; he offered Sheriff Gilmore a drink

"Calvin, normally, I would say no to a drink because I'm on duty, but today calls for more than one drink," he said, taking the drink and drinking half the content in one gulp.

"Mr. Hedley brought me this letter a few hours ago. It was shoved under his door by Sam. It is a confession of all he and Mertel had done to hurt, damage, and destroy Mabel, Mona, and your lives. It is quite revealing; please read," he pulled out the letter and gave it to Calvin. He read it out loud so Mrs. Cooker could hear.

Mrs. Cooker grasped when she heard the details about Matthew St. James' murder; she had always thought Matthew would not have disappeared on Mabel. Calvin read the letter in its entirety. Faces twisted in sadness, anger, and despair. Calvin was upset that Thomas had been a part of Mertel's sick games, "That fucking bitch," he said, forgetting momentarily that Mrs. Cooker had been in the room; he apologized.

Calvin returned the letter to Sheriff Gabriel.

"The other thing that occurred today is Mertel set Mabel's house on fire before she fled. She and Sam are on the run, and the police departments in a three hundred miles radius are looking for them. We'll get them, all of them, but I must caution both of you, your lives might be in danger," Gabriel said,

Mertel is an angry, desperate woman; she can commit murder; Sheriff Gilbert said to Calvin and Mrs. Cooker. Mrs. Cooker wiped away tears, "Gabriel, who else has seen this letter? She asked.

"Just us; I told Mr. Hedley some of its content; I wanted to make sure I told both of you first. I told Ned that Mertel and Sam escaped, and Mertel had set the house on fire before leaving; that is all he knows. I thought it would be best to tell your family some or all of this letter's content; I know Mona will be devastated by the news even though she knows nothing of her father. At least we know he did not abandon Mabel or her. The law will catch up with Mertel and her crooked father, Michael," he said with anger in his voice.

Mrs. Cooker was exhausted, burdened with the new revelations; after unburdening herself of so many old secrets, she sighed. Calvin wanted to hunt them down himself.

"What's going to happen next, Gabriel?" Calvin asked.

"Well, I'll write a complete report about the fire; the letter's content is evidence; I've sent out warrants for murder and attempted murder, theft, conspiracy to commit murder, and everything I could find to throw the book at them. I will dispatch two of my deputies to trace the riverbanks tomorrow. All four of them cannot get very far on the main roads without being spotted. I suspect they'll be using every back road or path within a two-hundred-mile radius." Sheriff Gilmore said. "Thank you, Gabriel." Calvin's voice cracked.

Calvin and Mrs. Cooker rode in Sheriff Gabriel's car to Mr. Spillman's Bar for a meal. Afterward, Sheriff Gabriel drove the short distance back to the station house to prepare his reports.

Mrs. Cooker had forgotten it would be a busy night at Mr. Spillman's Bar. Kelly, Jenny, Mrs. Baker, and Ned had been working hard. Mrs. Cooker promptly put on her apron and helped; it was not the right time to update them on what transpired at Calvin's house.

Mission accomplished; Wagon loaded, and everyone ready to leave after a long day at Spellman's Bar.

Mrs. Cooker said goodbye to Calvin and Steven Spillman; they were on the third round of drinks. Mrs. Cooker suspected there would be more rounds. She hugged them both; Steven promised to see Calvin home. She left them to reminisce about their shared past and current pains. It was good for Steven and Calvin; a lot of pain had separated the two good friends; they needed each other. Mrs. Cooker and the others drove off into the night.

Francine Cooker stared out into the darkness; Ned moved the reins to hurry the horses along. It was a gentle, steady ride back to the house; both man and beast were tired from the extra activities of the day. Everyone was tired, rode to the house lost in their thoughts, or dozing off as Jenny always did, but tonight she slept, not dozed.

Mrs. Cooker thought about Sam Cumberland's letter; all the new secrets revealed; she wondered what she should tell, what she should not. It was more secrets she did not want to have to carry around, now that she felt she had cleared out so many today speaking with Calvin. She felt a little cleaner than she had thought for some time; now, she felt dirty all over again with these newfound revelations. She felt like she could not get away from secrets that seemed to chase her down.

Francine's thoughts turned to Calvin; he was drinking the night away with Steven Spillman. They needed to ignite their friendship, to share their woes. Steven was perfect for that; they had shared so much already. Calvin had demons all over him; his family legacy seemed to be his punishment; just being born a Kimberley was a curse.

Francine pondered. What should she tell Mona and the others? Should they even know any of this? Francine felt the darkness creeping into her heart and her life. Francine Cooker was tired of pondering.

SEVEN

Escape into the Darkness

Mertel Fletcher stopped for the third time that evening; she had rested only long enough to eat the first two sandwiches she had taken along from Spillman's Bar that afternoon. Her feet were hurting from the long trek through the bushes along the riverbanks; she tried to stay out of sight of nosy people she might encounter who could give her whereabouts away. Mertel was desperate to put as much distance as she could between herself and the town of Fairbanks. She knew that Sheriff Gilmore had received the letter that the son of a bitch Sam had left under Mr. Hedley's door.

She hoped that the fire she had started at Mabel's old house had reached Mr. Hedley's and Mrs. Nelson's houses; that would make her day. Those two old meddling busybodies would also have to pay for how they had treated her over the years.

She cursed Sam, Thomas, Calvin, and Mabel for the mess she found herself in; it was entirely their fault; she saw herself blameless. If they had just given her what was hers, she would not have had to lower herself to such scheming manipulations. They had so much, she so little; all she wanted was a bit of what they had; was that too much to ask?

Mertel took her foot out of her boots and rubbed them; damn, she cursed; she was not used to walking long distances, but she would not walk on the main road to hitch a ride. She vowed not to be detected as she fled for her life. She would surely end up in jail, not something she could survive.

She did not think she had done anything wrong, maybe the murder of Matthew St. James, but she did not do that; it was Sam who had killed him with information from Thomas.

She put on her boots and started to walk; she had been walking for four hours already and would have to find a place to sleep. She cringed at the thought of having to sleep in less than anything but a soft bed, which she was used to; maybe she should have stopped at her mother's old house for more things before she fled.

Mertel was sure that Calvin Kimberley would give Sheriff Gilmore the location of her mother's house; he would come looking for her there first. Calvin had only visited a few times over the years, but he knew where the house was; she walked on. She stopped for a drink from the river; she missed that old bat Mrs. Cooker's lemonade. She would be having a hot meal if it were not for that stupid drunk Thomas Kimberley who had spoiled every one of her plans by killing Mabel and dying in the process; dumb ass, she thought.

She lamented about her situation. She had lived her entire life her way, and she got what she wanted. She took and gave nothing back; it had worked for her every time; why fix something that was not broken. She had learned how to be heartless, conniving, and cruel. She justified her self-centered existence; only her needs and feelings counted; she was a psychopath.

Mertel thought of her dead mother, Samantha, and wished she could kill her repeatedly until she had killed the memories of her vile existence; she believed Samantha was the root of her greed and selfishness. Mertel felt life cheated her. Samantha was not like Mabel, who cared and loved her daughter, Mona, and put her needs first.

As for her louse of a father, Michael McIntyre, why did he not fight for her, knowing she was his biological daughter, why did he not talk to her; they had seen each other often enough for him to recognize the resemblance; it was plain as day. Martel did not have the Kimberley features. She had dry sandy brown hair, narrow eyes, pencil-thin lips, and a shapeless body. The Johnson women, like Mabel, had it all—full lips, high cheekbones, sparkling brown eyes, long lashes, and beautiful petite bodies with curves.

She delighted in eliminating Mabel's one true love, Matthew, the father of her precious little Mona. She could not remember when she started to hate Mabel; was it from her mother Samantha, her so-called father Calvin, or Thomas; she was not sure, but she knew she hated her.

Mabel was born out of Calvin Kimberley's love for Monica Johnson sorted as it was in the details; she envied her, even if she did not know the truth. She pieced together all the cursing's over the years that her mother had given Calvin when he visited out of guilt.

Mertel pieced together rumors from the townspeople, especially the men whose lips loosened after consuming too much of her free liquor and family history.

She continued her trek through the woods.

Sam reached a small clearing and rested under an old tree that had partially fallen over; he kicked himself for not going into town one more time to get some food before he left, but that would have been too risky. He had to put lots of distance between himself, Fairbanks, and Mertel Fletcher.

He hoped that Mr. Hedley had seen the letter, but you never know with that man; he was busier than most men half his age, unlike the other men in town. He had watched the man over the years, had a great deal of respect for him; he thought he could have learned much from him if things were different. But Mertel had warned him not to get close to anyone; that was a mistake because he missed the opportunity to change his life and be a better man. Mr. Hedley always included him when Mertel was not paying attention; he learned a lot during those infrequent times. Things could have been different.

Sam reflected on the letter he left behind. He knew he could not go back to Fairbanks after his disclosures; except to go to jail. Murder, conspiracy to commit murder, theft, fraud and, lies—he was involved in all of it. He was guilty of being with Mertel when it occurred. He was a willing participant.

Sam had walked steadily for four hours; his stomach was growling loudly, announcing that it was time for a meal. He missed the succulent meals Mabel and Mrs. Cooker made. Three free meals each day made him grateful to Mertel for arranging them.

He reached a farm along the way, stole a chicken, roasted it, and ate it as if his life depended on that meal, and it did because hunger and exhaustion had taken a toll on him.

It was getting dark; there would be no light, except for the light of the half-moon; that would suffice. He intended to walk for at least another three hours or until his feet could carry him no further. That would give him a nine-hour lead-time away from Fairbanks, plenty of time to put enough distance between himself and Mertel if she had escaped before Sheriff Gilmore became aware of what had happened.

Sam believed Mertel might have gone to her mother's old house to plan her next moves comfortably when she discovered he had left; she liked to operate in luxuries. She was like a cat-snake anyway; she always landed on her feet and ever ready to slither away into a dark hole. If she decided to disappear and followed the path he took out of town, she would complain that her feet hurt, she was hungry, and she needed fresh clothing; he was glad he was not traveling with her.

Samuel Cumberland rested his head against a broken tree limb; he laughed hysterically at the absurdity of his situation and all that had transpired over the ten-plus years since meeting Mertel Fletcher.

He remembered when little Mona Johnson showed up to retrieve her mama's things after her death and the pompous looks that Mertel flashed when things were being taken from the house with Sheriff Gilmore and the others helping. Her yelling and screaming were no avail when items were loaded and driven away in Ned's and others' wagons. Mona had graciously left behind two of each utensil, two cups, two saucers, two bedsheets, two chairs— that sent Mertel over the edge. Sweet revenge, Sam thought.

Sam knew he should never have been involved with Mertel; he was equally guilty. He admitted that much in the letter. Sam wished he could take it all back, but it was too late. He burst out laughing until he cried, even though his tears were false.

.

EIGHT

Happiness Within Reach

Oh mama, I almost forgot, today I told Mr. Beatly that we would make a special thirtieth-anniversary dinner at Mr. Spillman's on Tuesday night for them. I told him we would host a private party with dinner and an anniversary cake, and Mr. Spillman would donate the champagne and space. He placed his food request. Is that okay?" Ned said, trying to change the subject to something nice to end the day, just as it had started.

Kelly and Jenny had nodded off in the back of the wagon, leaving Ned, his mama alone, for the rest of the ride home.

Francine Cooker was silent for the briefest of moments before she said, "That will be fine, Ned; we will prepare dinner for the Beatly's wedding anniversary; put it on the schedule.

Ned considered the moment was right to announce to his mother the serious subject of his engagement.

"Mama, with your blessings, I'm going to ask Jenny to marry me; I've picked out a ring at Mr. Beatly's shop."

Francine Cooker was happy for her son and Jenny; she was ready to hop off the wagon and do a jig right in the middle of the dirt road. "Ned, that's wonderful." She said.

Ned reached across the small space between them in the wagon and hugged his mama as tight as he could.

Mona had been looking out the window, waiting.

Jake watched Mona over the pages of the book he was reading.

Jake stirred in his chair. "You gone stare out that window all night until they come, aren't you?" "You want some lemonade?"

"Yes, they're late coming back tonight; yes, I would like some lemonade too, thank you," Mona said.

Mona turned back to the window; she saw the faintest hint of the horses and wagon through the darkness coming down the dirt road. Jake returned with lemonade.

"They're finally coming, Jake. Mona and Jake ran out into the night air to greet Mrs. Cooker and the rest.

"Hello, Uncle Ned. Why you so late? Everything okay?" Mona asked while walking over to the horses to hold their rein and pat them. She helped Mrs. Cooker down from the wagon.

Jake walked to the back of the wagon just as Jenny and Kelly were waking up from their nap. Jake unloaded the wagon to the kitchen. Sarah, Mona had helped Mrs. Cooker into a kitchen chair; she was exhausted. "Lord, what a day; I'm so tired," she said.

Jake was not much for showing emotions, but he hugged Mrs. Cooker and said, "Thanks, Mrs. Cooker. Ms. Henderson gave Mona and me lots of free time after we finished all quizzes. We got one painting each done," he looked proud of himself.

All of them sat in the kitchen and discussed the events of the day. Mona looked at Kelly, slumped into the kitchen chair across from Mrs. Cooker; she said, "Kelly, you okay." Kelly nodded and smiled.

"Mona, we are all tired. It was a madhouse at the Bar." Mrs. Cooker chimed in.

"I want to hear everything, Mrs. Cooker," Mona said, excited, though sorry she had not gone with them.

Ned countered by saying, "Okay, little Ms. Mona, we'll tell you everything tomorrow morning. I want mama to get some rest now; we are all tired; I'm sure you and Jake are tired too."

"Night, everyone," Jake said.

"Night," Mona said.

Mrs. Cooker went off to her room.

She poured a healthy glass of the Brandy Calvin had given her for Christmas and relaxed with thoughts about Herman. She looked at the rings on her fingers; she sure could benefit from his guidance, comfort, and strength, especially the comfort part. She laughed at herself, realizing just how much she had missed the comforts of a man's arms around her, the conversations, and someone to confide in and get advice. She had denied the need for such support until Herman's proposal. She needed and wanted Herman. Their friendship was a natural progression. She allowed her mind to think only of Herman and about sharing the rest of her life with him.

She fell asleep into sweet dreams about her and Herman.

Back in the kitchen, Jenny poured a fresh cup of tea for everyone at the table as they recounted the day.

Ned told them about the letter Sam left at Mr. Hedley's door for Sheriff Gilmore. He confirmed Mertel had burnt down Mabel's home; Mrs. Nelson witnessed Sam and Mertel separately fleeing to the woods like someone was chasing them. Thomas Kimberly had died, and mama visited Calvin to offer condolences. Mr. McIntyre stole monies from Calvin's family and the townspeople, and Sheriff Gilmore was hunting for Leila and Mr. McIntyre.

Jenny, Sarah, and Kelly were stunned; they asked several questions; Ned did not have the answers. He said he was in the dark as much as they were. They all agreed Calvin Kimberley was in the middle of the chaos.

"No wonder Mrs. Cooker went to bed; she must be exhausted mentally and physically," Sarah said.

"We'll just have to team up and make sure she does less work." Sarah chimed in.

"Especially since Thomas's funeral reception and Mr. Beatly's thirtieth wedding anniversary dinner will be at Spillman's Bar," Ned added.

Later, when Jenny and Ned quietly recounted the day's events, Jenny inquired about Calvin Kimberley's involvement.

"Well, from what the rumor mongers in town recently told me, Mertel is Calvin's illegitimate daughter with a woman named Samantha that used to live in town; something about Mabel's mother Monica, but mama won't talk about it. So, I try not to listen to any of the rumors; these townspeople would gossip about their mother, you know. Besides, Mona does not need to hear anything negative about her grandmamma," Ned said.

"Ned, unfortunately, those rumors are now affecting our lives, your mama's life; she looked so worried when she found out Mr. Calvin had left all that money for Mona. And the letter to Sheriff Gilmore showing up; something is wrong, I can feel it, and it all revolves around Mona somehow. And what of Mertel and Sam? Are they dangerous? Could they come back and harm us?" Jenny was very scared. Ned hugged her and said, "Jenny, you've got to stop worrying so much; everything you worry about is rumors and speculations."

"I know I shouldn't be so worried."

Ned nodded. "I love you, Jenny Slater."

The following day was business as usual.

The door suddenly opened; Sarah, Kelly, baby Sasha and the rest of the children trailed in. Both women looked exhausted. Mrs. Cooker startled everyone with her sudden appearance at the kitchen door. "How are you, Mrs. Cooker," Sarah asked.

"I am well. How are you feeling, Sarah?"

"I'm fine, Mrs. Cooker.

"Does anyone want tea?" Mrs. Cooker asked.

When everyone said, "No, thank you," she made a single cup, sat across from Mona and Jake, and enjoyed her brew.

The discussion around the table was about Mrs. Cooker's upcoming wedding and the weddings of Sarah and Jenny.

"Okay, folks, we need to get this kitchen cleaned up before Ms. Henderson gets here for your lessons; you all need to get tidied up; get your lesson books. Sarah, you need to rest before you have to go back to the Bar," she said and put her cup in the sink.

The door opened; Ms. Henderson entered.

The children greeted her in unison. "Good afternoon Ms. Henderson."

"You are, on-time Heather, "Mrs. Cooker said.

Congratulations, Francine, I heard the good news about your marriage to Herman."

"Thank you, Heather.

"They'll be getting married in two weeks right here; we are all going to help, Uncle George, too, when he gets out of the hospital," Mona exclaimed.

"Okay, children, that's enough; it's time to get cleaned up; go get your books so I can talk with Ms. Henderson and Mona," Mrs. Cooker said, rising from her seat.

Mona retrieved the paperwork and monies from her cash box. She and Mrs. Cooker discussed the budget, inventory, purchase orders, receipts, profit, and expenses, and she gave an account of all current funds.

Ms. Henderson smiled, "Mona, I am very impressed with your knowledge of the business and how it operates." she said.

"Mama taught me everything about this business, and after she died, I discovered books about keeping records and inventory and ideas for expanding the restaurant and bakery. She had already started the work; we are following through with her written instructions." Mona said.

Mrs. Cooker beamed with pride.

"I heard how you handled Mertel and Sam. That was very brave of you, Mona," Ms. Henderson said.

"I had lots of help and support, besides when I heard her accusing Mrs. Cooker of stealing my mama's money, saying it belonged to her, I was furious."

"We will begin expansion of the restaurant and bakery by investing three thousand five hundred dollars in construction materials, chairs, tables, and all the things we'll need. Our staff will be partners in the business.".

Ms. Henderson looked at Mrs. Cooker, shook her head up and down, and said, "Well, Francine, I am being schooled about the business by a ten-year-old, wow. What a report; very impressive, Ms. Mona Johnson; you are as sharp as your mama; she taught you well. Now, Mona, do you want daily, weekly, monthly reporting?"

"Weekly and monthly reporting," Mona replied.

"Mona, Jenny, and Ned will be running the business full-time with Kelly and Sarah. I will be winding down Heather, and with you in charge of bookkeeping, I am confident everything will be fine. How much would you like to be paid?' We will also give you five percent ownership in the business, Heather," Mrs. Cooker was bullish, surprising even Ms. Henderson.

"That is very kind of you, and Mona; if I take a five percent share of the business, I will not take a salary," Ms. Henderson said, still moved by their generosity.

"You are family Heather Henderson; we take care of family," Mrs. Cooker said.

Ms. Henderson put away her notepad. "I will start now with a system for tracking purchases, sales inventory, expenses, salaries, and banking."

Mona was happy.

Mrs. Cooker excused herself.

Mona turned to Ms. Henderson, "Ms. Henderson, I would like your permission to use my painting instruction books as part of my reading requirement. Mr. Beatly is sponsoring my art, and he bought me everything I need. Jake and I will use this table.

"Wow, Mona, this is a fantastic gift from Mr. Beatly. It looks like you have everything you need; it's nice to share your things with Jake".

"Thank you, Ms. Henderson," Mona said

The rest of the children came into the kitchen for their lessons.

The day ended positive, though Mona wondered what danger might be lurking to disappoint her.

NINE

Leaving It All Behind

Michael McIntyre and Leila Landers travelled off-the-beaten-path just south of the Alabama border; to a small town named Sundridge, population one hundred, fifty. He stopped at a gas station long enough to fill up his tank, eat stale food, get further directions, and continued their journey.

In his suitcase were two bags of the cash he had stolen from Calvin Kimberley and Fairbanks residents' savings. He had grabbed the funds from his office and home vaults, unbeknownst to Leila. Michael figured he had to think like a Pirate if he would survive his escape. He traded his freedom, lavish lifestyle, and family's respect for monies that did not belong to him.

The thought of prison crossed his mind. Jail belongs to other people, not people like him; he was a lawyer; he had put people in jail and bailed some of them out. He bailed out Calvin Kimberly many times, that shithead.

He thought about the charges that would come if he got caught for fraud, embezzlement, theft, breach of trust, and lifetime disbarment. He was sure that he would not see the light of day, nor would Leila. Still, Michael believed he, and his father before him, deserved the money he had taken.

The McIntyre family had kept that bastard, old Mr. Kimberley, and his dysfunctional family happy and out of trouble. He and his dad kept their dirty secrets, paid bribe monies, and covered the lies they wanted no one else to know. As far as he was concerned, Calvin Kimberley could go to hell.

He had busted his ass for it, continually working to keep Calvin's drunken ass out of jail, covering up his shit; now the tables turned.

"Damn," he cursed out loud, startling Leila, who had been quiet; he did not like it when she goes quiet; he did not want to guess what she was thinking; she was a chatterbox that drove him crazy. Why had she gone silent like a merry-go-round without the motor?

"What's on your mind, baby?" he shifted in his seat; his ass was beginning to hurt from the long driving.

Leila raised herself upright and cleared her throat.

"Everything is just so crazy, Michael; one minute we're making love on top of your desk, the next minute we're on the run. Should I be angry, sad, hurt.? I don't know."

She had been fuming in silence; Michael was not telling her about the stash of money in bags in his suitcase; she discovered the bags when he was out of the room. She was not sure if she should trust him. It was too late to second-guess.

Leila had her stash. She had siphoned off a large sum from Michael during her employment with him. She lied to her husband about not having enough money, and she scolded his wretched mother not to squander the upkeep money. She hated them and planned to leave, but not in the manner it happened, not as a fugitive. She exhaled loudly and puckered her bottom lip to show her disapproval. She hoped Michael noticed how broken she was.

Michael glanced at Leila.

"I know this isn't easy, I'm unhappy too, but we'll have to make the best of it. We will stop soon, get a room for the night, eat and rest." Michael still liked Leila.

Leila sank into the car seat like an unhappy child.

Immediately, Michael wanted to drag her out of the car and spank her; then he remembered her glowing red-hot naked ass, and he wanted to fuck her instead.

"Okay, we'll stop to eat and rest at the next place we see."

He had not thought about his wife since he has been on the run. She got the best of the deal anyway; she got the house and its contents.

She was a hand-picked religious woman. When Michael stopped sowing his wild oats, he discovered that his wife could not bear his children. She was not disappointed because she had heard stories that linked Michael to Samantha, Calvin, and Mertel and would not have cared to carry a child with such degrading family background.

Michael did not like his wife or what she represented; he did not like her church people. The last person he wanted to think about was Christina; he never wanted to see her again, Amen.

He looked at Leila sitting next to him; he hoped she was worth all his trouble; he smiled and reached for her hand.

TEN

Life's Twist and Turns

Francine woke up with the heavy heart she had gone to bed with the previous night; the glass of brandy had helped, but now she is alert with no liquor to dull her thoughts.

She raised herself and said her usual morning prayer. The sad feeling from the previous day still lingered. There were so many thoughts rushing through her mind; she could not focus. Francine sighed deeply, knowing that self-pity was not a pretty picture to carry around. She showered and headed for the kitchen to start her day; it was Friday, an important day.

Mona had gotten up earlier than anyone else in the house; she organized monies, invoices, and receipts of the previous days into respective envelopes for Ms. Henderson. She recorded the numbers noting expenses and income carefully.

She made up floats for the morning and afternoon, putting everything into a neat pile. Then she made up the envelopes for supplies they would need to purchase.

Mona placed the envelopes in the money box and put them in the closet. She wrote out a small list of all they had to do over the next few days, including filling the orders for Mrs. Plummer's fifty pies and Mr. Beatly's and Mr. Spillman's orders. The business was growing;

they had three regular clients plus the restaurant customers; it was time to hire more people to help.

Mona organized everyone's pay envelope just like her mama had done. Mona headed to the kitchen, where Mrs. Cooker quietly sang along with a song on the radio and cooking.

"Good morning Mrs. Cooker; I hope you slept okay," Mona said as she put down the pile of papers, envelopes, books in her hand on the small side table in the kitchen.

"Morning Mona, I slept fine. Just realizing I am no spring chicken, I got to take it easier. How did you sleep?" she asked as she seasoned fresh chickens for the next day.

"I slept like baby Sasha; I guess we were all tired because I don't see or hear anyone else getting up; yet. What would you like me to do, Mrs. Cooker? Mona asked, ready to help.

"Well, before you do anything, I want to see the first painting you did yesterday; you did do one, didn't you? I hoped you had fun; how was Jake? I want to hear about everything, Mona," Mrs. Cooker said, surprising Mona.

"Mrs. Cooker, it is not very good; it needs a lot of work; I was practicing," Mona said, trying to avoid showing the painting, but Mrs. Cooker was having none of that.

"Mona, honey, if you don't want to show it, that is okay, but your first painting is always going to be special no matter how you may think it looks now because you did it. One day you'll look back at it and cherish that first painting because it started your journey to becoming a great artist, as Mr. Beatly said."

"I would like to see it, Mona," Mrs. Cooker continued as she seasoned three large roast beef.

Mona excitedly rushed to her room and retrieved her first painting for Mrs. Cooker. She was happy that Mrs. Cooker was interested in her painting. She proudly mounted it on the mini easel and placed it on the kitchen table.

Mrs. Cooker looked closely at the painting.

"Mona, this is beautiful for the first piece of art. That is the Barn outback? And two of our cows in the garden? I am impressed, Mona; you should feel proud. Mr. Beatly recognized your natural talent. Are you going to give him this painting? We will be catering a special thirtieth-anniversary dinner for Mr. Beatley, his wife, and their son at Mr. Spillman's; you could paint them a gift."

Mrs. Cooker examined the painting.

"Are those little chickens? That is cute, Mona," she said.

"Can I decorate Mr. Spillman's Bar for the Beatly's anniversary dinner? Mona said, smiling, incredibly pleased with herself.

Ned walked into the kitchen.

"Good morning, Mama, good morning, Mona."

He looked towards the kitchen table,

"Wow! Is that your first painting Mona? That is beautiful," he said, moving closer to the table, seeing the painting for the first time; he picked it up.

"Thanks, Uncle Ned; Jake helped me with it; he's amazing" Mona was smiling.

Before Ned could say anything, Jenny came into the kitchen looking tired; she was rubbing her eyes, said, "Morning Mrs. Cooker, morning everyone. Who's amazing?"

"Morning, Jenny," they all said.

"I was telling Mrs. Cooker and Uncle Ned that Jake is a good painter; he'd got natural talent too," Mona said.

Jenny looked at Mona's miniature painting.

"Mona, you did this? Very nice," she said and gave Mona a great big hug.

The days following would be busy with Thomas Kimberly's funeral reception and the Bently's anniversary dinner. Everyone was preparing, cooking, and finishing. Spillman's Bar was where the celebrations would take place.

"Sounds like a lot of work to me; what extra supplies should I get? Ned asked.

"I think we should get two extra roast beef, three smoke portions of meat: turkey, bacon, ham, an extra bag of flour, sugar. We can spend an extra fifty dollars.

"Don't forget Mrs. Cooker and Mr. Hedley's wedding in two weeks; we got to keep track of that," Jenny said.

"Oh yeah, I almost forgot. Saturday, July 27th, 1947.

Mrs. Cooker looked confused as if she had forgotten the date of her wedding for a moment.

"We don't have to worry about that yet," she chimed in."

Mrs. Cooker had made an extra two dozen cornbread loaves and four dozen buttermilk biscuits; to make sure Mr. Hedley, Mrs. Nelson, and Mrs. Lindsay (who had not been in good health since Mona's mama's died); were fully supplied.

Mrs. Lindsay did not have relatives; she had outlived all her other family members; brothers, sisters, husbands, and all eight of her children. The grandchildren rarely visited. Mrs. Lindsay, Mrs. Nelson, Mrs. Baker, and Dr. Taylor were four of the town's original families. Mrs. Cooker took care of them in their old age.

Ned and Jenny would drop off food for Mr. Hedley and Mrs. Nelson on their way into town; the wagon was always packed with deliveries.

Another day; breakfast over; dishes cleared, washed, and put away. Sarah and Kelly made the sandwiches, Ned and Mona gathered up the eggs, placed some in the wagon, and kept the rest for the house. The last batches of pies, fried chicken, chips were finished and set aside to cool; Mrs. Cooker turned off the latest batch of potatoes, the cabbage and carrot stew that accompanies the roast beef dinner. Mona washed and cut up the lettuce, tomatoes.

"I'm glad Mrs. Cooker has timed out to rest; she does way too much. When can we start organizing for her wedding to Mr. Hedley; when is the date, Mona?" Sarah asked as she finished wrapping the last of the sandwiches and putting them away in the large cooler box.

"In two weeks, the wedding is Saturday, July 27". Mona replied.

ELEVEN

Life's Lemonade

Ned and Jenny started the first part of their journey in silence, recovering and catching their breath after an already very long morning. She tucked her purse between them on the seat to free her hand and took Ned's in hers. She did not want to seem too forward, but she claimed the man who had won her heart. She would be careful about the number of public affections they could show each other without being husband and wife.

In other words, Jenny was careful of the townspeople's gossip; no matter how innocent their actions were, she knew Mrs. Cooker would be fuming at her, Ned. So, she carefully held his hand but stayed on her side of the wagon; she was okay with that. Her body tingled just from the touch of his hands, the memories of their shared kisses; she was happy.

Usually, she would be nodding off in the back, lulled by the movement of the wagon, but she had to be fully alert because this is the first time they were getting the supplies on their own; she had everything on lists for each location; they were used to the routine.

"Ned, when we get to Maple Lane while you're delivering the pies, I want to see if I can find some decorations at the general store for Mr. Beatly's anniversary, your mama's wedding. Mona made a list of ideas to have our decorations for everything," Jenny said, trying to keep track of everything in her head, as well as on paper.

"Okay, it will take me at least half an hour to unload these pies, less with help from Samuel, his brother. Mona is so excited about everything; I am happy because I was kind of worried for a time there about how she would handle losing Mabel, but she is handling it like a champ. Thank you, Jenny, for taking care of her, being there for her; she loves you, Jenny, very much," Ned said, giving her hand a little squeeze, but he wanted to kiss her.

"You don't have to thank me, Ned; I love Mona. I loved her mother; she was a great woman. Besides, you cannot help but love Mona; she has been through so much. I just want to protect her like my own child or my little sister. Besides, as long as Mertel and Sam are out there, we have to protect her."

Ned stopped the wagon, turned to her, said, "Jenny, you've got to stop worrying so much about Mertel, Sam, all the other bad things, people out there; you'll go mad with worry, be very unhappy. I am not saying bad things do not happen; I am just saying we got to learn how to deal with life's lemonade and sweeten it as best we can. It is not going to be perfect, but we will make the best of it; together. I love you, Jenny." he gave her a quick hug for re-enforcement and started the wagon again; they were off.

Calvin Kimberley woke up to the first-morning sun hitting him square in the face; he grimaced against the light. He was unsure how he got into his bed or even how he got home; he tried to get up, but a wave of nausea, pounding, dizziness made him retreat onto the pillow. He held his head with both hands and squeezed, trying to stop the pulsing vibrations, but it was of no avail.

He vaguely remembered being with Steven at his Bar last night; he had closed the Bar with him; they had stayed, talked until the wee hours of the morning. Yet, for the life of him, he could not remember what happened after that; but he knew the moonshine Steven had brought out had something to do with it. He was never good with moonshine, but who was. It always put him on the floor with little recollection of what happened between the first glass and the last. Moonshine was the ultimate dysfunctional love-hate relationship anyone could have; they had been intimate friends for years.

Calvin had no choice but to surrender to his bed; all he could do was try to get out of the sun's path, which failed because he could not reach the curtains he had opened yesterday before Mrs. Cooker came. So, he baked, sweating out some liquor as the headache, nausea subsided enough for him to raise his head.

He looked around the room; saw that his jacket was neatly hung across the chair, his shirt, pants turned on the arms, Steven. He still did not know how Steven could have drunk so much. Yet, he got him home, in bed, undressed, and go home himself, when he could barely walk or have any recollection of the walk. Steven always could hold his liquor better than all of them even when they were younger; he was always quiet when he drank, observing everything, not at all like him or Michael. We were always trying to out-compete each other with our drunkenness, knowing Gabriel, Steven would save us from whatever calamity that could befall us.

He thought about Thomas's funeral, knew he had to see Pastor Hayley's again, made the final arrangements. Mrs. Beatly said she would order the flowers, the wreath for him; he thought that was kind of her; he paid her even though she insisted otherwise.

Steven, Mrs. Cooker said they were going to take care of the reception, even though he did not care to see most of the town's people, as Mrs. Cooker had said he should not stop them from coming to pay their respect. He guesses she was right; he would not try and argue with her; it was a losing battle. He wanted to pay her for the food, but she refused, saying it was the least they could do for the family. Mrs. Cooker continued to amaze him every day.

Calvin Kimberley looked up at the ceiling of his room and wondered what he would do; he felt lost, alone, empty. He thought he had nothing. No wife, children, and family to love. Nothing he possessed or owned was more important to him than those things; he had lost Mabel and Thomas. It seemed a final blow, reminding him how much he had lost in life. He was just drifting along in life, waiting for it to end; he had soured on life.

He saw giving Mona all he had as just a way of making up for all his failures. If only one thing he could correct, do right in his life, he saw this as it: his only redemption.

He closed his eyes against the sun, saw Monica smiling down at him; he wanted to go home to be with her, even if heaven dammed him to hell.

Calvin smiled, hugged his pillow, and fell asleep.

Three hours later, he was up again, washed, dressed in one of his more respectable suits; he had lost some weight, but it still fits him well. He took a final look in the mirror and saw that he was still a dashing gentleman of the South, albeit with a bit of wear and tear; he was still a handsome man.

For the second time since his death, Calvin went to Thomas's room, took Thomas's favorite suit from his closet. It was navy blue with a gold navy style double-breasted button and a white shirt; he got the tie, socks, underwear, and undershirt and packed them neatly in a bag. He went to his dresser again, found the cufflinks for the suite, his shoes. He looked around once more; saw the framed picture of Thomas, his mother, and him on the side table in happier times. Thomas must have been maybe five, just before everything fell apart for both; Calvin did not think he or his son ever recovered from that part of their shared history; he never spoke to him about it either, until recently. Calvin wanted Thomas to know, maybe to explain himself, but it was too late, too late.

He wondered then if he should contact his mother, but he concluded she did not care; she never returned to visit, write or sent a present to acknowledge his existence or birth. So, it did not matter now that Thomas was dead; the Kimberley's would all die quietly without any such fuss about love, acknowledgment, an outpouring of grief. They were a dying breed with no one to carry on the mantle in the family's name; he left the room before he was overcome by grief; closed the door behind him.

Calvin left the house in a hurry; he sped into town as if chased by ghosts that lived in his house.

He went to see Pastor Hayles first to make final arrangements. He thanked him and left for Dr. Taylor, who also acted as the town's mortician. Thomas looked like he was asleep; his face had a look of innocence.

Calvin needed to remain sober. He thanked Dr. Taylor, who told him he and his family would be at the funeral, and he would work with Pastor Hayles to make sure Thomas had a great send-off. Calvin left a bag filled with clothing. He handed Thomas' cufflinks directly to Dr. Taylor and thanked him for his compassion showed Thomas. Calvin Kimberley was almost in tears; his voice cracked under the strain of trying to speak.

"Calvin, it's my pleasure; from all accounts, Thomas was a good man; I have known quite a few good men taken down, out by what Mrs. Cooker, Pastor Hayes calls the Devil's Water. You'd be surprised by the kind words people have to say about your son; his kindness, compassion," he said, patting him on the back and then extending his hand to shake.

Calvin left the hospital moved by what Dr. Taylor had said about his son Thomas, whom he had to admit he did not know. He walked over to Mr. Beatly's store, feeling he would not be able to stay in the claustrophobic car in which he could sometimes hear his dead father still condemning him. He inhaled deeply; he had a panic attack at the thought of his father; he wondered when he would rid himself of the old buzzard.

He opened the door; Edgar was at the counter serving Mrs. Waverly: "Morning Calvin, I'll get my wife for you. Excuse me, Mrs. Waverley" he went to the back and returned with his wife.

"Is that you, Calvin Kimberley, my goodness. The first time coming back into town, I see one of my favorite students. How are you?" he heard a strangely familiar voice say, turning around to face him. It was Mrs. Waverley, his and Thomas's old schoolteacher; he had not seen her in ten years; he thought she was dead.

"Hello Mrs. Waverly, oh my, it's been years since I've seen you. I am fine, simply fine, thank you. How have you been, and how is your family? Where have you been hiding? He asked, crossing the floor to hug her; she was kind to him as a child, young man.

"Calvin, you always wanted to find out everything all at once," she said to his barrage of questions. "Well, Benjamin is gone about twenty years; two of the boys; Evan, Oscar died over ten years ago now; there is only Pamela left; she has two sons. Her husband died two years ago; I wanted to move back here; I never thought I would miss it so much; it feels good to be back. I am so sorry to hear about Thomas, Mabel; they were far too young to die; it is very tragic, very tragic indeed. They were good people, Calvin," she said, hugging him again.

Calvin Kimberley helplessly started crying in Mrs. Waverley's arms; he was once again that unhappy child; she consoled about his stolen candy, pencil, or book.

"Thank you for your kind words, Mrs. Waverley," he said.

"You'll see me at the funeral service tomorrow Calvin. Have a good day now," she said as the Beatlys emerged from the back.

"Thanks, Mrs. Waverley, and that would be very nice of you," he hugged her again, and she went back to her shopping.

Calvin turned and spoke to Mrs. Beatly.

"Everything will be delivered first thing in the morning to Pastor Hayles," she said as she looked at a note she had made in her order book.

"Thank you for everything, Mrs. Beatly; see you tomorrow." he left. His stomach grumbled, announcing its displeasure at not being fed; he looked at his watch. It was still early; he was ready for lunch; he walked over to Spillman's.

Mr. Hedley had gotten up early to check in on Mrs. Nelson; she was not feeling very well after the fire had been put out, and everyone had gone back to their own business.

They had sat talking in the back of her house on the table, the chair he had made for her years ago. They had also had dinner together because he had warmed up all the food Mrs. Cooker had sent for his dinner; it could have fed him and two other grown men; Herman was not a big eater. He had taken it over to share with her even though he knew she had plenty of her own. They had talked about this, that, but mainly about Mertel, Sam, if they would ever come back to Fairbanks.

They laughed until their sides hurt talking about what Mona had done. Mrs. Nelson said she heard all the commotion when Mertel was there trying to cook the food Mona had left behind and saw plenty of smoke to know that most of the food was burnt or wasted. She had heard Sam storming out of the house many times with Mertel shouting after him not to come back too late with her food. She said she made it a point to share everything she got with those around her, all except Mertel; she knew it irritated her; she felt her watching from the window.

After dinner, Herman packed up his picnic basket and made sure she was locked up safe and sound inside before he went home. There was not much that could make Herman Hedley unhappy these past few days; he was on cloud nine. There were too many good things despite the many bad that could not faze him.

He had finally won the hand of the love of his life; for the next two weeks, he would be walking on cloud nine before he landed amongst the stars in Francine's arms. He scolded himself for not doing it when Mabel had encouraged him; she always used to say,

"Herman, time won't wait on you forever, you know, or she'd say, Herman, when are you going to start living your heart's desire?"

Herman smiled at the memory of Mabel Johnson; she was all woman, had more balls than quite a few men he knew, she was special. He missed their confidential talks that taught him much at his old age. She had helped him with his business; it had turned into a five to ten men business with her influence, not the one, two three-person show as he had done for years; now he had more time for himself, made more money.

Mabel's best advice was for him to duplicate himself, train his people to do things his way; only. Herman was more successful now than he was his entire life, had more money than he knew what to do with; he wanted to spend it all on Francine, the family. Mabel was exemplary with every advice she gave him; even when he did not see it as possible, she had already worked it out in her head; the whole thing. He knew she would be happy that he finally proposed to Francine; she had been waiting a long time.

Herman tidied himself, dressed, made some coffee, headed over to Mrs. Nelson with a fresh pot, two cups, sugar, and cream, part of his morning ritual; now that he had volunteered himself to pick Mr. Beatly's vegetables from the garden, he was happy to do it. Mabel was so insistent on doing it herself; he only helped when she asked; she was fiercely independent, like Francine.

Herman always liked strong women; his wife was the weakest woman he ever knew, loved. He enjoyed a strong woman who made him passionate; his wife soon became an emotional, physical, psychological burden to take care of her every need without reciprocating. Do not get it wrong, he loved her, but he wanted to be taken care of too; he had married a princess who wished for everything to be done for her happiness and benefit. They had had one child, but his son Marcus had died when he was only three; she was never the same again; their marriage was over, yet he loved, took care of her until she died, never complaining once. As far as he was concerned, he had made his bed, would have to lay in it, get comfortable.

He knew it was unfair to judge any woman against Mabel or Francine; they were just rare, exceptional women; other women would pale in comparison. That is why he never stopped loving Francine after all these years; he was willing to wait his entire life, now it was finally happening.

Herman left his house through the back door, walked the short distance to Mrs. Nelson's, knocked; he could hear her singing in the kitchen; the door was already open. He put everything down on the table, walked into the kitchen.

"Good morning Nelly. How are you this morning? Hope you slept well," he said as he stood in the doorway.

"I'm fine, Herman; I slept like a baby. I did not realize I was so tired; so much has happened in the past weeks. I am getting too old for all this spectacle, turmoil. I'm glad everything is going to settle down, go back to normal; if there is a normal for around here," she said, wiping her hands after washing the few plates left in the sink.

Nelly started for the doorway; Herman backed up, went back out into the fresh morning sun; they sat, drank, chatted some more about the good ole days when things were simpler.

After about half an hour, he excused himself, went to pick the vegetables, put them in their baskets; he knew Ned would pulling up anytime now. Twenty minutes later, he had everything ready at the front of Mrs. Nelson's house; she had joined him, had taken a seat at the small set in front of her yard.

Herman spotted the wagon soon after they had sat down after washing and drying his hands in the bucket near the small set of Barrels he had set up for Mabel, Nelly to catch rainwater; they were full, almost spilling over. He got up anxious to see his soon-to-be bride; he started pacing like a schoolboy waiting to hear the test results.

"Stop pacing Herman; you'll wear your shoes out," Nelly said, laughing at her joke.

Herman laughed because he felt like a schoolboy who just got his first kiss from the girl he loves; he felt a little silly. When he did not see Francine sitting up front in the wagon, his heart sank; he became instantly concerned. Before Ned could come to a stop, he was asking.

"Morning Ned, Jenny, where is Francine. Is she okay? He held the rein of the horses; gave them the apples he had picked for them. He looked concerned; his smile was gone.

"Good morning Mr. Hedley; Mrs. Nelson, mama is fine; she stayed home to rest while Jenny, I make the early deliveries, pick up supplies. I guess mama did not want to come along for the long ride today; plus, we must get back in time for Mr. Spillman's lunch crowd. Sarah, Kelly, and Mona are getting the rest of the food ready, so when we come back, we can unload, repack the wagon to go.

"Thank you again, Mr. Hedley. The case is perfect for delivering pies; we're going to Maple Lane right now to deliver the first fifty" Ned jumped down from the wagon, shook Herman's hand, patted him on the back. He went over to Mrs. Nelson, hugged her, and then went for the baskets of vegetables while Jenny hugged both Herman and Nelly.

"We should be back in about three hours, hopefully not more; it all depends on how fast we can get everything done; it's going to be a long weekend," Ned said, placing the last of the baskets onto the wagon; he was ready to get going.

Jenny took Mrs. Nelson's food supplies into the house the way Mabel always did. Ned gave Mr. Hedley his.

"Ned, you just take your time," Mrs. Nelson said from her seat at the table. "We'll go see your mama; maybe we can help in some way," she was saying that for Mr. Hedley's benefit, he still looked worried.

Then, Ned, Jenny stopped, looked over at Mabel's burnt-down house, shook their head.

Then Ned said, "I'm so glad that fire never spread; we could have lost a whole lot of houses, endanger people's lives; that woman better not let me see her."

"You, us both; we couldn't do nothing to save it, just watch it burn, Ned," Herman said.

"We are just lucky; there was no wind, yesterday Ned. The Lord himself couldn't have saved our homes," Nelly said, looking over at the burnt-out shack.

"Sorry, Mr. Hedley, Ms. Nelson, we have to go now," Ned said, looking at the time.

"Yeah, I know; we'll see you later," Mr. Hedley said; he was already thinking the same thing.

They waved goodbye, Ned and Jenny were off; Mr. Hedley, Mrs. Nelson both went into their homes to get ready to visit Mrs. Cooker; he had picked up the teapot, cups, sugar, cream on his way home. He quickly put away the things Ned had brought; he was not hungry anymore; he was too worried to eat.

Herman was worried that Francine was taking on more than she should at her age; worried about what more was in that letter Sam left for Sheriff Gilmore; he knew she had not told him everything. He worried about Sam and Mertel; even though he told Nelly that they would never come back, but he was unsure even about that.

He locked up the house, hitched up his old wagon, went to get Mrs. Nelson, who was standing in front of his house; he got down; helped her up; they were off.

Steven had awoken that morning later than usual; he could not move at first because of the pounding in his head. He had almost forgotten the horrible feeling of being drunk; he had been sobered over the past five years, thanks to Mabel. He knew that he did not want to go back to that; he dreaded falling back into that way of life. It had been challenging the past weeks since Mabel's death, his inspiration for keeping sober. But he knew he had to stay sober; his life depended on it now; Mona's, Mrs. Cookers, the others. He felt they depended on him; he did not want to fail them; for the first time in his life, it was important for others to look up to him, respect him; all because of Mabel. So, he felt responsible for making sure that they were okay, just as they wanted him to be okay too. Besides, they were the only family he felt connected to; he felt love and appreciation; it was not just business.

Yet, when Calvin showed up, it brought back many painful memories and hurt he thought he had long ago gotten over. Also, Calvin was in such a state of grieving that he wanted to share his pain because, in many ways, it was pain and suffering that they shared and understood. He questioned if he was using Calvin's situation as an excuse to drink more.

Steven moaned as he willed himself into a sitting position on the bed. The grandfather clock in the living room stuck at seven-o-clock; it was an hour later than his usual wake-up time. The house was silent except for the tick-tocking of that old clock; he was anxious to get away from its loneliness and head for the Bar The Bar was his refuge; his home was a place he came to sleep, shower, and dress. He had been lonely since his father's death and his mother's languishing illness.

He was longing for the company of people; deep inside, he longed for a family of his own; that was Mabel's fault too. He was a happy drunken bachelor when they met; now, after seeing the joys that family brought to the men who came to his Bar, he felt a ping of jealousy. Yes, most were just useless drunken idiots most of the time, but when they brought their wives and children to have dinner at his Bar, he could see the pride and happiness they had being family men.

Their children adored them no matter how bad they were as men or fathers loved them; he wanted to experience that now before he died.

Steven sighed and tried to stand up; he was a little shaky, but he made it to the bathroom, washed his face, bathed, and got dressed. He staggered to the kitchen, took out some of Mrs. Cooker's sober-up concoction, drank half glass of it. The taste almost knocked him on his ass as it hit the back of his throat with a punch; he grimaces, almost brought it back up. The hot peppers, horseradish, garlic gave him another kick by burning all the way down to his stomach; he burped, releasing the smells of yesterday's meals as a reminder of his overindulgences. He went back to the bathroom, washed his mouth out again, he drank some of the leftover lemonade on his table.

He put on the kettle to make a cup of coffee as per Mrs. Cooker's instruction to drink something hot afterward to break up, activate her concoction. As bad as it tasted, he felt better already, quickly swallowed the coffee as hot as he could take it. His stomach rumbled in protest; he belched two more times; then had a bowel movement while breaking out in an intense sweat.

Steven left the bathroom, feeling confident that he would make it thru the day without an oppressive hangover. "Thank you, Mrs. Cooker," he said out loud. He wondered how Calvin was doing because he had drunk so much the night before he did not even know when he was home. It had been a long time since he had put a drunken buddy to bed; he was glad it was Calvin, no one else.

Steven left the house, headed for the Bar; today would be one of his busiest days; then there would be Thomas's funeral reception tomorrow. His walk was brisk but not hurried; he enjoyed the walk to the Bar every morning; it invigorated him.

He opened the back door, went inside, opened the windows, started wiping down all the tables, the counter, washed the remaining glasses from the night before that he was too tired, drunk to do. Then he opened the Bar's front door to let in the fresh air; then he went to the back door and propped it open. He was ready for anything the day brought, thanks to Mrs. Cooker's concoction.

At that moment, he thought he should buy some of her concoctions for his customers; they would appreciate him later for it once they got over the taste. The Bar was ready; he sat down with a tall glass of water; he was thirsty; he could have drunk a gallon.

Steven was about to get up when he saw Calvin crossing the street; he walked in, came, hugged him. "Morning Steven, thank you for getting me home to bed; I didn't even remember leaving the Bar this morning. You're a good man Steven, my brother for life," Calvin said, taking a seat beside him at the table by the window.

"You're welcome, Calvin, not a problem. I could not leave you alone; you could barely walk, so I drove you home. I think that helped to sober me up a little," he said, taking another drink of water.

"Can I get some of that water, Steven; I'm thirsty" Calvin shifted in his seat.

"No problem, Calvin," Steven said, got up to get another glass as Ned pulled up in front of Mr. Beatly to deliver his loaves of bread and other goodies. He noticed that Mrs. Cooker and Mona were not with them; he concluded they must be back at home preparing the rest of the food while Ned, Jenny, did the deliveries, picked up supplies. He brought a pitcher of water to the table, another glass.

"How you manage to be up so early, Calvin; I thought you'd be on your face for most of the day," Steven said, pouring two glasses of water.

"Well, I couldn't get out of bed for about three hours, but the extra sleep helped. I can't handle liquor like before; I think I'm getting old," Calvin said, picking up his glass of water, finishing it in one drink.

"You, me both," Steven said as Ned, Jenny came into the Bar with several carrying crates.

"Good morning Mr. Spillman, Mr. Kimberley," Ned, Jenny said as they entered and saw them sitting at the table. Calvin nodded his acknowledgment with a smile.

"Morning Ned, morning Jenny, how you two doing today. Where Mrs. Cooker, Mona? Steven asked, taking the tray with the bags of chips from Jenny. Then he led Ned to the back room with the rest of the things.

Jenny went back to the wagon for the baskets of chips later that night; she kept her eye on Mr. Kimberley, wondering why he was suddenly so frequent in the Bar. She was suspicious of his sudden interest in Mona, asked what was behind it. Jenny wanted to trust him, but her mind would not allow her; she realized she was overprotective.

"Well, mama is finishing up; I hope getting some rest; Mona is helping Kelly, Sarah finishes up everything for lunch, dinner today. We must deliver fifty pies to Mrs. Plummer in Maple Lane; it is our first delivery, plus we must be ready for Thomas's reception tomorrow. It's a little crazy right now," Ned said, putting down the carrying tray of pot pies on the table. Ned, Jenny walked back out together, came back with the rest of his order.

"Thank you, Jenny, Ned," he said, taking the last tray from her while Ned placed his on another table. "I guess we'll see you both later then," Steven waved goodbye with his free hand; they said their goodbyes to him, Mr. Kimberley, who sat quietly watching the whole thing unfold.

Calvin Kimberley watched them get up on the wagon and drove off towards the hospital.

Steven brought out two pot pies each, some chips on plates for both. He was ravished by hunger, knew his stomach would not make it to lunch; he suspected Calvin had not eaten either. They ate quietly over their lunch turned to breakfast, looking out the window of the Bar as the rest of the town woke up to a new day.

"These are good. They work hard, don't they? Calvin said after he had finished the first pie, he started on the second.

"They are the hardest working family in town; Mabel taught them everything they know about running a business. It seems little Mona is quite the little businesswoman herself; she takes no prisoners, like her mama. I suppose you heard about what she did to Mertel, Sam before they left town," Steven said, taking another bite of his pie.

"Various pieces of the story, what happened? Calvin asked, popping a few chips into his mouth, poured another glass of water for himself, Steven.

"Well, Gabriel said Mertel was so mad her veins were popping out of her neck, cursing, swearing" Steven was laughing so hard recounting the story he had to stop eating not to choke.

"Oh my God, she did all that to them; good for her," Calvin said, laughing his ass off too.

"Gabriel said if he hadn't gone with her, she would have gone herself anyway with Mrs. Cooker, the whole gang, or without. He said the look of determination in her eyes scared him, but he left respecting her more than most adults he knew. She is tough as nails under that sweet innocent smile, smart too. Calvin, your granddaughter, is the reason why the restaurant is still alive; she took all her mama's notes; everything she taught her made sure her mama's dream would not die. She's amazing; sometimes I can't believe she's only ten," Steven said, scooping the last of the pie into his mouth.

"Wow, she did all that; I wished I could have seen it," Calvin said, laughing a hearty belly-busting laugh as he finished eating the last of his chips; he was full, satisfied, and proud.

"Gabriel said it was something to behold all the adults rallying around her, Mr. Hedley, Mrs. Nelson, Mr. Spencer. His son Carlton and Mr. Parker were all there with their wagons, which stunned poor old Mertel. Sam just stood there looking at everything without saying a word." Steven could not stop laughing; he had tears running down his face.

"I heard Mertel burned down the house before running off, and Sam left a letter for Gabriel. What was that about?" Steven asked, hearing about the letter, but nothing else.

"That is more sorted secrets and accusations that I cannot reveal right now; later, I will decide how much to tell. This whole nightmare keeps getting worse; I am not sure anyone, especially Mona, needs to know what it said. She would be even more devastated than she is right now,"

Calvin and Steven talked for the rest of the morning about life's lemonade; it felt like old times, like twenty years had not passed between their last conversation; yesterdays.

Ned and Jenny stopped by the hospital to bring George, and the staff biscuits, gravy, cuts of ham, smoked bacon, turkey for breakfast, and a large pot of tea Mrs. Cooker had prepared for them. She had also sent lunch and dinner for the staff and George.

"Morning, old boy, you feeling ready to come home today, or you happy laying up around here being taken care of by these pretty nurses?" Ned asked as he entered the curtained section where George lay; went and hugged him.

"You know I could stay here, take all this pampering, but you also know I'd go out of my mind after a while just being laid up in here, no matter how pretty the nurses are. 'Morning Jenny, how are you doing today, pretty lady?" George asked as Jenny rounded the corner behind Ned.

"Morning George, how are you feeling today? Are you ready to eat? You want the works with some tea," she asked, going over to hug him.

"You know the works, Jenny; laying up like this, all I want to do is eat," he was laughing. So, Jenny went off to get his breakfast, and Ned brought George up to date about what time they would come back to get him up if Dr. Taylor said it was still okay. They left him eating his gravy, biscuits, bacon, ham, collard greens, and a large cup of tea. George was in heaven, smiling, thanking them as they left; they would see him later; he would be home soon.

TWELVE

Moving Forward Towards Destiny

Ned and Jenny's progress to Maple Lane was slower than expected because Ned did not want to damage any of the pies even though they were secure in the case in the back of the wagon. The journey northbound to the town of Maple Lane was a beautiful, picturesque ride filled with scents of Magnolia, Willow, Oaks, Jacaranda, Mimosa, and other trees on both sides of the dirt road.

It provided a spectacular view of color, scents of sweet flowing plants, and trees invading the nostrils. Jenny leaned back into the seat, getting more relaxed for the long ride. She did not want to bring up Mr. Calvin Kimberley's name again, but it bothered her more about the attention he was suddenly showing Mona and the family. Maybe it was because of what happened with Thomas, Mabel, he felt guilty, but she thought it was more than that. She knew within her very bone that some dark secrets lie within his actions; she also thought about how Mrs. Cooker had reacted to the money that he gave Mona.

"Are you okay, my love?" Ned asked, surprising himself and Jenny with his words; he smiled when she turned to look at him and reached for his hand.

"Yes, Ned, I'm okay, I'm just thinking," she said without revealing her thoughts; she held on to his hand.

76

"I know you're thinking, Jenny; you're always thinking; that's what I love about you. You're not just another pretty face around here; you've got looks, brain, that ass, woo wee; it's doubly fine" he was chuckling at his joke.

Jenny smacked him in the arm in play to show her protest about the comment he made about her ass; then she said, "It's about time you noticed, for a minute, I thought you were a completely blind man" she could not help but giggle herself.

He raised her lips with his hand, kissed it softly, then said, "Jenny Slater, you're the only woman I love, will ever love. I've loved you all my life" he gently lashed the reins as the horses increased their gallop to a steadier pace; he was getting concerned about time too.

Then he said, "You know you can talk to me about anything, right," he squeezed her hand gently.

"Yes, I know Ned; you're my best friend," she said and then changed the subject. "Isn't it so beautiful out here, so peaceful; the air is so clean, fresh" she looked deep into the forest of trees that surrounded them.

Ned stole a look at the beautiful profile of her face, saw a small worry line crease the top of her forehead; he knew that look well. Not much Jenny could hide from him, but he left her alone to her thoughts for now. They both had much to think about over the next couple of days, weeks; everything was happening so fast, furious; they all had to be careful about losing track of the essential things in their lives, like each other. They rode the rest of the way, talking about the business, what would be happening over the next week.

Minutes later, they enter the bustling town of Maple Lane with people moving about in every direction. Jenny could see the riverboats lining the dock embarking, disembarking people and goods at a rapid pace to continue their journey up or downriver.

Fairbanks had no docks, so none of these boats would stop in their town; slowly, everything came to Fairbanks by land. Ned pulled up in front of Mrs. Plummer's store; they both went inside to speak with her; get some help to unload the pies.

"Good morning Mrs. Plummer," Ned said when a plump woman in her sixties came over, gave him a loving hug like a mother to a son.

"Morning, Ned, I'm so glad to see you. So, sorry to hear about Ms. Mabel, Thomas; please give their families our condolences, that poor chile Mona. It is devastating. Now, who this beautiful flower, you brought with you," Sylvia said, smiling at Jenny, reaching out to hug her. "How's your mama, Ned."

"Thank you for your condolence, Mrs. Plummer; I will pass it on. Mama's simply fine; she is home resting, helping get the food ready for later; this is Jenny Slater, Jenny, Mrs. Plummer. Jenny is one of the owners of our company; she's family," he said, smiling at the warmth in which Mrs. Plummer embraced her.

"Hello Jenny, welcome to Maple Lane; great to meet you," she said, still holding her hands.

"Ned, where you've been hiding this beautiful woman, you know I'm looking for wives for my sons," she winked at Jenny.

"Good to meet you, Mrs. Plummer; it's a pleasure; I've heard a lot about you, your family. Congratulations on your hard work, the success of your business. We are looking forward to working with you," Jenny said, smiling with her. She liked Mrs. Plummer; she was a happy woman.

"Unfortunately, Mrs. Plummer, Jenny's already spoken for," Ned said quickly and then changed the subject. "Where are the boys, Mrs. Plummer? I will need some help to bring in all these pies; we have them in the case on the wagon; I cannot leave the case with you. Also, Jenny would like to find out where she can go, find some decorations for birthdays, weddings, etc."

"They're in the back, Ned. Why don't you get them? I'll show Jenny how to get to Mr. Timothy's shop; it's just a short walk from here," she said, grabbing Jenny by the hand, leading her back to the front door.

"Now, when you get there, tell Mr. Timothy that I sent you; he'll take good care of you. On the other side, there is also Mr. Smith about ten stores down: he is a little old cranky man, but he is harmless. You will find some things in his store too. If you want, I can send one of the boys with you too."

"Thank you, Mrs. Plummer; I'll be fine; besides, Ned will need all their help to unload all those pies so we can get back in time for the lunch rush at Spillman's Bar," Jenny said, getting her purse out of the wagon.

"Oh yes, I almost forgot; Ned told me about your pot pies; I've heard about them from others who passed through your town. Mr. Cooper could not stop talking about them when he came by to sell me a new stove, which he talked me into, a good thing. That stove is a wonder. I can do much more. I would like to order about fifty for next week Friday; twenty-five of each. Is that enough time to get an order in Jenny? How much are they? She asked, getting excited; she was smiling from ear to ear.

"Mrs. Plummer, you can get anything you want; we'll fill your order. The pot pies are fifty cents each wholesale; you can sell them for one dollar or more depending on your customers," she said; then she remembered the receipt Mona had made up to give to her for her purchase, record.

Jenny reached into her purse, took it out, and gave it to Mrs. Plummer. "You can pay me when I come back. We gave you a dollar off each pie because of the amount you're buying," she said, thanked her again before she left for Mr. Timothy, Mr. Smith shops.

"Thank you, Jenny," Mrs. Plummer said, watched as Jenny walked down the street towards Mr. Timothy and Mr. Smith before she went back into her store; she could smell the pies from the wagon's showcase; she knew she had made a good investment. Because at two dollars pies for a one hundred dollars investment, she could make up to three hundred dollars profit; it was a great deal.

Ned, Jack, Daniel emerged from the back of the store laughing, making all kinds of noise; they were on their way out the door as Mrs. Plummer came in; she smiled at them then said, "Don't you all be doing no playing around my pies now boys." She had a new glass showcase made for the pies that sat near the back of the store.

"We won't, mama," Jack said, pushing Daniel one more time before they got out the door.

All Ned could do was laugh at them; he missed not having a brother of his own to share with, but Jack, Daniel had become his brothers from another mother. They regularly played pranks on each other; Ned somehow always got involved; it was worst when George was around because he could find trouble in a teacup. That is when Ned remembered he had to pick George up from the hospital on his way home. "Hey guys, I've got to be back in a half-hour, or I'll be getting a whole bunch of grumbling from the ladies, so let's get this done fast, okay," he said, climbing up on the wagon.

"No problem, Ned; we'll get it done," Daniel said, pushing his brother one more time before the work started. They started another pushing match again. Ned just looked at them, shook his head. "You two act like two children. No wonder none of the women here will even date you; you're too old for all that playing," he said.

Daniel, Jack looked at each other, none too pleased. "We get dates, don't we, Daniel?" Jack said, hoping for some re-enforcement from his brother, but none was forthcoming. They pushed each other again; Jack is grumbling about Daniel, not defending their manhood.

Ned was laughing so hard he almost fell off the wagon. He had unhooked the ropes that held the case in place, carefully pushed it to the back of the wagon so it would be easier to take out the pies; they would take two at a time. They started, all playing ceased for the moment.

Jenny walked briskly towards the stores but could not help looking around at all the people, stores, and activities around her. It was exciting to be in a bigger town than Fairbanks, but she was a little overwhelmed as people passed with a quick nod acknowledgment of her presence. Five minutes later, she spotted Mr. Timothy's General store, went inside, waited for Mr. Timothy's to finish serving his customers, then approached him.

"Good morning, Mr. Timothy; my name is Jenny Slater; Mrs. Plummer said you would be able to help me with some decorations for weddings, anniversaries, birthday parties. Could you please show me what you have in stock; do you have some sort of catalog; so I can also make an order for what you do not have? Jenny said, extending a hand.

"Good morning Ms. Slater; nice to meet you; if you follow me, I'll show you what we have in stock," he said, shaking her hand, then led the way.

Mr. Timothy's store had everything; her eyes were darting back, forth across the shelves in the store to see as much as she could in the time she had. She could have spent half the day shopping, spending all her money. He took her to the second row of shelves, left her to select what she wanted. A moment later, he returned with a basket for her to put things in, told her if she needed help just to call him.

Jenny was delighted with the selection of decorations; they were from the big cities like New York, Boston, Washington, etc., because nothing like that was made anywhere around here. She picked up floral decorations made of paper, fake flowers, wreaths, quality colored, patterned, hand-painted plates, cups, white linen napkins with pretty-looking ring holders. She bought a set of fancy knives, forks, spoon, three sets of glass cake holders, tops, a dozen lace tablecloths, serving utensils, candles, holders of various sizes; before she knew it, she was going back, fourth from the shelf to the counter to drop off stuff.

She was calculating in her head as she shopped; she took one more look around and paid Mr. Timothy, who gave her a considerable discount for her purchase. She quickly looked in his catalogue; she ordered a wedding cake holder, four silver trays, four glass jugs, a rolling serving tray; she paid him in advance.

"Thank you, Mr. Timothy, for your kindness. May I please have a receipt for everything, please also put in the discount you gave us. I will be back in twenty minutes to pick them up," Jenny said, shaking his hand one more time.

"You are very welcome, Ms. Slater; thank you for your business. I will have these things packed up, ready for you when you return. Please say hello to Mrs. Plummer for me; tell her I will be by later for lunch," he said, reaching for a bag under the counter.

Then he said, "Ms. Slater, I would like to give you this hat, glove as a gift." He had put aside a beautiful little blue hat, matching gloves; he smiled, showcasing a few missing teeth in his head. The hatbox sat on the counter beside him.

"Thank you, Mr. Timothy, but I cannot accept such a beautiful gift," Jenny said, even though she loved the hat, glove instantly; it was another of her favorite color.

"Please, Ms. Slater, do an old man a kindness by accepting this gift. It is not very often a beautiful young woman comes into my store, spends over sixty dollars in my business. I can tell you are a businesswoman, will be an excellent customer for years to come. Are you new in town?" He asked when she hesitated.

"I live in Fairbanks; I'm just here to deliver some pies for Mrs. Plummer's business; we'll be supplying her pies, pot pies," Jenny said, still looking at the hat, gloves.

"Oh, so you must know Mr. Beatly then, Mrs. Cooker, my condolence to Ms. Mabel's family," he said, his smile deepening.

"Thank you for your condolence; it has been harrowing for all of us. Mr. Beatly is one of our suppliers, clients for our food business, but he is more like family; I live with Mrs. Cooker. We will be hosting the Beatly's thirtieth wedding anniversary dinner this coming Tuesday; that's part of why we need these decorations; mums, the word okay, sir. I should be back again next Friday with Mrs. Plummer's next order. When will the items from the catalogue be arriving?" she asked, picking up the hat; she placed it on her head, looked in the mirror; she liked it.

"It looks lovely on you, Ms. Slater. Please do say hello to Edgar for me, Mrs. Cooker; her food is legendary around these parts; good woman. Also, please give the family, Mona, my condolence about Ms. Mabel; she was a lovely woman. Also, your catalogue order will come in about two weeks, or would you like me to put a rush on it," he said with a laugh.

"That will be fine; I can get a rush; yes, thank you, I will accept your gift, Mr. Timothy; you are a very kind man," she said, putting the hat back on the counter.

He quickly put it in the hatbox along with the gloves, handed it to her, and said, "You are very welcome; I'll see you in twenty minutes; he was still smiling.

Jenny walked out of Mr. Timothy's store feeling empowered; she was just beginning to recognize the power her looks and body had over men. She saw how they looked at her and saw how they went out of their way to accommodate her. She finally understood what Mabel had been telling her all those years. Your brains and looks are your number one assets, she used to say.

Jenny crossed the street to find Mr. Smith's store, spent the rest of the money on more decoration items, and thought that Mr. Smith was not so bad; he just seemed lonely. He did not have as much as Mr. Timothy's, but his things were unusual; she liked them, so would Mona. She spent the rest of the money, collected the items, and her receipt, then left his store and back to Mrs. Plummer.

With every step, men tilted their hats, hoping to get a smile from her; she was not aware of her beauty or even had acknowledged it before today; Jenny had pep in her steps.

Ned and Mrs. Plummer's boys were unloading the last pies as Jenny came around the corner with her hands loaded with bags. Ned gave Daniel the two pies in his hand, rushed to help her put the bags in the back of the wagon.

Before he could ask any questions, she said, "Ned, we have to pick up the rest of the things at Mr. Timothy's before we go. He also gave me a hat, glove as a gift for being such a good first-time customer," putting the hatbox away.

Jenny went into the store to thank Mrs. Plummer, get the payment so they could be on the way. "Mrs. Plummer, thank you for recommending Mr. Timothy; he's a genuinely nice man; Mr. Smith seems a little lonely, but he was kind too. We got almost everything we needed. Oh, that smells so wonderful, Mrs. Plummer. What are you cooking?" Jenny asked as the various smells invaded her senses.

"Thank you, Jenny; I know you know good cooking; Mrs. Cooker, Mabel Johnson, God rest her soul are legends even around here. People talk, you know, oh Mr. Cooper saved two of his pies to have with his soup when he passed through town. I bought one of his stoves because of the way he talked about Mabel's pot pie. I just focus on soups, sandwiches, sweets, like cookies, tarts, now pies, pot pies, thanks to Ned. I am mainly cooking beef, chicken, vegetables, pea soups; every Friday, I do beef, chicken, or pork with rice dishes; I cannot manage much more than that at my age. But the business is growing; I am running out of food every day with many unhappy customers.

The boys help, my best friend, her children, a couple of more people, but the town is just growing so fast. There are more ships, more people; it is simply crazy around here sometimes; more food helps.

"How long have you been doing this, Mrs. Plummer? Are you going to train others to cook for or with you?" Jenny asked, taking a closer look at her place. It was cozy looking, inviting with large windows, curtains that made you feel like you were sitting in your

84

mother's kitchen. It only had about ten tables; on one side, a long table, stools offered extra seating.

Three large plants, several small plants; placed strategically placed around the room that added to the ambiance, the homeliness of her business. She had put in a new glass showcase for the pies; the front counter into the kitchen area had a carved handcrafted mahogany swinging door depicting a woman in an old fashion kitchen; it was beautiful.

"I'm trying, but it's hard to find the right people, so I'm teaching my sons as much as I can, but they're still too young, not always serious. I need a young woman like you who wants to run a business; you work hard, but it is your time, your money. Maybe my sons will marry someone like you, Ms. Jenny Slater; beautiful, smart, hard-working. Ned's a lucky man; he is a good man too; I can tell he is the one that won your heart. You don't have to say anything; I can see the way he looks at you," Mrs. Plummer said, handed Jenny the payment for the pies. "Ned, you ready to get going, or you, my boys, still fooling around," she said, winking at Jenny.

"No time to play today, Mrs. Plummer; I was just putting the case back in place, securing it for the ride back. I'm ready to go," Ned said, coming in to say goodbye. Jack, Daniel was right behind him, still nudging each other, fooling around.

Mrs. Plummer hugged Ned, then Jenny said, "It was a pleasure to meet you, Jenny. Ned, you take care of her, you hear."

"Thank you! Mrs. Plummer, I will," Ned said, punching Jack, Daniel, in the arm as he left.

"Thanks, Mrs. Plummer, see you next time. Nice to meet you, Jack, Daniel," Jenny said, waving goodbye as they left.

Ned helped Jenny up into the wagon and said, "Okay, where's Mr. Timothy's place from here? I don't want us to be late getting back" he took the brakes off the wagon's wheel and turned into the street.

"It's on your right, about two minutes down this road. I got a lot of things we can use for different special occasions. I also order items from the catalog. I hope everyone loves them, especially Mrs. Cooker and Mona." Jenny said.

"I'm sure they'll love them; you have great taste. You love me, don't you," Ned said, turning to wink at her in jest as he gave off with a slight chuckle. He was almost at their destination; he slowed down, breaking the wagon to a smooth stop right in front of Mr. Timothy's store.

Jenny put a frown on her face to protest his comment, then said, "We'll see about that; Mrs. Plummer is looking for wives for her sons; they're pretty cute too" she winked back at him, started laughing.

Ned stopped chuckling, saying, "That's not even funny, Jenny. I love them like brothers, they might be cute, but every woman wants a man, they still act like boys. I'm not worried; I think," he said, hopped down, went on the other side to help her down. "Milady," he said, extended his hand like a gentleman.

"Thank you, kind sir," she said, extending hers to him, but he scooped her up off the wagon, spun her around twice. They broke out into pearls of laughter that startled passersby, who looked at them as if they had lost their minds. "Ned Cooker put me down before people think we've both insane. You so crazy," she said as he gently placed her on the sidewalk; she straightened out her dress.

"Your wish is my command' milady," he said, bowing slightly; he had a mischievous smile on his face.

"And you talk about Jack, Daniel, really," she said, pretending disbelief, but she was smiling.

"Jenny, Mr. Hedley said a man should never forget how to have fun or to be fun; laughter will be one of the key ingredients in making a happy wife, so I'm sticking to his advice," he said, put a skip in his step.

"Come on, Ned, you're so silly. Let us get the stuff, get out of here before they think we're two mad people let loose in their town, from the mental hospital we saw coming into town," she said, walking into Mr. Timothy's store.

"Hi Mr. Timothy, thank you for packing everything up for us; you know Ned, my business partner Mrs. Cooker's son, you will see him with other family members when I can't make it," she said, grabbing bags as Ned, Mr. Timothy shook hands.

" Nice to see you, Ned, you've been here a few times with Ms. Mabel, your mama right; your partner is quite impressive; she came in here, without hesitation bought everything in one fell swoop," he said, picking up one of the six crates he had packed for easier transport.

"Mr. Timothy, you have no idea what a hard worker this beautiful lady is," he said; he suspected that Mr. Timothy was already sweet on his Jenny.

"I just met the lady, but I can tell that just from watching her shop," he said, helping them put all the things in the wagon, bid them a safe trip to Fairbanks, watched as they drove off down the road leading out of town.

"Nice man; I think he likes you, Jenny," Ned said, feeling proud that so many men of all ages liked, desire the woman that would be his wife one day. "You know Jack, Daniel, have had a crush on you for years, but they know that I've been in love with you for a while now, so they just put it out of their minds, but they're still disappointed. They say you are getting more, more beautiful every time they see you," he said, beaming with pride like he had won a grand prize.

"Well, I'm not your wife yet, so don't be so sure, Ned Cooker. You're counting your chickens before they hatch; you know what your mama would say about that," Jenny said, teasing him.

"Well, there ain't no chickens here. Anyway, I can't wait to see what you bought for the business; did you leave anything in the man store for other people to buy?" he asked teasingly.

"No, I bought out his entire inventory because it was just sitting there waiting for me; plus, he gave me a big discount for being a first-time customer, buying so much at once. He also gave me this beautiful little hat, matching gloves that I could not refuse. Would you like to see it?" she asked, reaching into the backside of the wagon. She grabbed the hatbox, took it out, and placed the hat on her head, the gloves on her hands, smiled. "Isn't it lovely, Ned?" Jenny said, turning around so he could have a better look.

"It's beautiful, Jenny; I think I'm going to have to keep two eyes on that little old man Mr. Timothy; he's a lot sweet on you," he said, taking another look at the hat and glove.

"Don't tell me you're jealous of a little old man now, Ned," she teased, put the hat, glove back into the box. "You have nothing to worry about, even though you've already counted your chicken before they hatch," she said, teasing some more.

"Okay, I surrender; my mama told me never to argue with a woman; I would always lose or be punished at a later date when I least expect it," Ned said, waving his handkerchief in surrender.

"Okay, now we have to organize the pick-up of supplies from the furthest to the closest," Ned said as Jenny took her list of supplies Mona had written out.

"Thank you, Jenny, for being so strong; I know it's a lot of pressure you've taken on to make Mabel's dream a reality; none of this could happen without you. You make me, mama, Mona, everyone stronger because of your strength. I'm so grateful for you," Ned said, almost getting emotional.

"Come on, Ned, we are all in this together; what about you; you are the backbone of this family. You work harder than all of us; Mabel used to say, "I don't know what I'd do without Ned" all the time; you were her backbone; she could depend on you for anything," Jenny said, reached for his free hand, squeezed it. "We are all in this together; everyone is important, Ned; equally."

"Well, as modest as you're trying to be, you are the center of all this Jenny, Mama too, but I'm hoping that once we start to grow, Mama will be doing less; I can see that she is getting more, more tired every day. I hope Mr. Hedley will help her slow down a little; take some time off, visit New York or Georgia or some other big city. Just to get away, see a different part of this big ole beautiful country called America," he said, looking over at her.

Jenny sat back in her seat and thought about the next couple of days; her mind was crowded with all they had to accomplish in the days, weeks, months ahead. She wondered whether it would be too much with so many people depending on her to be healthy. She did not wish to feel very weak, vulnerable to the whims of life, destiny. "I love you, Ned," she said, looking straight ahead towards their future.

"I love you too, Jenny," he said.

They drove the rest of the way in comfortable silence, Jenny thinking about the business, the supplies lists, Ned, Francine, Mona.

Ned about all that, getting George settled in at home, his proposal to Jenny, the secrets his Mama kept that could harm them, but Ned wanted to put the latter to the back of his mind; now was not the time for those thoughts, they would spoil everything. He knew that conversation was not over, not by a long shot.

They picked up all the supplies and returned home to find Mr. Hedley and Mrs. Nelson sitting in the kitchen, keeping Kelly, Sarah, and Mona company.

"Uncle Ned and Jenny are back," Mona announced when she ran outside to see who was coming this time. Mr. Spencer had dropped by earlier to check in on the family on his way to get supplies with his son Carlton who had a crush on Kelly, but she did not see it; he was too shy to say anything. Everyone knew because Carlton would get nervous every time Kelly was around; otherwise, he was a chatterbox with Uncle Ned, us.

Mr. Hedley, Kelly, Sarah, Mrs. Nelson came out to help; the children had gone in to wash their hands, clean up to help too. The children all wanted to see the decorations Jenny had bought for the business; they were excited because this was the part of the business they would help with; Mrs. Cooker had said maybe, it all depends on how they behaved.

Ned, Jenny pulled up, everyone started unloading before they could say hello to everyone by name. "Hello, Mr. Hedley, Mrs. Nelson," Ned said because the children, the woman, all started taking things off the wagon before Ned or Jenny could even come down.

"Wait, children, we have to organize where we are going to put all these things before you start moving them. Okay, Mona, Jake, make sure the children put all the decorations in the living room; we can look at them and organize them later. Kelly, Sarah put all the meats and things where they belong and get the children to help. Ned, Mr. Hedley, you know where the flours, sugars, potatoes go; okay, you know what to do," Jenny said, taking charge.

The wagon was overflowed with supplies, indicating business growth. Jenny remembered Mabel's number two rule; *you must spend money to make money;* her number one, *cash, is king; invest wisely.* She felt tired from the long journey;

THIRTEEN

Investing Wisely in Our Future

Mrs. Cooker woke up just as the noise level reached a fever pitch in the house; the children's excitement about the decorations Jenny had bought overwhelmed the conversation taking place in the kitchen over cups of coffee and tea.

Jenny had to eventually see what was going on after she had had her tea. They could hear her from the kitchen talking to them as she walked. "So, children, what do you think about all the decorations" she was asking as they all tried to speak at once; mostly, she heard they are great, Aunty Jenny.

Jenny said, "Okay, if you back up a little, I'll show you everything, and we could organize them at the same time. We will need some crates for storage, and Mona can do inventory please,". They all moved back. She started taking out stuff and putting them in piles according to the category in front of them.

"Yes, Aunt Jenny; I'll get the notebook," Mona said, rushing off, and returned two minutes later.

"Okay, these are fifty fancy cloth napkins, rings for weddings, anniversaries: special times. These are twenty beautiful large, small silver candle holders. These are fifty folded paper bells, balls with strings in five colors; ten reds, ten whites, ten yellows, ten blue, ten yellows" Jenny unfolded all five colors for them to see. That excited them; then she said, "These are the fake floral wreaths; ten each of the large, white, and red; four each of the small white, pink, blue, red, yellow; they could be hung or set on a table. She showed them fake doves, colored paper streamers, explained how they worked. She showed them the fifty special plates, knives, fork, wine, water glasses, ten serving spoon sets.

Then she said, "I have more things coming with another order; I'll show you those too because Mrs. Cooker says if you behave, this will be your jobs, decorations, but only if you behave, take care of these things."

Jenny went through everything one by one; after about half an hour, she restacked, organized the supplies, and put them aside in the storage boxes. Then she said, turning to them, "Okay, Aunt Jenny has to get ready to go."

The children protested, "We want to see more Aunt Jenny."

Mona was impressed, said "Aunt Jenny, these are amazing; they are going to make Mr. Spillman's Bar look like a dream for the Beatly's; I can't wait for them to see it," bubbling with excitement.

"Thanks, Mona, we can talk about the other stuff later, organize them into occasion's category...like weddings, anniversaries, birthdays, etc. But right now, your aunt Jenny has got to eat, get ready to go.

A few minutes later, Mrs. Cooker came out of her room, redressed, ready to go; she hugged Mr. Hedley, Mrs. Nelson when she saw them sitting at the kitchen table eating a piece of chocolate cake, having their tea. They had already helped Ned, Sarah, Kelly pack all the food into the wagon; covered them up for transport. She sat down to have a cup of coffee before they left as Kelly and Sarah filled her in on what happened while she was resting.

Jenny, Mona came back into the kitchen as Mona talked excitedly about all the decorations that Jenny had bought, how the Beatly's anniversary dinner will be so special, they will be so surprised;

then she hugged Jenny. "Thank you," Mona said after her long excited spiel.

Jenny gave Mona all the receipts, leftover monies in each envelope, and went to her room to refresh herself quickly and changed her clothes.

Sarah, Kelly flipped the schedule again; Kelly went off to breastfeed baby Sasha one more time before she left for the morning; three bottles of arrowroot porridge were left in the icebox for her until Kelly's return in the afternoon. She would return with Ned, George; Sarah would come back in the afternoon for the dinner rush.

Mona went, put away the envelopes for Ms. Henderson's bookkeeping, accounting; she knew she would be concerned about the new expenditures. But Mona, everyone had agreed it was an excellent investment into the growth of the business. And they saw the decorations Jenny had bought, loved them; Mona was convinced they were on the right path. Who does not like to feel important about a bit of fuss being made over them on their special day; that was a good investment in people and business.

Ned came and sat down at the table; he was tired; all the extra lifting, bending, pushing, and pulling took its toll on him faster than he expected; it was only ten-thirty. He had not had any time for himself over the past number of weeks; they were busy doing something every day since Mabel's death.

"Ned, you want something to eat before you go?" Sarah asked, looking over at him; she knew he must be hungry by now.

"Yes, please, Sarah; I'm starving; what you have over there, I can quickly eat before we go," he said, straightening up in his chair, ready to eat.

"We have biscuits, gravy, fried chicken, roast beef, mashed potatoes; we made some rice for the chicken and to go with the beef stew for dinner later.

"Sarah, give me the works; I worked hard this morning, real hard. We picked up twice the number of supplies, delivered more than ever; I still have lifting to do. We still have an hour, a half before we have to be at the Bar," Ned said; he hadn't eaten since seven this morning.

"Why don't we all have lunch before we go because, you know, as soon as we get to Spillman's, we won't eat or rest until after two or maybe three this afternoon? Let us just set the table, eat, and get going. Where are the children?" Mrs. Cooker asked, tried to get up to serve.

"Mrs. Cooker, please sit down; we will serve you, Mr. Hedley, Mrs. Nelson, children," Jenny said as she, Kelly, Mona got up to set both tables, serve out the food, quickly have everyone sit down to eat. They blessed the table, ate; then Jenny, Ned, Mona, Kelly, Mrs. Cooker left for the Bar.

Sarah, Mrs. Nelson, Mr. Hedley, the children cleaned up the kitchen; put away the dishes, leftover food.

Mr. Hedley took Mrs. Nelson home, went off to check on the supplies he had already ordered to build the new part of the Bar. He had also ordered some yellow bricks that would give the building a sturdy, modern look. He had gotten a fantastic end-of-year clearance deal; he could not refuse. This would be his gift to Mabel's dream, Mona, the new business, to his future family.

Herman was a wealthy man by any standard, but he was humble about his wealth; none of the townspeople or even Mrs. Cooker knew anything about his actual financial value. To be quite honest, Mr. Herman Hedley had invested wisely with several large companies years ago when he worked in New York City for a time.

His brother-in-law Charles Buckman, the husband of his only sister, was a wise, honest man who had encouraged him to invest in energy (Oil), transportation (Trains, Buses), and communications (Telephone service) companies. Still, it was his sister who was gifted at picking these stocks.

He remembered giving Charles those first hundred dollars, still not fully understanding the whole stock market business.

But he trusted his sister, Charles, with his life, his money; they were all happier for it. The next day he had brought the paperwork for three sets of investment at thirty-three dollars, thirty-three cents each; Herman was hooked. Each month, he set aside one hundred dollars and gave it to Cynthia, Charles, who had an impressive, growing investment portfolio.

Charles always used to say, "Herman, if you want to beat the man, get respect from the man, and get things done by the man for you. You'd better have more money than the man; you will be okay. Just always keep two eyes on the man, or he will try to rob you blind while plucking out your eye. So, you also must be smarter than the man always," he taught Herman everything he knew.

He taught him how to invest, withdraw his interest, turned it into cash, put it somewhere they could not reach. So, he would grow each investment to ten thousand dollars each time, withdrew nine thousand, leave one thousand to grow. He brought his money home to Fairbanks, built an underground safe. No one knew they were walking on hundreds of thousands of dollars when they entered parts of his living room, kitchen.

That was twenty years ago; both Charles and Cynthia had suddenly died in an automobile accident about two years ago but had left a small fortune for their two children, who were young adults by then.

Charles, Cynthia's children, still communicated with Uncle Herman, sending him new stock tips or just saying hello, catching up on things; he missed their parents terribly. Charles was his best friend, a man he completely respected. They had come, spent time in town but mostly kept to themselves, finding most of the town's inhabitants too provincial in their thinking.

However, they had loved and admired Mrs. Cooker, Mabel; Charles thought they would have flourished in New York instead of living in such a limited environment. But as Mabel had so eloquently told him, it was the limited environment that produced his brilliant, beautiful wife, children, and his fantastic brother-in-law; everyone else he admires sitting at the table or in their homes. This same environment nurtured more beautiful, exceptional people at a greater per capita rate than any big city.

Mabel had won her case; Charles promised to investigate land in Fairbanks just to be closer to this nurturing she was talking about; he had smiled a mischievous smile. At that moment, Herman knew he liked Mabel a little too much; his sister was none too happy.

But Mabel, however, was clever, picked up on his feelings, games, and dismissed any possibility by speaking about Cynthia's gift of picking the right stocks, building the family's wealth. Just listening to the conversation, Mabel had figured out that even though Charles had known about stocks, it was Cynthia who, once she learned how it worked and made their money.

Cynthia smiled as Mabel gushed about her talents, promised to sit down with her only to learn more about this stock thing, making a point that she does not wish to be alone with Charles. Cynthia always knew Charles was a little flashy, a bit of showboating man; she had to admit she used to like it; she thought it showed pride and confidence; now it felt arrogant. And yes, he was a good man generally, a great father who was always dotting on his children Olivia, Samuel. But he had wondering eyes, hands; she knew that, had spoken to him, Herman about it.

Herman had not given her advice one way or another but asked her if she could live with the 'Balance,' which stumped her. So, he explained 'Balance,' whether it is building a marriage, a business, a government, a country, or anything. The 'Balance' is what you can live with; fifty-fifty, eighty-twenty; one hundred percent, in the end, build something worth staying to fight for and then ask yourself what you are willing to give up to find that 'Balance.'

Mabel had empowered Cynthia that night; she was never the same again; Charles went into making Cynthia happy mode because, for the first time, the 'Balance' had shifted, not in his favor. The jig was spilled on that table that he would be nothing without his super talented, gifted wife who came out of a backwater town like Fairbanks. Yet Mabel meant him no harm; she inadvertently or maybe on purpose had 'Balanced' their relationship for the better; they became closer after that.

Mona's investing in her mother's dream brought up all kinds of memories for Herman about his sister, brother-in-law, their children; he missed them. All this, plus his wife's passing were still fresh in his head, his heart; he was not used to being alone, did not want to be alone anymore. Herman would tell Francine everything once they were married; it would all be hers, anyway, married or not.

He smiled to himself, stopped in front of Mr. Zimmerman to check in on the chairs, benches, tables he was making; the fabric would be in next week, they would be in a full-scale building mode in two weeks. He left Zimmerman's, went to see Pastor Hayles, set the date; he was not leaving anything to chance, not this time.

The day went, as usual, setting up for the lunch rush once they arrived at Mr. Spillman's; Ned, Kelly, Jenny, Mrs. Baker, Mrs. Cooker, Mona worked as a team.

Mona took Mr. Spillman his lunch and saw that Mr. Kimberley was again keeping him company, so she asked him if he would like to have lunch with Mr. Spillman. Mrs. Cooker had prepared a brunch plate for him that included a roast beef sandwich, fried chicken, a few biscuits with gravy that she knew he loved, and a salad.

"Yes, I will be eating too, Mona, thank you," he said, looking at his friend's plate longingly.

"I'm sure we have a few more biscuits with gravy left; they are not for the customers but our meals, Mr. Spillman, so I'm sure it will be okay. What would you both like to drink?" she asked, moving towards the back door.

"Ginger beer for me, lemonade for me," Calvin, Steven answered in unison; they laughed.

Mona did not have to ask Mr. Spillman anything. He was stuck on Mrs. Cooker's ginger beer; he said it cured his gas and ulcers. Mrs. Cooker said his stomach needed all the help it could get. That man punished himself. Mona returned a few moments later with two glasses.

The day went well as Jenny explained the lunch hour service to Kelly for the first time after organizing and preparing everything. Mona slipped back into the Bar for the plates; ten minutes later, Mr. Beatly came; then came the mad rush of workers descending looking like an angry mob.

Kelly handled lunch again like a seasoned professional, following Jenny's instruction with Mona helping her get all the orders right and flowing smoothly; it was easy to get used to the routine.

After lunch, everything cleaned up, and they had prepared for the late afternoon dinner crowd; Ned took Mrs. Baker along with Kelly, Mona home on their way to pick up George from the hospital. Mona was excited that Uncle George was finally coming home. Jenny, Mrs. Cooker stayed, rested.

They pulled up in front of the hospital; they went inside to get George. Mona ran inside first, was at George's bedside before the others to hug him. "Good afternoon Dr. Taylor," she said, almost bumping into him.

"Good afternoon Mona," Dr. Taylor said as Mona stormed into the room, hugged George.
He was giving George his final instructions for his recovery when Ned Kelly came into the room.

"Good afternoon Kelly, Ned; I was just cautioning George here about what he can and cannot do to make a full recovery. I did not see you this morning Ned, but it was wonderful of your mama to send so much food for the family, staff again; it is kind of her. Those biscuits with the gravy, the ham, collared green; wow, please thank her for me, for us. George, I will miss you, but I'll miss Mrs. Cooker's food more," he laughed. "George, you're in great company, the Nurses love you too, but I don't want to see you back in here anytime soon. Now, no more boxing, no heavy lifting for at least two more weeks, easy on the drinking; come back in two weeks for a checkup. If you start feeling any new pain, come see me right away; otherwise, you are free to go," Dr. Taylor patting him on the arm.

"We'll make sure Dr. Taylor he doesn't do none of that," Mona chimed in. "I'll watch him," she did the two fingers to her eyes than his, making everyone crack up.

"Well, George, you will be in excellent hands with Mona here. She'll report any discrepancy to me directly, right Mona?" he asked, teasing George, playing along with Mona.

"Yes, I will," she said, happy to be Dr. Taylor's spy to make sure George stays healthy.

"See that doc you got Mona here committing to spy on me; I'm sure I won't get away with anything in that house. It's a house full of women, except poor Ned here; the boys and their vote won't count," George said, extended his hand to shake Dr. Taylors.

"Thanks, Dr. Taylor; I'll see you in two weeks. Please say goodbye to your beautiful wife, Dr. Morgan, Nurse Terry. Where's Nurse Stella? I'd like to say goodbye," George said, sitting up in the bed; he had dressed, was ready to go.

"Nurse Stella went to see Mr. Fabien at his home to change his bandages. Yesterday he got a nasty slash on his arm when a tree branch he was cutting broke off and cut him on its way to the ground. Then he fell, broke his leg, it was a freak accident. Good thing his son was there to tie off the bleeding, help him to the hospital. Sometimes we make house calls for older patients; besides, I think she like his son Frank, a nice young man. Ned, I know you have to go so I won't keep you; All the best, George, Kelly, Mona, take care," Dr. Taylor said; Dr. Taylor shook his hand and started to walk to his office but stopped. Did the, I am watching you watch him eye thing to Mona; cracking everyone up, he left laughing too.

"Thanks, Dr. Taylor," they said; Mona picked up George's small bag while Ned, Kelly helped him to his feet, to the wagon.

George said, "Afternoon Mrs. Baker good to see," as he groaned in pain, hoisting himself with Ned's help into the back of the wagon. He was leaving the hospital the same way he came.

"Good afternoon George. How are you feeling, young man? Mrs. Baker asked, looking at all his cuts, bruises. "I'm glad you okay because this family couldn't handle losing another loved one; God he knows," she said, turning around to look at him again.

"I'm fine, Mrs. Baker; just a couple of cuts, bruises," George said, trying to get comfortable, downplaying his injuries.

"George, if you want to lay down, I have a blanket back there in the corner on your left. I know it's hard to sit up with broken, bruised ribs," Ned said, knowing George would try to play tough guy. But Dr. Taylor had already told him that George should not be putting a lot of pressure on that rib, so he needs to be lying down mainly for the next week on his back. That would not be easy for George, known as the "Walkabout" or "The Traveler," meaning he was always roaming here and there; George had to be out and see and understand what was happening. That was just George; he was curious like that about everything; he just had to know.

Mona pulled out the blanket before George could say anything, rolled only part of it to create a makeshift pillow; George reluctantly lay down on his back, bending his knee so he would be comfortable.

"Four against one," he grumbled, closed his eye against the blazing afternoon sun; Ned pulled off to drop Mrs. Baker, George home.

Ned helped Mrs. Baker down from the wagon and put away the food mama had given with her; unlike most people in town who went to church, Mrs. Baker was a Saturday Sabbath keeper. She went to church on Sundays like everybody else, but she also felt that keeping the original Sabbath was more critical; Sunday, however, she got her sermon, her communion with others in the faith. Friday night to

Sunday evening, Mrs. Baker did not work, handled money, ate what was already prepared.

When Mona asked her why she did it that way, she said it was God's time to communicate with her and she with him. Mabel and Mrs. Cooker respected her wishes; besides, they thought five days a week part-time was all Mrs. Baker should be working at her age anyway.

FOURTEEN

Home Sweet Home

When they finally pulled up into the yard, Mona yelled out, "Uncle George is home."

Mona jumped down from the back of the wagon.

Mona said, "Come on, Uncle George; let's go."

The children ran out of the house and gathered around the wagon: Kelly and Ned came; Sarah and Ms. Henderson came out to see what is going on.

"Uncle George," the children called out excitedly.

George eased himself into a sitting position, pushed himself off the wagon with the help of Ned. He insisted on walking himself, "Okay, family, don't be treating me like I'm disabled now" George extended his arms, the children hugged him. He groaned when they accidentally crashed into his ribs.

Ned saw his grimace, said "Okay, children take it easy on Uncle George; his ribs are hurt, so no lifting for now, at least for four weeks, okay" he did not want to alarm them too much. He just wanted to make them aware that Uncle George would not be able to horseplay with them for a while. "Plus, he is going to need your help to recover, get strong again, okay children," Ned said because he knew George would try to push himself long before his body could adequately heal.

"Yes, Uncle Ned," they said in unison, released George from their collective grip.

"Don't worry, Uncle George will be back lifting you, spinning you around in no time at all; your Uncle Ned just worrying like a girl," he said, chuckling at his joke; everyone laughed too, including Ned. But when he winced at the pain the laughter brought on, everyone stopped.

"Okay, see what I mean. Who is a girl now, Georgie" Ned said, taking a little pleasure at his friend's pain for calling him a girl. Then he said, "Uncle George will be living with us now, so you will see him every day, not to worry. He will need lots of rest, so I know you will be on your best behavior, right.

"Yes, Uncle Ned," the children said in unison.

Ned wanted to make sure the children understood how sick George was even though he knew George would still try to play the strongman, who cannot be hurt. Ned understood why George picked up boxing; he wanted to show that he could take a beating, give one too. He wanted to be able to defend himself against his dad or any other man. So, he concluded boxing was his ticket to becoming a better fighter and prepare his body for anything.

Ms. Henderson came, gave him a gentle hug, said, "George, it's so good to see you again; I'm glad you're going to be okay" she stepped back into the circle that had formed around him.

Sarah stood rooted to the ground; she did not want to hug him for fear of blushing in his arms, so she said, "I'm so glad your home; you look better since yesterday" she looked over to Kelly for some rescue. She felt her pulse quickened when she tried to look at George; she could not understand why she acted so, so, in love. It hit her like a ton of bricks; she loved George; it had grown so innocently. They were friends first, then playmates with the children; now, she yearned for his touch as a woman. Sarah blushed at her thoughts, hoping no one else saw it. Her longing for George had increased since their revolutions to each other in the hospital.

"Thanks, Sarah" George barely got in before he was interrupted by Kelly. He stole a look in Sarah's direction; his heart skipped a beat; he wondered how long he could stay around her being so vulnerable; he never felt this way before about any woman. So much so it even surprised him; he was a torrent of emotions he had never felt before; he wanted to scoop her up. George never saw himself as a married man to any woman anytime soon, but Sarah could drag him down to the pulpit without a protest from him, plus he just adored her boys.

"Yeah, George, Sarah's right. You look a hundred times better; let us just go in, settle you in your room; it's ready, you can rest," Kelly said, moving towards the door of the house.

"Okay, ladies, I'm at your mercy, but be gentle," he said, trying to crack another joke; he laughed, but his ribs protested again. "Maybe I should just go lay down a bit. That wagon ride shook all parts of me; I'm a little tender," as Ned again helped him to walk into the house without any protest this time. "Thanks, Ned ole pal, Mona," George said as Mona ran to the other side of George, held his hand.

"We are all here for you, Uncle George; we'll take care of you," Mona said, smiling up at him.

Kelly walked over to Sarah, wrapped her arms in hers; they walked into the house together; she knew Sarah was nervous about George being so close. They walked into the house; everyone crowded around George's bed as Kelly, Sarah, helped him take off his shoe, which was not tied up, into bed. After about twenty more minutes of the children asking questions about his injuries, being in the hospital.

George made it seem so scary in there; he talked about how big the needles are that they sewed him up with, the giant needle they poked him to get medicine into him.

The younger children's eyes bulged; they asked, "Did it hurt Uncle George?"

"Just a little, you just had to get used to it; besides, it didn't last long," he said, lying back on the pillow; he was more tired than he realized.

"Okay, children, hug Uncle George but just be careful, return to your work with Ms. Henderson. Sarah, can you please bring George a jug of water, a glass for his room; George needs his rest," Kelly said, ushering the children out of the room with many 'Oh do we have to go' coming from all corners, including Mona as they hugged him, reluctantly left.

"Okay, George, all your clothes, everything you will need is already in the draws; Kelly, the children will be here with you. Sarah, I will be leaving for the Bar within the hour with the rest of the food, but we will come, say goodbye first. George, please try, get some rest; I'll be back," Ned said, leaving the room to pack up the wagon.

Sarah had hurried from the room to get the jug of water, glass for George; she was glad she would not be in the house with him alone today. She could feel herself getting more, more caught up in her fantasy of George Morgan. It was fine when he only visited, but now they would be living under the same roof; her heart skipped a beat thinking about it; she felt wet again.

Her husband, Carlos Campbell, was the only man she had been with, but he never made her feel like this. She dreaded it when Carlos touched her from the first to the last time.

It was a natural longing with George, the desire she felt for him; it had grown in her unexpectedly without her being aware until it was too late. It even shocked, surprised her when she finally had to admit it to herself; strange how the heart is. She made so many promises to herself about never letting any man back into her heart; she never saw George until it was too late; her feelings had overwhelmed her.

Everyone had passed her in the hallway, so she knew she would be alone with him; her hands trembled slightly, spilling a tiny bit of water to the floor. The door was open; she hesitated at the threshold as if to enter would cause her to fall more into his world; she felt weak to him.

Sarah put on a smile to calm her racing heart. "Here's your water George, if you need anything, just call Mona or Jake; Kelly will be here too, but I hope she can get some rest too because of baby Sasha," she said, placing the pitcher, glass on the side table. She did not want to say too much to give away her nervousness or look too closely at him.

"Are you going to avoid looking at me all the time, Sarah?" he suddenly asked, then said, "You don't have to worry Sarah, I promise never to hurt you; this is where we belong right here this moment. I know it," George said, his eyes pleading because he knew she was afraid. "Can I at least get a hug before you leave me for the day; all I've done is dream of you lying in that hospital bed. Sarah, I love you," he said with passion in his voice she had never heard before; it moved her.

She went over to his bed, hugged him, said, "George, I love you too, but I'm afraid," she kissed him on the lips tenderly, then backed away when she heard tiny feet running down the hallway towards his room.

"Aunt Sarah, Uncle Ned said he'll be ready in ten minutes; he wants to have a snack," Mona said and then dashed off again just as quickly, not waiting for an answer.

"George, this is too crazy; I can't do this," she said, moving towards the door when he grabbed her hand.

"Sarah, I'm not asking you to do anything but trust your heart; don't you think it's hard for me too to contain what I'm feeling. I want to spend my life with you, our children, Sarah; lying in that hospital bed gave me a new perspective on life, what is important. I realized I want a family, need a family. I wanted someone to love, love me back;

I have never felt that way before, Sarah. I just adore the boys; you're a great mother, an amazing woman; I'd be lucky to have you in my life," George blurted out without even thinking. He felt vulnerable about sharing so much about, what was in his heart, but still felt safe with her.

Sarah moved closer to the bed, lightly rested her head on his chest, mindful of his injuries; she heard his heart beating faster in tune with hers. Tears came to her eyes.

George raised her head to look into his eyes as a fresh pearl of tear trickled down her cheek; he lightly kissed it away. "It'll be okay, Sarah, I promise," he said, kissing her gently.

Suddenly he felt an erection coming on beneath the sheets, He quickly tried to wrap it between his legs without her noticing, but it was too late as it rose to lightly stoke her elbow that rest on top of the sheets. His blushing made her realize what had happened; she stole a quick look, started blushing herself when she saw the beast that lay just beneath the sheet waiting for her; she shivered in anticipation, a little fear.

George immediately started to cover up his manhood with his hand, apologize. "I'm sorry."

But she stopped him with a boldly surprising comment of her own that shocked, excited them both at the same time. "George, I can't wait to be your wife, share myself with you," she said, placing her hands on his erection. She giggled like a schoolgirl, him like a schoolboy. They kissed again; she left the room before anyone got too suspicious; their fingers lingering over each other touch until they were released; they were happy to have found each other.

Sarah walked into the kitchen with a glow on her face; she tried to look busy to avoid any direct stares as if her face would give her feelings away; it would; she was smiling from the inside out.

Jake watched his mama intently; he knew something was different about her over the past couple of months; she was happier than he had ever seen her. She was singing, smiling to herself more;

he hoped it was because of Uncle George. He could tell that Uncle George liked his mama, not just in a friend kind of way either; he always spent time with her as much as he spent time with them. He noticed that when George came, it was playtime for his mama, too; George made sure of that; he was glad again because his mama was way too serious all the time. Jake thought she was still worried about dad finding them; she was never relaxed in town, always looking over her shoulders and searching faces. She had stopped doing that so much lately, but he still felt she worried about him. Sometimes Jake had to admit; he still had nightmares about his dad beating his mom. "Mom, you okay" he inquired, watching her over his math assignment; she was not the same woman that left the kitchen earlier for Uncle George's room, something had changed, but he could not put his fingers on it.

"I'm fine, Jake, just trying to make sure we have anything for the Bar," she said, making sure everything was out of the cooling box. She found two large salads, two more jugs of ginger beer, lemonade, started to take them out.

"Oh my, I forgot about those, Sarah; mama would send me back. I'll get the jugs," Ned said, taking another bite out of his sandwich; he was working on his second one.

Sarah shook her head; she did not know how Mrs. Cooker feeds him, everybody else; he was like two grown men in one the way he ate. Yet you did not see a stitch of fat on Ned; she was jealous. She took the first container of salad out to the wagon; then, the second, stored them in the cooling box, almost overflowing with food.

She went back into the house, went to see how Kelly was doing just to focus on something else. Unfortunately, Kelly was fast asleep with Sasha curled up beside her in bed; she looked at them, wondered if she could or would want to have any more children now. She knew George would wish to father children; he did not have any; she wondered if it would be fair or proper to get involved with him any further if she did not want any more. George loved children. She could tell by how he played with all of them in the house, any which came by; he was like a big child himself, him, Ned.

Sarah almost stopped by George's room again but decided against it, went back to the kitchen instead. Ned was eating the last of his sandwich, washing it down with a tall glass of lemonade; he got up, put away his plate, glass; got the two jugs to place in the wagon.

"Okay, everyone, see you later, Ms. Henderson. I will see you tomorrow; Mona, do not forget to tell Ms. Henderson about the extra purchases today, what we will be doing for the Beatly's, Mr. Kimberley. Now children remember Uncle George needs all his rest; Aunt Kelly is resting with baby Sasha, so keep it down, okay," Ned said, heading for the door with the jugs.

Sarah went over, hugged all the children, and told them to behave themselves, to help Uncle George, Aunt Kelly. Sarah left with Ned, and they were on their way back to the Bar, but today she did not want to be away from home; George was there.

They arrive at the Bar; the rest of the day went as expected; before they knew it, it was over; they were packing up for the night to go home.

Mr. Kimberley stopped by to speak to Mrs. Cooker about Thomas's reception, had given Steven five hundred dollars towards an all-you-can-drink night of boozing at the Bar. He gave Mrs. Cooker another five hundred dollars for the staff, whatever else she needed extra for the day.

The more Mrs. Cooker protested, the more Calvin insisted that it should go towards the business or staff for their hard work, commitment to Mabel's dream; whatever she wanted to put it to, it was up to her. She could think of it as a small investment for their future. He left, thanking her for caring about his son with tears in his eyes; she accepted it with a full heart, hugged him, and told him it would be okay.

Calvin Kimberley was sober as a judge, and she was thankful. She saw hope in his future, a fresh start; she hoped he was taking

SHADOWS OF THE PAST: TURNING POINT

advantage of; she knew it was going to be a battle because the demons of life never rested.

They went home tired; tomorrow would be another day.

Back at the house, the rest of the day had been quieter than anyone could ever remember in a long time. The children worked with Ms. Henderson until late afternoon catching up on work; they had missed fussing over George, spending time showing her some of the decorations their Aunt Jenny had bought earlier in the day. However, what the children had quickly learned with Ms. Henderson, everything became a teaching-learning experience.

For instance, when we showed her the fork, knife, spoon set, she called them dinnerware, etiquette utensils, cutlery for formal dining. She explained a formal dinner table could have up to eighteen pieces or more of eating ware; she proceeded to list them. Four kinds of glasses, liquor/sherry, champagne flute, water, wine (white and red); five types of plates or dinnerware, dinner, salad, bread, soup bowl, saucer, and cup; four kinds of forks, dinner, salad, seafood, dessert, three types of knives, dinner, butter, desert; four types of spoons, tea/coffee, soup, seafood, dessert. Finally, a place or name card, linen, napkin, and napkin holder. Also, there are additional things like carving forks, knives, spoons, cake and pie server, tongs, etc.,

After hearing all that, Jake could not resist commenting; he asked, "Do people need that much stuff to eat?" while the younger children nodded, looked on.

"No, Jake; that's just for very special occasions; I rather like using my fingers personally," Ms. Henderson said with a slight chuckle. Then she said, "Okay, boys and girls, I think that will be it for your lessons today. Let us clean up, put everything back in order, back to the kitchen to organize your books, homework, lessons for next week; everything is written on the caulk board." She got up off the floor with a bit of trouble because she had not sat on a floor for years.

Jake, Mona helped her up when they saw that she was struggling.

"Thanks, Jake, Mona," she said, stretched out her back; she left an hour later, just as Kelly was waking up from her nap.

Mona had spent time with Ms. Henderson updating her about their activities and how much extra monies they spent on decorations for the launch of the new part of the business. Ms. Henderson also talked about what else they could get in serving, eating utensils. Her formal dining lessons were highly educational, informative, timely; considering what they wanted to do, her input was priceless. Mona realized that Ms. Henderson was an anomaly in a town like Fairbanks; she was well educated, well-spoken, well-traveled, and very knowledgeable on just about everything. She could easily be a professor at any university or college in any small or big city, but she returned to Fairbanks after her education, travels, and adventures. Mona wondered why but thought it too forward to ask, which was unlike her. She respected Ms. Henderson, only asked her nonpersonal questions, but she was still curious. They talked some more about the budget, cost breakdowns, meeting next week as a team, that she would have a report ready for them.

Then Mona said, "Ms. Henderson, what would it cost us to get a safe? And I would like you, Jenny, to be responsible for this part of the business. I want Jenny to become the leader in the business; she is brilliant, she is like my mama that way; plus, she will be running the business when I go off to college as you did. I want to be a teacher, like you, but I don't know for sure yet," Mona said, feeling immensely proud to be following Ms. Henderson's path.

Ms. Henderson smiled, felt proud that Mona wanted to follow in her footsteps. "Mona, you have a great future ahead of you no matter what path you chose. You have so much going for you, Mona; I am proud of you. Now, as for Jenny taking on the bulk of the day-to-day finances, that is a great idea but let us ease her in slowly until everything else settled down. Plus, we need about a three to six-month financial window with the new business so she can see the complete picture with all the new numbers. She has so much on her plate now, running the day-to-day until the restaurant bakery opens. Besides, she handles all the monies for supplies, salaries, etc. Mona, we have to think about hiring more people to make sure you, the family, are not overwhelmed," she said, looking keenly at her.

"We will be hiring George to help with pickup, delivery; we are going to hire four servers for the restaurant bakery, three more kitchen staff to help with the cooking. We realize that with the new orders for pies in Maple Lane, we must hire at least two bakers to help, hopefully, one male one female. With the growth of the business, we can hire more people because we all want Mrs. Cooker to work less. Jenny is doing great; she has learned the business very quickly; I feel that she will take the lead more; you are right about putting too much on her too fast. Kelly is catching on fast, but the baby will slow her down until she gets a little bigger. I guess we will just have to take it one day at a time. Ms. Henderson, Jenny has an idea about putting some of Mrs. Cooker, my Mama's recipes, in a cookbook to sell; can you investigate how we can do that. We have over two hundred recipes we can put in many cookbooks; we want to start this as soon as possible. What do you think? Is it possible? And how much would we have to invest? It's essential that we have many streams of income," Mona said, excited to be sharing all their ideas.

"Slow down, Mona, one thing, day at a time, remember; I'll check out the cookbook opportunity; it's a great idea. Also, we will have to budget for new staffing support so we will have enough business to pay everyone. We also have to work out the cost per pie ratio for Maple Lane," she said when Mona interrupted her.

"Ms. Henderson mama had all those costs already calculated; now we just have to multiply supplies by product. She had all the cost for everything worked out; see" Mona handed Ms. Henderson her mama's notebook, turned to several pages to show the entire cost breakdown per item, all the cost breakdowns for the new business. "It's all here; this is what I've been working from," Mona said, flipping to the last page that her mama had written the day before she died.

"Okay, Mona, can I borrow this so I can create a proper budget with cost, income projection for the next three to six months. Your mama also kept track of every cost, all the income, so I will have her track record to follow. I should have done this already. Your mama was always like that about everything she did. She kept the best notes of any student I ever had; you are the same way, so much like your mom. I have lots of work to do for our meeting next week; I will return these notebooks on Monday. Are all the numbers for all recent sales in here too?" she asked, gathering up all her paperwork, the notebooks.

"Everything recorded, income, expenditures, salaries, investments for business building, miscellaneous expenditures to cover decorations and unforeseen items, and an emergency fund. All receipts and invoices are in the respective envelopes; all monies have totaled; everything is there," Mona said, feeling proud of herself for keeping track of everything.

Ms. Henderson smiled because she felt Mona would have been overwhelmed by now, but she was not, she seemed to have everything under control, but she still worried that maybe she was taking on too much for someone so young. She wanted Mona to have more of a normal childhood than she was having, be able to be a child, run, play, and not have so many adult things on her mind. A ten-year-old should not be as involved with a business and miss out on the critical freedom of mind that every child should have.

But no matter how Ms. Henderson felt personally, she was still proud of Mona, the family; she considered them very brave, fearless, taking on such challenge of expanding, starting new businesses. But after observing the steps Mona had taken with the guidance from her mother's well-researched, documented information in those notebooks, it seemed the natural next step. It seems Mabel Johnson had been training Mona for some time to take over the business, obviously not now, but destiny waited on no one. She packed up her bags and called back the children to say goodbye before leaving, hugging everyone, even baby Sasha, Kelly.

Mona ran to the back room to see if Uncle George was up. "Hi Uncle George, you okay; you need anything?" She asked, pushing the door open after giving it a slight knock. George was just lying there looking out the window into the yard.

"I'm okay, Mona, just looking at these trees, and never realized before they were so beautiful. When you are lying on your back and cannot move, you see the beauty you always take for granted. What you and the other children up to?" he asked, shifting in the bed.

Mona could tell that Uncle George was already getting restless because he was not good at lying around. "We just finished our lessons with Ms. Henderson; everyone's outside playing; so is Aunty Kelly, baby Sasha. You want to come, sit with me, Jake, while we paint. We can put a chair with some cushions out for you," she said, anxious now to get him out of the house, the bed.

"That sounds nice, Mona, but I think I want to stay in bed some more; my ribs are hurting more than I thought they would be by now. I guess I did bust them up badly; all the boxing I did must have done some real damage, but I never felt it before. My dad must have just finished the job of breaking them; it hurts like h...., I mean it hurts a lot," George said, trying to hoist himself up a little to fluff his pillows, fix them better behind his back. He grimaced with pain as it shot through his torso.

Mona rushed over to the other side of the bed to help him. She placed the pillows behind his head to be more comfortable; then, she gave him a glass of water because George looked like he was breaking out into a sweat. "Here you go, Uncle George," she said with a look of concern covering her face. "Can I get anything else, maybe some of that painkiller Mrs. Cooker gave you?" she said, about to run to the kitchen.

George reaches out to hold her hand. "No, Mona, don't worry, I don't want anything, thanks. Just keep me company for a while; tell me what is going on with Jake, Thomas, Serge, Margaret, Marie, Suzie. And why don't you show me your painting?" he said, resting his head back on the pillow.

Mona dashed off to get her painting; Jake's too; when she returned, she started rattling off all that had happened in the house. She told him how Uncle Ned and the boys had conspired to dunk her with a bucket of water. Mona was glad to have Uncle George back in the house because she always felt like he was her big brother, always looking out for her, over her.

They talked until Aunt Kelly called out, "Mona, can you and Jake come to help me set the table for dinner" from the Kitchen.

Uncle George struggled to take his feet off the bed and firmly put them on the ground before attempting to move; it was a slow, tedious process with George grimacing with each movement. The problem was he could not help but put pressure on the muscles in his lower stomach to move; that was where most of the pain started and ended around his ribcage. "Go get Jake and Aunt Kelly to come and help me, please, Mona" Uncle George looked a little embarrassed at not being able to lift himself into a standing position. The more he tried, the more pain shot through his body.

Mona ran off to get Jake, Aunt Kelly, she stopped at the back door to see if Jake was still outside, but he was already in the kitchen; so, she said, "Uncle George needs help getting out of bed" and ran back to his room.

Aunt Kelly called Margaret to watch baby Sasha in the small cradle in the kitchen and went with Jake, Mona, to help George. "George, why don't you stay in bed? We'll bring you your dinner; it's no trouble," she said, moving to the other side of the bed to cradle him under the arm while Jake, Mona, tried to maneuver into a better position to help him on the other side.

"Kelly, I don't want you guys to be following behind me, catering to my every need; Mona here already treating me like I'm deadly sick, close to dying. I need to move around a little, or I'll go stark raving mad, like old Mr. Walker, run-down main street butt naked like him," he said smiling; he was his ole mischievous self.

Jake said, "That's gross, Uncle George. I wouldn't want to see that" he made a face, laughed.

Then Mona said, "Uncle George, you are crazy, but not that crazy. I don't think this would be the same thing as Mr. Walker crazy; he's been crazy a long time" she looked at him as if trying to see if he looked crazier than usual. "Nope, you don't look crazier than usual."

Kelly looked at Uncle George, then Mona, said, "That would be a sight to see; George Morgan running down the main street butt naked. Dr. Taylor would have you back in the hospital by the time you hit the end of the street. Okay, children, let us get George up before he loses his mind because I wouldn't be able to explain this one to Mrs. Cooker" she was trying to contain her laugh. "Okay, after three lifts. One two three" they lifted, pulled Georges body up off the bed, which was no easy task. George was a big boy.

George stood up at first with a bit of wobble, but Kelly, Jake walked, supported him until they reached the kitchen while Mona removed any obstacle in his path, pulling out the chair for him to sit.

"Thank you, family; by the way, Jake, you've talent there, son. Mona showed me your painting; I am impressed. I loved it," George said as he got comfortable in the chair.

Jake became self-conscious, smiled, said, "Thanks, Uncle George, but I'm just okay. I'm learning, but I'll get better with practice" Jake was not feeling comfortable with all this attention, looked over at Mona.

"You both have talent, Jake. When you have a talent like that, you owe it to the world to share it. Next couple of months, when I am better, we will make a trip up to New York to see some of the master painters they have in the fancy museums they have there. What did Mr. Beatly call it?" He said, searching his mind for the word. "Yeah, I'll be your sponsor too," he was smiling, his biggest smile.

Mona let out a scream that startled baby Sasha, went, and hugged him. "Uncle George, you'll take me, Jake, to the museums in New York, really," she said, getting more excited by the minute because she had read about the great artist in the art books Mr. Beatly, Ms. Henderson had given them.

Then she said, "Jake, we are going to see paintings by famous painters and others in New York. Thank you, Uncle George, oh my God, we're going to New York, Jake" Mona started dancing around the kitchen.

Jake looked stunned, surprised at the same time; then, a small smile crossed his face. "Really, Uncle George, you're not kidding us, are you?" Jake asked, not wanting to let himself believe.

"Well, I'll have to ask your mama Sarah Jake; I'll have to ask Mrs. Cooker for Mona if they say yes, we can go for a weekend. Maybe your mama can come to keep you two out of trouble or maybe me out of trouble; either way, it will be good to have an adult with us, so we will not end up getting in trouble," George said, laughing at his joke.

But Jake, Mona knew he was not joking because Aunt Sarah, Mrs. Cooker, would never let Uncle George go off with us alone; not that they did not trust him, they did unequivocally. It is just that in their eye's Uncle George could not say no to us; they knew that. It would be like sending off three children off on their own; for the weekend: not a good idea. Do not get me wrong; Uncle George was very responsible, trustworthy, reliable, would protect us with his life; he is always there to help. He was independent, still working or looking for more work, making his own money; as the women would always say, a good catch. However, once Uncle George got around children, everyone lost track of the fact that he was an adult in the mix of children. If there was more noise in the house, Uncle George was in the middle or the bottom. He would often wave his white handkerchief in surrender; Mona was almost sure they were the first ones to bruise his ribs, but he never complained.

"Okay, settle down, Mona, Jake, just let me speak to your mama Sarah, Mrs. Cooker first; after everything settles down around here," George said, stretching out his long legs under the table.

"That would be a wonderful trip for them to take; that would be nice of you, George. And I am sure once everything settles down, it will be okay; I know your mama would go, Jake," she said, checking the pots of food warming up. "Well, now that's out of the way, come on, Jake, Mona; let us get dinner going so we can settle everyone down for the night. You know what to do; Uncle George is not going anywhere, he's home, now leave him be," Kelly said as they frowned, started setting the table.

Ten minutes later, they were all sitting at the table, blessed our food, and ate. Kelly had us help with the dishes, cleaning up the kitchen; even Uncle George had to dry plates. Even though he jokingly protested that he was an injured man, to which Kelly laughed it off, she said, "George, even if you had one arm, I'd still put you to work."

George believed her too because Kelly was like a super general; she organized like clockwork. Then she sent us all off to the bath, change into our sleeping clothes; Uncle George read our favorite story to us, changing his voice for each new character; he made it scary too. We were screaming, laughing so hard Aunt Kelly came out of the bedroom to see what was going on as Uncle George upped the ante by walking around like a mindless zombie Frankenstein with his hand extended, making strange sounds as we ran around him in circles. Which was not hard to do with his aching ribs; he walked stiffly.

Even baby Sasha was screaming, laughing from her basinet as the others ran around screaming with pure enjoyment; this was Storytime with Uncle George before bedtime, every time.

"George, you always have these children making a ruckus," she said, smiling at them; she was not even mad because even baby Sasha was enjoying all the excitement, would be right in the middle of that hot mess if she was old enough. She was screaming with glee along with the others.

Kelly went into the kitchen, checked on Sasha's bottle of porridge she had left to warm; she was trying to wean her slowly off the breast. Uncle George was finishing up a story; everyone went to bed afterward because everyone would be attending Thomas's funeral, reception at the Bar.

Mona had to admit she was tired too, so they all hugged Uncle George, went straight to bed, fell asleep promptly; the house was clean and quiet again.

Kelly left George sitting in the living room while she settled Sasha down for the night, lying beside her until she fell asleep; that was the last thing Kelly remembered; she fell asleep too exhausted.

George sat in the darkened living room alone with his thoughts; he had been thinking about his future, what he wanted. For the first time, George felt like a man, not a boy; he wanted a wife, a family of his own, and a home. George wanted to make Sarah and their children happy, prosperous. It was vital for him to be a man in their life; he was determined to be that man who would change their perception of what a man should be in a woman and their children's lives. Besides, Sarah did not need any more failed experience; he wanted to treat her as his queen. He caught himself because usually, he was not so soft, sentimental. Most women wanted him for his body, great sex from a strong man, especially married woman here, in Maple Lane. He provided discreet service as their handyman, slash secret lover; some wanted more. However, over time he was unhappy, feeling like a piece of meat, now hated to be called stallion even in jest. He wanted more than sex in his life; he wanted Sarah's passion.

FIFTEEN

Celebrations of Life

Mrs. Cooker was glad to see the lights of her home off in the distance. She was bone-tired; she just wanted to see her bed, get comfy in it. She wanted to celebrate a successful day with everyone because they all had worked hard to meet their first big order. She had to remember to speak to everyone about what we should do with the money Calvin gave them. It was a lot of money to put into the business; it was almost a half day's income for all their sales. To be quite honest, she did not even want to think about any more business for the day; she wanted a cup of tea, her bed in that order. She would make her tea, go to bed; that was the plan; she closed her eyes, hoping her mind would rest too.

Ned urged the horses forward with a quick lash of the reins that never touched their beautiful shiny black coats. They may not have been stallions, but they were beautiful horses that could have been champions in their own right if it were not for the injuries they sustained that would cost most horses their lives. Ned had taken them off the breeder's hands when he had wanted to put them down after a freak training accident broke one leg; the other was found to have challenges breeding champions for Mr. Booker's stables. Their futures were the glue factory, meat shop, or two bullets.

They had been faithful friends, his only mode of transportation. He was grateful for them because while he thought he was saving their lives, they had ended up saving him, giving him independence which many did not have.

Ned could see the house coming up into view, it looked hushed, but he knew everyone in there was probably tired too; what a day, he thought. He looked over at his mama, she had her eyes closed, but he knew she was not sleeping; she never slept in the wagon. Jenny and Sarah were fast asleep when he took a quick peek.

Ned knew that Sarah was trying to get used to all the hard work and long days; it was not easy, plus taking care of the children.

"You okay, mama? We are almost home. How are you feeling? You must be tired," Ned said, turning to his mama, who had now opened her eyes.

"Ned, we're all tired; I know you are tired too; if I weren't so tired myself, I'd want us to celebrate our first big delivery to Maple Lane, the launch of this new part of our business, but all I want right now is my bed," Francine said looking at her son who had made her so proud.

"We can celebrate anytime, mama; maybe after the Beatly's anniversary dinner. Everything is happening very quickly, but it feels good to be busy," Ned said as he pulled up into the yard, stopped.

No movement from the house-maid Ned suspected that everyone had fallen asleep, even Mona, Jake, who always stayed up to make sure they came home safe. It felt strange not to be greeted by Mona's Uncle Ned, everyone's home.

He dismounted, went to help his mama down from the wagon; she started to make her way into the house. Then he went around to the back of the wagon where Jenny, Sarah, napped. Strangely enough, Jenny always woke up as soon as the wagon stopped moving, but Sarah needed a little more time to orient herself after waking up.

"Let us go, ladies, we're home; don't worry, I'll bring in the things, just go in, get ready for bed. I know your bone-tired," Ned said, reaching up to help them to come down from the wagon.

"Thank you, Ned," Sarah said.

Jenny gathered her purse, belongings, paperwork that lay beside her. Sarah and Mrs. Cooker were already inside when Ned swooped Jenny out of the wagon, spun her around in his arms, planted a kiss on her lips with such tenderness she hardly felt it.

"Mr. Ned Cooker, you need to stop before someone sees us," Jenny said, giggling like a little girl.

"I don't care, Ms. Jenny Slater. I do not care if anyone sees us. This week is a week of celebrations; he kissed her again, this time deeper with more passion. He felt the beginnings of an erection and blushed.

Jenny giggled again; if she felt his erection, she did not comment or gave any indication that she did.

"I love you, Ned," she hesitated a moment then said, "All of you" She giggled again. There was no need for Ned to answer.

Jenny walked into the living room to see George still asleep on the sofa; she called, "Ned, Sarah, come help me get George back into bed.

"George, wake up; let's get you into bed," she was saying. George tried to open his eyes when Sarah and Ned walked into the room.

"Sarah, my love," he mumbled sleepily.

Jenny said, "George, wake up," she looked at Sarah, who had turned beet red. Jenny indicated that she should come. Jenny mouthed to her; *It is okay.*

Sarah said, "Yes, George, I am here; wake up so we can get you to bed," she was touching his face and gently stroking his cheeks.

George opened his eyes and said, "I was dreaming about you, Sarah," before noticing Jenny, Ned standing there watching them both;

they were smiling happily for them. "Hi Jenny, hi buddy," he said, trying to straighten up in the chair but winced.

"Hey, buddy, how you feeling? You've got to stop talking in your sleep, man," Ned said, taking a friendly poke at his best friend.

"I was talking in my sleep. I thought I stopped that long ago. Hope I didn't say anything incriminating?" he said, looking from Ned to Jenny to Sarah, who just stood there looking at him smiling.

"Well, you did start to talk about the time...." Ned said but was interrupted by Jenny.

"George, you didn't say anything incriminating don't listen to Ned; you were talking about Sarah, calling her your love," Jenny said, causing Sarah to blush again; George looked like his hand was in the cookie jar. "Come on, you two; I know how you feel about each other. It's been a year, right George, right Sarah?" she asked, looking from one to the other.

"Ned, I'll tell you again. Jenny is a witch. I am sure of it now. How could you have known a year ago? I just recently admitted it to myself, Ms. Jenny '*See Everything*' Slater," George extended his hand so Ned and Sarah could help him up.

"The children love you, George; you always play with the children, always asking Sarah to go with you and them on some grand adventure. It seems natural that they would bring you two together, sharing while looking after them," Jenny said in a matter-of-fact voice that sounded a lot like Mona and Mabel.

"Ned, I must say your Jenny is as sharp as a butcher's knife; she doesn't miss anything. We must be the luckiest men in Fairbanks to have two smart, beautiful women," George said, smiling with drunken love. Sarah smiled; she was happy; she did not pretend around Ned and Jenny anymore.

Sarah suspected Mrs. Cooker knew what was happening with her and George. She wondered how Mrs. Cooker felt about her having children before. How many more children would George desire? She was not sure about anything other than her feelings for George, which was OK with her. She was unhappy until George came into her life.

"You okay, Sarah? Don't worry about anything," Jenny said after they had helped George to bed. "Let us go, now Ned, so these two can have some time together before they fall asleep. Goodnight George. Sarah, should I keep the teapot on low for you?" Jenny asked.

"No, I'm okay; thanks, Jenny," Sarah said and sat beside George. Ned and Jenny left.

Ned returned and unpacked the wagon while Jenny made tea for Mrs. Cooker, Ned, and herself. She paused and made a food plate for Ned and put leftovers on the stove and in the icebox.

Jenny helped Ned put away the storage crates.

Ned put the horses in the stable, fed, and watered them. He brushed, put on their blankets, and popped an apple in their feed bucket as a treat. He patted the horses and left.

Francine tapped a tad of brandy into her cup of tea to help her off to sleep; her mind was what kept her up at night.

Ned and Jenny were alone in the kitchen. Ned ate the food plate Jenny had prepared for him. They talked about how the day had been at Mr. Spilliman Bar and Calvin Kimberley's liquor give-away to regulars who had run out of money for drinks.

Ned said he noticed Calvin holding a glass of lemonade throughout the night, and he remained sober; everyone else was drunk. Wives whisked their husbands away though some of them returned after they had performed their once-weekly three-minute husbandly duty.

"Thank you for the food, Jenny. I was famished," Ned said, looking at Jenny like she was dessert.

Jenny wiped down the stove and counters; she did not consider that work. Ned often looked at her in a way that made her tingle, but she was not about to give in to his or her desires; it would be too easy. Even though all she wanted to do was suck on those full lips of his that said kiss me, suck on me, nibble if you wish, her mind was awash with all the thought of what she could do with his lips. Oops, she thought she might have to change her underwear again; they felt wet. She had never felt any of these feelings before; her whole body tingled with excitement at the discovery; she wondered if Ned could see what was happening inside her body, inside her mind.

"Jenny, hey Jenny, are you okay? Jenny heard Ned breaking through her thoughts. "What you are thinking about Jenny?" he asked, putting the last of his meal in his mouth, washing it down with some of the ginger beer.

Jenny looked over at him, "You, your lips" she reached for his plate, glass; moved to the sink to avoid his eyes.

"Really, what about my lips were you thinking about, Jenny? He asked with complete amusement on this face; he wanted to kiss her as her bottom lip quivered slightly. She did not want to answer him.

Ned got up, went over to the sink to help with the dishes; he could feel the electrical charge that hung between them in the air, giving off unseen sparks. Ned's heart was full of love and lust he had to admit for Jenny, but he did not want anything to interfere with what they have or will have; there was no rush.

"Jenny, don't worry, I'll wait," he said, tilting her backward; he looked deeply into her eyes; he kissed the tip of her nose.

A tear fell from the corner of her eye, he wiped it away, but all she said was, "I know Ned, I know" she washed the dishes; he rinsed and dried them.

They finished up silently, enjoying the charge they felt as they touched ever so slightly. It felt like the lightest touch of a sudden breeze, yet their bodies heated up like a fire lay between them.

"Shoot, I forgot about ole Bessy, Fran, Pearl, Annabelle; they're probably still out by their spot. I got to go get them before they wander off; they are not always the brightest animals in the barn sometimes, other times they surprise you when you least expect it" Ned wiped his hand, started heading for the door.

"I'll come with you, Ned," Jenny said, drying her hand after wiping down the sink.

"Jenny, you don't have to. I know you're tired, why don't you go to bed," Ned said, but he knew she would come with him; it was part of their nightly ritual, he didn't want her to be uncomfortable. He tried to set Jenny's mind at ease; he wanted to be able to propose to her the right way, marry her, have a family with her; nothing was going to spoil that.

"I want to, Ned," she said, taking his hand in hers. They walked out under the moonlit night; a warm breeze lifted the leaves. They went to the pasture, found their cows Bessy, Fran, Pearl, and Annabelle waiting for them.

Jenny knew those cows could find their way home without help but liked the fact that Ned came for them every night and scratched them between their ears. Jenny swore they looked forward to their leisurely walk back to their enclosure because no matter how far apart they stood, they always came running, jostled for position to get their rub on the head first as soon as they saw Ned. "They like you, Ned; I'd be jealous if they were women," Jenny teased, taking Fran and Pearl by their ropes.

"Very funny, Jenny, you've got jokes," Ned said, reaching out to tickle her, which started her running around the cows, giggling for him to stop. He slipped between them, grabbed her around the waist; they both fell in a heap on the ground laughing hysterically.

Ned was on his back; Jenny lay square on top of him, looking down his face. She kissed him passionately like a cold drink of water on a hot day; you did not want to stop until every drop was gone; that is how she kissed him.

Ned responded in kind, drank from her like a man just emerging from the desert into an oasis. He was weak to her surrender; his loins expanded between her legs.

Jenny felt his erection moved higher, higher until it touched the tip of her vagina through his pants, her dress, slip, and underwear. She tingled all over as wave after wave of sensation washed over her; she moaned.

Ned let out a deep groan from within him that he did not recognize; for a moment, he covered his face to compose himself. Then he eased Jenny off him slowly, hugged her, helped her up, and they continued their walk. Ned knew that if he did not get a hold of himself or away from her, he would have a very painful erection all night. It had been a rough two weeks coming to terms with his feelings for Jenny and his body's sudden response to her.

He felt like he was on the verge of having an erection every time he came near her these days; he did not want her to think he had an erection all the time. He had difficulty keeping his penis from rearing its head; he felt they should suspend their nightly walks until he had better control. They reached the enclosure; their cows gladly went inside; they started for the house.

Ned stopped Jenny at the door of the house, looked into her eyes, said, "Jenny, I don't want you to think that all I'm thinking about is getting you in bed. I just do not seem to have any control over my body suddenly; it is not your fault; I am not blaming you for anything; it is me. I have no control over my own body, it scares me, so maybe we should not be alone so much for a while" Ned's voice cracked with emotions, his head lowered onto his chest.

"Ned, I am feeling what you are feeling too, it's hard, but maybe you're right; it would be best for us just to slow down a little before everything gets out of control," she said, reaching up to kiss him lightly on the lips. They understood what was happening between them; they went inside their beds after locking up the house.

Sarah bolted up from the bed, sat upright; she was startled from her sleep by a door closing in the back of the house. It was only then that she realized that she had fallen asleep cuddling with George. Nothing had happened, of course, but it would not have been a good thing if Mrs. Cooker or any of the children had found them in such a position, innocent or not.

She scolded herself for being irresponsible, but she did not beat herself up either; she had spent a fantastic night with George just talking and sharing. George held on to her like a drowning man holding on to a piece of wreckage in the middle of the open ocean; she felt the same way as if he was her lifesaver. They had fallen asleep in each other's arms, feeling safe, secure; she had never felt that feeling before. She felt safe in George's arms; she felt at home.

Sarah slowly unhooked her arm from under George's neck, eased herself up gently off the bed, trying not to wake him from his sleep; he looked so peaceful, kissed him tenderly on the lips and, left his room. Sarah smiled to herself as she snuggled under the sheet on her bed; she still felt the warmth of George's body on her left side where their bodies had touched. Her body raged with the excitement of being caressed by him; she was wet; he had not even connected yet; her body quivered with excitement she could not contain. She fell asleep, contented.

Francine sat up in bed. She did not remember much about the night before except that she had put a tad more brandy in her tea before going to sleep, not much else; she must have been exhausted. She kneeled to pray. She needed extra attention from the man above, for she had been experiencing difficulties going up and down on her old knees, and she had taken to praying while sitting on her bed.

It was a celebration day; Thomas Kimberley's life and death and Mabel's new special occasion services launch. She said a special prayer for Thomas and Mabel's souls.

Francine got dressed and went straight to the kitchen; it would be one crazy day no matter how she tried to cut or sliced it, and she was not talking about the food they had to prepare either. She noticed that amid the death, disappointments, depravity, old, new secrets revealed, love was in full blossom all around her—First Herman, then Ned and Jenny and George and Sarah.

She had lived long enough to recognize cupid's arrows landing into young people's hearts. Once love has smitten a heart, it becomes helpless to fight. She had seen sane, rational men and women lose themselves, sometimes becoming someone not even their mothers would recognize. Love can sometimes take over, and your mind will not be involved in any decisions you make with logic or reason attached.

Francine was happy for all of them, wanted them to hurry up, get on with it because she was tired of the games of trying to hide love, which she could not. She giggled when she remembered how Sarah had blushed at her suggestion of taking care of George. Something was going in Sarah's head that she did not want anyone to know about, but you could see the love, excitement is written all over her face. Francine could not blame her; George was a fine young man, good-looking too; she realized that he was just trying to find his path with no guidance that a good strong man would impart to his son. She was glad he had Ned's father in the early days when he and Ned were inseparable as boys; they were brothers who depended on each other.

Francine washed her hands and put on her apron; she would start the two large roast portions first, then chickens and ham. They had gotten one of Mr. Portman's smoked ham; she would be coating it with honey, mustard, and pepper mixture before she baked it. A typical holiday fare, but she would serve it at Thomas reception and the Beatly's anniversary dinner as appetizers or hors d'oeuvre as Jenny and Mona called them.

She had been doing all the new fancy things since she was a child helping her mama entertain guests. She blamed all those fancy books, magazines they had been getting from those cities up north; like they knew anything about dining etiquettes that the southerners did not teach them, she scoffed at all the foolishness. She considered the best food to be finger food; it did not need fifteen plates, glasses, forks, spoons, or knives to enjoy, yet she consistently enforced proper eating etiquette to everyone in the house. Except when it is her Finger Lickin Fried Chicken because everyone that tried to eat it with a knife, fork always ended up abandoning them, licked their fingers too; she enjoyed seeing that. That is why it was called Finger Lickin; her mama used to remind her when she would see people eating it to the bone. Francine took out the doughs for the loaves of bread, placed them to rest, get to room temperature.

Jenny, Ned, and Sarah woke up, came to the kitchen; they heard Kelly in the backroom fussing with baby Sasha.

Mona came in half an hour later, rubbing her eyes, surprised to see everyone already up and working away in the kitchen.

"Good morning, everyone," she said, going to get a glass of water from the jug on the table; she drank two.

"Morning Mona," they all said; then Mrs. Cooker looked closer at her and said, "You're thirsty this morning, young lady" she was mixing something in a large bowl on the center table.

"I could drink a gallon of water this morning, Mrs. Cooker; it must be all that salt we put on those plums we picked yesterday.

"I told you those plums not ready for eating; they're going to upset your stomachs; maybe not yours or Jake's but the younger ones." Mrs. Cooker shook her head in dismay as to why children never listen. Well, most adults she knew never listen either, so she gave the children a little leeway.

"Okay, ladies, we must make fifty loaves of bread today; once these roasts and chicken are done, we can start on the next, ten at a time; then we will do the big pot pies, then the mini ones. Ned, would you start cutting up the cabbage, carrots, and potatoes for the soup while I get these beef bones going. Mona, can you get the beans that have been soaking? Bring them here" she heaved the pot of soup bones she got from Mr. Kennedy into the boiling pot of water.

"Yes, Mrs. Cooker," Mona said, walking into the panty for the beans in the tub; she put the tub on the table.

"Mona, could you please go help Kelly and the children and take a peek at George; did anyone check in on him since last night?" she asked, turning on the stove to start the fried chicken.

"Not since last night; he was fine when I saw him last," Sarah said, to everyone's surprise.

"Mona, please checks in on George first, then can you help Kelly organize the girls, get Jake to help his brothers; they don't have to finish dressing until after breakfast, but they must have all their clothing ready."

Mrs. Cooker was in fine form; "Tell Kelly not to worry; we got everything under control here; make sure you got your stuff ready, too, young lady. Oh yes, I almost forgot Mr. Kimberley gave us five hundred dollars for Thomas's reception. He said we could use it for whatever we wanted. We can decide together, later." Everyone stopped in their tracks.

"But Mrs. Cooker, I thought we were doing this for free for him and Thomas," Ned was puzzled.

"I told him we were not taking any money for this, but he insisted, said he wasn't going to leave until I took it. The surprising thing was he was completely sober; I thought of all nights, last night would have been the night that I would forgive him having a drink or two," Mrs. Cooker shook her head from side to side.

"He never had a drink in his hand all night, mama. I saw him, watched him all night; even smelt his glass to be sure, it was just lemonade," Ned said, continuing to cut the vegetables into bite-size pieces.

"That's nice of Mr. Kimberley. He's been very generous; is he going to be okay, Mrs. Cooker" Sarah was concerned.

"He'll be okay, I hope; it's a good thing he's doing celebrating his son's life sober; lord knows…." She stopped herself and said instead, "I'm proud of Calvin; he's making some positive changes in his life. That is how death is; sometimes, it forces change; gives you a different perspective on life. You see what is important, the people who are essential to your happiness and wellbeing. We can talk more about this later; I just didn't want to forget," she said, popping in a dozen pieces of chicken into the hot oil.

Everyone started talking all at once. "Five hundred dollars for the business and us? Anything we want to do with it?"

Mona said nothing; she was puzzled by Mr. Kimberley's generosity to her and her mother's business. She went off to check on Uncle George.

She knocked on his door, heard a groggy "Come in" from him, pushed the door open with an enthusiastic "Good morning Uncle George. How are you feeling this morning; it is going to be a crazy day with the funeral, reception, and foodservice all in one day. I'm not sure if I'll be able to spend a lot of time with you today, but we should be back from the Bar by about six or so," Mona rattled off as she jumped up onto his bed to hug him.

"Wow, that sounds like quite a day; I guess everyone's up in the kitchen preparing food. I forgot today is Thomas's funeral; how you think Mr. Kimberley is doing; he did not look so well the other day in the hospital when Thomas died. Dr. Taylor was more worried about him than me. Mona, I have never heard a man cry like that before; I hope I never hear a man cry like that again. I felt sorry for him. I almost started crying myself, to tell the truth," George said, shaking his head.

"I don't know what's going on, but he's been very generous to me, giving me five thousand dollars toward my future; then last night, he gave Mrs. Cooker five hundred dollars to do anything we want with it for the business or us. I'm grateful, thankful, but I don't get it, Uncle George," Mona said.

"Look, Mona, don't be overthinking everything like you always do; just accept it as kindness, leave it at that. I am sure there is no sinister motive behind his giving you and your family some help.

Besides, Mrs. Cooker always looked out for him even when no one cared; she is special to him; I see how much he adores Mrs. Cooker, like a mother. Plus, I am sure there is a lot of guilt about your mother, even Thomas; he said many things the last couple of nights before Thomas died. It was painful to hear," George said, becoming serious all of a sudden.

Then he said, "Mona, life can be very messed up sometimes; I think we all know that. Look, I thought I would die alone in my father's house until I heard Ned calling out my name. Now, I am here with you guys; life's twist and turns you. Well, I do not have to say anything more, do I" George elbowed Mona.

"You ready to get out of bed, or do you want to rest some more, Uncle George? I can get Sarah and Uncle Ned to come to help you if you want; I have to help Aunt Kelly with the girls' clothes for the funeral later. Can you come, or are you still too sore?" she asked, backing up towards the door.

"I can wait until they have some time; no, I think sitting up in a church or on that wagon is still a little too much for me," George said, clearly uncomfortable.

Mona walked into Kelly's room. The girls were running around. Kelly was tending baby Sasha and clothes scattered on the floor. Kelly yelled at the girls with a promise of punishment. She turned around and saw Mona.

"Good morning Mona, thank God you came; would you please organize the girls? Help them pick out a dress for the funeral. They have had baths; put house dresses atop the funeral dresses to avoid a mess during breakfast. Please comb Margaret's hair; she's the one not done yet; thank you, Mona," Kelly was exhausted.

"No problem Aunty Kelly, that's why I'm here. Come on, girls; you heard your mama," she said. When she saw the disaster, Mona started to organize them, said "Okay girls, let us get your dress first, your socks, shoe over on one bed with the ribbons for your hair. What would you like to wear, Margaret? Mona asked, knowing she would pick her yellow dress or one of the versions of yellow dresses she had; yellow was her favorite color. "This one," she said, choosing the one with a bow that could tie in the back, one bow on the front; Mona put it aside, told her to find socks, ribbons, her shoes.

"Okay, Marie, pick one, you too, Suzie, let's hurry up, clean up before your mama's finished with Sasha," Mona said, starting to pick up some of the dresses, take them to their hangers.

Once they had all their clothes together, they came over to the pile of dresses, started hanging them up too. By the time Kelly had finished dressing Sasha, they had finished; Mona was braiding Margaret's hair, putting two ribbons in her hair that matched her dress. Margaret was seven, Marie five, Suzie three; Sasha was just over a year. Mona put the colored ribbons in each girl's hair, and they went out into the living room to sit, wait for breakfast with strict instructions, not to make a mess.

"Thank you, Mona," they all chimed before she walked away.

Mona wanted to check in on Jake and his brothers but thought better of it; she went to her room to organize her clothing for the day before returning to the kitchen. She put away the night's envelopes in her room after recording the numbers and managing the paperwork. Ned and Jenny had gotten extra supplies for today, but they still needed to get the eggs, vegetables from the garden, the one at her old home. Mona quickly picked out her dress, shoe, socks, ribbon and went back to the kitchen to get the eggs' baskets.

Then she went back for the baskets for the vegetables that were her job every morning to pick along with Uncle Ned, but he was busy cutting, chopping, dicing, shredding, and slicing this morning. It was all hands on deck; they were running a tight ship, as her mama would say. And for a moment, when she went back into the kitchen with the first basket, she swore she saw her mama in the middle of the chaos smiling; she almost dropped the basket, she stopped in her track, tears came to her eyes.

"What's wrong, Mona? Jenny asked suddenly, alarm by the look on Mona's face, which looked like joy, shock, and sorrow; she put down the dough she was preparing for the last ten pans to go in the oven.

"I just saw my mama standing right beside you, Mrs. Cooker; she was smiling. She was right there, right beside you," Mona said; she was crying now.

Jenny rushed over to her, wrapped her in her arms, taking the basket at the same time, slid it onto the table. "It's okay, Mona, you're going to see your mother all the time; I can feel her too beside me all the time. You said she was smiling with you; I know she is so proud of you, Mona, of us; you are making her dream come through today; this was one of them. She's got to be happy about that," Jenny said, sitting down, pulling Mona to sit on her leg like a small child.

"Do you remember that day we were at the house cooking? She was talking about growing the business after she bought the stove," Mona nodded. "Well, Mona, she talked to me about a lot of those dreams too, so I know how important this day is when we launch the business officially. But you know the most important place she is in all the time? Jenny asked; Mona nodded, pointed to her own heart and Jenny's. "That is right, Mona, your mother, is already right here in my heart, in all our hearts; I still talk to her every day. Did you know that?" she asked, looking at Mona closely, seeing a vulnerable child; sometimes, she forgets that she was just a child because she's so intelligent, determined, and forward-thinking. It was scary at times.

"Everyday," Mona was feeling better already.

"Mona, people might think I'm crazy if they see me talking to myself, but I find it comforting," said Jenny embracing her again as she rocked and cooed her.

"Thank you, Aunt Jenny; I feel better; you are right about mama. I talk to her all the time, too," Mona said in almost a whisper.

"Mona, we all talk to your mama. Trust me, chile, we all crazy in this house. Your mama Mabel left us a lot of wisdom to guide us.

Sometimes, I argue with her, too; she always wins with logic; I could never win an argument with her. I would hear her voice telling me and Mrs. Cooker; *you are never too young or old until you are in the grave*; then she would say something like, *I don't believe that stupid saying, you can't teach an old dog new tricks, who came up with that anyway. You have done so much in your life, and you learned along the way. See what I mean?* Her words are always in my head. I would be like, *Lord, help me, Jesus, this woman trying to kill me*, those experiences changed my life and opened my eyes," "Mona, this is part of your mama's celebration of life. Mona straightened up, thanked Jenny, Mrs. Cooker, and everyone; they finished the day's cooking and preparations with Kelly's help.

Breakfast prepared; the table blessed; they ate. Sarah and Ned got Uncle George to eat with the family. Excitement was in the air. For the children, it was having fun; for the adults, it might be a sad or happy day but one to remember.

The children washed the dishes, the women and Ned cleaned the kitchen, packed the wagon, and dressed for the day.

Mr. Hedley brought the vegetable for Mr. Beatly's. He packed the rest of the supplies and food into his wagon. Ned would make three trips, Mr. Hedley two, to carry supplies and food for Mr. Beatly's, Mr. Spillman's, and the church.

SIXTEEN

Love and Forgiveness Starts with You

Mrs. Cooker, Kelly, and the girls, Jake's younger brothers, were off to the church to help Pastor Hayles and Mr. Kimberley with any last-minute touches. Mrs. Beatly arranged all the wreaths and flowers that overflowed Thomas's coffin; she soon left to change for the service.

Calvin was looking at the various floral arrangements, suddenly burst out crying at the coffin when Mrs. Cooker came up behind him to ask if he was okay after he wiped his eyes, blew his nose.

"His mother sent a wreath, a bouquet for him," he said, pointing to the two beautiful red, white arrangements of roses. "I never told her about Thomas passing; how did she find out," he said, breaking down again.

"Word travels, Calvin, your family's name is known; a death is the kind of news that doesn't stay quiet for long." Mrs. Cooker said, looking at him closely. He was looking sober; well put together for his son's celebration of life, looking like his old dapper self; she felt proud of him.

"I mistreated her, Francine, I can't see her forgiving me; my father treated her worst, I allowed it, did nothing to stop it or protect her or Thomas," he said sobbing again; he shook his head in distress, dismay; disgust.

"Calvin, you can't do this to yourself, not today; this shows that she still loved Thomas. She must have forgiven you too to have sent such a beautiful wreath, bouquet. She just may come, you never know; with enough time wounds heal; the heart forgives," she said, patting him on the hand she held.

"It will all work itself out, Calvin, you'll see, but it all starts with you; forgiving yourself is the first thing that will invite others to forgive also. Calvin, this is a good start staying sober, clear-headed in honor of Thomas; I am proud of you. The healing always starts with you, Calvin," she said, patting his hand again, excused herself to go see Pastor Hayles.

Calvin Kimberley sat down on the church's front pew, repeated a prayer for his soul, the souls of all those he had wronged willfully or unwittingly; his soul was feeling more purged.

Then he heard an almost long forgotten click of heels that could only be but one person in his world; he turned around, there stood Thomas's mother, his ex-wife Cindy McCall Kimberley looking even more beautiful, polished than the first day he had met her.

Calvin Kimberley got up like he saw a ghost or got his prayer answered, ran into her arms before she could even do anything, started to weep. Before he knew it, he was asking her forgiveness, saying over, over again, "Please forgive me, Cindy, please forgive me; I'm so sorry" he was kneeling before her with his arms firmly wrapped around her legs.

Cindy, who had come early to say goodbye to her only son in private, stood motionless, shocked, moved by Calvin's display of feelings; she knelt with him holding him, they both cried twenty years of pain, hurt, mistakes away in each other's arms.

Cindy had hoped she would not see Calvin; she would be able to slip in; slip out without anyone noticing her. She had come to terms with her decision years ago to walk away from her son, Calvin, but she never again loved or remarried. She never had more children, breaking her parent's hearts.

She had spent most of the past twenty years traveling like a drifting vagabond from one place to the next, living off her parents' monthly stipend, causal work wherever she stays longer than two months. And every time her heartache for what she had lost in Fairbanks, she moved further away until she reached the shores of Europe; there she stayed for the past ten years. She had only returned about a month ago to bury her father when she heard the sad news about her son, whom she had not seen since he was a young boy. Now she came to say goodbye.

"I'm sorry too, Calvin, so sorry; will you forgive me," she said as tears ran down her perfectly manicured face.

They held on to each other like two people lost out in the middle of the sea, with only a tiny piece of wood holding them afloat. They stayed that way for the longest time until Calvin released her, produced two handkerchiefs, and gave her one. A proper gentleman always carries at least two; he had been taught. They wiped their faces and blew their nose; he helped her up from the church floor and ushered her onto the nearest pew.

"I forgive you," they said, broke out laughing; it was strange to hear each other laugh after all these years.

"Cindy, I'm so…." He was saying before she placed her fingers on his lips, took his hand in hers.

"Calvin, please don't repeat it; we both messed up, we both made mistakes we can't take back. I just wanted to sneak in here early, just say my goodbye alone, leave; I didn't want to see you because I didn't want to feel guilty about you, about Thomas…." She said before he interrupted her with his fingers on her lips.

"Cindy, you don't have anything to be guilty about; you were a great woman, a great mother, a great wife; I just couldn't see it. I was weak Cindy, spineless, stupid; especially with my father," Calvin said, looking deep into her eyes.

"I was so young, being a wife, having a child with no close family or a mother around, I was weak too, I just wanted to run away; from you, from your father; Thomas. I convinced myself Thomas would be better off, even fine without me, but I was not fine without him or you. I just kept on running because I was too ashamed for leaving, didn't know how to come back," she said, letting out a sob that moved Calvin; he reached out; held her again.

Calvin, Cindy sat crying together until they felt better; just holding on to each other was a part of the entire healing process. They both needed to forgive; each other.

Calvin closed his eyes, held Cindy in his arms as if she were saving his life; he had just prayed about her forgiving him; here she was. He would finally have a chance to try and make amends to her if that were even possible.

Cindy got up, walked over to her son's coffin, and started a new set of crying. She knelt beside it, leaned on it for comfort, support, saying "I'm so sorry, Thomas" repeatedly.

Calvin rushed to her side, brought her back to the pews when her wailing overwhelmed her.

Cindy did not expect to have so many raw emotions going through her; she had been steeling herself since the news of her father's death and about coming back to Fairbanks to see Thomas; now it was too late.

Her firm, I am fine façade came crumbling down like the walls were made from mud; she fell limp in Calvin's arms, drained of years of pent-up pain.

Calvin held her, knowing how she felt; he felt the same; like a lifetime of burden; guilt lifting off his shoulders. It left them both exhausted, like they had been through a war together that had lasted almost twenty-seven years.

"Thank you, Calvin," she said…."

"No, Cindy, thank you" he kissed her on the hand, then the lips because in his heart, he knew he did love her, despite everything.

Mrs. Cooker, Pastor Hayles, came into the church, walked over to them; Francine gasped because she would recognize Cindy McCall Kimberley anywhere; even at a distance, she still looked the same.

"As I live, breath, pray, I know about answered prayers, Cindy McCall Kimberley. My Lord, how have you been? When did you get here?" Mrs. Cooker asked, walking over to hug her.

"Mrs. Cooker, it's so wonderful to see you again," she left Calvin, rushed into Francine's arms.

"You look lovely; how's Ned, your husband? She asked to avoid her questions.

"Well, Ned's just fine; his father passed away a few years ago now; I'm engaged to husband number four," she said as Cindy picked up her finger to take a closer look at her rings. Mrs. Cooker was wearing most of her gifts from Mr. Hedley; it was a house vote; she had lost, so Cindy was a little surprised to see all her jewelry, rings. Mrs. Cooker did not like a flash.

Cindy was happy for her but a little jealous. She said, "Congratulations, Mrs. Cooker, these are so beautiful; they are stunning. Does Mr. Hedley have a twin brother?" she asked to a round of laughter. "You're both fortunate to find true love at any age; you are just glowing, Mrs. Cooker," she said, pulling her over to the pew.

"Thank you, Cindy; I feel fortunate; at my age too," she said, turning to Pastor Hayles.

Calvin stood up, said, "Pastor Hayles, this is Thomas's mother, Cindy McCall Kimberley," he said, making room for them to all sit.

"It is a pleasure to meet you, Mrs. Kimberley, finally; I am so sorry we are meeting under these circumstances. My condolence to you; your family. Now, if you will excuse me, I have a few more things I need to do before the service; if you have any special requests for the service, you can tell me when I return. Wonderful to meet you again, Mrs. Kimberley," he said; was off.

"You look wonderful; you haven't aged a day in twenty-plus years, Cindy. How is your father, mother doing?" Mrs. Cooker asked, sitting down on the pew with Cindy in the middle; she held her hand.

"Dad died last month; that's why I'm back, and then I heard about Thomas. I had to come," she said, about to start a new round of tears.

"Only God knows why he makes things happen good, bad; the only thing you need to know right now was that Thomas was a good man with a good heart born from two good people; you, Calvin. Sometimes life just deals you a bad hand; we must live with it. He is at peace now, Cindy; he is at peace; I hope that you two will finally find some peace yourselves; that is a good thing. Besides, you both cannot be going through life hurting like this; God knows what you both needed; love, forgiveness, yes indeed. Now I got to go check in on Kelly, the children. I'll see you both later," she said, hugged Cindy, get up, walked to the side door that led to part of the backyard of the church.

"Thank you, Francine; you were always there for Thomas, me," Calvin said, wiping new tears from his eyes.

"Calvin, I keep telling you, God's on your case; I am just a vessel; thank him," she said with thankful prayer in her heart.

Mrs. Cooker felt relieved as she walked out into the sunshine. She knew; hoped that this day would come when Cindy, Calvin would somehow come together; make amends. However, Thomas's body was not a part of her prayers, yet she knew God had his reasons; she rarely questioned his, but today she has some questions she could not voice to God, but he knew.

Jenny went into overdrive organizing Ned, Sarah, Mona, Jake, divided them into two groups: with Sarah, Jake, Mona in the Bar setting up, Ned, herself in the back kitchen arranging all the foods for the reception after the church service, funeral.

She had asked Mr. Spillman to put out three long tables at the Bar's far end, along with two large round tables. She instructed Mona,

Jake to cover the tables with the new table clothes she had bought and put out the six large food trays.

Mrs. Beatly had brought over several bouquets of large flowers to decorate the tables, Bar area; they placed some in ten small vases she had bought, arranged them around the room on the other tables, and two large ones on the food tables. Tall candles are set up on every table in beautifully decorated candle holders.

They put out all the deserts in their special serving trays, covered them up, left all the hot items warming on the stove, all the cold items in the icebox; Ned, Mona, Sarah, Jake left for the church; while Jenny stayed behind to finish up.

Steven Spillman hurried to finish preparing the Bar for his godson funeral reception. He had ordered extra liquor with Calvin's money and added quite a bit of his own to the liquored-up celebration. Steven had bought enough alcohol for every man and woman to have at least five drinks tonight. He had committed himself to not going home sober tonight either.

He scrubbed down the Bar, tables and even wiped the chairs; he had bought extra glasses and ordered additional blocks of ice to cool the wines, Champaign bottles. He had brought his suit but had his work clothing on, was racing to get everything done before he had to get going to the church; his mind was on Thomas, Mabel, Calvin, Cindy.

He had asked Calvin if he had contacted her but hadn't gotten a straight answer; he hoped she would somehow be there; it had been more than twenty years since he last saw her.
Cindy McCall was one of the finest women ever to grace Fairbanks; she was well polished, manicured like a perfect lawn, but she still could not touch Monica's or Mabel's natural beauty.
He remembered how jealous and bitter Michael had been when Calvin married her after Monica's death, thought it unfair that Calvin should always get all the most beautiful women only to destroy them.

Now that Steven was looking back into their past, he realized that it was more than youthful jealousy Michael carried for Calvin all those years ago; but he, like Gabriel, had caulked it up to the competitive nature of both men. They were all a little competitive back then, but Michael and Calvin were ruthless in their one-ups man's ship, conquest to have one notch up on their belts against each other. But he never knew Michael had such long seething hate for Calvin, working to destroy his friend or what they all thought was friendship. When you are young, you only see that kind of competition as youthful enthusiasm for women that was their only focus back then; women; how many they could get in bed. Many promises made even more, broken hearts, a slew of lies that impacted these women on fundamental levels all for their immature games, amusement; all of which still influenced their lives and others.

Steven shook his head, he did not want to think of how many lives they had callously destroyed along the way for their pleasure, enjoyment; the only person that stood out in his mind today was Cindy McCall. He wondered if she had heard about her son Thomas's death, was she even in North America; he had heard through the grapevine that her father was quite sick. Would she come back to bury him or her son, or would she still hold on to old hurt, old grudges?

Cindy never came to Calvin's father's funeral, but he figured she would have cursed the older man into his grave; that man gave her grief while she lived with them, so there was no love lost between them. He hoped that by now, she would have tried to forgive, try to forget, but how do you forget your child or husband; he was sure she had paid a hefty price, leaving.

Steven had not thought about Cindy for years but knew death had a way of refreshing your memories of people who once were in it; even briefly, she lasted maybe five years in that home.

Steven always wondered what made the people he knew with money homes so void of happiness, happy memories; they always seemed to be wanting, lacking, or missing something vital amid plenty.

Almost hungry or starving for more but never satisfied even after feasting on all their eyes can behold.

He considered himself, Gabriel, the most stable mentally, emotionally happier, more contented over these many years as friends, but Calvin, Michael always seemed unsatisfied with their life's lot, even with so much. Gabriel, I was like the poor bastard cousins that tagged along everywhere out of obligation as family comparing access to money. Still, we never felt within ourselves that we were poor or wanting of anything compared to them. We saw each other as childhood friends. We were boys having fun together; social status was not a factor in our interaction until someone made it so, usually an adult.

Steven had hired two young women to help him tonight in the Bar, Stacy Hampton, Marie Mullen. At first, he was a little reluctant about Mabel's idea, but with the Bar getting busier, he needed help; besides, she was always right. He had hired young Mr. Wilbert Turner to help around the place, do some cleaning here, there, but he had been having problems taking care of his sick wife, their two small children, keeping up with the work required.

He felt sorry for the young man, he needed steady help, but he told him once his family troubles were sorted out, he would still have a job to come back to; so, he hired Mr. Seymore Stanley, who was too old to be working but came steadily none the less; did his job even if it took a little longer. Mr. Stanley was in the back boiling large pots of water for the glasses to be washed as they came in; he had ordered an extra one hundred glasses, two large spanking new tubs to wash and rinse them in.

Steven heard the church bells toll ten-o-clock; he rushed to get changed for the funeral. Jenny and Mr. Stanley stayed back to watch the Bar while Steven was gone. He knew that Calvin would need all the support he could get; Mrs. Cooker and Ned would not be able to contain his guilt or misery.

Steven was far more worried about Calvin now that he had stopped drinking over the past two days, though he was happy for him. He was concerned because sometimes he felt his friend was almost trying to say goodbye.... like he was not sure he would see him again. Calvin was never the same after Monica's death and Cindy leaving; he just fell apart completely.

Steven had never envied his friend's station in life because he had a first-hand view of his life's interior that he did not always like seeing. And even though his, Gabriel's, Mrs. Cooker's homes were far humbler than Calvin's, he had found more love, kindness, acceptance in our four walls than he had seen in Calvin's own. He rarely went home until he had to; his father used to curse that he was running the streets like a criminal until all hours of the day, night even when he was young.

We had no idea until Calvin's mother died from the flu that his father was abusing her until Mrs. Cooker, Doctor Morgan intervened; Calvin was a wreck then, too, trying to kill himself at various points but called it having fun. He was utterly reckless back then, dangerous to himself, others; we thought he was the coolest. We were just as dumb as ass; youth, ego, testosterone, fearlessness somehow kept us alive when we all should be dead by now.

They would run across the bridge when the train was coming, which on several occasions almost cost them their lives; they just escaped death when they jumped off the bridge at the last moment when they realized they would never make it to the other side. Michael damaged his leg once when he hit a rock after plunging off the bridge; it could have been worst if he had hit it directly, but it was just a superficial injury that made Michael scream like a girl; cry like a baby. His father was none too happy, squarely blaming Calvin for almost costing his son his life.

We never let him live it down; Steven laughed at the memory that seemed a lifetime ago; it was. Nothing was the same between them or ever would be again; still, he missed his childhood friendship with the men who had contributed to shaping his life. He felt sadness at a loss.

They had shared so much of their life; suddenly, their lives seemed on separate, distant paths. He went to get dressed for his godson's funeral and the rebirth of his friend Calvin Kimberley. People were starting to make their way to the church; as they gathered, the hushed whispering could be heard throughout the building as they realized Thomas's mother, Cindy McCall Kimberley, was sitting at the front pew with Calvin Mrs. Cooker, Ned, Mrs. Hayles.

Most of the townspeople had never seen her; only a few remembered her from twenty years ago. Most had thought she had died because a woman getting up, leaving her husband and son behind, was unheard of in those days, but they had heard stories through the rumor mills over the years that made them sympathize with her plight.

From all accounts, Mr. Kimberley Sr. was a brute; they blamed him for driving her away; they blamed him for most if not all their problems even though he has been dead for many years now. They just never liked him; even in death, he garnered no sympathy from the lot.

Pastor Hayles came in; the service started while everyone took their seats as the choir sang swing low sweet chariot coming forth to carry me home; the congregation joined in. Pastor Hayles provided a stirring sermon that garnered many Amen throughout the congregation as Calvin; Cindy silently cried, holding on to each other as if they were the only ones left in the world.

Steven went up to give his godson eulogy; he was touching as he spoke about Thomas's birth, youth, and young adult life. He talked about Thomas's kindness to the elders, children in town, his generosity to strangers, and his willingness to help anyone who needed help. He spoke about his smile, his boyish good looks, and that he trusted everyone, even those not deserving of it. He talked about Thomas's drinking and how it devastated his life and how he still found time for a kind word or a smile for anyone in distress. He spoke about his loving heart, a willing hand ready to get dirty when work needed to be done. He talked about how Thomas gave money to those in need that no one heard or knew of except those he helped without fanfare. He spoke about how he felt; he failed him when he needed him most while he wallowed in his self-pity that he wanted another chance to make it up. Steven wrapped up his eulogy with "Thomas Malcolm Kimberley was a good man, who made some mistakes, but gave so much in return. Rest in Peace," he said, leaving the pulpit in tears.

The service ended. Everyone joined the procession and walked to the Kimberley's family plot at the nearby cemetery; Thomas was finally at rest.

Mrs. Cooker announced that the reception would be held at Mr. Spillman's Bar; they were all invited to bring their families; she had to beg Cindy to stay for the reception; she did.

Mr. Hedley, the rest of the family gathered around the Kimberley's. Ned asked if Calvin wanted him to drive him, Mrs. Kimberley, back to the Bar, but they decline, opting to walk back to the Bar with the rest of the townspeople on foot; they held each other's hand.

The townspeople came up to them one by one, gave their condolence, tried their best to support them even if it was just for show; they appreciated it. It was a little overwhelming for them both, but they held their head high because their only son had touched so many people.

Steven rushed back to the Bar because it would quickly become a nightmare once the liquor started flowing; he could hardly keep up, so he recruited Ned, Seymore to help him behind the Bar, while everyone else took care of the food for the Kimberley's; the town's people.

Jenny had set up a special table for Mr. Kimberley, his direct family, which turned out to be only Cindy, asked Mona if she wanted to serve them their meal, drinks.

It seemed bizarre that Mona, of all people, would be serving them, but she held no more hostility towards Thomas Kimberley or his family; anymore. In her ten-year-old mind, all she heard was how much Thomas Kimberley loved her mother; yes, it still stung, but she knew it was an accident and not a malicious one.

Mona did not fully understand everything about love, but she knew her mama still loved her father even after he had disappeared without a word, even though she did not want to talk about him; she heard her crying herself to sleep many nights. She had kept the ring he gave her safe, sound in her jewelry box wrapped in a special piece of tissue paper all these years; that said a lot.

Mona knew for sure that her mama loved her father until the day she died, believed that she was still waiting for him to come back someday, maybe they were in heaven together now, Mona thought. She went into the kitchen for the special trays of food prepared for their table; the table had been set with knives, forks, spoons, plates large, small with napkins.

"Good evening, Mr. Kimberley, Mrs. Kimberley," Mona said when she came to the table with the first tray of food.

"Good evening Mona, thank you so much for all your help. Meet Thomas's mother, Cindy McCall Kimberley. Cindy, this is Mabel's daughter Mona Johnson" he said, looking extremely uncomfortable even as he tried to smile through his grieving discomfort. A look of shock cross Mrs. Kimberley's face. She realized Mona Johnson did not know her connection to Calvin Kimberley; or the twists and turns that brought them together. The irony of their intersecting life was not lost on her.

Cindy extended her hand to shake Mona's tiny hands. "Hello Mona, it is a pleasure to meet you; I'm so sorry to hear about your mother. How are you doing?" she asked, not sure what to say; she was the spitting image of her mom.

"It's a pleasure to meet you too, Mrs. Kimberley; my condolence to you also. I am trying to take it one day at a time, as Mrs.

Cooker says, but sometimes it is tough, but I feel she is with me every day. I saw her standing in the kitchen this morning when we were getting the food ready; she was just standing there smiling with me; she was happy," Mona said in a matter-of-fact voice as she looked closely for the first time at Cindy Kimberley.

Mona noticed the makeup she wore; she looked so fancy, especially her clothes, because no one wore anything like what she was wearing around here, not even in Maple Lane.

So, Mona said, "I like your dress, Mrs. Kimberley; I've never seen anything like that, ever" she had a sparkle in her eyes.

"Mona, you have exceptional taste; the dress is from Paris, the purse, shoes from London; the jacket is from Greece. I traveled a lot over the years, but I'm homesick; I'm thinking about coming back, especially now that my mom is alone with my father passing last month" she cleared her throat because she almost started to cry again. When she realized she had lost her father, son in less than one month, everything was happening so fast that she felt exhausted. And now finding Monica's, Calvin's granddaughter Mona hosting her son's reception after her mother's Mabel tragic death at her son's hands; it was almost too much for her.

Cindy had re-entered the world of lies, secrets she wanted so much to escape, had. Still, she looked at little Mona Johnson, and she could not find it in her heart to have hatred against her for the past that had forced her to run away from her child to keep her sanity.

"Are you okay, Mrs. Kimberley?" Mona asked, watching many emotions cross her face; joy, love, pride, shame, fear, embarrassment, hurt, guilt, anger, hope all in a flash. As if she remembered a lifetime of memories, she wanted desperately to remember, forget.

"Yes, Mona, I'm fine; thank you for your kindness, Mrs. Cooker's, the entire family to me, my son, Calvin; we are very grateful, appreciative for the support," she said, taking a long drink of wine to calm her nerves. Cindy felt just sad for everyone; Mabel, her son, Mona, Calvin, Monica, her parents, even herself because we had all lost our innocence during this journey on the road of life together in little ole Fairbanks, USA.

She has been to dozens of cities in over twenty countries, and she always hesitated or dreaded to come back to Fairbanks. Her parents never really forgave her for leaving Thomas behind; she had to go.

No, Cindy, be honest, you wanted to go away, and Calvin's father paid you generously to give his precious idiotic son a child, an heir to his empire. You went away and lived handsomely.

Cindy never told anyone about the arrangement she made with Calvin's father, not even her parents; only Michael McIntyre Sr., the Kimberley's lawyer knew the truth. So many things ran through her mind.

"Cindy, are you okay? One minute you were talking, the next you are looking so far away," Calvin said, a little concerned. Mona stared at Cindy,

"May I get you water?" Calvin said, pouring water from the new glass water jug.

"Thank you, Calvin; I guess I'm a little overwhelmed by all this; first my dad, then Mabel and Thomas; it's all too much. My stomach is a little upset too," she said, taking the water from Calvin and drank; her mouth was dry.

"Mrs. Kimberley, I'll get you soups; that is just what your stomach needs to settle down. Excuse me," Mona said, walking toward the back, dodging men, women, children along the way. Mona thought Cindy Kimberley looked like she had a world of things on her mind; it was not just Mabel's or Thomas's recent deaths.

Mona could not put her finger on it, but she could not help but notice the look of stunned disbelief that briefly crossed Cindy's face when Mona was introduced or Mr. Kimberley's nervousness in doing so. Maybe everybody was simply crazy with raw nerves.

There was sorrow, pain, hurt, disappointment, shame on their faces; they also beat themselves up for their own reasons.

There seemed to be too many secrets, missing pieces of information about her life, family, past that she did not want to think about tonight or what they knew or did not know. They were celebrating life after death, not death after life; she took the bowls of soup to the table then went for the small servings of fried chicken, roast beef, other selection for their table.

But before she left their table for the night, she said, "Mr., Mrs. Kimberley, I hope you find peace with Thomas death, like how I'm finding peace with my mama's" she said about to walk away but stopped, turned; went over to Cindy Kimberley, hugged her. "My mama used to say sometimes a hug can make almost anything better. Good night" she said, walked away into the crowd.

"Good night Mona" they both chimed together, watching her disappear into the crowd; Calvin exhaled; he was holding his breath. Cindy had tears running down her face; Mona's gesture moved her.

"Calvin, she is gorgeous, charming, kind, generous, and smart. Wow, she doesn't know, does she, who she is to you?" Cindy asked, already knowing the answer.

"No, Cindy, she doesn't know, neither did Thomas or Mabel. That is why this is so painful," Calvin said, pouring another drink from the bottle; he had permitted himself to get drunk after staying sober most of the week since Thomas's death. But now that Cindy was there, old, new demons; feelings of guilt washed over him, feelings he had thought he had dealt with long ago.

Calvin's stomach grumbled as prangs of hunger pains announced themselves; even with the noise in the Bar, music in the background, they were sitting close enough for Cindy to hear his stomach; burst into laughter with him following suit. They picked up their spoons, said a little prayer, ate; they were both famished.

On the far end of the table, a condolence book was set up; it was not what Cindy expected; she was overwhelmed by the number of people who came to pay their respect to her, Calvin. At first, the atmosphere around her baffled her because it seemed more like a party than a funeral reception.

When Calvin explained that it was a celebration of Thomas's life, not his death, she seemed relaxed; also, Steven brought a bottle of her favorite wine, his favorite whiskey, two glasses, left them on the table with a small ice container. They sat together watching the crowd, quietly spoke about their son. She had missed his growing up into manhood.

Calvin told her about what kind of young man he was but had to admit that he had been in a drunken haze most of the past twenty years and talked about his failings as a man, father, and husband. Calvin was not kind to himself, faulted himself for all that had happened to destroy all their lives; tears spilled from his eyes; all Cindy could do was hold; comfort him. She was just as guilty, too, if the truth is known, even guiltier, so she kept silent; she had no right to judge anyone.

Mr. Cobbler played quietly in the background as men, women, and children streamed into the Bar that was now bursting to capacity. The children stayed in one corner closest to the back kitchen with Mrs. Nelson, Ms. Henderson eating, generally enjoying themselves.

Mona, Jake, Jenny, Sarah, Kelly, Mrs. Cooker, Mr. Hedley, Mr. Spillman, Ned all worked together to make the night a huge success. By eight-o-clock, they had started packing up; all the food was gone, given away, or sold out.

Mr. Hedley took Mrs. Nelson, Kelly, Sarah home with the children, including Jake and Mona. Then he came back to help pick up, drop off all the extra supplies, decorations; they had been washing, drying, stacking; organizing everything so that it is ready to go.

Mr. Spillman sent Mr. Stanley home after they had given him dinner, food for Sunday; he smiled, thanked Mrs. Cooker, Jenny, and shook Ned's hand for being so kind to him.

Steven looked like he could sleep for two days, but he was still smiling because it was the best day the Bar had ever had. Even with all the free liquor generously given away, the men spent freely into the wee hours.

Calvin, Cindy Kimberley came, thanked them all by eight-thirty. "Mrs. Cooker, Jenny, Ned, thank you so much for all your love, support today; I don't know what I would have done without you. Thomas would be so proud. Steven, thank you, I'll never forget," he said, hugging Mrs. Cooker, Jenny, then Steven, shaking Ned's hand.

"Mrs. Cooker, how can I ever thank you, your family, Mona; she is just wonderful; you're an amazing woman to take care of her," Cindy said, radiating warmth, love with her hug.

"You are very welcome, Cindy. It was our pleasure to do this for Thomas; he was a good man. Mona is an extraordinary little girl; she is very loving and forgiving. She is sharp as a tack, kind; we love her very much. I hope you're going to stay in town for a little bit before you're off again," Mrs. Cooker said, holding her close, looking into her eyes. "It's time to let go of the past, Cindy, build on the future; there's nothing you can change in the past, but you can make the future better" She hugged her again.

"You are right, Mrs. Cooker. We have all made mistakes haven't we; I hope for a clean slate," she said, reaching out to shake Jenny's and Ned's hands.

"Good night, everyone," Calvin said, taking Cindy by the arm; they walked out of the Bar into the night together. They walked back to the church, wobbling slightly; when they got to the car, he put her in the passenger seat, and they drove back to the home she had not seen in over twenty years. She would sleep in the master bedroom that they once shared; he is one of the guest rooms; they were little more than strangers at this point.

Mrs. Cooker and the family packed up all the stuff for their final trip back home in the wagons. Steven said goodnight to them, hugged Mrs. Cooker, and said, "Thank you, Francine. It was a very successful day. Ned, you are the best, Jenny wow, what can I say?

You're an unstoppable general" he watched as they boarded the two wagons and drove off.

Steven closed the Bar an hour later after the last of the stragglers left; he did a final sweep, checked the back doors, shut the windows, turned off the lights, locked the door, went home. He felt proud that his godson's life was a celebration; it had brought his parents Calvin, Cindy back together, if only for this.

.

SEVENTEEN

The Tides of Change

No one spoke on the ride back to the house; they were all too tired; even though they had lots to say about the success of the day, they were just too tired to voice it. Ned whipped the horses gently to move them along at a steadier clip; he knew that everyone wanted to see their beds; they still have all these supplies to put away that would take all of them about half an hour or more.

Ned saw Mr. Hedley's wagon up ahead; he appreciated him more every day; without him, it would take three or more trips back, forth to the Bar and an extra two hours to unload everything after the women had faded out. Ned was looking forward to George becoming part of the team, taking some pressure off him. Lost in his thoughts, Ned looked back to see Jenny taking her usual nap; she must be exhausted; all he wanted to do was scoop her up in his arms, put her in her bed, tuck her in.

Francine looked out into the night. Her mind was going over the day's activities; she was pleased with everything that happened, especially Cindy Kimberley, showing up for her son's funeral. She seemed more comfortable by the end of the night. However, she wondered what Cindy was thinking concerning Mona. Francine hoped that Cindy had truly healed, came to terms with the past because she knew when she left, she was very hurt, angry, bitter; Mona, Thomas were just small children, she sighed. They were finally home at last.

Kelly, Sarah, Mona, Jake, and George greeted them at the front of the yard. Mrs. Cooker hugged George, walked him into the house, ordered him to take a seat at the kitchen table, and said, "George, you know you can't be lifting anything heavy with your busted-up ribs. You want to end up back in that hospital, being waited on hands, foot by those beautiful nurses, right? She looked at him. "George, we'll be working you soon enough, then you'll be praying for some rest, but right now, you need to get lots of rest like the doctor said. How was your day?

"Just fine, Mrs. Cooker, just a little restless, you know I'm not used to just sitting or lying around," he said, stretching out his back.

"I know it's hard not being able to move around the way you use to, but it's just for a little while, George, but you got to give your body time to heal. You are a fortunate man from what Dr. Taylor said about your injuries; God is watching over you, George Morgan. Now, you had enough to eat today.

"Yes, Mrs. Cooker, I couldn't eat all that was left; that was for two men, not one," he said, chuckling. "But it was all very delicious; I just don't have much appetite these days; my eye's bigger than my stomach," he smiled.

"George, I remember when you could eat that and more. You must be in love," she blurted out, stunning poor George into silence. "Love must be in the air because everyone in this house is eating slow, all except the children. I know they just too tired these days to eat as much; that is normal, I suppose," she said, putting her purse on the shelf with the other business papers, envelopes from the night's sale at the Bar. She went to the sink, washed her hands, filled up the kettle, put it on the stove.

"Mrs. Cooker, it's difficult to sit, stand, lie down, and sometimes to eat and go to the bathroom. I never realized one broken rib could affect so much of my body, movement," he said, shifting in his seat to make a point.

"And you want to start lifting all kinds of heavy things; you can't even sit up straight or crooked for that matter or even use the bathroom comfortably," she said, hearing Mabel's words in her head about needing somebody like Mr. Hedley in her life to help her.

As she looked up, Herman walked into the kitchen with his arms full of supplies heading into the living room with Jake, Mona behind him. Ned came in next with the storage crates, put them in the corner; Kelly, Sarah, Jenny came next; carrying a handful of pots, pans, serving trays, etc., put them away in their rightful places. Forty minutes later, they had emptied the wagons, and Ned had put away the horses, went for the cows; we were all sitting in the kitchen having a cup of tea.

Jake, Mona went off to bed but not before everyone thanked them for their help throughout the day, making the first special occasion, Thomas's reception, a huge success.

Mr. Hedley and Mrs. Cooker retreated outside; and stayed for a while; they understood each other's needs. Francine felt free to love again; she permitted herself to welcome companionship into her life. She was relieved that she would not spend her last days alone.

"Herman Hedley, I love you, I suppose I always have; I'm feeling very blessed to have you in my life; thank you," Francine said, kissing him.

"Francine, you make an old man's heartbeat like a young stallion; I can hardly wait two more weeks to have you completely."

She kissed him again to stop him from talking.

"Let's discuss that tomorrow; tonight, I want you in my bed."

"Would you like me to ditch the wagon down the road, come back, and sneak into your bedroom" he winked at her—they burst into laughter.

"Herman Hedley, I never heard such a delicious idea in all my life; you naughty old man you," she said, clearly enjoying their play.

"Thank you, Francine, for loving me and allowing me to love you. Now go get rest; we will see each other tomorrow; we have lots of plans to make," he said, kissing her again before he mounted the wagon, drove off, waving goodbye; he was a happy man.

Francine watched him disappear into the night, went back inside, said goodnight to her family, and went to her room. Tonight, she did not need any help to sleep; sleep was already upon her by the time her head hit the pillow.

Ned helped Sarah put George back into his bed; it was getting a little easier because George could help himself more, but George felt twice as heavy after a long day like Ned had had.

He said, "Goodnight," left Sarah talking to George, and he went back to the kitchen where Jenny was finishing wiping down the tables. Kelly had already gone off to bed; she was almost sleeping on the table when they had tea.

Ned helped Jenny finish wiping down the tables, locked the doors, turned off all the lights, walked her to her room; they hugged, kissed before she went to her room and he to his; they were both tired.

The house was quiet; everyone was asleep except George and Sarah; she was tired too; their conversation did not last long before she was yawning so much that George took pity on her and told her to go to bed. Which she reluctantly did because falling asleep again in his room was not an option; she kissed him quickly and went to her bed.

Mona lay in bed, looking up at the ceiling, waiting for the house to be still. Her mind was racing from everything that had happened during the day. She thought about the Kimberley's, how odd they behaved at the Bar.

She wondered why Mrs. Kimberley went away and never came back for her son or even to visit.

Mona was glad the day went great; for the Beatly's anniversary. Dinner. She hoped Mrs. Cooker, Uncle Ned, and Aunt Jenny would have a beautiful wedding day.

For a moment, she wondered how many villains she had in her life; she only knew about Mertel and Sam, the Beast. She was the only Johnson left in Fairbanks; her mother, grandmother, and great-grandmother were all gone.

Most of all, she wondered why they all had only one child each and what happened to the fathers of the children; where did they go? She had more questions than answers; When she asked her mama or Mrs. Cooker, they avoided the questions. They told her just enough to make her feel good about the answers; it was complicated, and she was too young, Mona was told. Mona wondered at what point the truth became complex.

Mona sighed; she had heard adults double talk all her life. She yawned twice; she fell asleep, still wondering what she would have to unravel one day about her family's past that was so complicated; she floated off into dreamland, where her mother awaited her with open arms.

Jenny jolted from a dream where she was running, from what or whom she did not know. She was sweating; her heart was racing; so was her mind, but she could not materialize any other memory from the dream. She reached for the glass of water she always kept on her bedside table and drank deeply. She tried to lay back onto the pillow and relax, but her mind was now alert; there would be no more sleeping for her; she got up, went to the window, and looked out into the backyard. She could tell that the sun was just about to rise over the mountains on the other side of the house.

The grandfather clock in the living room struck five-o-clock; she could hear the birds gathering on the fence to start their morning fishing for worms; the early bird gets the worms.

Jenny opened the window to let in the crisp morning air. She inhaled several deep breaths trying to recall her dream. She wrapped her arms around herself, looked out into the semi-darkness; the moon was still lingering in the skies above; she observed the magnificence of the night; she felt its mystical pull that called out to her. The moon seemed reluctant to relinquish its hold, but the sun illuminated the night, busting the moon's hold on the world. The moon became a mere shadow in the sun's presence; the stars lost their luster.

Jenny got dressed in yellow; she needed extra sunshine; the yellow dress did the trick; then, she went into the kitchen.

She put the kettle on, started preparing breakfast, get dinner organized; she wanted Mrs. Cooker to be well-rested. She went out to the coop, gathered two dozen eggs for breakfast, then went back to the kitchen, washed her hands, cut up the bacon, sliced the ham, started to fry them.

She mixed the flour, sugar, baking powder, butter, and buttermilk for biscuits; and put that aside. Then she puts water pots on, one for the cream of wheat porridge, one for the grids, one for the collard greens.

Jenny walked over to Mabel's radio, turned it on, just low enough to hear it in the kitchen; it brought her comfort, great memories whenever it was on. She envisioned Mabel dancing around the kitchen; Mrs. Cooker panting and dancing along, and saying, *"Chile, you gone kills me with all this dancing, I thought we were here to cook; not dance."* *Mabel would say, "It's all the same, Mrs. Cooker. It is called providing the joys of life by cooking and dancing."*

"Good morning Aunt Jenny," Mona said, walking into the kitchen expecting to see Mrs. Cooker.

"Morning Mona, how did you sleep, sweet pea," Jenny wrapped her in a cocoon.

"At first, I could not sleep, Aunt Jenny, because my mind was just racing about everything that happened yesterday. First, feeling like mama was right here with us, I think she is pleased about everything. Thank you, Aunty Jenny, for working so hard to help make mama's dream become a reality," Mona said, holding on to Jenny as if she were a safe shelter from the storms of life.

"I know what you're talking about, Mona that's what happened to me too; I guess it's what they call an adrenalin rush after effect that happens when you slow down or stop after a crazy day. Your body is tired, but your mind is still racing full speed ahead," Jenny said, letting her go and going back to the pots on the stove.

"I know what adrenalin is; Ms. Henderson did a word lesson with us two weeks ago. It's when your heart is beating so fast you don't feel pain or anything else; you're stronger, faster; at everything," Mona said, excited to be using a word she had learned.

Then she said, "Aunt Jenny, I've been thinking about how happy mama was when I saw her yesterday" Mona was pulling out the chair to sit down but decided to get up, help with breakfast. Today was their day off; most Sunday service missed them because they were tired from expanding.

Jenny looked at Mona's tiny little face, saw the free spirit of a ten-year-old excited about using a new word, happy about her mama's memories. She seemed at peace; she was so resilient. Jenny marveled at her sheer strength in facing, dealing with her mother's death.

"What would you like me to help with, Aunt Jenny?" Mona asked, moving over to the other side of the table, "Are we going to cook today so Mrs. Cooker can rest?" she went to wash her hand.

"Yes, Mona, I would like Mrs. Cooker to rest today because I know she is tired; if we can all work together, she won't have to do anything today once all the food is done. I personally just want to go back to bed after breakfast," she said with a small smile on her face; Jenny could feel that her body needed the rest too.

"Aunt Jenny mama used to say that you are the smartest woman in this town; she was right," Mona said, putting on her little apron, wiping her hand.

"Mona, your mama, was special to me, to all of us, and I'd do anything for her and you. Mona, I have been so impressed with you how you have handled all of this; your mother's death, funeral, the business, Mertel, and Sam. Your mother would be proud; I am pleased; we are here for each other. Now let us get this food going; oh, before you do anything else, you want to give George a quick check to see if he is okay. Then you can come back, help with these biscuits. Should we make some gravy for the biscuits? Jenny asked, moving quickly between pots putting in the collard greens, cream of wheat, grits now that all the waters were boiling.

"Yes, to gravy…. It is Uncle Ned, Uncle George's favorite. I'll be back, lickety-split," she said, racing out of the kitchen.

"Morning, Uncle Ned, I'm going to check in on Uncle George," she said, stopping long enough to give him a quick hug.

"Morning, Mona," Ned said as he watched her storm down the hallway. Ned walked the few steps to the entrance of the kitchen, was surprised to find Jenny alone mixing, stirring, tasting, looking like a seasoned veteran; he just stood there, watched a moment, then said, "Morning beautiful, need some help," moving towards the sink to wash his hands.

"Morning handsome, yes, I'm hoping that we can finish breakfast and dinner so Mrs. C won't have to do anything today but eat and rest. I got most of the breakfast going; can you please peel some potatoes; cut them up," Jenny said, putting on two frying pots to get the eggs cooked.

Ned went over to her, gave her a hug, a small kiss on the lips. "Thank you, Jenny; you're amazing," he said, not wanting to let her go, but he heard a herd of tiny feet running down the hallway. Suddenly a look of concern crossed his face as he realized his mama was not up yet.

Just then, he heard the crack of her door, her voice telling the children, "Morning children, slow down before you knocked over someone or something" her voice was firm but not angry.

"Morning, Mrs. Cooker," they all said before they ran outside to get their first round of playing in before breakfast; Jake followed behind, looking a little tired.

Mrs. Cooker walked into the kitchen to see Ned and Jenny looking like they just got caught with their pants down. "Morning Jenny, morning Ned; it smells wonderful in here, Jenny. Oh my, I'm sorry Jenny, I overslept this morning; I guess I was more tired than I thought," she said, moving to the sink to wash her hands.

"Good morning, Mrs. Cooker. We want you to rest today; no cooking for you at all. I got breakfast almost finished; I got dinner cooking; once Sarah and Kelly come, we will have everything done in no time. Are you planning on going to church today?" Jenny asked, turning the bacon and the ham. "Ned, could you please get your mama some tea" Jenny put in the second batch of biscuits to bake.

Thank you, Ned and Jenny; I was so tired this morning I almost did not come out of my bed, but then I smell all this delicious food coming through my door. Jenny, you make me, your mama proud Chile, Mabel too. Where is Ms. Mona? I know I heard her little voice earlier; thank you, son," she said, taking her teacup from Ned.

"And yes, I think I will go to church today; we have so much to be thankful for" she sipped her tea, put the cup down.

"I sent Mona to check in on George; she'll be back any minute now. Mrs. Cooker, you need to rest up today; you've been going all week long," Jenny said as Ned hauled out the bag of potatoes, took out about three dozen, started peeling, cutting them up. She took the first of the biscuits, rolled them off the baking dish into the waiting wire rack.

"Mrs. Cooker, I would like you to try this; I put little cut-up pieces of bacon in them; plus, I put in some finely chopped peppers, carrots, celery. It is my new recipe. I figured people love them on one plate; why not put them together, charge a bit more. I only made six batches to see what everyone thinks," Jenny said, walking over with two on a plate forcing Mrs. Cooker to sit back down. Then she said, "Would you like to try it with some gravy?" she asked, reaching for a small bowl.

"Jenny, I'm so glad you're taking the initiative to put out your recipes; this looks delicious," Mrs. Cooker said, taking a small pinch off the side. "Good Lord Jenny, this is delicious. Ned, have you tried this?" Mrs. Cooker said, taking another bite as Jenny put down the bowl of gravy and fork. She poured the gravy on, took a forkful. "Jenny, the customers are going to love this. Ned, you've got to take a bite," she said, sinking the fork in again, taking another bite.

"Thank you, Mrs. Cooker; that means a lot to me," Jenny said, beaming with pride.

"Chile, I could eat this all day, the gravy's got more bacon, the pepper is perfect; it's wonderful," Mrs. Cooker said as Ned came over, had a forkful, then a second.

"Jenny, these are great; they are going to be one of our biggest sellers. I like the crunch of the carrots, celery, you know me; I love my bacon. We should call it the Bacon Veggie Biscuits; these are good with or without gravy," Ned said about to finish what was on the plate.

Then Mrs. Cooker said, "Ned, I said taste, not dine, you can get more later," taking the fork from his hand, she was laughing at him.

"Jenny, I hope you made more than six batches because you know I can eat six of them by myself; these are good; wow, I'm very impressed," he said, going back to his peeling, cutting.

"Well, since you have everything under control, Jenny. I think I'll go back to my room and prepare my church clothes," she said, getting up from her chair.

Kelly and Sarah walked into the kitchen together, followed by Mona, George. "Good morning Mrs. Cooker, morning Ned, Jenny. It smells amazing in here." Kelly said, going to wash her hand.

"Thanks, Kelly; today is Mrs. Cooker's day off; she is going to get her clothes ready for church after breakfast. We are going to prepare breakfast, lunch, and dinner together; breakfast is almost made. I started dinner; the beef stew is on, the roast chickens, beef are waiting to go in the oven after the last two batches of biscuits are done," Jenny said, putting some more butter, salt, and pepper into the grits. Then she sweetened the cream of wheat porridge, got Kelly to cut up one of the six loaves of bread she had taken out, which had been cooling on the shelf, and butter them.

Sarah washed her hand, put on her apron, and started helping Ned by washing the potatoes, putting them in the pot to cook.

"Mrs. Cooker, do we have to come to church with you too, or can we stay home? Mona chimed in as she helped George to the table; Mona wanted to spend some time painting today, or a least try.

"No, Mona, no one has to come to church with me, but I've got so much to be thankful for right now; I got to go give a little extra thanks to the Big Man upstairs. Okay, ladies, I will leave you in charge. I cannot remember the last time I did not cook a meal in this house.

I'm looking forward to just eating today, Jenny, that new biscuit recipe; I could eat it all day; it had me licking the fork," she said, laughing as she went to her room.

"What new biscuit recipe, Mrs. Cooker talking about Jenny; are you holding out on me?" George asked, looking across the table at the pile of biscuits on the rack; he licked his lips. "What, no sample for Georgie?" He asked, looking like someone stole his pet dog. Everyone knew George loved food, was not himself when he was hungry; he could eat like two grown men, Ned. He looked over at Ned, who was about to crack up watching George protesting like a child. Then he said, "Ned, I can already tell you've gotten a taste; look at your face you still got gravy at the side of your mouth," he said, feeling good he had busted Ned, who had sat quietly peeling; cutting potatoes not saying a word until now.

"George, all I'll say is that we've got a new favorite to sell. I think we should call it the Bacon Veggie Biscuit; with or without gravy, it's good, perfect. Besides, I only got a taste from mama's plate" he glanced at Jenny, then George.

"Mona, why don't you get a cup of tea for your Uncle George? I'll fix him up a sample of the new biscuits I made up this morning with some gravy, so he can stop whining," Jenny teased, looking at Uncle George like she was mad before they all burst out laughing, including him. George pouted his lips for good measure.

"Uncle George, your pouting is not a pretty sight; only baby Sasha pouts around here," Mona said, chuckling at her joke. She put his cup of tea down as Jenny brought the sample biscuit plate, gravy which did not look like a sample; it had four biscuits cut up, four forks.

"Okay, everyone, you can stop what you are doing; go try the biscuits since George is acting up; everyone can get a small taste until breakfast is ready.

George picked up one of the forks, sank it deep into the biscuit, scooping up all the gravy he could get, put it in his mouth, he chewed, savoring it. "Oh, my Jenny; I'm in love," he said, reaching for another forkful. George was making all kinds of food sounds as he ate.

Mona grabbed a fork as Sarah and Kelly came over for a taste themselves; the table was completely silent as they all ate one each of the delicious treats while Jenny; Ned looked on.

"This is yummy, Aunt Jenny, really amazing; I want more," Mona said, licking the extra gravy off her fork.

Kelly, Sarah just kept nodding their heads in agreement as they ate all their samples, leaving nothing behind on the plate, not even gravy; they had mopped it up with the last of their biscuit.

"Jenny, that was delicious; you just made it up just like that; you've got talent. The customers are going to love it; it's like a whole meal in one biscuit; I love it," Sarah said, went back to boiling the potatoes in batches.

Kelly was the slowest eater in the house, but when she was finally finished, she licked her finger twice to get any extra gravy off from the last round of mopping up; she looked disappointed the sampling had come to an end. "Jenny, your husband is going to be the luckiest man this side of the Mississippi; oh, my goodness, I can't wait for breakfast. Let's go, people; I'm hungry," she said, went back to buttering the bread after rewashing her hands.

"Thanks, I hoped you'd like it; now Mona, let's set the table, finish up and rest today" Jenny started getting out the serving bowls;

she popped the roast, three whole chicken in the oven. Then she called out, "Ten minutes to breakfast" a few moments later, the children guided by Jake stormed into the kitchen; were promptly told by their mamas to go wash their hands.

Everyone commented about Jenny's biscuits; we decided to add them to our menu, slowly growing.

Ned took Mrs. Cooker, Sarah, Kelly, the children to church while Jenny, George, Mona, Jake stayed behind to rest; relax. Ned, Jake had help Uncle George out to the backyard to sit in the gazebo; he said he was going crazy looking at the same four walls; Jake stayed with him; set up the paints and easels to paint all day if they wanted.

Jenny, Mona finished cleaning up the kitchen, put all the food on the stove under low heat. Then they sorted out all the decorations they would use for the Beatly's anniversary; set those aside in two crates, then they took out three sets of plates, cups, glasses, cutlery for their table setting; put those in a crate. They organized all the serving bowls, plates, platters, glass water, and juice jugs in the third, placed all the napkins, tablecloths, name place holders, candleholders in the fourth.

All the items for their first-anniversary celebration dinner had been organized, set aside in one corner of the living room. At the same time, the rest of the supplies occupied the other side of the room. It was quickly realized they need to have a separate storage room for unique occasion supplies. They had taken up almost half of the living room; we had not noticed because we were so busy.

Mona, Jenny spent the next hour planning, organizing, mapping out the entire day of Mr. Beatly's anniversary, giving everyone a job. Even Uncle George, who was assigned everything except lifting, Mona was sure he would not be impressed with being the head of decorations with the children but would silently protest because they would leave him at home by himself if he did.

The Beatly's dinner would start promptly at five with; music played by Mr. Cobbler, finger foods, followed by soup, salad, main course, the dessert would be their anniversary cake, homemade ice cream.

They would be served at their table by Jake, Mona; their Champagne would be sitting chilled in the silver bucket; Mr. Spillman would come over; pour their drinks. The package also included brandy for him, red wine for his wife at the end of their meals, a small bouquet with any special gift the husband wanted to give; an expensive bow-tied Cuban cigar box would arrive with the wife's gift.

Everyone would be dressed formally in their Sunday best suits, special dresses, giving the dinner a quality high-end feel; Mr. Spillman loved the ideas when we told him what we planned. He thought it would be very classy; set a new standard. We kept everything as a surprise for Mr. Beatly and his family.

"Mona, I don't think we missed anything, do you? And later, we can discuss all of this at the meeting; go over the children's role with them. We can also start including George in the meetings," Jenny said as they looked over the list one more time together.

"Aunt Jenny, I think we covered everything; then some. Yes, Uncle George should start coming to the meeting; maybe he has some ideas about Maple Lane, what is needed there for us to expand on; he is always there," Mona said, packing up the books, papers, and envelopes.

They had counted the money from yesterday and added it to the accounting book; they had two, one they kept at the house; one that moved between the house and Mrs. Henderson's containing the same information, updated daily.

"We'll talk about what to do with the money Mr. Kimberley gave to Mrs. Cooker, work on a budget for a safe, the cost to build a storage room. What did you think of Mrs. Kimberley? Was she nice; her clothing looked expensive; I have never seen anything like that except in those fancy magazines your Mama used to get. I never really got to talk to her; it was so crazy yesterday. Mrs. Cooker introduced us quickly during the madness," Jenny said, looking at Mona now.

"Mrs. Kimberley seemed to be a nice lady from what I saw, but as you said, it was crazy yesterday; she seemed a little distracted, maybe overwhelmed by everything. I do not think she expected all of what happened yesterday. I do not think anyone did, not even Mrs. Cooker. She said her clothing came from all over Europe, England, France, Italy, Greece; she's been traveling all this time, but she looked like she missed being in America; she seemed lonely even when she talked about other counties." Mona did not know whether she should talk about Mrs. Kimberley drifting off in the middle of their conversation and Mr. Kimberley's concern.

"Wow, to be able to travel like that would be fantastic, but to never come home to see my son in over twenty years or my family; I don`t know if I could do that," Jenny said, stretching out her back. "I suppose she had her reasons for not coming back here, but I can`t imagine a reason or reasons I would leave my young son behind, my husband or life. I can`t judge, but it must have been a fairly good reason; I guess we`ll never know that little piece of secret, will we, Mona" Jenny said, getting up from her chair. "Mona, go spend some time enjoying yourself now. I`m going to go take a nap; I need it," Jenny said, kissing Mona on the forehead; headed down the hallway towards her bedroom.

"I`ll see you later, Aunt Jenny; you look like you need rest; I`ll be outside with Uncle George and Jake. I`m sure Uncle Ned should be home soon from dropping off Mrs. Cooker, the others," Mona said; getting up herself, she started to head for the door after putting her stuff on the shelf for the meeting later.

Mona went outside and found Jake, Uncle George, in the gazebo; the seats had cushions to make George more comfortable. Jake was trying to teach him some basic color combinations on some of the test papers Mr. Beatly had given Mona to practice. It was a cute picture to watch Jake teaching George to be delicate with a paintbrush, but Mona knew George would not be able to sit up and paint for an extended period. Mona knew it was George's way of showing that he was interested in what they were doing; he knew Jake appreciated his support.

Mona picked up her easel and placed her strategic base colors on it; white, blue, yellow, brown, green, red, black palette. She picked a medium frame to paint a picture of Mr. Beatly's store for their anniversary gift.

Uncle George had given up on the painting lesson with Jake; he was lying back on the cushion with his eyes closed, legs on the small table that had been off to the side; he was dozing, snoring lightly in the background behind us.

Jake was busy creating a new piece, utterly absorbed; they spoke very little but worked solidly for the next hour when Uncle Ned came back, pulled up the wagon close to the Barn; they waved to him as he dismounted, unhitched the horse, gave them water, food; started to brush them down. Then he went over to the apple basket, plucked out four apples for them to have two each; he took off their bridle; released them into the meadow along with the cows to run wild; they were in for the night.

Uncle Ned decided to leave George right where he was napping; he looked at our paintings; said, "You two are getting so much better. I'd like a picture painted for my room. I'll even pay you both for them," he said, looking again at our newly started picture. "By the way, Mr. Hedley will be bringing home the family after church; I'm going to take a nap myself. Where is Jenny? And how long had George been sleeping?" he asked, stepping down off the last step of the gazebo to go to his room.

"Aunt Jenny is sleeping; Uncle George been out for about an hour, maybe a little less," Jake said, turning away from his painting to look at George, then Ned.

"Aunt Jenny said she was exhausted after we organized the Beatly's anniversary stuff; had a planning meeting. We are still having our regular meeting with everyone later, but because this is our biggest week, we must be organized, with everyone doing their part, even the children and Uncle George. It's going to be a lot of work, but we'll be fine," Mona said with confidence.

"Well, I'm glad Jenny's resting; mama got a chance to rest too," he yawned. "And I'm going to go get some rest too; I'm exhausted. Come wake me if you need me," he said, walking back to the house.

"Okay, Uncle Ned," Mona, Jake chimed together, burst out laughing; they went back to their painting, enjoying the quiet Sunday morning, early afternoon while Aunt Jenny, Uncle Ned, George slept.

The rest of the day went by slowly because they were not watching the time; the family was brought home by Mr. Hedley, who ended up giving a progress report when all the adults, Mona, children met.

They discussed `various aspects of the business, the week's activities, did the accounting, collectively decided to put the five hundred dollars from Mr. Kimberley into the business.

Jenny, Mona explained the plans to the children for their anniversary party duties, explaining that George, Mona, Jake would be in charge of decorations, serving, the others would run the kitchen as usual. Everyone understood their job responsibilities.

They ate dinner together and talked for a while before Mr. Hedley left while the women seasoned all the meats and put them away; everyone went to bed early. They knew no one would rest in the house again until next Sunday; that was fine with them because it was a sign of success, so they went to sleep excited about life; their weeks ahead.

Steven Spillman looked out the window of his Bar; it had been a slow evening, he had closed doors, was cleaning up from the last of the stragglers who had stopped by; he usually did not open on Sundays. He would not come in today but decided last minute to check in anyway on that old icebox he had in the back storage room because the water had to be drained once a day, or it would flood the floor.

He had opened the back, front door of the Bars to air out stale smells that lingered of men's armpits, women's perfume, foods, spilled liquor that mingled to make a new smell. He was just in time to pour the water out onto the flowers Mabel had planted for him out back; she said it would be relaxing for him when he needed a little rest before the chaos of the day started. Mabel was right.

Mabel had gotten Mr. Hedley, Mr. Zimmerman, to make a chair with padding so he could lie down, rest; it became his favorite place, meticulously took care of the flowers.

Steven went inside, feeling her spirit around him; he missed her, but he thought she was happy with all that had happened. He locked the doors, turned off the lights, started for home, smiling because he was thankful for the day Mabel walked into his Bar; life; changed it forever.

Calvin Kimberley woke up with a start and sat up in bed; he was uncomfortable in this bed but would sleep in it over the next two nights to make sure Cindy would be comfortable during her stay.

It had taken him quite a bit of convincing to get her to stay, had surprised her with breakfast in bed on Sunday morning. Making coffee, orange juice, eggs, and bacon; toast with a fresh loaf of Mrs. Cooker's bread; he had picked a few roses from the garden his mother had planted what seemed like a lifetime ago. It had been years since he had looked at the garden, much less picked anything from it. It had painful memories that he did not want to face about the past. But recently, he found himself slowly taking walks through it, really started to appreciate its beauty, tranquility; he felt the love of his mother there.

He reflected on their first conversation in this house after so many years, how she was shocked that he lived alone, cleaned the house himself, even knew how to cook.

To which he reminded her how much time he had spent around Mrs. Cooker's kitchen, how she had had him cooking, cleaning, helping her out with all her dishes when he was there. All the children that lived or went there came away with all these skills, boys, or girls. It had finally rubbed off; he was grateful because he would not starve to death or live in a pen.

They avoided talking about his father but told her about his descent into alcoholism after everything that happened; she had left but made sure he did not blame her or wanted her to blame herself. He told her he understood why she left; he did not fault her in any way, nor his father; he solely blamed himself. He felt at peace with his honesty with Cindy.

Cindy sat up in the bed, looked around the room she once occupied with Calvin as his wife, and saw nothing had changed, not even the sheets and blankets. It was like the room was a time capsule. She was not sure if she wanted to sleep in this room but decided she had to face the demons of yesterday; she swore last night she heard footsteps coming down the hallway or was it her imagination.

Her heart skipped a beat as old memories came flooding back; she flashed back in time, watching the door as if the monster were once again coming in. She shook her head at the memory, knew her mind was just playing games with her; she tried to reflect on her conversation with Calvin yesterday.

Cindy had told him everything about what she had done in her travels, all that she did, even about how she felt before she left, but she did not tell him about his father or his deal for her to go away. However, she knew that he would find out about it if he went through those boxes of files he had taken out of Michael McIntyre Jr. and Sr.'s office. It was all in there somewhere because she only dealt with his father's lawyers after leaving; they sent her the money directly.

She did not tell him either about the numerous times his father had come to her room drunk, rambling, trying to hold her down when Calvin was not there. Each time she called for Ms. Ruby or Mrs. Chambers, their lifelong housekeeper, Ms. Ruby always came running, loudly stating she was coming, which still scared him off.

Cindy was sure Ms. Ruby knew what was happening but could say nothing directly, only speaking in parables that Cindy only understood later. She would recall her saying things like, "People can't live under this kind of stress long before they plum lose their minds;

kill someone or themselves. You got to know what your limits be before they crack" she would look at me with such sadness in her eye's; like Mrs. Cooker always did.

She became increasingly frightened to be alone in the house with Mortimer as Calvin slipped deeper into drinking. Cindy was left to fend for herself with a new baby, surrounded by help, a monster that lurked just behind her bedroom door. She had tried to be happy at first with the birth of Thomas. He was a dream baby, never giving her any trouble, as if Thomas knew at birth; she was already under duress, did not want to add to it.

It was not long after when Ms. Ruby caught him one night when his drunkenness made him too slow to hear her approach. She noticed Mortimer trying to hold Cindy down on the bed; while Thomas lay beside her crying, she shouted, "What's going on, Mrs. Kimberley, you, okay?"

As Mortimer straightened himself out, he said, "It was just a misunderstanding, Mrs. Ruby. I just wanted to hold my grandson, but Cindy said I was too drunk" he staggered off. Mrs. Ruby stayed with them for the rest of the night, talking gibberish until Cindy, Thomas, fell asleep.

The next day when that spiteful old buzzard sobered up, he spoke to her as if nothing had happened the night before; she despised him; still cursed him even in death. Cindy blamed him as well as Calvin for driving her away from her son, this home. Plus, knowing that Calvin did not love her, he had abandoned her. His father preyed on her vulnerability, loneliness, anger. He was a vampire trying to suck off her; she had to escape before it was too late; that was her rationale back then.

The next day Mortimer brought McIntyre Sr. to the house; they decided she should leave for her own protection, but she would have to part with Thomas. Cindy was devastated; it became a choice of stay and possibly be raped, lose her mind, kill him or herself, or leave Thomas behind. He sweetens the deal by agreeing to pay her off for a lifetime of silence; her son, who was a Kimberley after all, should remain there. It was sick, maybe selfish, she knew, but she saw it as her only escape to a better life and her sanity. Cindy agreed; the checks never stopped even after Mortimer died; she became a miscellaneous expenditure on their books.

She remembered wanting to claw his eyes out near the end before she ran after he had offered to pay her to go one more time; she took it. By then, she had already hated Calvin and hated his father even more; she began to resent having had Thomas, whom she loved. So, she left.

Cindy silently wept; her memories had kept her a prisoner for over twenty years; now, with Thomas's death, she was forced to face all the demons of the past she had left behind. She suddenly felt empty; her heart ached; she felt alone once again in her marriage bed that gave her no pleasurable memories.

She thought about how much she had loved Calvin, despite their far from perfect marriage. It was a lifetime ago, yet her heart fluttered when she saw him crying, begging her forgiveness. She wanted to kiss him, throw herself into her arms, but she did not; she wondered if coming back here was the right thing to do; she had scolded herself most of that first day and night.

Cindy wondered if Calvin would ever leave Fairbanks; he did not have anything left except maybe Mona; it was apparent she did not know who he was to her. More secrets and lies; there had been so many already she did not want to be involved in more; she had to leave. She felt the webs encasing her, the madness seeping back into her mind.

Cindy got dressed, packed her small bag that only contained one change of clothes, sat at the mirror to comb her hair, and put on her makeup. The look in her eyes said run, never look back, but she hesitated. There was a knock on her door; she knew it was Calvin.

EIGHTEEN

Mabel's Dreams

Ned woke up earlier than usual; he had gotten nine hours of sleep the day before. Besides, his body was not taking no for an answer; as soon as he hit his bed, he was asleep. He was excited about the day because his ring for Jenny may arrive; he would pop the question after dinner.

He would speak to his mother again out of respect; besides, in every way, his mama was Jenny's adopted mama, he would have to ask her if she were not his mama anyway; country folks had all these rules around marriage. He had finally made the decision that had rattled around his brain for a long time; he loved Jenny Slater, could not wait to marry her.

Ned finally understood the electricity thing that Mabel talked about when he found the right woman. She had said there would be a physical, electrical charge between them, unseen but felt that would also act as a magnet. At first, he did not believe her about people magnet; he understood the North and South poles magnet's science, magnets people built, but not the magnet of the soul, heart, mind, and body.

The good girl in love with the bad boy or the good boy in love with the bad girl or how completely opposite people can love each other; all to the dismay of everyone around them, it was a puzzle for sure, at least to him. But then he saw it all around him as he looked more keenly at the people, couples he encountered in life. The soft-spoken ladies with the crustiest men in town or the men with the wives who cursed or beat them all the time in public and private; the lifelong friendships of the bully and his tag-along (s), were examples he saw clearly in his everyday life.

Jenny was not his exact opposite, but she was more assertive than he was, more outspoken, asked more questions, motivated. He was steady, reflective, a reserved observer, she an active observer. Yet he felt they fit together like perfect puzzle pieces; he got up to bathe, dressed. It would be a busy day without him clouding his mind with thoughts of love and its mysteries. He headed for the kitchen; he was hungry.

Jenny rolled over in bed thinking about the next two days, worried that they would be able to do everything they needed to do to make the Beatly's anniversary dinner a success, still do everything else. Yes, they had planned everything out and organized everyone, but she was Murphy's Law believer about whether something could go wrong …. plan for everything; so, she went over everything one more time in her mind, okay more.

She started when she left her bed to the night when they would be packed up and leave Mr. Spillman's. The two days had become a long list of things to do, people to coordinate in her head. She ran the list of activities from A to Z; then she ran her what-if plan to protect her from Murphy, but she knew life had a way of messing up the best-laid plans; so, she said a little prayer for the extra measure before she left her bed.

Jenny was an efficient woman, but she understood the importance of prayers in everyone's life, so she prayed, mainly because she considered her life a miracle of chance or God's plans. The Chance was her mother dying, and she ended up with a wonderful woman like Mrs. Cooker.

Jenny thought it was God's plan for Mrs. Cooker to befriend her mother after she had seen Dr. Morgan from a vicious beating by her father. That caused her mama to lose another of Jenny's siblings to miscarriage and even her death two years later in Mrs. Cooker's home.

Was it life chance or God's plan? She had no suitable answers for that as a practical woman, so she chose both, left nothing to chance alone. Jenny looked out the window, lamented all the forced changes they had survived over the past number of weeks: Mabel death, then Thomas, uprooting Mona, Sam and Mertel kerfuffle, and them burning down the house, the letter which she did not know the content of, Cindy Kimberley showing up, Mr. Kimberley's generous gift to Mona, the hug, Mrs. Cooker, and Mr. Hedley's engagement; those are just the one's she knew.

One thing Jenny had grown up to learn was that Fairbanks, as small a town as it was, had secrets upon secrets that were whispered but never spoken out loud. She could not help but notice the whispering that went on around the Kimberley's when people realized that Cindy Kimberley had returned to town to bury her only son Thomas.

The town's people came, paid their respect to her and Calvin, but many unasked questions hung in the air between the condolences and prayers for the family. They wanted to know why she left, felt entitled to know, but no one dared ask.

Jenny got up from her bed, took out her clothes, bathed, and dressed for the day; today would be a long day of shopping for the supplies needed for the week. Mrs. Cooker, Kelly would make the anniversary cake; she would pick up the Beatly's gifts for their gift exchange that Thomas, Serge, Marie, Suzie would carry to their table. She had to remember to pick up extra bacon, celery, and onions for the new biscuits that the family wanted on the menu; it was a hit at breakfast yesterday; she left her room for the kitchen.

Francine Cooker woke up feeling good about the day; her anxiety over the past few days seemed to have eased from her mind, the soul just as quickly as it had come for its all too frequent visits lately. She started to wonder if Mabel and Herman were right that she needed to get away sometimes, take care of herself, or be taken care of. She was starting to feel a little overwhelmed by recent events and the secret that accompanied them.

She looked around her room; saw an entirely all too organized life that never held any new adventures for herself; her entire life as an adult revolved around taking care of others. Not that she neglected herself; okay, she had to admit that she did in some ways because she felt obligated. Now she felt no obligations except for Mona, who was in great hands with Jenny, Ned, the rest of the family; she could go away for a little, the world would not fall apart without her.

Francine smiled, started singing 'Give me that old-time religion, give me that old-time religion, its good enough for me' on her way to the bathroom to bath, then dress; start her day.
She felt filled with the joy of the Lord after yesterday's church service, it had been a sad place to be for the past number of weeks, but she felt renewed by Pastor Hayles's message of forgiveness, letting go, letting God work it out for you.

Pastor Hayles talked about forgiving oneself and others to find true peace; it was a journey no matter how you cut and slice. It seemed like all the good townspeople of Fairbanks came out; it always happened right after someone's unexpected death, relatively young. It was as if they said to themselves, 'Oh my God, that could have been me; I need to make some changes, so they came to church for about a month then disappeared back into their past patterns, lifestyle; she'd seen it all the time.

Death's sudden and silent descent on those around us always makes our lives and those we love defenseless. Still, as with everything, humankind takes even this for granted. Francine's mind was rambling on from one thought to the next, asking essential questions she did not want to answer just yet; she was evading them.

Francine wondered if she could just go off into her golden years free to enjoy it like other women her age. Would she be held responsible equally with Cindy, Calvin, his father for being duplicitous in the mess that is Mona's legacy, by God, the universe? The road to hell is said to be paved with good intentions; she had lived a lifetime of good intentions; it had become a very slippery slope a long time ago. She went to the kitchen, her one safe place where only food and cooking occupied her mind.

Mona stirred in bed, opened her eyes slowly; she dreamed about painting at the gazebo; her mother was there watching her, laughing and clapping her hands. Mona remembered that the painting in her dream looked like the one she already painted.

Then it hit her of the day when the bag of potatoes broke open; Uncle Ned went chasing them down in front of Mr. Beatly's; that is what her mama was cracking up about in the picture.
Mona remembered the day now; Mr. Beatly came out to help after he had a good laugh himself; he decided that is what she was going to paint. After all, Mama's business had started with Mr. Beatly; he was her first supplier and customer. Her mama's dream had started there; it would be a fitting painting with special meaning to them.

Mona slipped out from underneath her sheets, went to the window, flung it open as the crispness of the morning air rushed in, chilled her slightly. The mist on the blades of grass still lingered as if waiting for the morning sun to dry up what the plant did not absorb during the long night. The shades of the morning sky beckoned at Mona to paint it; she almost ran out with her easel, paints, canvas to capture the beautiful colors the rising sun made.

Mona went to her closet, took out her green dress, matching sweater, lay them on her bed, bathe, dressed, and left her room.

Uncle Ned was already sitting at the kitchen table with a cup of tea, ham sandwich he had already made before anyone else was up. He was putting the last piece in his mouth, pouring another cup of tea from the pot on the table.

Jenny was busy slicing up bacon, ham for frying. Ned got the eggs. Mona walked into the kitchen, cheerful, bubbling with joy.

"Good morning, family," she said, going over to Mrs. Cooker; planted a kiss on her cheek.

"Good morning Mona, don't you look just beautiful this morning in your green dress," Mrs. Cooker said, slowly spinning her around, looking at her cute matching ribbons neatly tied in two French braids.

"Wow, look at you, Mona, you look gorgeous; mama, it looks like Mona got a hot date," Ned said, laughing. Then he said, "You could give Cindy Kimberley a run for her money this morning, Mona; all you need now is a purse, hat, some white gloves; you could have come off that boat from France with her," he said utterly enjoying himself, now.

Jenny said, "Don't mind your Uncle Ned Mona, only God knows how he gets dressed every morning; he's color blind, you know. Besides, men do not know anything about fashion, especially your Uncle Ned here," she said, giggling. "You look beautiful, baby; are you going to town with us later?" she asked, still slicing.

"You know that's right," Mrs. Cooker said, laughing too.

"Mona knows Uncle Ned's just pulling her leg, so don't you two gang up on my dressing. A man only needs three sets of clothing; working clothing, two or three for going out, and church suits, ties, three shoes to match, that is it," Ned said, getting up from the table; he was still smiling.

"That's his papa talking right there," Mrs. Cooker said with a giggle.

Mrs. Cooker looked happy and rested. Everyone look rested

"I'm going to go milk them girls before we get going; they were looking heavy since last night," Ned said, talking about our cows Bessy, Fran, Pearl, and Annabelle, changing the subject. Then he said, "And we will need eggs for breakfast. We will need at least six dozen for everything in the house, Mr. Beatly's usual three dozen daily, another dozen to divide between Herman, the others. That is a lot of eggs all of a sudden; we should be thinking about buying some more egg-laying chickens, maybe a couple more roosters; build a bigger coop? It just dawned on me. What you ladies think?" Ned asked, suddenly serious; he was always serious when it came to business.

At least that is what Mona's mama had said the first time she worked with him; she said they could joke, laugh but when it came to performing, he was all work; it was true because Uncle Ned seemed to have two modes; work and play even the other children knew it. They knew that when Uncle Ned was working, there was no playing, well, most of the time, and that was because Uncle Ned was a kid at heart.

"Well, that sounds like a great idea Ned, we can get Herman to put the chicken coop together today; you, Jenny, can get them on your rounds today; we've got the portable chicken coop out back that can transport fifty chicken at a time, remember. Mona looks in your mama's book; see how much she paid for the chickens from Mr. Bean, please? Mrs. Cooker asked Mona; she was off.

"Jenny, we need to get more help for you, Kelly, Sarah in the kitchen; I think we should bring in Mrs. Morgan now to learn the recipes. We are making over three hundred pies per week now; we serve food five days per week; lunch, dinner, now special occasions celebrations; it is a lot for five adults, will get much busier for Mona, you. George will be helping Ned soon to ease his stress a bit, but we still got to consider our health and well-being along the way. So today, I am going to talk to Mrs. Morgan. I think Sally Simon, she is a nice young lady, saw her at church yesterday. I like her; she is alone now since her mama died; remember; she is looking for a new job. She says she is tired of those men at the mill talking to her like she does not have a brain in her head; she could do all their jobs in her sleep, better than them too. What you think?" Mrs. Cooker asked after her long ramble.

Mona could hear everything as she went to her room to get the books, envelopes of cash; she had plum forgotten to do any of her usual accounting this morning. She realized that she had awoken with Mama, painting, the dream, and nothing else; she grabbed a stack of papers, envelopes and returned to the kitchen. She sat down at the table to look up numbers; do the accounting, bookkeeping.

"Mrs. Cooker, I think you right, we should bring them in as soon as possible, we're growing fast, we are barely managing as is, everyone is tired; I'm tired, I know you're tired, even Mona looks tired. What you think, Ned, Mona, about getting two more people to help us in the kitchen," Jenny asked, looking from Mona to Uncle Ned.

"Yes, because we do have extra money we can use, really need the help; everyone is working so hard; let us just spend the money that will help us the most. Besides, after tomorrow night we will be so busy we will have to hire at least two more people anyway, remember Mr. Cobbler will be on our payroll when we have these special occasions. Mrs. Cooker Mama bought the chicken for half-price from Mr. Bean at seventy-five cents per chicken; I think we will get the same deal from him. She made a note here off to the side 'buy more get better price'; she had bought three dozen the first time, five dozen the second time, seven dozen the third time, so on. Uncle Ned, you forgot to calculate how many chickens we also use every week on the menu; our family's food; chicken sandwiches, pot pies, roasts, fried that add up to sometimes more than one hundred chickens per week. That's a lot of....." Mona said and started clucking around the kitchen like a chicken; she could not resist.

Ned, Jenny, and Mrs. Cooker burst out laughing as Mona continued her loud clucking around the kitchen, turning her arms into little wings, plucking at Uncle Ned. They were in an uproar when Kelly and Sarah walked in; they looked at each other, then at the mad scene before them because Aunt Jenny and Mrs. Cooker had started clucking like a chicken too.

"Good morning, family. What kind of craziness is going here?" Kelly asked as she, Sarah burst into laughter; they could not help it; they had gotten used to expecting anything from this crazy, lovable family every morning they got up.

"We're doing the chicken dance with Mona, trying to decide how many more chickens to buy," Jenny said, clucking a few more times before becoming self-conscious of how ridiculous they must look. Yet she did not mind because she was in good company as Mrs. Cooker, then Ned let off their last set of clucks before they stopped; slumped into the closet chair still laughing.

Kelly just kept looking at them as if to say; it is way too early for no chicken dance before my coffee; I do not think so. "I am certain there isn't no house in the whole of the United States of America woke up to the Chicken Dance this morning. "Mona, you started all this madness?" She asked Mona looking all serious for a moment. Then she said, "Come hug me, Mona. I love you for being you; the chicken dance Mrs. Cooker, indeed" she stretched out her arms; Mona clucked one more time, raced into them; they held each other hugging; then she hugged Sarah, who stood just watching the whole scene unfold.

"And this was all about deciding on buying more chickens? Sarah asked, trying to get clarification as she released Mona to get a cup of tea.

"Well, it started as a discussion; Mona got up, started walking around clucking like a chicken, flapping her wings, so we join her. It was great fun; sometimes, you must be like a child to be a child of God. Kelly, Sarah, you got to learn how to do something rash, spontaneous, crazy; life is too serious already," she said, clucking again, which sent Jenny off into another chain of laughter because Mrs. Cooker's clucking was the best.

Kelly could not help herself. She started laughing again, cluck once, then twice; said, "I hear you, Mrs. Cooker" she clucked again; they all had a final laugh before they finished their conversation about the chickens.

Jenny wiped tears from her eyes, straighten her dress before she said, "Okay, all you Cluckers, let's just buy fifty more chicken before we all break out into more chicken dancing" she went back to her cutting.

Mona sorted out the envelopes for the supplies, lunch, dinner float, an extra twenty-five dollars for the Beatty's dinner, of course, fifty dollars for the chickens. Jenny, Sarah, Kelly, Uncle Ned, Mrs. Cooker continued with breakfast, started making the dough to put aside to rise for the loaves of bread and pies for tomorrow.

Jake was up, wanted to help, so he went with Ned, Mona to gather the eggs, milk the cows, get the chicken coop ready. First, they got the eggs; then milk Bessy, Fran, Pearl, and Annabelle to make fresh butter and cream. Neither Kelly nor Sarah liked churning butter because they said it was very labor-intensive, so they investigated a newer, more modern model.

Then they moved the coop onto the wagon; Ned realized that they would have to make two trips to get everything, so he decided to get the chickens first, get them out of the way. So, Uncle Ned took off with Jake, Mona to get the chickens, roast portions of beef, smoked meats, all in the exact location, while Jenny worked on the food with the women.

Mona, Jake squeezed up on the front seat with Ned; it was their first trip with Uncle Ned; they were excited because Uncle Ned was so much fun to be around. Half an hour later, they were at Mr. Bean's farm; it was just seven in the morning, but Mr. Bean was already out on his farm raking and giving a feeding of leftover veggies to his chickens and roosters, and turkeys. They roamed freely around his farm guarded by some dogs that looked like they could rip your throat out, but they were gentle beasts who came up to Uncle Ned for their daily rub on the head.

Mr. Bean was happy to see Ned as always; they shook hands, talked business while Jake, Mona played with the dogs. "Ned, the only problem with getting you all these chickens right now is I'll need help gathering them together. Fifty you say, you want them all right now," Mr. Bean said, scratching his scraggly beard, his bulging belly; Mr. Bean did not look like a bean but more like a turnip, round in the mid-section with sticks for legs.

"We'll help Mr. Bean. No problem with that," Ned said, pointing to Jake and Mona.

Mr. Bean looked at Ned then Jake, Mona "I know little Mona isn't afraid of nothing, Jake, that's Ms. Sarah boy right, he's old enough, yep he can help too. You got the scoop on the wagon Ned?" he said walking toward the second Barn which had most of his egg-laying hens.

"Yes, sir," Ned said, ready to go.

"Okay, let's get going" he opened the door; Uncle Ned called us over.

"Come on, Jake, Mona, let's get going," he said, following Mr. Bean into the Barn.

We packed the chickens into the coop until all fifty were locked up and ready to go. Five roosters with their leg tied in the wagon, twenty Cornish hens for the Beatly's dinner, and the family in a small box. Uncle Ned paid the bill.

Mr. Bean gave Jake a baby rooster, Mona a baby chick of their own, instructed them how to care for them. They thanked him for their gift, promised to take care of them; Mona named her chick Chickpea; Jake called his rooster Monster because he kept pecking him on the fingers.

They travel next to Mr. Portman for all their smoked meats; then they popped by Mr. Kenneth for two sides of beef before they started to head back home by nine-o-clock. It had taken them two hours to get everything; the wagon was loaded to capacity as chickens, roosters, Cornish hens voiced their displeasure at being cooped, tied up; it was a symphony of bird sounds.

Uncle Ned and Jake talked about boys' stuff while Mona watched the beautiful scenery they passed as the wagon moved steadily along the gravel road. The trees bowed gracefully under the weight of multiple shades of green leaves. The flowering trees released the last of their scented flowers and leaves, floating softly to the ground to wilt and turn into food.

Mona inhaled deeply, capturing the scents in her nostrils; she exhaled feeling refreshed, then inhaled deeper, filling her lungs. They were ten minutes away from the house when they saw Mr. Hedley just up ahead, moving at a quick clip; Ned lashed the reins to get the horses moving faster to catch up, never touching the horses. She still could not do that yet; every time she tried, she hit them; she concluded that Ned was just a master of his reins, his horses, their master, loved them.

They always responded to him differently from everyone else; she noticed; everyone else did too. He had saved them from certain death; they were loyal to him for that; he cared for them, showed them kindness, they remember, showed him back loyalty; lovingly nudged him when he came close. Sometimes they seemed to be talking to him when they saw him first thing in the morning, came over to encourage him, strange as it seems. They had a great relationship with George, too, because he was always kind to them and had spent a lot of time with Ned during their healing and recovery process. Mona decided she would learn how to paint Uncle Ned's two horses Nelly, Bertha; give it to him as a gift.

Uncle Ned was almost upon Mr. Hedley; he looked over his shoulders when he heard the fast-approaching wagon; smiled when he saw us.

Uncle Ned pulled up beside him. "Morning, Mr. Hedley. How you doing this morning?" he said, smiling at his soon-to-be father-in-law and mentor.

"Morning Ned, Jake, Mona, you are all up, out early this morning. I can hear chickens, so I assume you went to see Mr. Bean, he quickly surmised. And I guess we will need a bigger coop right away; Ned, we will need our farm one day soon to grow all our food for Mabel's Restaurant Bakery; it is growing fast. Mona, what you think?" he asked as he, Uncle Ned, slowed down their horses as we approached the path into the house; he let Uncle Ned go first.

"I'm fine, Mr. Hedley, I got a baby chick from Mr. Bean today, and Jake got a baby rooster. How are you today?" Mona asked, raising her voice, getting ready to jump down off the wagon to show off her baby chick to the other kids.

"I'm just fine, Mona, just fine, thanks," he said, pulling up behind Uncle Ned.

Thomas, Serge, Margaret, Marie, and Suzie came running up to the wagon before it even stops; Marie and Suzie were screaming with excitement as Mona held up the chick for them to see from the wagon; she jumped down as soon as it stopped.

"Look at what Mr. Bean gave me, a baby chick. I'm calling him Chickpea; he gave Jake a rooster; he's calling him Monster because it keeps pecking," Mona said, proud of her new pet.

"Can I hold it, please, Mona?" Suzie asked, coming closer but backed away when Chickpea chirped.

"She won't hurt you, Suzie, hold out your hands out," Mona said, gently placed Chickpea in Suzie's outstretched hands, who giggled with delight; then she passed her to Marie, then Margaret.

Jake had come down from the wagon but was still smarting that his roosters had pecked him a few times. They quickly gathered around him, his roosters who looked mad at being held for so long; he looked like Jake, mad. "I don't like this rooster; he's bitten me at least four times," he complained before anyone could say anything.

"Can I have him then?" Serge asked.

"No, I said I don't like him, not that I don't want him, Serge," Jake said, more than a little annoyed.

"Okay, can I at least hold him, Jake, please" Serge pleaded, stretching out his hands as Jake tried to release his rooster into Serge's hands. But the roosters had other ideas, saw it as an opportunity to leap to the ground, and ran across the yard as if running for life. All the children, including Mona, scrambled after it.

Ned, Mr. Hedley watched from the back of the wagon, trying to decide if they were going to put all the chickens temporarily in the old coop or take time now, expand the one they had or make a new bigger one. It was a lot of chickens, so for now, they just took down the coop, which weighed a lot more with fifty chickens, proving Mr. Hedley stronger than even Ned expected; they placed it by the permanent chicken coop.

"Those chickens were way heavier than I first thought they'd be, Ned," Mr. Hedley said, stretching out his back; there was a good reason he was in construction until this age; he took care of his body.

"Yeah, Mr. Hedley; you're a strong man; I'm impressed," Ned said, following his lead, stretched out his own back.

"Ned, you only got one body, so you have to take care of it, you'll have a young wife one day to hopefully help wreck it too, but if you take care of it, I'll take care of you. And Ned, you have got to stop calling me Mr. Hedley, just call me Herman; we are family, been for a long time.

"Okay, Mr., I mean Herman; you go inside if you want; I'll get the rest of the stuff," he said, walking toward the wagon.

"Let us just finish up together, we can go in; I got the veggie for Mr. Beatly's, I know you've got to deliver the loaves of bread, pies, etc.; I'll help you do that; the women can focus on the food for tomorrow; the rest of the week. Besides, it will give us some time to talk," Herman said, patting him on the back.

"I'd like that, Herman. Thanks," Ned shook his hand.

Mrs. Cooker, Jenny, Kelly, Sarah, George came out when they heard the children screaming, running wild in the backyard chasing Rooster. Uncle Ned, Mr. Hedley had just put down the coop, were talking, walking back to get the rest of the stuff on the wagon.

Mrs. Cooker said, "Children settle down before you give that rooster a heart attack. The poor bird was not used to all this attention he is getting, all their little hands coming at him, that bird's use Mr. Bean's quiet farm.

"Good morning Herman," Francine said as he walked over, planted a kiss on her cheek, and hugged her.

"Good morning Mrs. Hedley, morning ladies, morning George. How are you feeling today?" he asked. He reached out, held Francine's hand, smiling like a silly lovesick puppy.

"Morning, Mr. Hedley," Jenny, Kelly, Sarah said together.

"I'm fine, Mr. Hedley, feeling better every day; plus, I have a wonderful family of beautiful women taking care of me. What more could a man want; I have got everything," George said, smiling with mischief all over his face.

"Well, George, as long as you're not a fox in the henhouse, you won't get shot," Ned said, cracking up at his joke while he patted his best friend on the back.

The women cracked up, but Sarah's heart skipped a beat; she thought she would not have minded if George the Fox snuck into her coop at night; she blushed at her thought.

"Ned, you know that this fox will only break into the best coop in town to find the best hens," George said, starting his bantering with Ned.

"You know the best farm has the biggest guns; best hens for the picking," George bantered.

"That's why you'll get shot, probably in the butt too, running away," Ned said, laughing even harder.

"Okay, you two, that's way too much information for my ears; all I can say is just be careful who's farm you turn up on both of you; you will be shot; people around here are very protective about their hens," she said laughing at her joke…."Now what help you need, Ned, so we can go inside, get delivering these goods to Mr. Beatly's; you, Mona, Jake, Herman can eat some breakfast. We had to feed the children; you know how they are when they don't eat on time; it was a madhouse," Mrs. Cooker said, walking towards the house.

The children were still chasing the tiny rooster. He was outsmarting all of them, pecking fingers that came too close as if its life depended on it.

"You guys leave that poor rooster before you give it a heart attack; poor bird, it must be scared to death," Ned said as it ran off into the bushes out of their reach, safe.

"That's one smart bird," George said as all the children came back, sulking after the futile chase.

"Mona, can I hold Chickpea? Margaret asked.

"Me too," Chimed Thomas, Margaret, who had not held the chick, were holding out their hands to be next; Chickpea just looked on quietly from Mona's hand as more hands reached for her; she chirped.

Mona placed Chickpea in Thomas's hands first, then turned to Jake, said, "Jake, don't worry, he'll be back soon" she walked over and hugged him; the others came over, hugged him too.

"I'm fine, I don't need no hug, he's just a stupid bird anyway; who cares," Jake said, turning away; he never liked the public show of affection like Mrs. Cooker, not even from his mama. They all backed off because when Jake was upset, you just had to leave him alone; they started towards the house to get something to drink.

"Okay, everyone, grab something from the wagon that you can carry into the house. George, why don't you come to help me get some juice for the children? I know they're thirsty," Mrs. Cooker said, seeing him walking towards the wagon. "Also, let's get all the foods on the wagon to deliver to Mr. Beatly, Mr. Spillman; children, come wash your hands" she was almost in the house.

Ned, Herman, Kelly, Jenny, Sarah, the children all grabbed something off the wagon, took it in to the house; until it was empty. They transferred the veggie from Mr. Hedley's wagon and packed the loaves of bread, pies, pot pies, and chips for delivery; then Ned got the eggs, put them in the wagon.

They went inside; Ned, Mona, Jake, and Mr. Hedley ate breakfast while the children did their homework and assignments before Ms. Henderson came; Jake was still upset about his rooster and did not say a word for the rest of the morning.

Soon after Uncle Ned, Mr. Hedley, Jenny left to make deliveries; George, Sarah sat down with the younger children to help them with their homework. Mona, Jake went to the gazebo to paint until Ms. Henderson came; she finished the Beatly's gift. Kelly, Sarah, Mrs. Cooker started cleaning, washing, seasoning the meats to put in the icebox to marinate. Mrs. Cooker baked the cake, put on the vanilla icing, and decorated the cake with tiny white pearl-colored roses, white ribbons, crimped waves. She wrote Happy 30th Anniversary, Mr. & Mrs. Beatly in Gold after mixing the icing with a small amount of finely ground safflower.

Francine carefully set aside the three-tier cake, started on the other cakes to be served over the week; chocolate, vanilla, and lemon. She set them aside to cool while she prepared the icing. Kelly and Sarah made the fillings for the pies, with the last of the blueberries, peaches, and apple for the crumble pie, and set them aside to cool. She seasons the Beatly's, families, Cornish hens; she stuffed them with a mixture of wild rice, apples, celeries that they always enjoyed, set them aside in the icebox.

They retired to the living room to rest after everything was in order; left the beef stew slowly cooking, the vegetables steaming over a pot of water, rice. Mr. Hedley, Ned returned soon after; Mrs. Cooker got dressed to go with Mr. Hedley into Maple Lane; he had another surprise for her. She went reluctantly only after Jenny insisted that they had everything under control, ready for tomorrow.

Later, Ms. Henderson came to give the children's lesson; then, she met with Mona, Jenny to discuss the budget and all the business's financial components. She had organized the income, expenditure report, recorded every penny. She breaks down the cost of every one of our food items from raw material to finished products; she said Mabel was right to buy everything in bulk to get the best price. She broke down all the: current, future staffing salaries, food supplies, building supplies costs, calculated our business growth increase of over one hundred percent, gave us a total of seven thousand dollars cash on hand.

She also set up a different set of bookkeeping for investment, donations for the business, such as Mr. Kimberley's five hundred dollars in a separate category called miscellaneous emergency funds to be used only for extreme emergencies. They set prices for the unique service; Dinner for two includes a three-course meal, wine/liquor, dessert, twenty-five dollars, two adults, two children, thirty-five dollars with a cake add three dollars. Ten people, one hundred dollars. Twenty people, two hundred and twenty dollars. One hundred people would cost nine hundred and fifty dollars, including finger foods, salads, main course, dessert, a three-tier cake for the occasion, and five more cakes of various flavors, decorations, three pies, and ten bottles of wine for the tables. The prices she came up with sounded reasonable, quite affordable for what they would get; we would be paid handsomely for our work. They wrapped up the meeting with a commitment to purchase another stove, a safe, to hire two staff right away. Ms. Henderson left soon after; the rest of the day, the entire family rested in preparations for the rest of what would be a crazy week.

Mrs. Cooker, Mr. Hedley came back bearing boxes upon boxes of dresses, shawls, hats, more jewelry; Francine seemed overwhelmed, but Herman just had this stupid happy smile as if he had just won some grand prize or something.

Mr. Hedley, George, and Ned expand the coop; he had popped by his house to get changed, his toolbox, chicken coop wiring, some pieces of wood. Three hours later, all fifty chickens were in their new homes with plenty of hay bedding. The coop was twice as big now, as they expanded the old chicken coop instead of building a new one. The yard became a sonata of chickens, roosters who had their little section in the coop; they were too aggressive to be in the same space as the chickens all the time. They just got together to do their business; otherwise, they did not always get along.

Mr. Hedley went home after that, saying he had to check in on building supplies, which were due any day now. He said by next week; they could start expanding the restaurant walls without disturbing business; he was still waiting for the construction tarps to keep the dust to a minimum. He also recommended young Mr. Daniel Dillinger to do the signage and give us an excellent price. Mr. Hedley left after giving his soon-to-be wife a hug, a kiss, making her promise to rest for the rest of the day, which was futile. But we had his back on that request, made sure she never touched the kitchen again until she sat down at the dinner table to eat.

Mrs. Cooker just did not know how to relax, so we pushed her, insisting that she show us everything that Mr. Hedley had bought for her. After the show and tell, we hung up, put away everything where she wanted it, left her to rest.

Jake's little rooster finally came back into the yard and pecked his shoes to get his attention. Jake scooped him up; a small smile returned to Jake's face; Monster pecked him only once since that time. They all went to bed early.

NINETEEN

Building on Tomorrow

The hysterical noise coming from the roosters and chickens announced the morning had arrived, but it was not their usual sounds, Ned; immediately knew something was wrong. He quickly put on his robe and shoes and ran out to the backyard just in time to see a fox running off with one of their chicken in its mouth, as the rest ran around clucking for their lives. The fox dodged under the far bush as it spotted Ned coming towards the coop with an old broomstick in his hands.

The fox looked back one more time to ensure he was not being followed and slowed its pace to a steady trot. Ned pretended pursuit, but he knew he did not have a chance at getting the fox, so he went to inspect the damage done. One chicken lay dead with a broken neck; the other chickens and roosters seemed scared to death, still wary of the fox's return.

Ned knew then they had to get a couple of dogs back in the yard to protect their chickens; he took up the chicken and brought it into the house. They would have an extra chicken to cook this morning, so he turned on the stove to make a pot of tea because everyone would be up soon; he also put on a pot of coffee for Kelly, leaving them on low. Then he went to bathe, dress, get ready for the day; he wanted to find out if the ring had arrived today, but he did not want to distract Mr. Beatly from his special day; he went back to the kitchen for his tea.

Jenny had heard the commotion coming from the backyard and got up when she heard Ned rushing out of his room like a bat out of hell; she quickly bathes, dressed, and left her room, stopping at the back door to look outside. She saw feathers all over the yard; the chickens and roosters looked around them as if watching for danger. She went to the kitchen, found Ned sitting at the table drinking a cup of tea, looking dismayed.

"Morning honey, what's going on outback?" she said, grabbing a cup off the table, getting a cup of tea herself; that is when she saw the dead chicken in the sink.

"A fox happened, he killed one, took off with another, but that's it; we have to get a few dogs just to protect our chicken; we have too much to lose now," he said, rubbing his head.

"A fox, I haven't seen a fox around here for a while; they certainly found out about our new chickens quickly; I guess it's all that extra clucking they're doing. How quickly can we get these dogs because you know that that fox now knows where he or she can get a free meal, who would not come back for a free meal" Jenny said, trying to keep it light because she knew Ned was not taking the loss of even one chicken well. She could tell he wanted to harm that poor little fox; he was that serious about protecting our hard work, business.

Ned was still frowning, so Jenny went over, kissed him just before Mrs. Cooker rounded the corner, said, "Good morning Jenny, Ned; I heard a whole bunch of ruckuses in the backyard this morning; what was going on" she asked, reaching for a cup to get her tea; then she saw the chicken. "Foxes," she said, seeing the dead bird.

"Yes, mama, we will have to get some dogs to watch over the chickens, or he'll be coming to have dinner every day; we can't afford that. I'll go see Mr. Barns later about two of his guard dogs," Ned said, finishing his tea; he got up, got the bag of potatoes to start peeling.

"Well, as long as everyone in this house is okay, I can overlook a chicken or two; but we can't afford to lose anymore," Francine said, washing her hands, putting on her apron.

"Okay, Jenny let us get this party on the road; let us bake the roast beef, chickens, start the beef stew. I will start making the fried chicken; we will get the potatoes on as soon as Ned is finished. Then we will do all the loaves of bread, then the pies, after we can make the sandwiches for the lunch rush," Mrs. Cooker was saying.

Mona walked in just then, yawning as if she could still use some sleep. "Good morning," she said, going to the sink to wash her hands; she was not her usual perky self.

"Morning Mona, you still look tired, Chile; didn't you sleep well?" Mrs. Cooker asked, taking a closer look at her. "You look a little pale Mona, are you sure you're okay" Mrs. Cooker checked her forehead to make sure she did not have a fever or anything; she was cool to the touch.

"I'm fine, Mrs. Cooker; just feeling a little tired, that's all. I'm hungry," she said, sitting down at the table.

"I'm with you, Mona; I'm hungry too," Uncle Ned said, putting down his knife.

"Ned, you're always hungry; Mona, I'll make you, Ned, some sandwiches so you can feel better. Did you eat all your dinner last night, Mona?" Jenny asked, going to wash her hands; she took down the bread, cut off pieces of the roast beef, bacon in the icebox, and warmed them up in a frying pot, gave her a cup of tea.

"Thank you, Aunt Jenny," Mona said as Ned came over to sit beside her.

"Thank you, Aunty Jenny," Ned said, smiling mischievously at Jenny, then he turned to Mona, whispered, "Thanks, Mona, they wouldn't have fed me until later; they'd make me starve, work me to the skin, bones."

Mona giggled. "Uncle Ned, you're so silly like a willy," she said, taking a drink from her tea; she burped. "Excuse me."

"What are you whispering to Mona about, Ned," Jenny asked, bringing three sandwiches to the table, two for him, one for her.

"Uncle Ned is just saying he would be skin, bones around here if he didn't eat all the time," she said quickly, blessing, taking a bite of her sandwich.

Jenny said, "That's because your Uncle Ned has got a hollow wooden leg that all the food he eats falls into. Besides, your Uncle Ned could eat Annabelle all by himself," she was laughing as she went back to the cooking.

Mrs. Cooker joined in, "Jenny, you know that's right, Mona, don't listen to anything your Uncle Ned say when he hungry," Mrs. Cooker said, laughing herself; she started frying the chicken.

"That is okay, Mrs. Cooker. I know Uncle Ned is just pulling my leg," she said, finishing her sandwich. "I'm going to check in on Uncle George," she said, running off down the hall.

Mona reached George's room, lightly knocked before she opened the door as George was trying to get out of bed; he pulled himself up off the bed, groaned loudly.

"Good morning Uncle George; you need some help," she said, rushed over to help him.

"Morning Mona, I'm okay, thanks; it's not hurting as much as before. I'm going to brush my teeth, bathe, dress; I'll be out soon," he said, walking towards the bathroom.

"Okay, Uncle George, we're all in the kitchen," Mona said, turning around. She started back towards the kitchen, almost bumped into Sarah, who was just about to come to Uncle George's room.

"Morning Mona, how is George?" Sarah asked, stopping in mid-stride.

"Morning, Aunt Sarah, Uncle George is fine; he's on his way to bath, dress," Mona said, wrapping her arms around Sarah's as they walked to the kitchen together. Kelly came out of her room just then; she was tiptoeing, trying not to wake baby Sasha or the others.

"Morning Mona, Sarah, how's George feeling this morning?" she asked, walking up behind them.

"Morning Kelly," they said together, then Mona said, "Uncle George is feeling much better; he's getting ready."

They walked into the kitchen together. "Morning everyone," Kelly, Sarah said together.

"Morning, "ladies, how'd you sleep?" Mrs. Cooker asked, turning from her frying to look at them.

They went to the sink, saw the chicken, washed their hands, put on their apron, went to take out the dough for the bread, pies, pot pies out of the icebox. They started to roll, cut, load the dough into their baking pans, ten at a time, put them to rest, then into the oven; they needed fifty loafs today.

"I slept fine, Mrs. Cooker. I am excited about today; so are the children; they cannot wait to be helping with the business finally. Is that the work of a fox?" Sarah asked as she continued to roll out the pastry for the pies.

"Yes, I chased him off this morning," Ned said.

"And the girls can't wait to be the Beatly's gift bearers. I could hardly get them to bed last night; they're excited," Kelly said, beaming with pride.

Jenny removed the roast beef and the ten chickens from the oven; they were perfectly baked. They finished up the food and started breakfast as the children started coming into the kitchen. They had breakfast, and the children were sent off to get dressed while Mona and Jake packed the wagon for the first delivery.

Mr. Hedley was right on time with the vegetables from mama's garden; he was beaming; looking years younger than before. Mrs. Cooker said yes. They packed Mr. Beatly's order, the decorations, supplies for their dinner; Uncle Ned and Jake went to deliver those things while the women finished up.

Mr. Hedley stayed, worked on securing the coop, Mona helped Kelly with the girls, boys, then went to get dress; they all had to wear their Sunday best to the restaurant today, even Uncle George.

Two hours later, we were all packed up in both wagons heading for Mr. Spillman's Bar for a long day; Mr. Hedley would return home after dropping us off to get dressed, drop off food for Mrs. Nelson, rest.

Uncle Ned, George looked so handsome in their suits, Kelly, Sarah, Jenny looked glamorous in their new dresses. Mrs. Cooker was wearing one of the new dresses Mr. Hedley had purchased for her just yesterday; she looked amazing decked out in her new dress, jewelry.

They arrived at the Bar; Uncle George, Mona, Jake, the children set about decorating the Bar area, a table that the Beatly's would have their anniversary meal. They put on the white lace tablecloth, set the table following Ms. Henderson instructions for a formal table setting using the new: silver cutlery; soup bowls, bread, salad, dinner plates, wine, liquor, champagne flute, water glass, water, and juice jugs, napkins; the candles, etc. Then they decorated the public space with paper wedding bells, angels, several vases with fresh flowers, and paper streamers in blue, white, pink.

They tied white ribbons into bows on the three chairs, and then they cordoned off space with more white streamers, which separated their dining space from the rest of the Bar. They placed the large silver ice bucket on a small table next to their dinner table, along with the silver serving trays they would use later.

Finally, Mona put her painting on a small easel on the serving table, covered it up; she hoped they liked it. Jenny came, put the cake on the table, the small silk Chinese screen that blocks the cake from prying eyes. She complimented our work before she quickly went back to the kitchen, her preparation.

Everyone operated like a well-oiled machine because they had planned everything. They finished up; Uncle George, Jake took the children for a walk, with strict instructions not to get dirty from Sarah;

Kelly or they would be sent home. Then Mona walked over to Mr. Beatly's to pick up his presents so they could wrap them up in the silk wraps they had bought for gifts.

"Good morning Mr. Beatly; I've come to pick up your presents so we can wrap them. Mr. Beatly, you, your wife, are going to be so pleased with your surprise dinner," she whispered, looking around to make sure Mrs. Beatly was not in the room.

"Morning Mona, don't you look beautiful today; oh, don't worry, I sent Mrs. Beatly into Maple Lane to pick up some supplies with Charles, so she won't accidentally find out what's going on before time. She just thinks we are going to dinner, but she has no idea what is going on. I have three gifts for her; from what I've read, the thirtieth anniversary is represented by pearls; so, I want to get your opinion about my gifts," he said, taking out four small jewelry cases. "I want to give her these first," he said, opening a tiny pink silk box that contained a set of white pearl necklace, bracelet, earring set; the second box had a black pearl set in it,

"Wow, they're so beautiful, Mr. Beatly; I've never seen a Black Pearl before," Mona said, stunned by its beauty.

Then he opened the third box. It contained a set like Mrs. Cooker but with diamonds, red stones, his wife's favorite color. "Red is her favorite color. What you think, Mona?" he asked, looking at the box containing the necklace, erring, and ring. He looked anxious, like he was not sure it was enough.

"This is beautiful too; I love the red stones. What are they called?" she asked.

"These are Rubies, Mona, after my wife saw Mrs. Cooker's gift from Mr. Hedley; I had to do something extraordinary, or I'd be sleeping on the sofa for the rest of the year, maybe more. I cannot blame her; she is loved, put up with me for thirty-plus years.

Besides, when we got married, we never had money to have a honeymoon; now I can buy her something to say thank you for all these years," he said, almost becoming emotional.

"Well, Mr. Beatly, I'm sure she'll be impressed; we have a few surprises for both of you too. We're so excited to do this for you, your family; remember dinner starts at five sharp," she said as he closed the boxes, stacked them, and placed them in a small bag for her to take.

"Mona, I'm excited too; I know she'll love it, be happy, we'll be on time. I'm closing up by four, so we can get ready on time," he said, moving from the counter to pick up something else to give her. "Mona, this came in yesterday; this one is for you; I want you to give this to Jake to start his painting supplies" he said handing her two packages with their names on them.

"Mr. Beatly, thank you, you are so kind to us, but I want to pay for these. I have money," Mona said with gratitude, appreciation for his kindness but felt overwhelmed.

"Mona, please let's not talk about money; you two have a natural gift; I want to do this," he said, patting her on the hand.

"Mr. Beatly, I don't know what to say.... thank you, I'm sure Jake will be grateful too," she said, taking up the packages to go before she became overcome with emotions.

"Oh, one more thing, can you tell Ned to come by, see me when he gets a chance. We'll see you later, Mona," he said, walking over to the other side of the counter, a customer.

"I'll tell him, Mr. Beatly, thanks again, see you later," Mona said, walking out into the sunshine, across the street to the Bar.

Mona gave Jenny the gifts from Mr. Beatly; Jenny put them aside to be wrapped later. "Thank you, Mona; is everything ready inside?" she asked, looking at the packages in her hand.
"What's that? Jenny asked.

"It's gifts from Mr. Beatly for me, Jake; I think it's more painting stuff. He won't take any money for them; he's been kind; I hope they like my painting," Mona said, smiling.

"I'm sure they will love it, Mona, it's perfect; a painting of their business is a beautiful gift. I like the fact you put your mama, Ned, in the picture. I'm sure they will remember that day every time they look at the painting," Jenny said, stretching out her back; she sat down on the chair. They had everything organized for lunch; she was resting before the mad rush.

Mrs. Cooker, Mrs. Baker, sat quietly talking in the nook; Kelly, Sarah was, sitting in the Bar; while Kelly fed baby Sasha; she was there too, Mrs. Nelson would be by to help her with Sasha later.

Then Mona found Ned, giving his horses Nelly, Bertha some apples, water; they had hay in a container off to the side. "Uncle Ned, Mr. Beatly wants to see you when you get a chance," she said, watching as his eyes light up like a light bulb. "Is there anything else you want me to do?" Mona asked, ready to go back into the Bar to see what else Mr. Beatly had bought for her, to wait for Jake to return with Uncle George, the other children.

"Thanks, Mona, but I got everything under control," he said, giving Nelly Bertha one more apple before he went to go see Mr. Beatly.

"Okay, Uncle Ned, I'll see you later," Mona said, leaving him; she went into the Bar, sat down at the table with Aunt Kelly, Sarah to open her present, said "Aunt Sarah Mr. Beatly gave me this for Jake" she gave Sarah Jake's gift.

"Mr. Beatly is a saint; he amazingly generous; I'm sure Jake will love whatever he's given him," Sarah said, putting the package away.

Mona opened her package to find another set of new paint colour; ten new medium canvases rolled up in the package; she was pleasantly surprised.

"Nice, new paints, canvases; that's very nice of him; Mr. Beatly is serious about being your sponsor Mona, he is taking Jake under his wings too," Sarah said, looking at the new paints.

"I told him about Jake, how well he paints. I wanted to buy Jake a painting set, but he won't take my money," Mona said, focusing on the new colors of paints.

"You should see the gifts that he bought for Mrs. Beatly; she's going to be so surprised, by the gifts, by dinner. He said if he did not do something special for her this anniversary, he would be in the doghouse for the rest of his life. He also said Mr. Hedley's gift to Mrs. Cooker was an inspiration for all his gifts," Mona said casually.

"Yeah, Mr. Hedley blew me away with his gifts; I would have never believed he was such a romantic; he impressed everybody. Wives, girlfriends will be expecting more from their men," Sarah said, shaking her head; Kelly agreed, nodding.

Mona got up to put her paints, canvasses away with her small purse in the corner along with everyone else's stuff; they sat, spoke until people started coming in.

Ned finished feeding Nelly, Bertha, washed his hand, walked over to Mr. Beatly; he was excited that his package had arrived; he walked into the store just as Mr. Beatly finished with several customers.

"Good morning, Mr. Beatly," Ned said, extending his hand to shake his.

"Morning, Ned, how are you doing?" he said, reaching for a small package under the counter; he gave it to Ned.

"I'm fine, Mr. Beatly, excited. Are you ready for tonight? I hope Mrs. Beatly doesn't suspect anything," Ned said; taking the package, he started to open it.

"Nope, she doesn't suspect a thing; I just gave Mona the gifts I bought for her; she seems more excited than me about tonight," he said, fishing for more information.

"That's good because we want it to be a surprise for you too; everything is ready, so I'll get Jake to come by with your lunches," Ned said, indicating that they did not want him to come by the Bar either until it was time.

Ned opened the jewelry case and saw the Amethyst, diamond necklace, and earring set; then he took out the ring, a large Amethyst stone surrounded by tiny diamonds. "This is beautiful, Mr. Beatly," Ned said, looking at the set.

"Ned, you're a fortunate man; he only had this one left, didn't know when he would be getting any more; he said someone had come in to enquire about it a week ago. Fortunately, his policy is, he who pays first gets jewelry. I know Jenny will love it; I'm impressed you are doing this; congratulations, Ned," he said, shaking his hand again as Ned repacked his gift.

"Thanks, Mr. Beatly," Ned said, paid him as another customer came into the store; he shook Mr. Beatly's hand again.

"You are very welcome, Ned. I'll see you later," he said, went to serve his next customer.

Ned left the store, walked back across the street, he went, tucked Jenny's gift under the seat of his wagon. Then he went back to help, smiling like he had some top-secret information.

"Good morning, ladies, morning Mona," Mr. Spillman said, coming into the Bar from the back room. "Wow, the room looks beautiful; the Beatly's will be very surprised; I'm surprised, stunned with what you've done," he said, walking over to look more closely at the setup.

"The place looks so classy; I can tell you guys bought the best of everything; I almost didn't recognize my Bar.

He walked over to the small table; asked, "Mona is this one of your paintings under here. Can I look?" he asked, pointing to the easel.

"Sure, Mr. Spillman; I just finished it last night. It's my first real painting; I'm just hoping they like it," Mona said, feeling proud.

Mr. Spillman lifted the small white sheet that draped the painting. "Oh, my Mona, this is beautiful; they will love it. You said this is your first painting; Mona, you are a natural. It looks like his store. Is that your mother, Ned, with the wagon? That is brilliant; he will love it, wow," he said, chuckling. "They will love it. I would like to commission a piece; what do you charge for a painting Mona? He asked, draping the sheet once again over the painting.

"Thanks for the compliment Mr. Spillman but I'm not charging them; it's their anniversary gift from me. Mr. Beatly bought all my paints, supplies, says he is my Patron of the Arts, sponsor, at least that is what he calls it. I couldn't believe it; there were so many supplies," she said with the wonder of a child. "I'm very grateful to him; Jake is teaching me what he knows; he's amazing, much better than me," Mona said, looking serious talking about her painting, Jake's.

"I would like one for the Bar; you just tell me your price when you're finished," he said, walking over to the table the ladies sat.

"Mr. Spillman, I can never charge you; you are family," Mona said, hugging him. "You are the reason why mama's dream is going to become a reality. So, I want to paint quite a few paintings for the Bar, restaurant bakery; if that is okay with you," she said, sat down looking at him across the table.

"Thank you, Mona, that would be wonderful, but I would still like to help you, Jake, with your artistic aspirations; what did Mr. Beatly call it," he said, trying to remember the word.

"Patron of the Arts and Sponsor," Mona said, smiling.

"Yes, Patron of the Arts and Sponsor for you, Jake; Mona, your mother, was very special to me; I'm so very proud of you," he said, getting emotional.

"Wow, thanks, Mr. Spillman; Jake will be so over the moon. Can I tell him, Aunt Sarah?" Mona asked, beaming.

"Thank you, Mr. Spillman; that is kind of you. Jake will be excited; he is quite good," said Sarah, who had been sitting listening to the conversation between him, Mona. Sarah could hear the love he had for Mabel in his voice; she looked at Kelly as he spoke; she knew, saw, and heard it too.

"I understand, Sarah; you don't have to explain; you're a great mother; Jake is a fine boy."
Steven Spillman cleared his throat, changed the subject because he knew he was becoming too sensitive.

Steven said, "Oh yes, I almost forgot I have the wine, champagne chilling in the back, a nice bottle of Whiskey for Mr. Beatly. I know he likes Whiskey." Steven said, confident he knew his customers, friend.

Kelly waited until Sarah and Mona had finished speaking and said, "Mr. Cobbler will be here before five. He'll be playing by the time they arrive;" she was just finishing up feeding baby Sasha under the blanket that covered her breasts.

"Mr. Spillman, would you like your lunch now?" Mona asked, getting up to get his meal.

"Thanks, Mona; I'm famished," he said as Mona got up. "Can I sit with you, ladies?" he asked before he sat down.

"Sure, Mr. Spillman; I'll go get the children's lunch ready too; we should all eat something too. George should be back with them anytime now; it will get crazy in here in about half an hour. Excuse me," Sarah said, getting up to go too.

He nodded.

Mr. Spillman looked around the Bar one more time. "Mabel would be so very proud to see all this," he said, trying to hide the emotions in his voice. "These decorations are beautiful. I just can't believe this is my Bar; it looks so different, so elegant," he said, turning back to Kelly.

Kelly was burping Sasha on her shoulder. "Mona, Ned, George, the children did an incredible job; they will also be serving the Beatly's their meal," Kelly said, looking around herself. George will be serving them all their drinks, like at an authentic restaurant. Mona, Jake will be dedicated to serving their meals, the older children are their ushers, smaller children will bring in Mr. Beatly's and Mrs. Beatly's wrapped gifts. We bought a bouquet for her, a Cuban cigar case for him that we have taped with a red ribbon. Jenny and Mona sat down; they planned the special anniversary night to be unforgettable.

"We will take their lunch to them; we do not want them to be at the Bar until the dinner party starts; we want it to be a total surprise for Mrs. Beatly, and their son, and Mr. Beatly. None of the customers can know who the celebration is for until the Beatly's are already here. We know how people gossip; we are not taking chances." Kelly said.

Steven Spillman was impressed with the women in Mrs. Cooker's home, whom Mabel had taught well.

Mona went and got the inventory sheets with the day's menu; she sat down beside Mr. Spillman and silently went about her task.

Kelly excused herself and put Sasha in her bassinette to help Sarah with the children's lunch, eat, and get ready for the lunch rush. Sarah would be out front; she knew it would be crazy all day because more women started coming in with their children during the day. Ms. Henderson did not have to tell them that the business had grown. She could see it for herself because every day, new people came in, more women. They had become comfortable coming into the Bar without their men; it had become a place for the family than for men only.

"What's that you're doing, Mona," Mr. Spillman asked between bites; he was watching her intensity.

"This is our daily inventory menu tracker; mama always kept one for every day of the business; I have all her notes, income, expenses statements, budgets, goals, the dream book.
We are just following her plans, but it could not happen without everyone working so hard, loving mama, what she started; she loved, respected you too, Mr. Spillman. She had all these plans for you, the Bar; she felt she had to do everything she could to repay you for your kindness, generosity," she said gently with such intense seriousness he stopped eating for a moment; she never looked up until she finished.

Then she said, "Mama always talked about the importance of loyalty, that it is the foundation of everything we hold dear, she used to say. I understand now; she was right; she could see things most people could not. I miss her, but I feel her with me all the time. Sometimes I see her, but not like a creepy ghost or anything. She is usually just standing there, smiling with me. Is that crazy, Mr. Spillman?" Mona suddenly asked, stopped talking.

But Steven was sitting there stunned and speechless by most of what had come out of Mona Johnson's mouth; she was wise beyond her years.

So, Steven said, "No Mona, I don't believe you're crazy because I would be crazy right along with you; I feel her too, sometimes swear I see her," he said, stopping himself; thankful he was not going crazy if so, he was not alone. It was also a good thing he does not drink anymore like he uses to because he surely would be a complete wreck by now. Somehow, he had still been able to restrain himself even with the few over-indulgent episodes with Calvin for Thomas, him for Mabel.

He smiled then said, "Mona, your mother will always be with me, with us; always," he was fighting back his emotions because her words had moved him.

"I know Mr. Spillman; she's right here with us today; she's smiling, saying thank you. I feel her," she said, sending a shiver down Steven's spine because he knew it was true; he felt her too.
He resumed his eating, contemplating the deep conversation he just had when George, the children burst through the front door in a sea of noise. George told them to settle down before they got him in trouble with their mothers.

"Let's go say hello to Mr. Spillman, then all of you go outback, wash your hands before lunch" he scooted them over to our table.

"Morning, Mr. Spillman," they said together, looking a little more deshelled than when they had left but still clean.

"Morning children, you did an amazing job decorating for the Beatly's dinner; they'll be pleased. You all look so wonderful; are you excited about helping?" he asked, looking at how dressed up they looked.

"We're going to bring Mrs. Beatly's gifts from Mr. Beatly to her, Jake; Mona is going to serve their food on silver trays," Thomas and Serge yelled out excitedly; they could barely contain themselves.

Then Margaret, Marie, Suzie said in unison, "And we are going to bring Mrs. Beatly's gift,

"I'm sure you'll all be great; I'll be watching everything," Steven said, smiling because they made him even more excited than he was before. They had created a special occasion that people would not soon forget; it was quite beautiful, he thought. It fitted that it now became a part of Mabel's legacy.

"Thanks, Mr. Spillman," they said collectively; they had already started to fidget.

"Okay, that's enough talking; off you go to wash your hands…." Uncle George said, chasing them off. He was just in time to see their mother, Sarah, Kelly coming into the Bar with trays of sandwiches, potato chips; Ned was bringing a tray of cups, Jenny two jugs of juice.

"Lunch," they screamed, running towards the back sink to wash their hands, be first back at the table.

"Slow down," Kelly, Sarah yelled as they stampeded towards the door; they knew everyone would not get through at once.

George was still trying to finish what he had started to say but decided not to bother because no one listened to him anymore, not adults or children.

Jake was standing there just watching all the craziness that went on around him with his usual cool head; Mona knew he felt way too old for his brothers, the girls, but he had to watch out for them anyway. He did not mind most of the time, but sometimes they drove him crazy; he felt forced to spend too much time with them, but that is what family was all about.

"Jake, I have something for you from Mr. Beatly; come here," Mona said, waving him towards the table. She quickly went for his gift.

Jake walked over and sat across from Mr. Spillman, who was busy trying to finish his meal before all the children returned. When he looked up from his plate Jake, his eyes made four. "I hear you are quite a good painter, Jake; have been teaching what you know to Mona," Steven said, taking a long drink of his ginger beer.

"Just a little, sir, I'm still learning; we're both learning," Jake said, not liking the fact that Mona kept running off her mouth about his painting, which he thought was just okay.

"Well, you have quite a fan in little Mona; you two have been painting together every day," he said, taking the last bite of his meal.

"Yes, sir, I like painting, but as I had said, I'm just learning; Mona's exaggerating, you know how little kids are," Jake said, becoming more uncomfortable.

"Mona exaggerates? No, maybe a little overexcited, but I've never heard her exaggerate" he could tell Jake was not comfortable talking about himself. Steven saw himself in Jake, painfully shy, unsure of himself, confident but still insecure. He smiled because he could tell that Jake had a tiny boyhood crush on Mona. It reminded him of his childhood crush; he finished his meal, drank the last of his drink.

"Jake, I would like to be your Patron of the Arts and Sponsor, if that's okay with you? Steven reaches out his hand to shake Jake's, who sat dumbfounded at his seat, not moving.

"Mr. Spillman, I don't know what to say. Thank, thank you for your kindness," Jake stammered, clearly surprise still all over his face.

"Jake, if Mona, your beautiful mama, say you've got talent, I believe them, I'm willing to invest in your talent. All I want in return is for you to give it your all; okay, Jake," Steven said, then he shook Jake's hand excitedly as if they had just signed a million-dollar business contract. Steven felt connected to Jake by youthful experience; what would he do with all the money he was making? He had no children of his own; giving to Pastor Hayles Charities did not seem enough now.

Then Steven Spillman said, "Thank you, Jake, for allowing me this opportunity; I'll see you later," he gathered his plate, glass; headed for the kitchen's backdoor.

Jake sat watching Mr. Spillman until he exited, so he did not see Mona at first when she came back, stood beside him; he was looking still in shock.

"Jake did Mr. Spillman tell you, did he tell you; he wants to be your Patron of...." Mona was saying when he interrupted her.

"Yes, he told me....," he was saying when she interrupted him.

"And Mr. Beatly gave me this for you earlier," she said, thrust it into his hands; Mona was all excited now, she sat down beside him.

Jake took the package, put it on the table, and slowly opened it. There, wrapped in a large brown piece of cotton cloth, was a complete paintbrush kit, a large box of paints, and twenty rolled-up canvases of various sizes along with a few new painting instruction books neither had seen before.

"Wow, this is amazing," he said, got choked up; he did not want Mona to see; he opened the paint kit box; saw a note neatly folded on the top.

Dear Jake,
I have ordered a carrying case similar to Mona's for you, but my associates had no more in stock; it will be delivered in two weeks. Until then, please enjoy your gift, paint a beautiful picture of the world, Fairbanks; its beautiful town with beautiful people.
Sincerely,
Mr. and Mrs. Beatly

"Oh my God, that is so wonderful of him," Mona said, not thinking he interrupted her.

"Thank you, Mona; this is all so surprising. At first, I was furious at you for running off your mouth. I don't know what to say; how can I ever repay them, repay you, Mona," Jake said; he was smiling, his eye's sparkled with happiness.

"You're welcome, Jake," said Mona, smiling because Jake was smiling; she was thrilled.

And that was a good thing because Jake did not smile much. He was always serious unless Uncle George, Ned, was playing with him. Everyone else was laughing, but most of the time, he was serious.

After the children ate lunch, the tables cleared; ten minutes later, the Bar became a mass of men coming in for their meal. Jake, Mona helped Sarah, Kelly with service in the front, bringing all the orders back to the customers.

It was Jake's first time; he seemed a little surprised and overwhelmed by the number of people we served in those two hours. I do not think we stopped at all—the lunch menu was consumed with no leftovers.

Today, however, Mona could tell it was already a bonanza of a day with many gifts, blessings; it did not stop there because there was a steady flow of women, their children, each enquiring as to why the Bar was so decorated.

The women became too excited when Jenny explained that they were hired to make a surprise wedding anniversary dinner for a couple in town. She could not reveal the couple's names because it was a surprise. She explained that they did birthdays, weddings, anniversaries, any other kinds of dinner party or celebration a customer wanted. It included dinner/dessert or up to a six-course meal, drinks, decorations; prices depend on the number of people if it is semi-formal or formal.

The women left with broadcast news to spread in town, beyond its borders; the men had already started to talk before they had left, saying that they know their wives or girlfriends would love something like this.

Steven Spillman watched as Jenny and Ned spoke to the enquiring customers who were already impressed, sold when they saw the elaborate set up of plates, decorations, candles, cake, etc. Steven could tell that this would quickly become a successful part of their business; he could see the excitement in the women, their children's eyes; they wanted their surprise party. The children looked thrilled when told they could also have a dinner birthday party with decorations, cake too; they immediately asked their mothers if they could have one for their next birthday. And quite a few of the men looked worried already, knowing their drinking money would be diminished when their wives found out about this new way to demand them spend their money.

Tentatively they had ten children's birthday parties booked, another five-anniversary dinner request. Jenny and Ned instructed them to come in early between Tuesdays to Saturdays, speak to one of them, book their day, pay for their personalized package.

They had strategically set the wheels of free-market advertising into motion through successful word of mouth, see for a your-self campaign that people did not even realize was happening. They were successfully using psychological, emotional means by using potent stimuli. They knew to want; superseded all other emotions, needs.

When most people had slowed down, Steven called over Ned, Jenny, said, "Congratulations to both of you, this is the most impressive series of marketing, advertising I have ever seen in my life. I'm sure this will be a great success; I'm proud of both of you, the whole family, Mabel too," Steven said, shaking Ned's hand, giving Jenny a quick hug; he was just so emotional all day, he even surprised himself, he excused himself.

The Mabel Affect, he thought as he walked to the back room, away from everyone before he started crying like a child; he needed some time alone because the day was overwhelming him emotionally for the first time since the early days of Mabel's death. The strange thing is he has felt her around him all day, for a few days now. Since Thomas's funeral especially, that is why he could not lie to Mona, because sometimes he felt a little crazy himself about her mother's presence around him. At first, he thought he was going a little crazy, but his conversation with Mona made him feel better; he was grateful he was not alone in missing her.

Steven Spillman composed himself, suddenly had the exact déjà vu moment he had had with Monica, feeling her presence around long after her death, he suddenly felt her too; he shivered.

He found a clean cloth, wiped his face, and had a shot of whiskey to calm his nerves. This was not the time to fall apart over loss and regret.

He picked up a damp cloth and wiped the tables down; the Beatly's would arrive soon.

The children had been doing their homework quietly in the corner closest to the kitchen; they did not look impressed that they still had to do it. But as soon as Mr. Cobbler came in, they greeted everyone and started playing. That was their signal to put everything away and get ready for the Beatly's arrival; they were excited now and could hardly contain themselves.

Later, Mrs. Cooker, Jenny, Sarah, Kelly, and Mrs. Baker exited the kitchen and stood in a line. Uncle George stood at the front door with Thomas, Serge, and Margaret, ready to seat the family; and follow behind to serve their first drinks.

The Champagne and wine had been chilling in the silver ice buckets for about an hour; they had a small bottle of sparkling cider for their son. Candles on the tables had all been lit; the ribbon barricade had been partially removed to allow them entrance and separate them from the rest of the Bar. Mr. Spillman had changed his clothing, now wore a very sharp suit; he was smiling, ready to bring George the bottle of Whiskey to open for Mr. Beatly.

Mona and Jake stood by, waiting to serve the first round of meals. Aunt Jenny had the trays to start serving each course.

TWENTY

Surprise and New Beginnings

Mr. and Mrs. Beatly arrived on time.

George announced, "Welcome to your thirtieth-anniversary dinner, Mr. and Mrs. Beatly—Mrs. Beatly, this is your husband's surprise gift to you; please allow us to seat you."

George allowed the children to take each of their hands and lead them to their seats.

Mrs. Beatly, their son, even Mr. Beatly looked stunned beyond words from when they entered the Bar. Mrs. Beatly managed to say, "Honey, you planned all this for me" she was beaming from ear to ear; she kissed him more passionately than even she expected. Their son giggled because he had never really seen his parents kiss like that; she blushed, looked even more beautiful in her new dress.

Mr. Beatly turned slightly off colour. He was caught off guard by his wife's public affections. He said, "It was Ned's idea to have a special dinner, but I never expected this; I am blown away myself. Happy Anniversary, honey! I love you. Thank you for being the most wonderful wife in the world," he kissed her again.

"I love you too, my darling," she said with tears in her eyes.

The children walked them to the table, seated them.

217

"May I pour you a glass of Champagne, some sparkling cider for your son?" George asked when there was a break in their talking; he popped the cork, filled their flute, their son's.

"Thank you, George," he said, reaching for his wife's hand.

Everyone raised their glasses. Mr. Beatly toasted his wife and son and their life together. "To my wonderful family; without you, I would not be the man I am today. Thank you."

They all drank, already drunk from the excitement.

Mona then went to their table, asked them if they were ready for their appetizers, and went to get them from the kitchen; everything was lined up to be served. Jake and Mona served the Beatly's a six-course dinner.

Mr. Cobbler played quietly in the background for the next two hours once they had finished their meal. Mona removed the silkscreen from in front of their anniversary cake, gave them a chance to see it, cut it themselves. This was another big surprise they did not expect; Mrs. Beatly became overwhelmed, started to cry as Edgar Beatly embraced his wife of thirty years, thanked her again. They looked more in love with each other tonight than ever before; the candlelight flickered off their faces as they renewed their vows, love for each other. They cut their cake; Jake and Mona served them with a side of ice cream topped with Mrs. Cooker Blueberry preserves.

The Beatly's cuddled closer to each other at the table, had fed each other throughout their meal; Charles giggled numerous times as his parents showed public affection to each other; he was happy to see them happy. At the end of their meal, Thomas, Suzie, Marie, Serge lined up to bring out their gifts one after the other; Mona asked Mr. Beatly to say something about his gifts.

He cleared his throat before he said, "Mrs. Suzy Beatly, I would like to thank you for being my wife for the past thirty wonderful years. I know when we first got married, I could not afford a proper wedding, ring, honeymoon, or home, but you loved me anyway. Thank you. You loved me when I had nothing but a dream, a few dollars, no easy way of getting there, but you stuck it out with me, through feast and famine. Thank you. Today I hope that we will have another thirty years together; I hope that today, in the future, I can make up for all I didn't have to give you" Edgar had tears in his eyes; his voice had gone husky and tender. Then he said, "And this watch you gave me this morning will be a reminder of every second of joy you have brought me, our son," he hugged her, kissed her again.

Suzy Beatly hugged her husband, would not let him go; everything was perfect, her life was perfect; she could not thank Mrs. Cooker, her family for this beautiful experience that she would never forget. She muttered an "I love you, Edgar," wiping tears.

Mona signaled Serge; he came forward with her bouquet. Suzie came with Mr. Beatly's cigar case; they giggled like young lovers. Then Marie, Margaret, Thomas came with their second gift; Thomas with Mona's painting, Marie, and Margaret, with the first two jewel case containing the white and the black pearl sets, gave it to them.

"I can't believe there is more," Suzy exclaimed before she opened the first box containing the white pearl set. "Oh, my goodness, Edgar; it's gorgeous. Thank you, Edgar." He took the box from her hand, put it aside, and asked her to open the next.

Suzy slowly unwrapped the silk cloth, opened the box, gasped when she saw the second set of pearls in black. "Oh Edgar, these are so beautiful too. You are one crazy man Edgar Beatly," she said.

Edger stopped her and said, "Suzy, I have one more gift to give," he looked towards Mona, who sent Thomas for Mr. Beatly's final gift of the most refined bottle of Whiskey from Mr. Spillman.

Then came Mrs. Beatly's last gift.

"Suzy, this is the gift I've always wanted to give you from the first day I met you," Edgar Beatly said, watching her reaction as she opened his final gift to her.

Mrs. Beatly let out a scream when she opened the jewelry box and saw the ruby, diamond necklace, erring, and ring set.

"Edgar.... I do not know what to say. Thank you," she said and started to cry as he took out the necklace, gently put it around her neck, and slipped the ring on her finger. She put the erring on herself as it had a beautiful clasp on the back. "Edgar, this is the best day of my life, thank you," she said, hugging him again.

Mona brought over a small handheld silver mirror, gave it to her, said, "You look beautiful, Mrs. Beatly."

"I concur with Mona; you look beautiful, you are very welcome, Mrs. Beatly; I'm grateful you're happy; I'm a happier man for that. I must thank Ned, the family for helping to make this anniversary unforgettable. When he said they would do a little anniversary dinner party, I never envisioned anything like this. I am blown away; I cannot even think of how to repay them. Look at all the decorations, the children; this is a production, not a dinner," he said, looking around the room smiling. It was the first time he took the time to look around during all the excitement. "Wow, I'm moved beyond words," he said.

"Me too," his wife said, holding each other's hand.

The children gathered in the middle of the room, said "Good night, Mr. and Mrs. Beatly; we wish you another thirty years of health and love."

Before they left, Mr. Beatly thanked everyone for a beautiful evening. He promised to hang Mona's painting on a wall in his store.

"Mrs. and Mr. Beatly, thank you for allowing us to celebrate your wedding anniversary with you. It was our pleasure to do this for you, your wife," Mona said, smiling.

It had been a successful day. They packed up the wagon to start their journey home.

The children, Kelly, baby Sasha, Mona, Jake, and Uncle George, who was looking more pained as the night dragged on, fitted themselves into the wagon. Mrs. Cooker and Mrs. Baker squeezed into the front seat with Mr. Hedley, and they were off.

Mr. Hedley, Ned, would be making several trips to get all the supplies back to the house tonight, so they loaded up Ned's wagon while waiting for Mr. Hedley's return. They also stacked things under the light out back so they could load the wagons more quickly. Soon after the Beatly's left, they could remove the decorations, return them to their boxes, containers. The streamers were taken down and carefully rolled up for the next time.

They left the bouquets on the tables but removed the candles, their holders. They folded the table clothes; put away the silver bowls, jugs, trays, cutleries after cleaning, drying them carefully.

Jenny took Mr. Spillman his meal that they had carefully covered up because he had no time to eat all night, said to him, "Mr. Spillman, thank you again for all your support in making this night a success, sir" she hugged him quickly surprising him, her-self; she had never hugged him before.

"Jenny, you are very welcome. Thank you for doing this for the Beatly's; I'm sure they will never forget it; I'll never forget it," he said, looking around the Bar. It was like night and day once the decorations were gone. "Mabel is just smiling down at us; I can feel it; she's very proud of all of you, me too," he said, his voice was strained.

"Yes, she is Mr. Spillman; we all feel her; Mona's been seeing her too," she said, becoming emotional herself. "We are very proud of tonight, very proud....and the children were just amazing; they were so excited," Jenny said, realizing too late that tears were running down her cheeks.

Mr. Spillman hugged her again, said "Those are tears of joy, right, because if they're not, I'm going to tell Ned to have a strong talk with you" he burst into laughter at his lame joke; he was not that funny he knew.

"Okay," she said, smiling up at him; she felt overwhelmed by the work, emotions suddenly. "We're going to finish up the cleaning, finish packing up to go; we'll probably need about three more trips to get everything back home.

"Jenny, I had no idea you had brought so many supplies today, but I can see how much work you all did to make this happen for the Beatly's. I'm impressed with the way you introduced the business to the Town's people; it was quite brilliant, quite brilliant," he said, looking at several storage crates stacked neatly by the far wall.

"Mr. Hedley will be making us a storage room so we can put all these things in safely in a secure location. We bought quite a few things for this new part of the business; I think we will quickly recover our investment with about five jobs. Plus, create a new stream of income for the business; this is what Mabel had been planning; she wanted to make your Bar famous," she said, looking around.

"Well, Jenny, she had done that already, but today it went into the legendary stratosphere. Everyone who came into this bar today will never forget what they saw or heard; they will want this amazing experience themselves. It was classy, elegant, creative, thoughtful, intimate, personal, emotional, loving; that is just some of the comments I heard people making throughout the day. Trust me, I listened to people as they watched and talked; they were just as astonished as the Beatly's'; me. I predict that every woman, child in this town, will want to have a birthday or anniversary dinner party here; I have never seen the women in this town so excited about anything. Congratulations on all your hard work you, the entire family, have done since Mabel; Mona told me about her dream book, how you are all following it.

"Mr. Spillman…" she started to say.

"Call me Steven Jenny," he said, watching the remaining customers while they talked.

"Ever since Mona remembered, took those books out of the old house; she started reading all of them, realized that Mabel had written the entire plan for the business for the next ten years.
So, she started planning it out, then asked us to have a meeting and told us her plans to continue her mother's dream.

"Mabel had spoken about some of her plans," Steven said, remembering Mabel's many talks with him.

"Yeah, at first, I was kind of thinking how without Mabel, it would be impossible, but after Mona spoke that first Sunday morning, we were so dumbfounded. That was it; we all said yes, here we are. She's soft as feathers, tough as nails all at the same time; she surprises me all the time," Jenny said, shaking her head.

"I had the most remarkable conversation with her yesterday, today; I swore I was talking to Mabel for a moment; I've been feeling Mabel in the Bar all week. It's crazy," Steven said, glad he was finally having a talk with Jenny that didn't have to do with the business.

"It is happening to me too, so we all must be crazy," Jenny said but was interrupted.

"Excuse me, Steven, can we get another round over here," one of the men from the table in front of the Bar said.

"Mr. Spill…. Steven, I'm going to get going; we still have some work to do; thank you again for everything," Jenny said, shaking his hand.

"I'll see you later, Jenny; thank you," he said, walking away to serve his customers.

Jenny, Ned, Sarah packed everything up into both wagons; they left with Sarah, Jenny stayed with the final load. Finally, Ned came back; they packed up the wagon, went home. When they finally arrived, everyone came out to help, including Mr. Hedley.

Once they had put everything away, Mrs. Cooker called everyone into the kitchen, filled glasses for all the adults with Champagne Mr. Spillman had given her to celebrate their successful day; she also opened the bottle of sparkling cider for the children.

Then she made a toast, said, "I would like to thank each of you for making this day a great success. Children, thank you for making this a memorable day for the Beatly's anniversary; you all did fantastically, so you each will be getting a special treat. Mona, Jenny, Ned, I am so proud of your work to make this new business a wonderful addition; people cannot stop talking about it. Kelly, Sarah, Herman, thank you because, without your help, we could not do all we do. George, you looked so handsome today, do not worry, you will be working hard soon enough but thank you for today. I want to thank each, every one of you for committing to a dream. Finally, I want to make a toast to Mabel Johnson, whose vision has brought us together on this path. To Mabel, to Dreams," she lifted her glass, they clicked each other's glasses, drank.

We sat around recalling events of the day, joking, laughing, feeling good about our accomplishments until the children started to yawn, then Kelly, Sarah. Uncle George barely looked like he was hanging on. He winced every time he tried to laugh; the pillow Sarah had put behind his back seemed to be providing less, less help as time went on.

"I can see that it's way past these children's bedtime, some of you adults too," Mrs. Cooker said, winking at Kelly, who looked like she could curl up on the kitchen table, sleep with no problem. Serge, Marie, Suzie, the youngest all dozed in their seats; no one had noticed during the boisterous celebration they were having over their day.

"Okay, everyone takes a child; let's help get them settled in bed," Mrs. Cooker said.

"No, Mrs. Cooker, you need to sit down, rest, spend time with Mr. Hedley before he goes," said Jenny.

Ned helped George, who could not get up from the chair without help. "Thanks, Ned," he said, feeling lame; he felt helpless against the pain in his ribs now.

Jenny took Marie; Kelly took Suzie; Mona was already holding baby Sasha; Margaret walked behind, dragging herself under her own steam. Sarah picked up Thomas, and Jake picked up Serge.

Francine and Herman said goodnight. Everyone was tired after an exciting day.

TWENTY-ONE

Love's A Sweet Fruit

The roosters in the yard cock-a-doodle-doo several times as the sun rose over the Eastern horizon; it was just bringing its light onto the far side of the property. The sun was beginning to push away the black of the night with a promise of a new day, of new light as it slowly crept along the skyline.

Jake's rooster, Mona's chick, pecked around the base of the back door as if hoping their young owners would open it to carry them around for most of the day again. They liked the view from a hand once they knew they were safe, but still, they looked for them nervously in the sea of tiny feet and hands. They stayed close to the coop for the night. At the crack of the first cock-a-doodle-doo; they were at the door waiting.

The house awoke slower than usual; the previous day's wear and tear had everyone in their beds rolling over one more time. Even baby Sasha was quiet.

Ned sat up in bed when he heard the roosters' cock-a-doodle-doo for the third time; he reached for the shopping bag he had brought in from the wagon the night before. He had not had a chance to talk to anyone since he had gotten it, not even George. But George was in so much pain he just wanted to get him to bed.

Ned understood the importance of the doctor's instruction implicitly, keenly now, so did George, who did not look so tough or strong as he kept claiming. He helped him undress down to his briefs, got him in bed as Sarah popped in with a fresh jug of water, an ice bag for his hurting ribs. Ned excused himself and left Sarah to take care of George as instructed by his mama; he smiled a pained smile when he saw her. "Good night Ned, thanks," they said as he left.

Ned had found Jenny putting around the kitchen giving the tables a final wiping down; she looked beautiful in her dress, but he could tell she was tired. "Jenny let's go to bed, baby," he said, walking over to her, wrapping his arms around her; he kissed her on the lips long, hard, passionately surprising himself, shocking her. He wanted to ask her right there to marry him, give her his gift, but he wanted it to be more special than that—something just for her.

So, Ned said instead, "I love you, Jenny....I love you very much" he hugged her again, holding her tight against his body for a few minutes. Then he let her go, took her hand, said, "Let's go honey; let's go to bed" he walked her to her room, opened the door, kissed her once more, closed the door behind her when she went in.

Ned was caught up in his memories of saying goodnight to Jenny last night, how all he wanted was to scoop her up in his arms, take her into that bedroom, and make love to her; whatever that means, he was still a virgin. No, he did not want to admit it....who would; men and their lies.

Ned's heart was in full blossom, bearing fruits for Jenny; he was ready to make her his wife, share a marriage bed with her; he shivered at the thought, grateful they would be learning together.

If push came to shove, he could always ask George for advice because the women just kept coming back for more from good ole Georgie Porgy pudding and pie; that had kissed a lot of girls and made them cry. None had won his heart until Sarah, who had not gotten any of his pudding and pie yet. He quickly decided no because Sarah was way too cautious and modest, even if George was slick as a fox. He was rooting for them because he had never seen him in love or his buddy George so careful around a woman; Sarah was good for him.

Ned made up his mind; today, he would ask Jenny to marry him before it gets too crazy. Their next big event was his mama's fourth wedding to Herman; that would be another long wild day for all of them. Maybe they should close the business for the day because he knew no one would be willing to miss Herman Hedley and Francine Cooker's wedding to work at the Bar. Few people on their deathbed wished they had spent more time working.

It had been an extremely trying month punctuated by newfound love, deaths, funerals, weddings, anniversaries, betrayals, forgiveness, renewals, and change. It had been a lesson about time, how it did not wait for anyone. That time always marched on with or without you. It was a reminder to live every day, dream now, because tomorrow was not promised. That was Mabel's most crucial lesson; live life now; Ned finally got it.

Jenny rolled over in bed; she looked out the window saw the sun slowly coming up, but she did not want to get up yet. She still felt tired, especially after the adrenalin rush of yesterday's excitement and Ned's passionate kiss that kept her awake for part of the night. She wanted him to come to her room, cuddle up, hold her, nothing more, but she was lying.

Sure, Jenny," she giggled to herself because she had to admit it to herself; cuddling was not all she wanted. He had made her tingle all over with that kiss that sent her mind, heart, body racing into overdrive.

Jenny smiled, sat up, stretched out her back; she had started to feel pain in her muscles. She realized that cooking was a demanding job; you had to love it to do it. She stretched out her back again then got up, concerned that she was feeling so sore, but she knew her body was telling her it needed more stretches and rest. Which she knew it would not get, at least not today or anytime soon, that is for sure.

Jenny felt like she was caught up in a tsunami, swept away by events she could not control. She held on in the swirl of madness, hoping it ended with her and Ned finally finding their way to each other, rescued from the storms of their lives.

She went to the window and opened it wider it was going to be another beautiful day; the air was crisp, clean but still had the muskiness of the earth, woods.

She sensed Ned was up; the morning air always reminded her of him, earthy, woody but with a crisp, clean, fresh air smell that promised a new day. She did not want to think about Ned right now because Ned had her stomach in knots, twists, which left her dreaming, her body trembling, wet, longing; they were all new feelings.

Jenny had other things on her mind, like Mrs. Cooker's wedding on Saturday; that will be a massive production by itself. Plus, the pies for Maple Lane, plus Mr. Beatly and Spillman's weekly supplies; it just never ended; she was tired, already running everything through her head.

She walked to the bathroom to bathe, dress, get her day going because everyone depended on her to be healthy, even Mrs. Cooker, especially Mona.

Mona had become her driving motivation for all she did now; that child's strength inspired her. They were both motherless and fatherless…., but they had each other, understand when no one else did. They were orphans in the world.

Jenny's mind was racing….all the time, but try as she may, she could not get the tender ripeness of Ned's lips off her mind. She frequently lapsed off. Dam, she thought, felt out of control of her feelings, discovering her body through its betrayal. "It was a stupid kiss," she said, scolding herself one more time when she could not get the kiss sensation off her mind.

Jenny quickly escaped the confines of her room, mind, for the open kitchen hoping that an early conversation with Mrs. Cooker or Kelly or Sarah or Mona or even Jake would wash Ned out of her head. She entered the kitchen stopped in her tracks when there sat Ned drinking a cup of tea, looking like she felt tired, yet his smile quickly materialized as soon as he saw her.

Ned got up, came to her, wrapped his arms around her, said, "Good morning Mrs. Cooker, how did you sleep, my beautiful wife to be" he was not himself this morning. He kissed her passionately again like he did last night; she swore she felt she had to change her underwear again.

Jenny backed up and put the back of her hand on his forehead. "You feel alright there, Ned; you're acting a little strange," she said, looking at him more closely, seeing his bloodshot eyes. She had never seen Ned so affectionate without worry someone might see them; something was different about him this morning.

"I am in perfect health, maybe a little tired, but in excellent health, of sound body and mind.
My mind has never been more precise about what it wants," he said, kissing her again before releasing her. "You've been on my mind all night Jenny. Want a cup of tea? He asked, reaching for a cup on the table; he poured it, handed her the cup, she sat down beside him.

Jenny took a sip of her tea without saying a word for a moment, then she said, "I've been thinking about you too, Ned; the kiss last night, now this morning, wow. I'm overwhelmed by them; you can't keep doing that to me" she took another sip of her tea.

"You're right, Jenny, but I can't say I'm sorry because I wanted to do it, so it would be dishonest to apologize. I hope I'm not offending you in some way; I don't want to feel like I'm violating you in any way; please forgive if I have...." Ned said, starting a rambling apology.

"No, Ned, it's nothing like that; it's simply hard, that's all. You make me feel things I have never felt before; I just do not know what is happening with my own body. Every time you touch me, kiss me, you look at me; my body…." She stopped herself because she was unsure if she wanted to tell Ned so much when she did not understand her body or what was happening.

"I'm confused, Ned; my body, you, have got me in a state of confusion. I'm having thought of you only a wife should have Ned" she covered her mouth, blushed at her own words; she couldn't believe she was so bold; forward.

Ned took her hands in his, held them to his mouth, and kissed her fingertips. "Jenny, I love you, I promise you with all my heart, I only want right by you, I feel the same way, with those same feelings. You're not alone with what you're feeling…." He was saying when we heard Sarah, Kelly coming down the hall talking about yesterday; they straightened themselves even though it was not necessary because they knew; everyone knew it seemed but Ned and Jenny.

"Morning, you two, Jenny; I thought you'd still be sleeping after yesterday. I was so tired I don't even remember if I said my nightly prayers before I crawled into bed," Kelly said, reaching for the coffee pot.

Sarah yawned involuntarily. It was apparent she could still use an hour or two; they all could.

"I'm still tired, could use a half-day of sleeping for sure," Sarah said, taking the cup from Jenny, who had poured her tea. "Thanks, Jenny" she drank deeply of the hot tea, hoping to wash away sleep, gas in several gulps before she let out a small burp.

"You know what they say; no rest for the wicked; this week work is going to whip us into Olympic shape or break us," Sarah said, bringing their attention right back to why everyone was up when they should instead be rolling over in bed a few more times.

"I guess we might as well talk about the rest of the week; I was thinking earlier we have got to close the business for mama's wedding

Saturday because everyone that's a part of the wedding works for the business or with the business. All of us, I am sure Mr. Hedley, already spoke to Mr. Beatly and Spillman. If everyone agrees, we will have to put up a sign today. What you all think?" Ned asked, taking another cup of tea.

"Do we have a choice? Everything will be happening right here at the house anyway, right; the wedding, the reception, but not the honeymoon, I hope," Sarah said, giggling.

"Sarah," Jenny said, breaking into a giggle too.

"Ned's right, we can't have the business open, be here; besides, we'll have to do everything so that Mrs. Cooker doesn't have to do anything for her big day," said Kelly sipping her coffee.

"And to do that, she can't be in this house...so how are we going to do that? That is the question. Ned, you know your mama, how are we going to do that?" Sarah asked, looking around the table.

"How about we get her to stay with Mrs. Nelson for the night? We get Gracie to go there Saturday, style her hair, do her makeup, get her dressed, comes back here for the ceremony, reception. It will only work if your mama agrees, Ned. What do you think? That is the best I can come up with" said, Jenny.

"Well, that sounds like a great plan, but will she do it? That is the big question," he said, rubbing his temple. Suddenly, a light bulb went off in his head. "We have to let Mona ask her; she's the only one she may give into; get Mr. Hedley to back her up. If those two do not work, we do not have a chance. Mona is the key to the outcome; once she starts on about how she does not want Mrs. Cooker to see any of the decorations, she will do guilt, guilt, and guilt. And I know Mona will bring out the other children who she would get to surround Mrs. Cooker with endless *Please Mrs. Cooker, Please Mrs. Cooker.* That is brilliant now that I think about it," Ned said, leaning back, feeling proud of himself for solving what could be their most significant challenge to the day's success.

"That sounds like a great plan Ned, I'm sure if anyone can get Mrs. Cooker to do something, it's Mona, the rest of the children as backup," Kelly said, getting up to get another cup of coffee she needed today. She wanted to take the afternoon shift today to get some more rest, but Sarah looked like she had gotten less than her. They had all been working hard; it showed on them; Jenny, Ned, and Sarah looked tired, Kelly just felt tired. But she was the happiest she had ever been in her life; her children were too safe and comfortable; that was all that mattered.

Sarah was only partially listening to the conversation she had drifted off into her mind remembering last night. She was still wearing her pretty dress after putting the children to bed; she wanted to make sure George was okay before going to her room. Ned was just leaving when she came through the door; she said goodnight to him before she said to George, "I wanted to check in on you because you looked like you were in a lot of pain" she poured a glass of cold water for him. "How are you feeling?" she asked; she handed it to him.

"Thanks, Sarah, I'm feeling a little better now that I'm lying down; it was pretty bad there for a minute, but it's nothing some rest won't cure," George said, raising his head slightly to drink.

She had spent part of the night lying beside him as he slept; listening to his breathing, she missed the comfort a man brought to the loneliness of the night. She believed that man or woman should not live alone or be alone; she still had strong principles for staying or leaving if it was not what brought happiness and safety.

George made her feel safe, comfortable, loved, wanted, desired, but she was not pushing it; neither was he because they knew what they were feeling; there was no rush for anything. They had kissed a few times, but that was all; they talked, grew to love each other as friends.

"Sarah….she is daydreaming again," she heard Jenny saying as her mind came back into focus.

"Are you okay, Sarah; you want to get some more rest? Jenny asked her becoming concerned now.

"I'm sorry, my thoughts just drifted off. What were you saying again," she said, looking around the table.

"Those must have been some nice thoughts the way you were smiling; want to share them with us?" Kelly asked, teasing her best friend; she had a look of complete mischief on her face; then she started giggling because she could not hold back anymore.

"Oh, you got jokes first thing in the morning," Sarah commented, breaking out into laughter herself because she knew thoughts of George had her in La La Land recently; she did not like it but could not help it. Her feelings for George crept up on her heart like a bandit in the middle of the night. He had stolen her heart before she even knew it was missing. She awoke one day only to realize it was gone; it was now in possession of George Morgan, the bandit.

"What else we have to get done for Mrs. Cooker's wedding aside from getting her out of here; I'm ready to get going," said Sarah nudging Kelly in the process; she loved Kelly for being Kelly.

"Ned, do we have white paint, so can you do the gazebo? Maybe we can have the ceremony out there. We can have the dinner in the kitchen here or maybe even bring the tables outside; the reception in the living room," Jenny asked, hoping to get comments from everyone.

"We do have some leftover paint in the barn; I can do it tomorrow; today, I have something I have to get done," Ned said so cryptic that everyone looked at him, but no one asked; Ned was always secretive.

"We shouldn't plan to put everything outside until Saturday morning when we can check the weather. Otherwise, outdoors will be beautiful; we can decorate the yard from the house to the gazebo; Mona, the children will love that," Sarah said, getting up to pick up a piece of paper from the notebook, started taking notes.

"We have to do all the decorating, the cooking, the cake, the cleaning; Mrs. Cooker can't do anything from Friday midday," Jenny said.

"Ned, you and George will be in charge of taking care of Mr. Hedley, Sarah can you, Mrs. Nelson, take care of Mrs. Cooker. I'll take care of all the children," Kelly said.

"Do you think we can get Mr. Kimberley to drive Mrs. Cooker from Mrs. Nelson's here in that car of his?" Ned asked; he was sure that his mother had invited Calvin; why not utilize his car? He was sure he would not mind. Calvin Kimberley adored his mama.

"That is a great idea, Ned. Can you ask him please," Jenny said while Sarah noted it on the piece of paper. "Oh, we have to talk to Pastor Hayles tomorrow about the ceremony; ask him if he could come a little earlier on Saturday," she said, grabbing an apple off the table; took a bite.

"We'll get all our supplies today; we can do almost everything in the house; we only have three days to get everything ready," Jenny said, ready to wrap up the meeting; get going on today's cooking.

"I think we have everything covered, Jenny," Sarah said, finishing her notes, then said, "What do we need to do now, Jenny?" Sarah asked but was interrupted by Kelly.

"Hey Sarah, would you like to work this morning or this afternoon?" she asked, "You look a little tired."

"I'll take the afternoon if you don't mind; I think I'll take a morning nap with baby Sasha today," she said, yawned while she was still talking; they all broke out laughing because the yawn had said everything.

"Okay, Sarah, not a problem, take care of George," Kelly said, winking at her, laughing some more.

"I couldn't sleep, Kelly, even though I was exhausted; yesterday was so beautiful, so special; yes, we did it, but when I was watching Mr. and Mrs. Beatly and the customers.

They were in awe, and I was too, really in awe; yesterday was magical; it just kept running through my mind," Sarah said, looking tired, but her mind was still sharp. You could tell by the excitement in her eyes; voice.

"The feedback Jenny, I got from people yesterday was amazing; women were almost in tears. They were saying how lucky Mrs. Beatly was; the gifts he bought for her wowed them, made them a little jealous too. The men just kept looking at all the kisses Mr. Beatly was getting from Mrs. Beatly; they had never seen them publicly affectionate like that. We have about ten orders coming in this week. Trust me; those wives were already spending their husband's money," Ned said, laughing at his joke.

"I got the same response from everyone that spoke to me too. We did a great job; I am proud. The most important thing is that Mr. and Mrs. Beatly completely enjoyed themselves; I do not think they stopped smiling, laughing, talking all night. They were happy; I know they appreciated, were surprised by what we did. The children were amazing; I want to give them something special for all their help. What do you think they would like?" Jenny asked, looking from Kelly to Sarah. "What about money?" she asked, already convinced; because which child did not like their own money.

"Money is good," Kelly said, getting up for a glass of water. She would be wired all day.

"I agree, and money is always a perfect gift; maybe Ned can take them into Maple Lane next week so they can buy their things. I know they will like that," Sarah said; she got a glass of water instead of more tea.

"I like that idea, Sarah; I'll take them to Maple Lane Sunday on our day off after the wedding; it'll be a good rest, a surprise for them," Ned said, reaching for the leftover pot pie under the wire mesh on the table.

"Okay, it's settled, so let's get going then," Jenny said. Everyone got up to start the preparations for the day; they had all their supplies, thanks to Ned, who picked up everything yesterday.

"Morning, everyone," Mona said as she walked into the kitchen; they all turned around.

"Morning, Mona," they said.

Then Jenny asked, "How did you sleep, Mona? She walked over, hugged her, and then went to the sink to wash her hand; put on her apron.

"It took a while to fall asleep; I was still too excited about everything that happened yesterday; I was excited for the Beatly's; they looked so in love; they were kissing all the time.

It was kind of yucky but nice; I guess that's what adults do when they're in love," she said, reaching for an apple on the table.

"I'm hungry. Can I eat something else?" she asked, devouring the apple in five bites.

"We've got some leftover pot pies on the table if your Uncle Ned hasn't finished eating all of them," Jenny said, putting on a series of pots on the stove, turned it on; she was ready to cook.

"I only had two or three of those pot pies; your Aunt Jenny knows a hungry man is an angry man," Ned said.

"Mona, we were discussing Mrs. Cooker's wedding on Saturday; we want you to convince her to leave the house Friday night, stay with Mrs. Nelson, get dressed there, we'll get Mr. Kimberley to pick her up in his car; bring her here. *You have to say, we the children want to surprise you with our decorating, and we don't want you to see it before the wedding*," Jenny said, filling another pot with water.

"Okay, Aunt Jenny, I can do that. How will Mr. Hedley get here?" she asked, taking another bite of her pot pie; she poured a glass of water for herself.

Kelly, Sarah had washed their hands, put on their apron; they had taken out the doughs for the loaves of bread; pies. They were greasing, flouring the baking pans; line them up to one side of the table.

"Your Uncle Ned will be taking care of that; he'll help him get dress; bring him to the house for the wedding; we can ask Ms. Henderson to drive him," Kelly said as they started rolling out, cutting the dough to place them in the pans; they had twenty pans ready to go into the oven.

Jenny had put on the pot pies ingredients to start them cooking; she had the large roast beef, ten chickens in the oven baking; the smell of onions, garlic, fresh thyme perfumed the kitchen, soon the entire house.

"Mona, we were thinking about having the wedding in the gazebo, the back yard depending on what the weather will be like on Saturday, but we can still decorate the house even if we go outside. You, Jake, Uncle George; the rest of the children will be in charge of all the decorating," Jenny said, stirring the pots in front of her.

"Oh, before we forget, Mona, can you make a small sign for the Bar saying we're not going to open on Saturday. It will be too much to do mama's wedding; run the business. Can you please do it this morning? We want to put it up today," Ned said, eating the last of his pie; started peeling.

"No problem, Uncle Ned, I can do that," Mona said, taking another pie.

"Excellent, we have everything in order," Sarah said; they were rolling out the dough for the pies, filling pans. They settled into their tasks of getting all the food ready. Jenny turned on the radio; they always worked better when music was in the background.

Mrs. Cooker rolled over in her bed again; she could not find the energy or strength to leave, nor did she have any desire to; she acknowledged to herself that her body was tired, real tired. She could smell food cooking in the kitchen as it permeated her room; that made her feel less guilty for not getting up to help. It was the smell of food that finally woke her from her sleep; it smelled good; she was feeling good that Jenny, Kelly, Sarah, Ned; she was sure little Mona was right there in the middle of the mix taking care of business, plotting.

Maybe they were correct in wanting her to do less; her body was indeed telling her they were.

It was getting harder, harder to do the same things she used to breeze through with plenty of excess energy; now, she fought to just get out of bed. At first, she blamed her worries on her mind, but it did not hold water anymore; she was getting older in her mind and body.

Francine was thinking about her upcoming marriage to Herman. Her mind was now focusing on that; she was not sure because they had not had any time to discuss their plans or what is next. Should she live with him or him with her; she had no idea what Herman or the children were planning; she did not like being not in control or aware of what is going on.

Francine Cooker knew she was a control freak; even lying in bed now while everyone was cooking took strength not to get up, go take over; but her body would have stopped her in her tracks anyway; fatigue had taken over. Herman, the family that had taken over her life, was now sending her into a whirlwind marriage she was not sure she wanted, but it was too late to back out now; at her age, she could hardly become a runaway bride, where would she go?

She laughed to herself at the thought of she, Mrs. Francine Cooker, a runaway bride; she looked at the ring Herman insisted she wear all the time; she did it to make him happy.

Mabel had always complained about her not being willing to allow others to give or do anything for her when she was such a natural giver. Mabel's words came crashing into her head; "Francine, you've got to give yourself permission to live too; you're not too old for some sugar, you know," Mabel had said. Francine giggled because she felt like she could use some sugar now, not like the kind of sugar she wanted when she was younger, but it was sugar, nonetheless.

She had been feeling happier since Herman's proposal; she had tried to act casual about it, but she found herself laughing, smiling, and singing a whole lot more despite herself.

If she were honest with herself, she would admit she had been longing for the touch, the companionship of a man more and more. She was old, not dead. Yeah, she had written off any possibility of remarriage at her age, but the loneliness of her life in recent years; made her realize that her life was quickly passing her by; she was lonely.

It was not just the pressure of carrying the family; she missed having a man in her life. She missed the love, missed the affection, missed the sugar raw, refined, or caramelized, missed the companionship, missed the conversations, missed the comfort, and missed the care. She wanted all of it; only a husband could take her away from her sometimes overwhelming life.

Francine's mama used to say that even older people need some sugar; it helps keep the blood circulating, the heart beating. Even King David asked for a young virgin to warm up that crusty ole body of his. Some people may say he is a dirty older man, but you will do anything to live another day with a bit of joy in your life or memories when you are that old. When you are that old, all you have is your imagination anyway, any sweetness you can squeeze out of what is left.

"Everybody needed a little sugar in their lives sometimes," Francine repeated; she smiled at the memory of her mama, Mabel. Her mama was right, so was Mabel; she missed them both, especially their wisdom.

Francine felt like a young girl in love, realized that it was not that she had not loved Herman all her life; it is just that they were such good friends, best friends; it just never happened until now.

"Oh my God, I'm getting married on Saturday to the man I've always loved," she said out loud just to make it real, as if the rings on her finger, the jewelry on her dresser, were not enough to convince her.

What happened over the past week still had her mystified; she was suddenly caught up in a whirlwind of romance, emotions that she could not control; she did not want to. For the first time in a long time, she was happy, happy to have a man back in her life; Herman really in her life; he was always there ironically.

Francine Cooker sat up. She suddenly felt energized, excited, something she had not felt in a long time. Her mind felt free for the first time in a long, long time. It was like finding an escape from your own life; she got up.

She looked at the new dresses Herman had bought her; the girls had hung them up so she could see them; decide to wear them soon, or they would be lost in the back of her cabinet.

She chose the pink dress with the tiny red rose; it was a soft, flowing, pretty little dress, worn only in the big cities. She put it aside, went to the bath, prepare for what would be another long day. She was glad that she could depend on Jenny, the others. For the first time, she felt if she were not there, things would not fall apart. She put on her cooking clothe, headed for the kitchen even though she suspected they would try not to let her raise a finger; they would try.

Mona sat at the kitchen table doing yesterday's accounting, making up all the envelopes for the day. She started making a list of all the decorations they would need for an outdoor versus an indoor wedding; she realized that they would have to buy some more paper bells, angels, hearts, streamers. If they were going to do Mrs. Cooker, Mr. Hedley's wedding right, create something unforgettable, they needed more decorations.

"Aunt Jenny, can we please get some more wedding decorations for Mrs. Cooker's wedding. I think another twenty-five dollars will do it?" Mona asked, looking at her with her best pleading eyes.

"Why do we need more decorations, Mona," Jenny asked, removing the pot pie fillings from the stove to cool; she put on the pot for the fried chicken.

"Well, if we do Mrs. Cooker's wedding outside, we'll need more paper bells, angels, hearts, streamers; it'll be fantastic, Aunt Jenny: Mona said.

240

"What will be beautiful, Mona? Morning family," Mrs. Cooker said, coming into the kitchen.

"Your wedding; it'll be stunning when we do the decorations; that's why you can't be here when we do it," Mona blurted out; she focused on her list, so she did not see Mrs. Cooker look of surprise on her face.

"What you mean, I cannot be here, Mona. Where will I be?" Francine asked, reaching for a cup of tea.

"Well, the children, Uncle George, I want it to be a surprise, so you can't be here to see it until you're going to get married. You can stay by Mrs. Nelson's," she said, looking up from her list for the first time; she ran into her arms and hugged her tight. "I'm so excited you're getting married Saturday, Mrs. Cooker. It's going to be the best wedding ever," she exclaimed; she started dancing around the kitchen.

"Slow down there, Mona, my heart isn't ready for all this excitement so early in the morning today," she said as Mona twirled her around one more time; she was laughing, enjoying Mona's excitement, enthusiasm. She sat down at the table, trying to catch her breath, then said, "You're all up in here conspiring against me, isn't you; Ned, what's going on?" she asked in between trying to catch her breath; Mona brought her a tall glass of water.

Ned looked guilty but said nothing. He just kept peeling his potatoes.

"Mrs. Cooker Ned's not in charge of decorating, the children, Uncle George, I want you to be surprised when you see it like the Beatly's were. Did you see their face when they walked into the Bar; we want you to be surprised like that," Mona said, dancing around again. "It's going to be amazing," sitting down this time to finish her list.

"I just want a simple little wedding Mona, not all this excitement," Francine said, taking another drink of water.

"We do not have excitement, Mrs. Cooker; we're having your wedding; it'll be just family anyway right, it'll be good practice for when we do have a wedding. You'll be doing it for the business too, Mrs. Cooker," Mona said as everyone looked on, not saying a word, they were all nodding their heads.

Mona had skills, Jenny thought. "Mrs. Cooker, it will be so much easier for them to surprise you if you're not here," Jenny said, piping in her two cents; she took out; added some more chicken to the pot.

"So, let me get this right, on Friday, you want me to go stay with Mrs. Nelson, get dressed there, then come home for the wedding; where will Herman be? She asked, wondering what she got herself into when she said yes.

"Mr. Hedley will be picked up; you will be picked up too but not together. All that's been taken care of, so you don't have to worry," said Jenny, who was finishing up the last batch of fried chicken, packing them to drain.

Kelly and Sarah were focused entirely on filling their pot pies. They had fifty loaves of baked bread; they did not want to get tangled up in how to get Mrs. Cooker to her wedding. Mona and Jenny were tasked to pull it off, or it was game over.

"Please, Mrs. Cooker, please, can you just let us surprise you; we have everything planned out already. Everyone will be so disappointed if we don't get to surprise you the right way, please, Mrs. Cooker," Mona said, putting on her best pouting lips, sad eyes for sympathetic effect. Mona was working it like none of them could have; they could tell Mrs. Cooker was hesitating.

"Does Mrs. Nelson know about this?" she asked, wiping her forehead. She was getting hot from all the heat in the kitchen; it was not from the stoves.

"Mrs. Nelson knows everything" Mona kind of lied because she knew Mrs. Nelson would say yes when told; then said, "Aunt Sarah will be with you to help you get dressed, Gracie will come by to do your hair, make-up too; you'll see it'll be perfect, all you have to do is say yes" Mona was determined, but Mrs. Cooker was stubborn.

"I don't know about all that, Mona; I did say something simple, right," Mrs. Cooker said, looking around the room.

"It will be simple, Mrs. Cooker, but we want it to be simply beautiful for you, Mr. Hedley; if you don't want to do it for yourself or us; then do it for my mama please because you know she'd be doing this too," Mona said bringing out the big guns by talking about Mabel, her mama.

That did it, Mrs. Francine Cooker conceded. "Okay, I can't believe I let you blackmail me; you're ruthless Mona Johnson, just ruthless," Mrs. Cooker said, smiling because she had already decided to give in to them. She wondered what else they were up to, but that would also be a surprise.

"Thank you, Mrs. Cooker," Mona said, jumping up off her seat to go hug her; everyone looked like they were relieved because Mrs. Cooker's corporation was vital to the success of the wedding.

"You've back me in a corner using Mona to twist my arm with her cuteness; what can I do to help out?" She asked, rising to wash her hands and put on her apron.

"We have everything under control, Mrs. Cooker, finished today's menu, about to finish breakfast; just sit down, relax. Mona, please set the rest of the table. " Jenny said, placing another bowl on the table; started to fill another.

The children came to the kitchen door; Margaret had Baby Sasha; Suzie and Marie followed her. The boys were just behind them; Serge was still rubbing his eyes; Thomas yawned, looked as if he did not want to come out of bed; Jake looked ready for the day.

"Morning," they said, coming into the kitchen and sat down. Baby Sasha started crying as soon as she saw her mother, so Kelly washed her hands, dried them, took her to give her some breast. That would soon be over because Sasha was becoming all teeth, ready to try them out on most things that got in her mouth; she laughed when Kelly screamed out in pain.

"Morning, children, breakfast will be ready soon; everyone slept okay after yesterday," Jenny asked as she finished setting out some of the serving bowls filled with food.

Sarah finished up the final ten batches of Jenny's new biscuit recipe, put them out to cool on the wire rack in the corner; it was a new addition to the kitchen, thanks to Mr. Hedley. Then she excused herself to use the bathroom; see about George, whom she had left sleeping in the wee hours of this morning. She could hear the conversation behind her as she walked down the hallway towards George's room; she felt him pulling her deeper into him, especially now that he was so close.

Sarah, at first, did not want to admit that he had stolen her heart, but it was beating now like she was in a race the closer she got to his door. She hesitated before she knocked; she was excited, scared as old demons of her ex-husbands' charming beginnings quickly ran through her head.

It was happening less but still popped its head up every now, then whenever she doubted herself or George or what they feel. She knew George had been sincere all this time; this is what Mrs. Cooker asked her to do, take care of George while he recovers. That is the least she could do; besides, he is family, a part of this home; she knocked louder, hoping it drives away all her doubts and fears.

She opened the door to find George sitting up shirtless on the edge of his bed, looking better after his rest; he turned around.

"Morning Sarah, how are you this morning; I felt you in my sleep when you left. I felt your kiss," he said, getting up off the bed to grab a shirt out of the draw.

"Morning George, you did, did you. You were snoring hard last night, sleeping so deeply; I did not think you would notice. I'll get one for you," she said, crossing the short space to get him a shirt from the cabinet; it was closer to the door. She got it, walked back towards the bed, and gave him his shirt; he pulled her close, kissed her on the forehead in a tight embrace. "Thank you, Sarah; I appreciate you being here for me, for last night," he said, breathing into her ears.

"I'd be so lonely without you here, Sarah" he moved his head to look into her eyes; George felt his manhood move beneath his pants; he steadied his mind to control his potential embarrassment. He wanted her to know what he was feeling was not just physical; he was not about to let his penis get ahead of his mind; Sarah was more than a sex or fun thing to him; he had had plenty of that.

"You could never be lonely with Mona or the other children or Ned around. It's just because you're injured why they're giving you a break; you know it," Sarah laughed, trying to walk away from his embrace, but he held her.

"The children are great, but I desire the company of a woman who's also a friend to laugh with, cry with, grow with, and fall asleep with. That is really what not being lonely means," George said with a clip in his voice.

Then they heard the call to breakfast coming from the kitchen; they walked out together.

Sarah was glad she did not have to respond to his last statements because George had her mind in disarray, her heart beating with hope, but she did not want to dare anymore of what her thoughts had already given. The feelings of a possible future with him, a life with him, made her stomach do somersaults. They entered the kitchen together. The family greeted George; they sat down to eat breakfast as a family.

The rest of the week passed as most of their week passed these days; they were busy running a growing business and their lives in the small pockets of time they had. Mr. and Mrs. Beatly looked more in love than ever before when we saw them; they could not thank our family enough for helping them to have some of the most incredible memories of their lives. They were still overwhelmed by the magnitude of our gift. They gushed about how their son Charles was talking about the food, decorations, and music.

Mr. Beatly had put up Mona's painting in a prominent part of his store for everyone to see; they beamed with a loving new appreciation for each other, Mrs. Cooker's family.
Everyone congratulated them on their anniversary, asked about the experience and how they became our walking, talking advertising billboard.

The Townspeople could not believe that they had received such a wonderful gift from our family until Mr. Beatly explained he was hoping for a simple dinner for their thirtieth anniversary; they were just as surprised as everyone. Edgar told them he, especially his wife had no idea what they had planned. They were even more impressed; they started booking their dates. Fairbank families came out in droves; by the end of the week, they had more than twenty new dates for their unique occasion service.

Friday morning, they gathered in the kitchen, had their final meeting before the wedding, mapped out their plans. Jenny, Ned, would pick up all the supplies in Maple Lane when they dropped off the one hundred pies. Jenny wanted them to buy more plates, cutlery, etc. For the business now, they had twenty pre-paid package services ranging from two to twenty people. Their unique occasion service was an instant success; they all agreed they had to invest more in it to grow.

They would also stop by Mr. Kimberley and ask about his car to transport Mrs. Cooker to her wedding at the house; he agreed; said he would be honored. It seemed Cindy was still in town, would be staying for the unforeseeable future; they were trying to work out twenty-plus years of not seeing each other and the mistakes they had made; she was extended an invitation too.

Sarah and Kelly would stay behind to finish baking and get the rest of the food ready for transport.

Mona, Jake, Uncle George would stay to organize the supplies for the decorations, cutlery, etc. They organized the children and laid out the plans for tomorrow, each of their roles; they were excited to be a part of another special occasion, especially; because of Mrs. Cooker, Mr. Hedley's wedding.

Ms. Henderson suspended all lessons on Friday to give the children time to help with the wedding preparation; she would be there to help on Saturday; she was filled in on our plans.

Mrs. Cooker awoke most of the week to her entire family in the kitchen cooking away; even George got up to help peel potatoes with Ned in moderation; he became pretty handy with a knife.

They tried their absolute best for Mrs. Cooker to wake up to breakfast, allowed her only to work the morning and early afternoon at the Bar. However, once she was home, they had no control, so she cleaned, cooked whenever she was bored; always, rest was a foreign word. Mr. Hedley arrived early.

"Morning family, morning, my love, I have to get to Bar to receive delivery of some supplies. Here are my pre-marriage gifts for my beautiful bride." He dropped off several boxes and dashed off with only a quick kiss.

"Thank you, Herman," Mrs. Cooker said once again, taken aback. It was a huge box.

They sat at the table in anticipation, wondering what Mr. Hedley had brought for her now; Mona could not contain her excitement, asked as he left, "Mrs. Cooker, can we please see what's in the box" Mona was already moving to make room for her at the table.

"My goodness Mona, you're more excited than me," she said as Mona bounced up, down on her chair. She placed the boxes further on the table, moved the small one, investigated the shoebox with cream-colored silk shoes, tiny pearls around the edges, and then opened the top of the big one.

Underneath layers of tissue paper was a lace, silk cream-colored dress; she took it out of the box; held it up. It was a full-length long sleeve silk dress with lace around the neck, shoulders, breast area. It had small pearl embellishments along the neck, across the breast, down the back where larger pearl-like buttons closed the back; it was a very modern cut, absolutely beautiful. There was also a tiny headpiece still in the box. Francine saw the note, picked it up, and read it out when they kept looking at her like she held a State secret.

"To my beautiful wife to be Francine, something old the broach from my grandmother, then mother, something new the pearl bracelet, neckless, and something blue the hairpins. I was not sure about something borrowed, so I am leaving that up to you, the family. See you tomorrow for the rest of our lives. Love Herman. She opened the small box to see its content, showed them the broach.

"Oh my Mrs. Cooker, that's a beautiful gift; the dress, the jewelry, the note; Mr. Hedley is such a romantic," Jenny said; her mouth had dropped open; tears came to her eyes; she was the romantic of the family.

"Mrs. Cooker, you got to try it on; it's beautiful; I have something for the borrowed part of the wedding," Mona said, getting up off her chair, ready to help.

"How did he know your size; of course, the shopping," Sarah said, answering her question, then she said, "Does Mr. Hedley have a brother about forty years younger, Mrs. Cooker" breaking everyone into laughter.

"I'm asking that too, Sarah," Kelly said, giggling some more. But became serious, said, "Wow, Mrs. Cooker, Mr. Hedley, he's in a class of his own; he just keeps coming with more surprises every day. Ned, George, you two paying attention to how to treat your wives," Kelly teased.

"Seeing how happy your mama is, Ned, I'd marry Mr. Hedley myself if I could," George said, taking the sting off Kelly's words; they broke out laughing harder.

"You're so silly, Uncle George. You can't marry Mr. Hedley," Mona said, giggling again at what he said.

"Mama, you got to go try it on, see how it fits; it's a beautiful dress; beautiful gifts," Ned said, feeling happy for his mama, Herman, who seemed to have been waiting for his chance to pour out his love with gifts of gratitude.

The pressure was too much, so Mrs. Cooker went to her room with Sarah, Jenny while Mona went to her room to retrieve her mama's Mabel pearl earrings for Mrs. Cooker to wear.

The dress was perfectly tailored for her; a small veil that looked more like a cute little hat was in the box. It had layers of lace in the back that fell just below the nape, one flip-down panel with tiny pearls across the end of the lace to cover the face; it was beautiful, elegant, Mrs. Cooker was stunning. They pinned the blue hairpin at the side of the headpiece.

That is when Mona stepped up, looking serious, said, "Mrs. Cooker, you look so beautiful; the dress fits perfectly. Mrs. Cooker, I would like you to please wear these tomorrow" Mona placed the pearl earrings in her hand. Francine Cooker looked down at Mabel, one set of pearl earrings; tears came to her eyes.

Mona continued, "When I brought mama's jewelry box here, I found these pearl erring in it; I'm sure if my mama was here, she'd want you to use them too" she hugged Mrs. Cooker, Mrs. Cooker hugged her back as tears ran down her face.

Jenny, Sarah both had tears in their eyes, trying to hold back the emotions that caught them off guard with Mona's request for Mrs. Cooker to wear her mother's earrings.

"Don't cry, Mrs. Cooker; she's so happy for you, Mr. Hedley; she's been waiting. She used to say; I do not know what is wrong with Mrs. Cooker if she cannot see that Mr. Hedley is head over heels in love with her until he is stupid. And I do not know what Mr. Hedley's waiting for; he will have one foot in the grave before he says anything to Mrs. Cooker. Don't they know times a ticking? I'd laugh when she said that, but I knew it was true that she loved you both," Mona said with the wisdom, the memory of an elephant.

"I'd be honored to wear them, Mona, thank you," she said, hugging Mona again, put them in her ears with help from Sarah; poor Jenny was still crying.

Kelly knocked, opened the door only to walk into a tear fest; she said, "What's going on? Why's everyone crying" she walked over to them. "Oh, Mrs. Cooker, you look stunning."

"Thanks, Kelly, I don't know why they're crying, but I am crying because Mona just asked me to wear her mama pearl earrings. They're perfect; thank you again, baby, they're beautiful," Francine said, smiling. She turned to look at herself in the full-length mirror as the others stood around her. "I must say Herman's got great taste, style too, he knows what I'll like but wouldn't buy for myself. Very much like your mama Mona" she turned around to look at her aging behind, liked the way it looked in the gown.

"Are you going to make the children, Ned, George, see it before the wedding or let them be surprised like everyone else?" Jenny asked, wiping the last of the tears from her eyes; she was in love with love. "I think you should surprise them too," she said, voicing our opinion with nods.

The rest of Friday flew by at a rapid pace that accompanied too many things to do.
After the deliveries, pickups the family went into full-scale production, reached the Bar to provide the week's final service before the wedding the next day.

They went home earlier than usual because all the food sold out; families flooded Spillman's Bar for their meal until the following Tuesday. Mr. Spillman said he would also close on Saturday and open again on Monday to be at the wedding; he would provide all the liquor they would need.

The Beatly's said they would close by noon to be at the one o-clock ceremony, were giving them six bouquets, plus the bride's bouquet; Ned could pick it up Saturday.

Mrs. Nelson had been told the day's plan and agreed to host Mrs. Cooker, the bridal party. Mrs. Cooker would be dropped off with minimum protest at Mrs. Nelson's after breakfast tomorrow as a compromise.

That night the excitement of the next day faded as fatigue took over after they had done all the preparations for the wedding; they temporarily stored all the extra decorations in the last unoccupied room in the house; only kept the ones that would be needed.

They went to bed thinking about tomorrow, everything that needed to be done, but most of all, they just wanted everything to go well for two people that they all loved; they deserved to be happy. All evil thoughts faded into the night.

TWENTY-TWO

Life Grants Wishes

Saturday morning. The house is alive before the sun. Jenny Kelly, Sarah, Ned, George, Mona, and Jake busied themselves with making various miniature pot pies, biscuits, fruit pies, and cakes.

George and Ned made mashed potatoes and potato salad. Jenny made a big pot of soup to last the day and into the night.

Francine came into the kitchen. "Good morning," she said and moved toward the washbasin to wash her hands and put on her apron.

George pulled out a seat for Mrs. Cooker.

"Mrs. Cooker, this is your official day off. We will serve you," George said.

The table was covered with a lace tablecloth and set with silver cutlery; he poured her tea from a fancy teapot with creamer and sugar.

"Thank you, George, you don't have to go through all this trouble for me," Mrs. Cooker protested.

Mona reminded Mrs. Cooker about her hairdresser's appointment with Mrs. Nelson.

Kelly called out, "Breakfast in ten minutes."

"Ned, would you please bless the table," Mrs. Cooker asked as she poured herself another cup of tea.

"Lord God, thank you for this special day with my family. We ask you to bless my mama, Mr. Hedley, as they start a new life together today; remember everyone at this table, bless them, grant them their heart's desire. Remember those that do not have a meal today, thank you for this meal; bless those who made it. Amen,"

His prayer was beautiful.

"Amen," they all said, then Mrs. Cooker said, "Ned, that was just a lovely prayer, son."

Then Mrs. Cooker turned to Jenny and said, "This breakfast is wonderful; I could get used to waking up every morning to breakfast like this."

"Thanks, Mrs. Cooker, learned everything from you and Mabel; I'm grateful that I can survive on my cooking skills," Jenny said, taking another biscuit off the plate.

"Jenny, you are a fantastic study; I'm proud of you. I am proud of every one of you. All of you women here will make fine wives for the decent men in Fairbanks". Mrs. Cooker winked. The women giggled. Ned and George looked at each other curiously; George tried not to laugh; his ribs were still sore, and he did not wish to laugh himself back into Doctor Morgan's care. Belly laughs, and quiet sighs sounded around the breakfast table.

"Anyone wants seconds," said Jenny raising from the table.

"I want seconds," said Jake, Thomas, Margaret, and Suzie, in unison. "I'm full, Aunt Jenny, thank you," Mona said.

Mona enquired if she could help with clearing the table.

"Sure, Mona, you can come help," Jenny said.

Jake went off to see his brothers; Kelly followed behind to make sure things go well. She heard baby Sasha crying. She quickly bathed, changed, and breastfed Sasha.

"I'll go hitch up the wagon, mama," Ned said.

George washed his hands. Jenny stole a look at Ned.

Everyone was ready to start the day.

"Mrs. Cooker, you should let down your silver hair more often; it beautiful," Mona said, folding and putting her wedding dress back into the box along with the broach and her mama's earrings. Every item Mrs. Cooker needed for her special day was packed and ready, including a Bible.

"Mona, I am so happy; my wedding ceremony will be right here in this house, the simplest wedding anyone can have around here," Mrs. Cooker said.

Jenny knocked and entered the room.

"Mona, I come to help Mrs. Cooker get dress," she said.

"Okay, Aunt Jenny; her wedding dress, jewelry, veils are all in that box," she pointed out. "And her new shoe, slip, bra, panties, handkerchiefs are all in the travel bag over there along with her perfume, face, body powder, and bible. I do not think I forgot anything. Did I Mrs. Cooker?" she asked about to walk away towards the door.

Mrs. Cooker walked over to her, said, "Thank you, Mona, for all your help; I'm sure everything is in there. I love you" she hugged her tight to her breast.

"You're welcome, Mrs. Cooker; I love you too," Mona said, hugging her back.

"Thanks, Mona," Jenny said as Mona left the room.

"Mrs. Cooker, I just…." Jenny was saying when she was interrupted.

"Jenny, I want you to call me Francine, especially when we're alone; we're all adults; besides, you'll be my daughter-in-law soon, even though I've raised you like my own child," she said, picking up her herbal concoction of powder, cornstarch, herbs to put under her arms. She had made one for every adult in the house, wow did it help, especially the men who had reluctantly taken it. BO (body odor) was not a nice thing after a long day of working on the farm; around here, she said we worked hard, it would smell on us; she was right because

254

sometimes Ned, George, Mr. Hedley bath two sometimes three times a day.

Jenny looked stunned when Francine said daughter-in-law, but she was slightly behind her, so Mrs. Cooker did not see her face. How did she know that? She wondered, "Okay, Mrs. Francine, Francine, I just wanted to thank you, wish you the best, happiest life you, Mr. Hedley, could have. I hope you will take more time off to enjoy yourself; allow Mr. Heed ... I mean Herman to take care of you, no fuss. I can tell that he just wants to do everything for you," said Jenny. She was so emotional her voice was hoarse when she spoke; she did not mention the daughter-in-law bit.

Francine Cooker wiped her fingers on the towel, walked over to Jenny, wrapped her arms around her, and looked into her eyes. "Jenny, you are the daughter I never had, even though it was a tragic circumstance why you are here; I'm grateful every day to your mama for giving birth to my son's future wife," she said. Now Jenny could not help but show her surprise, she started to say something, but Francine put her fingers on her lips, released her from what we famously call her 'Grip O Hug.' "Jenny, you don't need to say anything, honey; I'm so happy for you, my son, that you have found each other. I can see that you love him, that he's stupid in love with you too," she giggled. "It's charming to watch, but we're tired of watching now; we want action," breaking out into laughter again. "Seriously thou Jenny, I do not want you or Ned to wait; life's too short, we don't know how many years we've been promised on this earth. You must grab all the joy you can while you can; if nothing else, this is the most important lesson Mabel harped at me, especially about Herman. But she always said nothing happened before it was time; it took Mabel's death to accept some happiness into my life again. Jenny, it has been an honor taking care of you, being a part of your life; your mother was the sister I never had; I love; you," Francine said, looking into Jenny's eyes.

"Thank you, Francine; I do love Ned very much," she confessed for the first time to the woman who had been her mother, would one day become her mother-in-law, her only family.

"Mabel used to talk to me too, but she was always waiting for Ned to act. She'd say he can be slow as molasses when it comes to making up his mind," Jenny continued, sniffling back tears.

"Yes, Mabel, saw things ten miles away. I know Ned loves you too, he's just unsure of himself, but he'll come around. Once he makes up his mind, there is no stopping him; he is like a bulldozer," Mrs. Cooker said, holding Jenny's hands. Then she said, "Jenny, everything is going to be alright, especially because of all the change that's been happening, that's my belief." she said.

"Francine, please wear one of the new dresses, Mr.….Herman gave you," Jenny said, wiping the last of her tears.

"Thank you for everything, Jenny. I know you'll make Ned a great wife; I'll be proud," she said, slipping on the soft peach-colored dress and putting on her shoes.

"Francine, you look beautiful. I am so happy for you and Herman; you have made him the happiest man alive. He hasn't stopped smiling since you said yes," said Jenny looking for her purse to put her other things.

"That is the thing, Jenny, Herman has always been in my life; I always loved him as my best friend, my confidant but not my lover; I do not know why, when I did, I dismissed it with, we're friends. But that is the exact reason I should have given him a chance long ago because he was my best friend; that is where all great relationships start. So do not worry," she said, getting her sweater; she never leaves home without one.

"Thank you, Francine," Jenny said, hugging her again.

"You are very welcome, Jenny, now let's get out of here before everyone has a fit," she said; Francine picked up her purse. Jenny grabbed the boxes, the travel bag; they left the room together.

Ned left the kitchen with George to go hitch up the horses. After that, George followed him back to Ned's room because he wanted to talk; George sat down on the bed while Ned changed his shirt.

"I can't believe Mona outed us like that...." George was saying before Ned interrupted him.

"George, I'm glad she did; we are not fooling anybody; besides, I'm going to ask Jenny to marry me tonight anyway.

George looked a little surprised. "So, you made up your mind, nice; I'm so happy to you, both of you," George said, standing up to shake his hand and smiling.

"Thanks, George, I am so happy. I cannot wait any longer. Jenny is driving me out of my mind; I cannot be around her alone anymore. Now's the right time so I went out, bought her a ring and necklace. I'm going to tell mama today when I drive her to Mrs. Nelson's," Ned said, getting the jewelry box out and showing George.

George took it in his hand, opened the box. "Wow, Ned, this is beautiful; Jenny's going to love it; be blown away. This must-have cost you a pretty penny. Did you see Mr. Beatly's gifts to Mrs. Beatly; he must have broken all his piggybanks with those rubies, diamonds, and pearls. I guess he felt he had a lot to catch up for. I never thought Mr. Herman had it in him either. Ned, I'm happy for you," he said, closing the box, giving it back.

"What about you, George? How long are you going to let Sarah wait? She is an amazing woman, a great mother; I can tell she is crazy about you. You have been spending a lot of time together lately. What's going on?" Ned said, buttoning up the rest of his shirt; he put Jenny's engagement gift back in the draw.

"I don't know Ned; I guess I'm a little afraid that I won't measure up to the kind of man she, the children, need. They had such a bad experience already with her first husband; I do not want to rush her," George said for more of his benefit than Ned's.

"George, I know you, I know you care about Sarah, she cares about you; the children love, adore, respect you already. What more do you want? What are you waiting for; we are not getting any younger, George, my friend. Besides, Sarah will be good for you, you for her; you know it. Maybe that is what you are afraid of; maybe you just want to hold on to your bad boy bachelor image. Just maybe, but are you willing to risk finding that one woman that loves and adores you, George; I hope not," Ned said, tucking his shirt in. He was ready to go.

"I think I'm ready to settle down. I have some money saved up, stashed away, but becoming a husband with a wife; three boys is a little overwhelming, you know," he said.

"Yeah, I know that George, I would be a little afraid too, but think about life without Sarah, those children since you have met them, and how empty it would have been. You have had so much joy being around them, being around her, growing slowly to love them; how much would you miss them if they were gone. That is the question you should be asking yourself, George," said Ned smiling at his friend. He patted him on the back; they started for the door.

Jenny had relieved Sarah so she could change to take Mrs. Cooker to Mrs. Nelson for her appointment; Mrs. Cooker was sitting at the table, talking to the children before she left.

Sarah changed quickly into a simple dress, rushed out of the room, almost collided with Ned, George in the hallway. "Sorry Ned, I didn't see you; Mrs. Cooker is ready when you are," she said, fiddling with a zipper on the side of the dress that had started to give her trouble. "Sorry George, you okay? I'll come back, help you get together after we're all done," she said in her most causal voice; she was nervous.

"Thanks, Sarah. It's okay; we'll all be busy today, that's for sure," said George trying to seem just as causal, but Ned could feel the electricity between them in their body language.

"Ned, you ready?" Mrs. Cooker called out from the kitchen.

Jenny had already put her things in the wagon; they had packed enough food to keep everyone at Mrs. Nelson's happily fed until their return for the wedding. She also made a basket for Mr. Hedley, who she knew was still running around with his own business.

"Coming, mama," Ned said, quickening his steps. "Got to go; I'll be back within the hour, George, if you want to talk some more" they reached the living room; the decorations were already stacked in small piles.

Mona, the children, stood up; she said, "Uncle George, are you ready to start; the weather will be beautiful all day" she walked over to Mrs. Cooker.

"Mrs. Cooker, you're going to be so surprised; it's going to be magical," she said, hugging her again.

Ned, Mrs. Cooker left; everyone else went into full-scale cleaning, cooking, and decorating. Baby Sasha's was placed in her bassinette to keep us company while putting the decoration around the house and in the back yard.

Mr. Herman had brought ten long staked kerosene oil lamps that would be used to light the path to the gazebo, around the dinner tables that they would bring out, set when Ned returned. He had also brought twenty-six-foot-long bamboo stakes that he put a hole near the top that they would be able to tie the paper bells and; streamer on.

Jake would dig tiny holes to put them in, creating a paper canopy leading to the gazebo.

"Okay, team," Jenny said. "Children, I want you to start cleaning up your rooms, put away your clothes so we can sweep, mop. Kelly, Sarah, and I will get going with the main cooking until Uncle Ned comes back. Mona, Jake, Uncle George will start making; decorating the canopy leading to the gazebo and the gazebo itself. Then they can start with the area where the dinner tables will be, the rest of the yard, then the house; by that time, you guys will be able to help after you've finished your rooms" she was watching the roast beef out of the corner of her eye's she wanted to cook it three-quarters of the way; finish it later.

"Everyone knows what they have to do; Thomas, Margaret, please don't forget to clean up the bathrooms, all of them. Mainly give the sink, tube a little wash; they are mostly clean already. Just give them a once over. Remember, we don't have a lot of time; we have three hours to have anything ready; to get ready ourselves," Aunt Kelly said, taking out another pot to give to Jenny for the beef stew.

"Okay," Thomas said, then Margaret said, "Okay, mama" they went off together.

They all went in different directions to their assigned duties; prepared the house for the most momentous day they ever had.

Ned sat beside his mother, looking at her from the corner of his eyes, was happy to see her smiling; she had genuinely smiled so few times of late; it seems all that bothered, ailed her was way in the back of her mind.

He wanted to tell her, but the timing did not seem right on their drive to Mrs. Nelson to celebrate her special day; so, he was taken a little back when she quietly asked, "Ned, when are you going to ask Jenny to marry you?" she turned her body towards him for good measure; looked into his eyes.

Ned was so shocked he almost fell off the wagon, but he realized there was not much he could keep from his mother's very discerning eyes. "Well, mama, I was going to tell you this week, but with everything, I kind of just wanted you to have your special day. I want to ask her tonight," he whispered back. "I bought her a necklace, ring set in purple. It's sitting at home in my drawer right now as we speak," he said, finally glad he told her or more as she told him.

"Oh, Ned," she almost yelled, "I'm so happy for both of you; I was just telling Jenny that you would once you made up your mind. I gave her my blessings; I am giving you too. I am so happy for you both; this is the best wedding, birthday, or any day gift I could ever get. Congratulations, son; make sure you ask her before the wedding so she can wear your gift. I am so proud of you, son; oh my, Mabel will be one happy woman in heaven today. Now, if we can only get George, Sarah, to stop their dance," she said.

"You know about them too?" Ned asked; she was uncanny like that. "Thank you for your blessings, mama. It means the world to me, to us; I love her very much. I can't wait to make her my wife," he said excitedly. Now he lightly lashed the horses for them to move faster.

Ned dropped his mama off and went in with her to Mrs. Nelson's; he only stopped long enough to hug and kiss her; he went over to see Herman.

"Morning, Herman," he called out from the backyard as he went to pick a few vegetables that they needed for the cooking today. He did not want him to do anything today either but knowing Herman Hedley.

"Morning Ned, how's everything, everyone doing? Must be crazy in the house by now," he said, wiping his hand on a dishtowel. Then he said, "Ned, all you had to do was ask, I'd bring the vegetables you needed."

"It's a little crazy, but mama is finally out, over by Mrs. Nelson getting her hair done. We just need a few things. Besides, you are not supposed to be doing anything today but getting ready for your wedding. I will be back later to help you finish dressing; get you to the wedding on time. Calvin will be picking up mama, Sarah, Mrs. Nelson to bring them to the house." Ned said, rushing around the garden to get everything; go.

"You sure you don't need anything or help Ned," he asked, ready to give him a hand.

"Thanks, but I'm finished now, Herman," he said, plucking up the last of the cabbage he needed for the coleslaw. He went over, shook Herman's hand, said, "Thank you, Herman," he said, smiling ear to ear.

Ned put the baskets in the wagon and went to Mr. Beatly to pick up the flowers, Mr. Spillman's liquor, ice, tubes; he still had a lot of work back home to do.

Thirty minutes later, Ned started back home within the hour. His mama was getting her hair gone, having a great time catching up with Gracie, who filled her in on everything that the Townspeople talked about their gift to the Beatly's, other news.

Ned arrived to find George, Jake, and Mona decorating the gazebo and making the canopy that led halfway in the yard.

Sarah, Jenny, Kelly, worked on the food; almost everything is done or halfway cooked. They began to put the mini pastries, cakes, and other finger foods they had prepared on the silver trays.

The children were in the living room tying paper bells, hearts, and angels into the holes Herman had drilled into the bamboo stake. So, George, Ned could place them in the ground; put the streamers on before standing them up.

They moved the four large folding tables tucked into the corners of the kitchen; places them in a line on the sheets of wood Herman had put down. Jake and Mona covered them with the new tablecloths.

Jenny and Kelly quickly arranged bouquets for each table; they also made small bouquets and tied them to poles. The two strings of lightbulbs that hung in the yard were not enough. Large and small candles were placed around the house, on holders, and the tables; they put all three large standing candles near the table that held all the food. The liquor table was placed under the tree closest to the house; the tubs with broken pieces of ice were placed on either side of the table. Once all the cooking, decorating, cleaning, organizing was done Kelly, Sarah took their children to bathe, get dressed; Mona went off to her room, took out her prettiest dress.

George went back to his room to bathe and dress; his ribs felt much better than a few days earlier.

Jenny turned down all the stoves in the house, left the oven warming, did not pump any more air into it to fuel the embers. She was about to go to her room when Ned came in from the backyard. "Jenny, can I talk to you for a moment," he said, taking her hand and leading her to his room. He opened the door. Jenny wondered what he was up to but said nothing. She just followed his lead; he sat her down on his bed; went to his draw extracting the jewel case.

Jenny sat watching Ned curious behavior, was about to say something when Ned got down on one knee, said "Jenny Slater, I love you with all my heart, I would love for you to be my wife; would you marry me?" he said, opened the jewelry box, removed the ring; held it in his hand. Then he said, "Mama's given us her blessings too, so you don't have to worry."

Jenny was stunned; she looked from the jewelry box to the ring to Ned, said: "Oh Ned, yes I'll marry you. It's beautiful; it's an Amethyst, my favorite," she said as tears began to run down her face.

Ned slipped it on her finger, impressed that she knew the name of the stone, said: "This is the first in a long list of promises I make to love, cherish you, Jenny; I hope that you will wear this today as a symbol of our love for each other" he said kissing her gently on the lips.

She looked at the ring, then wrapped her arms around him and said, "Ned, I love you with all my heart" she kissed him passionately as a well of yearning burst its walls; all her emotions came gushing out. She could feel her nipples perk up, hardened, her body released fluids that flooded her panty; she tingled all over with an urgency to make love to him, but she pulled away, knowing that their wedding night would be worth the wait.

Ned suddenly became aware that his penis had risen into an uncomfortable, embarrassing erection; he feared Jenny would see it.

But instead, she gently put her hands on it and said, "I'm feeling it too, except you can't see mine," and they both broke out laughing over shared intimacy with each other.

Ned stopped laughing, said, "That's just one of the reasons I love you, Jenny Slater."

But before he could say more, she said, "Because I have a female erection," she was smiling her most mischievous innocent smile, trying not to laugh.

"That too, your crazy sense of humor cracks me up; female erection indeed."

Ned put his hand atop hers, over the rise in his pants. Jenny reached in, took it out of his pants, gently removed her underwear, surprising Ned and herself, and brought him down on her. In one piercing action that brought a muffled scream and moans and groans of ecstasy, Ned penetrated her jewel. They rocked back, forth in awkward movements that betrayed their inexperience and innocence. Ejaculation exploded, and it ended as suddenly as it had started.

Ned inhaled. "Oh my God, Jenny, I didn't mean for that…" He trailed off.

"You didn't do that; I did that, and it's okay, Ned. All of this is scary for me, too; everything is happening fast. I have no regrets. I feel I have been waiting a long time for your tender touch, hear your whispers and feel your heartbeat. I did not want to wait a moment longer; Jenny's arms tightened around Ned.

Ned wiped the sweat from his brow and kissed Jenny long and hard. "Thank you for sharing yourself with me; I would have waited a lifetime to have you, Jenny Slater.

Jenny was in a daze as she walked the short corridor that led to her room; her body tingled all over as she still felt Ned inside of her. Part of her could not believe she had made love to Ned before their wedding, but she felt no guilt or regret, just surprise at her bold action.

She looked at her finger and the ring box in her hand. The diamonds surrounding the Amethyst bounced light off the stone and gave the deep purple an extra glimmer; she smiled and entered her room to dress.

Jenny chose the beautiful, full-length deep purple gown Mabel had bought her two years earlier that had sat in her cabinet all this time. She had loved it instantly but had protested that she had nowhere in Fairbanks to wear such an elaborate gown.

All Mabel said was, "Maybe not today, but a woman should always have something extraordinary, beautiful in her cabinet she can pull out; wear when a special occasion happens. Do not worry, Jenny, you will look beautiful in it. If Ned and all the men do not notice you in this dress, we will take it back, get something else," she had joked. Jenny looked at the dress now with a new sense of awe for Mabel Johnson.

Come to think of it, Mabel had bought them all formal gowns, the children's suits, and dresses with room to grow for Christmas gifts; it was as if she was preparing them for a big event.

She picked up the dress Mabel had given her and hugged it; more tears fell; then she put the dress and the jewelry box on the bed.

Ned and George were the first to be dressed and out of their room; they walked around the house and lit all the large standing candles. They made sure they were not close to any windows, curtains, or in danger of toppling over by accident.

The living room walls had tiny little hooks that held several paper bells, hearts, or angels on them; a bell hung over the kitchen entranceway. They went outside, checked on the decorations, started putting the bottles of beers, wines, Champaign, the closed juice dispensers into tubs of ice.

They had not spoken anything personal until Ned said, "George Jenny accepted my marriage proposal; she's going to wear my ring, the necklace" he was smiling from ear to ear.

"Congratulations, man, you're a fortunate man Ned. Jenny's a fine woman; strong, smart, beautiful; she is sexy too," he said, knowing it would get a rile out of him; he was teasing him a little.

265

"You better watch your mouth, Georgie; that's my future wife you're talking about," Ned said, fully aware his friend was only partially joking.

"Come on, Ned, very few men in town are blind; Jenny's all woman, no disrespect intended; I'm happy for your old man. You know Jenny's safe, she's my sister, you're my brother; I'd die or kill for both of you," he said, shaking his hand then hugging his best friend.

"Thanks, George. I'm excited, somewhat anxious because I can't keep my little head behaving itself around her like before; I'm a little embarrassed," Ned said as George broke out into a roaring laugh that sent a shot of pain into his ribs; he winced and stopped laughing immediately.

"Serves you right for laughing at me," Ned chuckled.

"I'm not laughing at you; I'm laughing at me, okay, maybe you too because I'm having the same problem with Sarah. I can't even control it, Ned; that's a first for me; at least not for many years, many years now anyway," he said with confidence. "I think I'm in love with Sarah; no, no thinking here, I'm in love with Sarah," George said, looked at his friend smiling at his acknowledgment.

"I know George, you've been bit by the love bug; weren't you listening to mama, Mona this morning. I know you are still wondering when it all happened because you just woke up one day, knew you loved her; when, it was not important anymore. It happened to me; I'm happy for you, Sarah; the boys will be happy; they love you too, especially Jake," said Ned as he straightened out the tablecloth on one of the tables.

"Thanks, Ned, we are two fortunate men; it's all because of your mama's love; kindness," said George as they walked over to the wagon to move it out of the way. They had staked off an area for wagons, Calvin's, Ms. Henderson's cars further from the house, away from the backyard.

Mona, Jake would quickly decorate Calvin's car before they brought out his mama. Ms. Henderson would bring Herman home after they helped him dress so everyone would be in place.

The backyard looked beautiful, with ten of the bamboo stakes making up the canopy that led to the gazebo; the other ten were strategically placed throughout the yard. The now white freshly painted gazebo gleamed in the mid-morning sun; the white paper streamers, bells, angels, hearts that hung from the intricate trellis design of the gazebo gave it an exquisite look.

The gazebo was not the same gazebo he had grown up seeing; he marvels at what some new paint could do for something so old. They finished their final to-do list; were happy.

Mona came out of her room, headed to Jenny's; she wanted to see if she was going to wear the purple gown her mama had bought her; she knocked on the door; went in.

Jenny was standing in front of her mirror, looking at herself; she had tears in her eyes again.

"Hi Mona, you look beautiful baby, how do I look?" she asked, turning around to show that the gown floated on air.

"Oh, Aunt Jenny, you look so beautiful, it's perfect; mama would be proud," Mona said, walking over to her; she took her hand; saw the ring.

"You're just in time to help me," she did not get to finish before Mona yelled out.

"Uncle Ned asked you to marry him. I knew it. He loves you; I am happy for both of you. One more wedding," she said, started dancing around taking Jenny with her; she held up the ring again. "It's beautiful, Aunt Jenny," she said, stopping her jig.

"Yes, he did; I said yes, I am so happy, thanks, Mona. Can you help me with the necklace, earrings" she said, going to her bed, picking up the box.

"Wow, Uncle Ned pulled a Mr. Hedley; I'm impressed," Mona said, taking the box; she was nodding her head; her eyes sparkled with excitement.

"Mona, I was so surprised when he gave me a ring, then the jewelry box. I think I floated today" she giggled like a little girl, Mona, right along with her.

Then Mona asked, "When are you going to get married, Aunt Jenny?" as Jenny sat on her bed so she could put on the necklace.

"We didn't talk about that yet, Mona, everything happened so fast, but we have to focus on Mrs. Cooker, Mr. Hedley; today it's their day," she said as Mona finished putting in her earrings.

"Thanks, Mona," Jenny said, getting up from the bed to take another look.

"Jenny, you look so beautiful; let's go find Aunt Kelly, Sarah; show them," said Mona grabbing Jenny by the hands.

"Hold on, Mona; I want to put some lipstick on," she said, rushing to her dresser; it was a deep mauve color; she pressed her lips together; they went through the door.

Kelly's room door was wide open when they entered; the children were the first to see Jenny; Margaret said, "Aunt Jenny, you look amazing; mama come look," she was urgently calling her from the other room.

"What's wrong, Margaret...?" She saw Jenny standing there with Mona. "Oh, Jenny, you look wonderful, the gown. She stopped in her track, then ran up to her. "Ned asked you to marry him, oh my God, Jenny; that's wonderful congratulations, I'm so happy for you, Jenny" she hugged her, then pushed her back gently to take a good look at the jewelry she had on. Then she said, "Wow, he went all out, Jenny; it's beautiful" she hugged her again.

Then the children yelled out, "You're going to marry Uncle Ned," they ran over to her excitedly.

Kelly picks up her ring finger for a closer look. "Oh Jenny, it's beautiful, you look beautiful, royal; purple is your color, girl," she said, speaking over the noise the children were making.

"You look so beautiful too, Kelly; your yellow gown fits you; everybody looks great," she said, looking around at all the children in their nice suits, dresses. The boys had come into the room.

Sarah came into the room after hearing all the commotion. "What going on?" she asked, looking at Kelly, Jenny hugging; the children gathered around them.

But before anyone could say anything, Suzie yelled out, "Aunt Jenny's going to marry Uncle Ned," Jenny nodded.

"Jenny, that's wonderful; I very happy for you, Ned; congratulations," Sarah said, walking over to hug Jenny as Kelly released her; tears now running down their faces.

"Thanks, Sarah; I got my prayer, my wishes," Jenny said, hugging Kelly back into the fold.

Then she said, "I have two sisters I always wanted; now the man I have always loved. I'm thrilled," she hugged them closer.

Jake came to the doorway, watching all the excitement, but he was not looking at Jenny, Kelly, or his mom; he was looking at Mona; how pretty she looked in her new dress.

They heard a car horn; everyone turned and looked towards the side door; they had almost forgotten about the time; they all marched out of the room towards the backyard.

Ms. Henderson was just pulling into the yard in her father's car; it was a classic 1941 Ford Custom Coupe; she said she did not like driving it because it reminded her of losing her parents all too soon. She never said much about them, but Mrs. Cooker had told Mona that the. Hendersons had been killed about a year after he had bought that car. They had been on a trip when the yacht they had been on with friends sank in a sudden tropical storm off the coast of Florida. Their bodies have never been recovered; Heather has never been the same since; she finished school, traveled on and off for years but returned to Fairbanks to live in the home she grew up in. She was still single, completely financially secure after her parents had left her millions of dollars in assets, money. She was very private but was a wonderful woman who spent her time providing private lessons for various students around town; she also tutored children whose parents could not afford her services but had brilliant children. She also privately fully funded numerous students from Fairbanks to pursue higher education with no fan fair. The money she was paid by people who had it was promptly returned into the hands of those that did not, in the form of writing supplies, books, paper, snacks, clothing sometimes, food for the family at other times; each needy student was given a selection of books to begin their little library.

Mona would shake her head when she looked at Ms. Henderson when teaching them after learning more about her. To look at this wonderful woman, you would never know that she was independently wealthy, generous, had changed so many people's lives because she made no fuss about what she did. Those who knew; knew, but most people in town had no idea unless she touched their lives. They were asked not to mention what she did; she wanted to be anonymous; they agreed, thankful for her kindness.

Heather Henderson had come early to help the only people she had left that she felt like family. She was happy and excited to be a part of Francine's big day; her parents had been to all her weddings, but she had missed two during her schooling and then travels. She walked into the backyard, ready for the day's excitement. Hopeful in her heart that love would touch her life too, she too longed for some future sugar to sweeten her life.

TWENTY-THREE

Weddings Engagements and Renewed Love

Calvin Kimberley drove into the yard with his father's 1937 Chevrolet Sedan and parked beside Heather's Coupe. He opened his door, stepped out, rushed around to the other side of the car to open the door for Cindy, then for Mrs. Lindsay.

They walked up the short path, stopped in their tracks when they saw the elaborate decorations. "This is better than some of the stuff I saw in those big fashions, star magazine; it's simply beautiful, makes me want to get married again. Isn't it beautiful, Mrs. Lindsay?" Cindy asked, looking around.

"It is; magical," Mrs. Lindsay said. Ned and George stood there looking very handsome in their suits. "Afternoon Ned, George, you young people did a fine job for Francine and Herman. I can feel the love that went into this; the town's people should see this, then they'd be wagging their tongues off." Then she said, "Ned, help me to a seat. Will you, my boy? Your gran can't stand up like she used to."

"Afternoon, Mrs. Lindsay; I have a seat for you right over here," Ned said, allowing her to scoop her arm through his.

"Mrs. Kimberley, can I take you to your seat," George said, extending his arm to escort her to her seat in front of the gazebo; which had twenty wooden folding chairs, four long benches decorated with

271

streamers; they would be returned to the dinner tables after the ceremony.

Just then, all the children, Jenny, Kelly, and Sarah, came pouring out into the backyard; Jenny stopped them, said "Afternoon Ms. Henderson, Mr., and Mrs. Kimberley, Mrs. Lindsay; okay Mona, Jake, why don't you go get the decorations quickly for Mr. Kimberley and Ms. Henderson cars; do it right now that they are here already" she directed the other children to sit until everything had settled down, but they wanted to help too.

Jenny, Kelly, Sarah went over to Calvin and Heather to thank them for their help. "Don't you ladies look beautiful today? The place looks amazing; wow, I'm impressed, impressed," Calvin said, looking around one more time.

"I agree, you all look amazing, and the yard. Just splendid," Heather said.

"We are grateful that our first special occasion wedding is for Mrs. Cooker, Mr. Hedley; it'll give us a good practice run; it will be a complete surprise for both of them," Sarah said, looking around pleased with all their efforts.

"We are very proud, but we must confess it was the children, with the help of George, Ned who did all the decoration with Jake, Mona as team leaders," Kelly said as Mona, Jake came out with the decorations for their cars.

"Hi Jake, hi Mona, I hear you two are the creative minds behind these beautiful decorations; I'm very impressed, it looks like a picture in one of them fancy magazine Cindy is always talking about," said Calvin watching the pride Jake, Mona felt for their work.

"Thanks, Mr. Kimberley," they said together, excused themselves to go finish the cars; this way, they would not have to travel with Uncle Ned, Aunt Sarah; they could stay home.

"Mr. Kimberley, would you like a drink before you go?" Kelly asked; he nodded; she led him to the table with all the juices, liquor.

He was sober today. Ned had already given; Ms. Henderson, Mrs. Lindsay, Mrs. Kimberley something to drink.

The Beatly's came next with their son Charles, Mrs. Baker, who lived just down the road from their business; they greeted everyone at the drink table; Mrs. Beatly said, "The decorations are so amazing, if I get married again, I'm hiring your company. Ladies, you have outdone yourselves; Francine and Herman are going to be so surprised. I know she hasn't seen any of this," she said, looking around, taking a closer look at the gazebo. "Oh, the Gazebo; it's lovely," she gushed; she could not help herself; she wanted to take a closer look.

"It's the children with Ned, George, Jake, Mona as lead; they did a wonderful job," Jenny said, offering Mrs. Baker and the Beatlys a drink too.

"I'll be back," she said, excusing herself to go say hello to Mrs. Lindsay, Cindy, also taking a closer look at the gazebo.

Ned extended his arm, said, "Mrs. Baker can I take you to your seat" he smiled his most charming smile; she took his arm.

"Thank you, Ned, you're such a charmer; excuse me, I go rest my old bones on one of those seats. Ladies, I didn't tell you how lovely you look today" she walked off on Ned's arm; they could hear her saying. "This is so wonderful to see all you children taking care of Francine, Herman like this; they deserve it; those two are meant for each other; after all these years," Mrs. Baker said as they walked towards the chairs.

"Ladies, I think I'm going to have to remarry my wife after today because she'll be talking about this as much as she's been talking about our anniversary dinner.

Jenny said, smiling. "I hope that once I'm married, I'll have thirty years with my husband; that happily ever after story," she said with the sparkle of love in her eyes.

"Sometimes it is not all happily ever after, wine, and rose Jenny, a good marriage takes lots of work; even I have been in the doghouse more than a few times over the years. But this anniversary, you made me look like, feel like Prince Charming; thank you for that, ladies," Edgar said, taking a drink of his lemonade; his throat had suddenly become dry from all his emotions.

Mona, Jake started on the passenger side of each car; they were pleased with their collaboration results; so was everyone else.

"Let's tie two hearts on the door handle of the back door and then tie a piece of ribbon on it; it'll float when the car is moving," Jake said, grabbing two from the box along with the streamers and scissors.

"And let's tie the streamers on the front door handles, the angels on the front hood ornaments, and two bells on the back bumper," said Mona getting more paper angels, hearts, bells from the boxes.

They finished up, stepped back from the cars; it was perfect with not too many decorations.
Mona turned around, called out, "Aunt Jenny, we're done; come, take a look" Mona was walking around the cars to make sure everything was secure; they would not come undone during the ride, too, from Mrs. Nelson and Mr. Hedley.

"This looks wonderful; you two have a talent for this; thank you so much for all your hard work," she said and hugged Jake, then Mona once she finished inspecting the cars. "Everything is ready," she said as the grandfather clock inside the house struck noon.

"That's our cue for Sarah, Ned, to go pick up the bride and groom, Heather; you ready," Calvin asked as he walked over to Jake, Mona, and Jenny.

Heather walked over, said, "I'm ready."

"So am I," said Ned smiling, ready to go.

"Give me a moment, Mr. Kimberley. I'm going to get Mrs. Cookers bouquet, Mr. Hedley lapel flower," Sarah said, running into the house. She had gotten so caught up in the conversation with Mr. Beatly, Kelly, Jenny she had lost track of time.

They turned as they heard the wagons of Mr. Spence with his son Carlton, Mr. Parker.

Then they saw Mr. Spillman's driving his beaten-up old 1937 Ford Stake Bed truck coming down the dirt road towards the house. He was sentimental about that truck because he could have more than afford to replace it; trice, he more than had the money.

They parked or hitched in the designated spot, walked up the pathway into our little paradise; they were all men, but they equally appreciated the work; were awed by our efforts.

Carlton was the first to speak. "Good afternoon ladies, Mr. Kimberley, Ms. Henderson, Ned, Jake, Mona," he said, looking around. Sarah had just come out of the house with the bouquet, lapel flower, but he was looking at Kelly. "And I must say everyone looks so beautiful; Jake, you look very sharp in your suit," he said, reaching out to shake Mr. Kimberley's, Ned, and Jake's hand.

His father, Mr. Parker, Calvin, Ned shook hands, and they had a brief conversation before Calvin, Sarah left. "Gentlemen, we are going to pick up the bride; we'll continue the conversation later," he said, opening the car door for Sarah.

They left to give Mrs. Cooker and Sarah the most time to finish dressing. Mr. Hedley would be easier; then Heather would be shuffling off with Ned.

Jenny could tell that Carlton was nervous around Kelly because he always rambled on, so Jenny invited Mr. Spencer, Mr. Parker to have a drink, wove her arms through theirs, and walked them over to the liquor, juices leaving him, Kelly standing there.

Still nervous, Jenny heard Carlton saying, "Wow, when this family does anything, they do it right, big; this looks like a Walt Disney Fairy-tale wedding Ms. Kelly."

That boy was raised with old school manners; Jenny thought as she walked away; it was Ms. Kelly this, Ms. Kelly that; she liked it.

"Thanks, Carlton; would you like a drink?" she asked, not wanting to be alone with him, even out in the broad open daylight.

Besides months ago, Kelly had acknowledged to herself that she had some powerful feelings for Carlton Spencer. They had only talked over the past year, but she felt safe with him, protected; he was not a small man. He was tall, big, meaty, packed with muscles all over, yet Carlton was a gentle man, kind to all the children. The children came to know him during his frequent travels to Maple Lane to do his and his father's business.

"I'd like a beer if you have one," he said, surrendering to Kelly as she looped her arms through his and walked him over to the drinks table for a bottle of beer.

Pastor Hayles drove up in his covered carriage; his wife and children opened the doors; jumped out, running into the yard, yelling "This is amazing" before their parents could disembark.

They waved a quick greeting to everyone but made their way over to Ned, Jenny, who was having a conversation before he took off to get the groom. Pastor Hayle's children joined the others.

"Oh Jenny, Ned, the yard looks enchanted," Mrs. Hayles said, hugging Jenny, then Ned; her husband did the same.

"I agree your family outdid themselves this time," Pastor Hayles said, looking around.

"Thanks, sir, the children worked hard to do all this. I was just about to go pick up the groom and bring him back; Calvin, Sarah has gone to help Mrs. Cooker dress, bring her back here," Ned said, turning to Jenny to give her a quick peck on the cheek.

"Honey, it looks like you're going to have another wedding here soon" Mrs. Hayles looked down, spotted the engagement ring on Jenny's finger. "Oh, Jenny, that's a beautiful ring. Is it an Amethyst?" she asked, then said, "Congratulations to both of you; love's just pouring out of this home."

Jenny was nodding yes to her questions, said "Thank you, Mrs. Hayles; it's a wonderful surprise; we don't want to make a fuss on their day; we'll have our day," she said as Ned started walking towards the car.

"I'll be back," Ned said as Heather got in the car."

"Mrs. Hayles, Pastor Hayles, would you like something cool to drink?" Jenny asked, moving towards the drinks table; later, everyone would help themselves, but they would all be served their first drinks for now.

Jenny served them; they joined the conversation with Carlton, his father, Mr. Parker. Then she, Kelly excused themselves to go check on the food in the kitchen but removed the clothes off all the finger foods; Kelly announced, "If you would like something to munch on before the wedding, please help yourself.

Then Jenny asked, "Kelly, could you please prepare a small plate each for Mrs. Lindsay, Mrs. Baker, Mr. Spencer, and Mr. Parker? And serve them at their seats. And can you please ask Jake and Mona to serve the smaller children once they are seated? I'll check on the food," she thanked her.

Jenny put the wedding cake on the cake table.

She placed two large candles and two bouquets in the centre of the table. Then she looked around the yard; everyone conversed in groups, the women near the gazebo, the elders sitting together, and the children focused on their snack.

Kelly was sitting on one of the backbenches talking to Carlton. They were smiling the; *I'm in love with you*, smile at each other that Jenny recognized; she is predicting a fourth wedding.

"Aunt Jenny, Aunt Jenny," Mona said as she and Jake hurriedly walked over to her; the clock had just struck twelve-thirty. "What else would you like us to do before Mrs. Cooker, Mr. Hedley gets here," she asked; Jake was right on her heels.

Jenny looked around. "I don't think there's anything left to do Mona, you, Jake, have been amazing. Thank you both," she said in a group hug. She kissed Jake on the cheek; he blushed, then she kissed Mona too so that he was not too embarrassed. "I don't know what we would have done without both of you two. Everyone cannot stop talking about your decorations; it is wonderful; you should be proud, got the children organized, and work together. I am just going to take all the little plates into the kitchen when everyone is finished eating. We have half an hour to relax; why don't you two go relax; eat something," she said, sending them off.

"Thanks, Aunt Jenny," they said, ran towards the food table.

Jenny walked around, collected the used plates, and went into the kitchen to put them in the sink she had filled with hot water, soap. She picked up the wedding cake knife, the server took it outside, placed it on the table. Then she went to her room for a bit of rest; she lay on her bed, closed her eyes.

Mona and Jake stood at the food table, carefully tried to choose one of everything; they were hungry; took a glass of lemonade each. They went and sat on the bench behind the second row of chairs to keep an eye on the other children; both Kelly and his mom warned them all about getting dirty or getting into any fights. They looked so cute in their little suits, fancy dresses; it was as picturesque as any royal wedding Mona thought; Jake looked so handsome too.

"Mona, we make a great team; I hope we get to do this again soon," he said, looking around at their handy work; they had designed this; it was magical.

"I think this is just our first of many more weddings to come yah, Aunt Jenny, Uncle Ned will be next, then your mama, then Kelly," she said, looking at him to get his reaction.

"My mama, what you mean?" Jake said, looking a little concerned. "Marry who?" he asked, puzzled.

Mona could not believe Jake was so clueless about love you had to draw him a map; he is a boy, boys can be so ignorant all the time, but she thought Jake was different.

"Uncle George silly, don't you see how they look at each other, how your mama's happy all the time now, she's singing, she's dancing, smiling all the time. She gets tongue-tied around Uncle George; he gets tongue-tied, stupid; it's written all over them," she said in a matter-of-fact way that was classic Mona.

"They're just friends, Mona, yah we love Uncle George, especially Thomas, Serge but I don't think...." Jake was saying, but then he reflected on the last few weeks since their visit to the hospital for George, him coming home to live with us. That morning after, when she came home, she was different; she looked happy, not so stressed, or worried, she did not seem afraid anymore, had stopped looking behind her as much.

He looked at Mona closer this time; she always managed to surprise him with her keener than ordinary observation, like she was looking right through people, seeing their intentions ahead of time. It was a little bit creepy that she could look at something, access it so quickly; he wondered more than a few times if she could see thru him, into his heart. He was a mix of emotions he did not yet understand; he thought girls were still yucky but not Mona. With Mona, he could sit with her forever, just talk; she was cool for a girl.

"I guess you're right; they have been acting pretty giggly lately; mama's been drifting off a lot lately too; they've been talking for a long time now," Jake said, concluding she was right.

"Aunt Jenny says that's called courting a lady; all men should know how to do that, like Mr. Hedley. Aunt Kelly says he's the king of courting, should be teaching a lesson to men in town; she says it could be a business, get paid to do it," Mona said.

Jake giggled. "I can see it now, 'Mr. Hedley's School of Courting' with men lined up to pay their money for lessons" he was bent over with laughter.

"It's a great idea; there are finishing schools for women; why not a school for men, how to behave with and around women," said Mona. Then she asked, "Would you be happy if Uncle George married your mama?".

"Yeah, I'd be happy; Uncle George is cool; if he makes my mama happy, I'd be happy for her, for them; she deserves someone who can take care of her; she takes care of people," he said.

Jake had been worried about his mama. Before George, his mama was afraid that his father would find him and his siblings and carried them away.

"Aunt Kelly is in love with Uncle Carlton and he with her; they don't know how to admit it to each other, but it'll come," Mona said, looking over at Kelly and Carlton sitting on the other bench.

Jake looked at Kelly and Carlton; he could not see what Mona had seen; he saw two adults sitting down having a conversation. But when he looked closer at them smiling, looking relaxed and comfortable, he wondered if that was a show of love.

"I guess I'll take your word for it, Mona."

"You'll see Jake, you'll see," she took Jake's plate and glass and walked off.

Jake watched all the adults around him; they laughed, joked, and having a great time already. Then he heard Ms. Henderson's car as she parked it off to the side.

Mona came out of the house just in time to see Mr. Hedley, Uncle Ned, Ms. Henderson walk into the yard.

Mr. Hedley was wearing a cream-colored suit, a shirt with a red rose in the lapel button, a red handkerchief in his pocket. He stopped dead in his track, looked around the yard in utter amazement; he was speechless for more than a few minutes. "Oh, my Ned, I don't know what to say; this is so beautiful; it's amazing. Francine is going to be speechless; I am at a loss for words. Wow." he said, looking around; then he saw the gazebo; he gasped.

Everyone came over to greet Mr. Hedley, shake his hands, and congratulate him again; he was overwhelmed.

Pastor Hayles said, "Congrats, Herman, this day will be unforgettable for so many reasons" he shook his hand; his wife hugged, kissed him on the cheek; she was very fond of Herman.

Mr. Beatly was next; he said, "Herman, I can't think of two people that deserve all this more than you two: congratulations, old man. Your family sure know how to throw down for a party; I think I'll have to marry my wife again because of you; Francine now" he shook his hand, hugged him.

Mrs. Beatly came up next. "Don't mind him, Herman; we're so happy for you, Francine, your family; this is just wonderful. You look very handsome," she said, hugging him, kissing him on the cheek.

Cindy was next. "Herman, I understand you have set the standard by which all men in town will follow; your family, all that they have done for you, Francine, I'm awe-struck. I have been all over Europe, been to many weddings, many fancy parties but I have never seen anything like this. Not even in those fancy magazines for the stars that rich people purchase."

His old friends all surrounded him; they just hugged him, shook his hand, they had already congratulated him, wished him happiness, but they all had been waiting for this day.

"Herman, would you like to have a drink; maybe we could all have a drink," Ned said, spotting Steven at the drinks table; he was way ahead of him, making drinks for everyone.

"Yes, and Ned, thanks. I could use a little something for my nerves," Herman said, followed behind him. Steven had already made his way over to the table and had started making drinks for all the men, ladies so they could give him the first toast; he started distributing them as soon as they arrived.

Steven shook Herman's hand; was ready to make the first toast. "Herman, I would like to make this first toast to you, Francine, your family; I wish you all the love, joy, happiness two people could ever have," he said, clicking glass with him; everyone took turns.

"Thank you, family, this is all so beautiful; Francine is going to love it; I love it. Thank you, I feel like the richest man in the world," Herman said, looking around, really seeing everything for the first time, all the work. A tear emerged from his left eye and slowly trickled down his cheek.

The children had gathered around on the periphery of the gathering. "Herman, the children, did all the decorations with Mona, Jake as the lead, George, I help them a little," Ned said, smiling proudly. George had been sitting watching all the excitement but had come over for the first toast.

Herman put down his drink. "Come here, give me hugs, children; thank you. Mrs. Cooker will be so happy; I'm so proud of all of you," he said as they gathered in a circle; and the group hugged. "Jake, Mona, I'm so captivated with your imagination, creativity; you two have a gift, all of you. Thank you for all your hard work," he said, hugging them again; everyone's generosity moved him.

"It was our pleasure Mr. Hedley to do it for you, Mrs. Cooker; we wanted it to be special for both of you," Mona said.

"We hope you both love it," Jake said, finally speaking.

"Love it; I think it's the most beautiful thing I've ever seen, Jake. I'm overwhelmed; it's breath-taking," Herman said, hugging them again, holding both close to his heart.

George had been hanging back talking to everyone; he finished his drink, asked Steven to fix him another; that's when Ned noticed that Jenny was nowhere to be seen, so he asked, "Kelly, where is Jenny?" Ned started for the house; it was getting close to that time for his mama's arrival.

"She was here about ten minutes ago; she must be inside," Kelly said, nursing her drink; alcohol was not her friend.

Jenny was not in the kitchen or the living room, so Ned headed for her room, rapping on the door several times before he went in. He saw her lying on the bed; she looked beautiful even when she was sleeping; he sat on the bed beside her, gently kissed her. "Jenny, it's time to get up, baby," he said, kissing her again.

She opened her eyes, smiled when she saw him. "Oh my God, I fell asleep. Is Mrs. Cooker here?" she asked, shot up from the bed.

"It's okay, Jenny, she not here yet; I just wanted to find you; everyone's here already," he said, getting up so she could get up from the bed.

She went to the bathroom, used it, washed her face, brushed her teeth again. "Let's go," she said, opened her door.

"One minute Jenny," he said, took her into his arms again, kissed her. "Thank you, Jenny, for all of this," he said because he knew without her, none of this would be happening.

"Ned, this is my thank you to Mrs. Cooker, Mr. Herman, for always being there for me, all of us," she said, taking his hand.

They heard Mr. Cobbler's voice; he brought a few of his friends to play for the wedding; it was their gift; they set up; Eugene set up his bass cello awaiting the bride's walk down the aisle.

Ned, Jenny reached outside just in time to see Calvin driving down the road to bring Mrs. Cooker to her wedding; he beeped the horn several times, warning them of their arrival.

The children scrambled to line up; Suzie, Thomas, Margaret, Jake, Serge; Marie would escort the bride; would be the ring bearers. Mona, Kelly, Sarah, Jenny would be Mrs. Cooker's bride maids; Ned, George were Herman's best men; Calvin would give Francine away.

Ned, Jenny went over to shake their hand, welcome them; George had already given them a drink, Steven had made up one of the favorite concoctions for the men; just the men; he was going around refilling their glass.

When Jenny saw that, she knew the soup would be the perfect first course to reopen their suppressed appetite.

Pastor Hayles took his position in the gazebo; Ned lit the candles around it; everyone took their seats but turned to see the bride coming from the car. Ned, George took their positions beside

Herman; the women rushed over to the vehicle with the children. Jenny had collected the ring pillows on their way out of the house; placed them in Marie Serge's hand.

Calvin pulled up just behind the house so that Mrs. Cooker could not see anything until she rounded the corner with the bridal party.

They gathered around her "Mrs. Cooker, you look so beautiful," Kelly said; they all nodded in agreement.

George quickly came over, escorted Mrs. Nelson and Gracie to their seats, and retook his position in the gazebo; the music started.

"Are you ready, Mrs. Cooker? Jenny asked, organizing the children once again.

"Mrs. Cooker, you look amazing," Mona said; she would walk right in front of the bride, her escort, just in front of the ring bearers.

Eugene started playing Here Comes the Bride on his bass cello, and the possession started towards the house and gazebo.

Calvin took her arm in his and started walking; the children and women lined up in front of them. Mrs. Cooker round the corner of the house; stopped dead in her tracks "Oh my Lord, what have you children done," she gasped, genuine surprise written all over her face.

Calvin started walking again. "They wanted to give you a little surprise Francine; are you surprised?" he asked, patting her on the hand that wove through his arm.

"This is more than a little surprise Calvin; this is magical," she said, looking around as she walked; her head was bobbing left, right, trying to take it all in. She was smiling when she saw Herman, her son, George standing in the gazebo; the gazebo never looked so beautiful; she almost started crying.

"Now, now Francine, no tears, no tears; look at your husband to be he's so proud he's about to burst," he said as she took her handkerchief, wiped a tear from her eyes.

284

Everyone stood when they saw her coming down the aisle smiling; her bouquet had red, white roses, a long cream-colored satin ribbon that matched her dress, Mr. Hedley's suit.

They reached the gazebo; Calvin released her with a kiss on the cheek; they stood in front of Pastor Hayles. "Please be seated, ladies and gentlemen," he said; they sat.

"Dearly beloved today, we are here to join this man, this woman in holy matrimony. Is there anyone here that can find any reason why these two people should not be married today, speak now, or forever hold your peace?" There was silence.

"Who gives this beautiful woman away?" Pastor Hayles asked, panning the small crowd.

"I do," said Calvin smiling.

"And who gives this man away?" he asked again.

"I do," said Ned beaming.

"Francine Millicent Cooker, do you take this man to be your husband, to love, cherish, honor him in sickness, in health, for better or for worst forsaking all other from this day forth till death do you part? Pastor Hayles said.

"I do," she said, wiping a tear from her eye.

Mr. Herman Foster Hedley has prepared his vows for his wife to be," Pastor Hayles said, indicating to Herman.

"Francine, I have loved you all my life; we have been best friends, confidant since childhood; you have been a source of strength, support, love, encouragement to me; I promise to love, honor, cherish, adore, take care of you for the rest of our lives. There is no other woman that I could forsake you for in sickness, in health. I promise to love you for the rest of our lives; I do," he said, wrapping up his vows.

"Can I have the rings, please?" Pastor Hayles asked; Serge gave him Francine's ring, Suzie Herman's; he started to pray. "Lord, I am asking you to bless these rings as these two beautiful people come before you in wedded bliss; bless them, bless their families, give them long life, marriage in your name; Amen. They all said Amen.

Pastor Hayles gave Herman a ring, said repeat after me, "I Herman Foster Hedley take this ring as a testimony before God; and man of my love, commitment to you."

Herman repeated, put the ring on Francine's finger; then Pastor Hayles repeated the same for Francine; gave her the ring, she repeated to him and placed it on Herman's finger.

Then Pastor Hayles said, "Who God has brought together, no man breaks asunder. I now pronounce you husband, wife. You may kiss your bride," he said as they kissed.

Cheers went up from everyone as the bride; the groom turned to face us; they looked so happy.
Everyone had a little bit of rice and confetti in their hands; once they started coming down the stairs, they released the tiny pieces of paper, rice in waves after wave over their heads.

Mr. Cobbler, his friends, started playing some songs that Mona did not recognize, but it added to the festivities.

George, Sarah escorted them to their seat at the table; as soon as everyone got up, their chairs were moved back to the table for seating. Steven popped open several bottles of Champagne, poured theirs first; then he went around the tables; even the children got a small taste.

Ned gave the first toast. "Please join me in making a toast to two of the finest people here in Fairbanks. Mama adopted Papa; I wish you all the love, joy, blessings, happiness that life can give you both. Thank you both for teaching me how to be the best man I could be, being role models for all of us," he said, clicking their glasses; they drank.

"Thank you, Ned," they said.

Then Jenny stood up and said, "Francine, Herman; thank you both for being you; you have both impacted my life in so many ways I wouldn't know where to start. I wish you love; every happiness in life," she said, becoming emotional she sat down; then excused herself; went to the kitchen to start serving their food.

Mona spoke next, then Kelly, Sarah, George, who all got up to help in the kitchen as the toasting went on and on.

They brought in the trays off the table, served out the entire finger foods onto small plates, and took them to everyone on the tables; then they went to get the small bowls of soup and served those next.

The atmosphere was a celebration with the family where everyone talked, laughed, drank, and ate while complimenting the bride, groom, and family. Jenny's mini-finger foods were a big hit.

After some time, Jake, Mona, Margaret took out the three salads; served them at the table, starting with the bride, groom.

Ten minutes later, they put the rice and peas, vegetables, sliced corn all in large serving bowls, started serving those to each person. Then they carved up the roast beef, roast chickens, ham, put them all on serving trays along with the fried chicken, and served each person.

The children, Ned, George, the women gathered in the kitchen; their meals were served; they went back to their seats at the table, eat with everyone else. They had set out numerous gravy boats on the table for everyone to help themselves.

"Children, this is the best meal I have eaten that I never cooked in all my life," Francine said, looking around the table as everyone was busy eating, talking, laughing, having a good time. Then she said, "Jenny, thank you for making sure everything runs right; I love you all," she said, becoming emotional.

"You're welcome, Mrs. Cooker, I mean Mrs. Hedley. What should we call you now?" Jenny asked, smiling.

"Well, Jenny, this is my fifth last name. Sometimes I am not even sure what to call myself," she said, giggling from the two glasses of Champagne she had had. "Now it's, Mrs. Hedley," she said, kissing her new husband, who smiled with pride that she would carry his name only. It would be hard to get away from Cooker; everyone knew her now as Mrs. Cooker.

Everyone had finished eating, sitting, enjoying each other's company, including the band.

Jenny, Ned, Kelly, Sarah, George got up, started taking up the plates off the table, stacking them carefully in the kitchen sink. They would give everyone some time to digest their meal before cutting the wedding cake, serving dessert.

They served several more rounds of drinks again, with Steven making more of his unique concoctions, opened more Champagne pouring generously.

Eugene Cobbler, his friends, went back to their instruments with their drinks, started playing some soft music at first; they played songs like; *Unforgettable, You Belong to Me, Heart and Soul, Tenderly, I Went to Your Wedding, I'm Yours, Be My Life Partner, Hold Me, thrill me, Kiss me.*

Herman got up; said, "May I have this dance Mrs. Hedley?" he asked, kissing her on the hand.

Francine giggled and said, "I would love to dance, Mr. Hedley" he took his bride to the dance floor that we had created. They had their first dance. Others soon joined them after the first song; the party began.

They then played livelier music, hoping to encourage everyone to the dance floor; the children ran and took it over; after four songs, Herman, Francine returned to their seats.

It was getting dark, so they turned on the stings of light, lit all the kerosene lamp stakes, all the candles, which gave the backyard a soft glow but still provided enough light to see everything.

"I love you, Francine; you have made me the happiest man alive," Herman said, kissing her one more time.

"I love you too, Herman; you've made me very happy," she said, taking his hand, looking around at the beautiful group of people who came to celebrate this day with them.

"Francine, I'm going to go speak to some of our guests; I'll be back, my love," Herman said, kissing her on the cheek. He stood, walked over to where Mr. Parker, Mr. Spencer, Mrs. Nelson, Mrs. Lindsay sat talking; she could not hear, but there were many more congratulations, pats on the back.

She looked on the dance floor and saw the young adult, older ones alike; Cindy and Calvin looked comfortable with each other; maybe they could find their way back to each other, Francine thought.

Kelly, Carlton looked very cozy; she knew there was a budding relationship there, but Carlton was painfully shy, like Ned; it took some time for him to act too. George, Sarah danced slower than the music playing; they looked like they were in their world. Ned, Jenny looked like young love; they talked while they danced; Jenny just glowed in her purple gown; she looked royal.

The children weaved between them, having fun. Everyone was smiling, laughing, giggling after one too many drinks; the children were just themselves. They never needed anything to get them having fun.

Francine did not notice Mona until she said, "Mrs. Cooker, I mean Hedley, I'm so happy for you, Mr. Hedley; mama's here smiling, dancing with us" Mona hugged her tight; she had tears of joy.

"I know Mona; I feel her too; she's been with me all day. I want to thank you, Jake, for all your work and amazing imagination. I would have never in a thousand years think of all this; when you said you all wanted to surprise me, surprise us. This is more than a surprise, baby; this is....it like a fairy-tale. I am sure even Walt would be mesmerized with you and Jake's work, maybe even a little jealous. Yes, I know the others helped, but this came from you, him, very extraordinary. It's like a magical enchantment; it looks even more beautiful with the candle, torch lights; whose idea was that" she asked, looking around.

"It was Jake's, Uncle George; once, Aunt Jenny suggested we take this outdoors, but it was a team effort. We wanted to give you, Mr. Hedley, a fairy-tale wedding because you both deserve it. You both do so much for us, for everyone all the time we wanted to do something for both of you; something you would never forget," Mona said with the excitement of a child with a new toy; she was holding her hands.

"Well, Mona, I have been to a lot of weddings, had a few myself; even been to some rich folks' ones, none of them could even come close to this. You, Jake, will be in charge of decorations for the business; if that is okay, we will pay for you both. This is work, lots of work; you should get paid for it," Francine said, hugging her again. "Now, where's Jake? I want to thank him myself too," she said, looking for him, but he was on the dance floor with Mrs. Nelson. He was taking turns dancing with all the older women just to get them out of their seats for a song or two; that was so sweet, Francine thought.

Then they saw Ned coming off the dance floor with Jenny heading for them; he asked, "Mrs. Hedley, my I have this dance?" he bowed, extended his hand like an old fashion gentleman.

Francine smiled at her son, proud that she had raised a fine young man who would be a husband soon himself with a wife and children. "I would love to, Mr. Cooker," she said, getting up, taking her son's hand. "Mona, Jenny, I'll be back; I'm going to dance with this handsome young man; don't tell my husband if you see him," she said, winking at them; Ned escorted her to the dance floor they were enjoying the moment.

"Thank you, Ned; you, George, the women, and the children have given us such a wonderful gift. I feel blessed, very blessed; I keep looking around; I cannot believe this is our backyard. Our little old gazebo has been transformed into all this wow; it seems so enchanted even now. Everything is perfect, the food, the music, all our family, the decorations, and the cake is remarkable.

"Well, mama, I just followed the women's instructions, directions, did whatever they wanted me, George, to do; it was a labor of love, I can assure you, mama. Everyone wanted to play their part in making this day special and happy for you, Herman; the children couldn't wait for you to leave," he said....

"I noticed; they just about put me out this morning," she said, laughing.

"They were just excited; they all knew what they had to do. Suzie, Serge were so nervous about not remembering or getting it wrong; they had poor Mona, Jake almost pulling out their hair when they wanted to rehearse over, over again," he said, laughing.

"Those women are pretty sneaky because I didn't have a clue about any of this; they're good.
I just wanted something simple at home, very low-key, did I mention simple," she said, smiling.

"I'm not complaining, mind you, because this is simply beautiful, I will never forget; talk about a wedding to top all my other marriages, this is it.

"Mama, I'm glad we could do this for you; it seems like everything just fell into place for this to happen. Jenny coming up with the idea, me telling the Beatly's we would make their anniversary dinner, then your wedding; soon mine. It's like we got an opportunity to showcase the business while showing people we care about love," he said, not wanting to distract from her night with the official announcement of his engagement to Jenny.

"Jenny said yes, oh congratulations Ned; why didn't you say something," she said, thinking about him, Jenny.

"No, mama, today is for you, Herman; Jenny, I will have our day too very soon," he said, spinning her around.

Ned felt a tap on his left shoulder, stopped as Mr. Kimberley stepped up, asked, "Ned, may I have this dance with the lovely bride," looking from Ned to Francine.

Ned bowed gracefully, passed his mother's hand to Calvin's; they began to dance; he went back to stand with Jenny, Mona.

"Francine, I have never seen you look more beautiful, happy. Congratulations again to you, Herman; he's a great man; they don't make men like him anymore," he said.

"Thank you, Calvin. He is one of a kind".

"I'm looking around, thinking if I were ever going to get married again, I'd hire your family; this is amazing. Cindy cannot stop talking about the decorations, the overall presentation, the food, you know how she loves these sorts of things, and all this is her world. She says she's been to exclusive weddings that didn't even come close to this; she's completely spellbound, blown away," he said as the music played softly in the background.

"I live here, Calvin; they did all this behind my back, planned everything; they told me nothing, sent me away, but you know that, knew more than me. They conspired together for two weeks, but I can't see how or when they had time to plan the Beatly's anniversary, my wedding at the same time; and do everything else," said Francine looking closer at Calvin himself.

"How are you, Cindy doing, Calvin; you look much more relaxed, more at peace; I'm happy to see that. I was hoping that you two at least tried to talk out some of your pains, hurts; it's been a lifetime," she said, looking straight into his eyes.

"Well, Francine, ever since Thomas's funeral when you told me that I had to forgive myself so others can forgive me. I was so troubled about him, about Mabel, about Mona, about Cindy, about everything I was not sure I wanted to live; then Cindy showed up. We have been talking about the past; it is a lot of pain, but it is very healing. Most of all, Francine, I couldn't have survived without your love, support, forgiveness; thank you," Calvin said with tears in his eyes, raw emotions in his voice.

"It's okay, Calvin. We all have things we regret, should have done, or did not do. It is all a part of our journey; we all have a chance to change course. Even this wedding, I did not want to even think of Herman as more than my best friend and confidant, but who else would love me more than my best friend over our lifetime. Life is rather bizarre like that sometimes, will hand you a fresh start when you least expect it. This feels like a fresh start for all of us, don't you think, Calvin?" she asked, but she already knew the answer; yes, it was.

"It feels like one Francine, it feels like one," he said, looking over at Cindy, who was dancing with Herman; he had forgotten how much she loved dancing. He watched her and realized he could fall in love with her again. They had talked, talked about this, that, her travels, life in Europe; his despair, troubles with Michael McIntyre; why the boxes in his living room.

"Calvin, are you alright?" Francine asked. He seemed a thousand miles away for a moment.

"Sorry, Francine, my mind just drifted off," he was saying, but she interrupted.

"You are thinking about Cindy? Love is a funny thing, Calvin. You can't control love".

"I know Francine; it's just that there seems to be so much distance between us, so many secrets still. She wanted to know if I had gone through the boxes, suggested I burn them all because it is all the past, not always a good one. I could not disagree with her, but maybe there are things I should know; I think I want to know. I'm confused, Francine; those boxes all feel like Pandora's box; maybe that's why I've hesitated every time I go to open one," Calvin said with a perplexed look on his face. "I'm sorry, Francine. I shouldn't be talking about bad memories on your special day," he apologized, feeling bad now.

"Sometimes the bad memories help's you also to remember the good ones, Calvin; you can find happiness; just let go of the past; set your house in order, forgive and forget. I agree with Cindy. You can do nothing about what happened in the past unless you change it. You know there is nothing good in those boxes," Francine was saying just as Herman walked over with Cindy.

"Calvin, may I steal my beautiful wife away for the next dance? I will exchange her for your equally lovely wife. Cindy, we don't say ex or ex's around here like most big-city folks because around here, you'll always be Mrs. Kimberley," said Hermana laughing at his joke, but he wasn't kidding; they knew it.

"Sure, Herman, but I may have to steal her back for one more dance later; congratulations to both of you. Thank you, Francine," said Calvin and kissed her on the cheek.

Calvin took Cindy's hand and danced with her.

The band suddenly stopped; Kelly asked, "Could everyone please gather around the wedding cake so that the bride and groom can cut it? We can serve dessert." She started to walk towards the table with the cake when she noticed Carlton staring at her with love, longing; she recognized that look; she had felt it herself.

Maybe she, too, would get her heart's desire. "Come on, Carlton, let's go," she said, holding out her arm. He hesitantly wove his arm through hers; their flesh tingled with the touch of the other; they knew they had found each other.

Everyone gathered around the cake; Herman and Francine fed each other the first pieces amid clapping, toasting, and drinking.

No one at the table could deny that Mrs. Cooker's team had planned, timed, and executed the presentation and service like some of the world's best maître d's at the finest dining establishments in the world.

Mrs. Cooker got everyone's attention. "Wow, can you believe it? I'm speechless," she said. "I agreed to Herman's over-the-top marriage proposal, under pressure (it was a five against one situation)." (Clucking). "This beautiful engagement ring and other jewelry Herman presented me must have cost a small fortune." (Chuckles and clucks). "The only thing I asked for was a simple wedding at home; after all, I already had three marriages more than most people." (Clucks). "I am the proudest woman, mother, and wife in Fairbanks. Jenny and Ned, congratulations on your engagement; I wish you the best in your future together," applause. "To George, my son; Jenny, Kelly, Sarah, Mona, my daughters, and all my children, thank you all for this unforgettable day. And finally, Herman Hedley, I love you today as I have always loved you; you were my first love since grade four when Penelope Stevens stole you away. I still love you," Mrs. Hedley-Cooker said to a standing ovation of claps and laughter.

Herman kissed his new wife.

"Well, ladies and gentlemen, I don't think I can top that speech or try to; all I can say is that I am overwhelmed with all this" he waved his arm around the yard. "The kindness, love, and support we have received from our family and friends are touching; I will never forget it. Ned, Jenny, I have watched you two grow into two fine young people; I wish you a lifetime of happiness, congratulations. Kelly, Sarah, Mona, Jake, children, thank you for your gift of love. To Mr. Cobbler, your fellow musicians, thank you for setting the mood" (Chuckles). "Francine has been the love of my life, my best friend and confidant, and now my wife" (Chuckling). "I remember Mabel at this moment; she always thought we were meant for each other; I thank her for that. I will always love you, Francine, always and forever.

Francine stood up to hug and kiss her new husband. (Cheers, laughter, tears).

The evening was warm with a light breeze that stirred the leaves and caused the streamers to twirl.

The band returned to playing, and the adults returned to dancing; the children were running around the yard playing tag between the dance floor, the gazebo, and the yard.

Kelly sat at the table with baby Sasha and talking to Carlton. She gave baby Sasha a tiny taste of the cake icing; she had been slowly introducing different tastes, textures, and flavors to her.

"Sarah, I think I want to go lie down for a little bit," George said, getting up. She got up, helped him to his bed, and made him as comfortable as possible. She stayed with him for a while, keeping him company until he fell asleep, he was tired, plus a few too many of Mr. Spillman's unique concoctions will do you in every time.

Sarah returned to the kitchen to find Jenny washing dishes; she had her apron on, had taken off her ring; put it on the table. Jenny was a workhorse, Sarah thought, put on her apron to help; before long, they were breezing through the piles of dishes that had accumulated on the tables, counters, in the sink.

"Congratulations, Jenny; it's been so crazy today; we haven't had a chance to talk. I'm happy for you, Ned," she said, stopped to hug her.

"Thanks, Sarah; he completely shocked me when he asked today; I'm a little overwhelmed by everything; it's turned out better than even we had hoped. I am proud of our work; we make a great team together. You will be; next, you know; George will ask you any day now, I know it. He's crazy about you; I know you are about him; besides, it's getting harder, harder for you two to hide your feelings," Jenny said, resuming her washing.

"It's that obvious, uh?" Sarah asked, resuming her rinsing, stacking. "I'm scared, Jenny. I have been married already; I have three children already. Do I want much more; is it fair to George who has no children of his own," she said, rambling on with just some of her self-doubts laid out before Jenny.

Sarah stacked dishes upside down on several clean towels to dry because there were so many of them.

"Sarah, George knows all of that; it hasn't stopped him from getting close to you, your children; besides, George adores your boys; they adore him. He has always put your children; first, all the children in this house George calls his children…." Jenny was saying when she was cut off.

"That's my point, Jenny, but none are his," Sarah said with a bit of coercion in her voice.

"Sarah, that is the point; George would protect with his life all the children in this house just like he would his own; there is no difference in his eyes. George started out caring about your children, spending time with them, sharing with them, and bonding. You happened way later, and I think both of you did not even know it was happening until one day you both woke up one morning, said to yourselves, I love that man, I love that woman; when did that happen. Am I right? Jenny asked, draining, rinsing out the sink, setting fresh soapy water for another batch of dishes; Sarah did the same but minus the soap.

"Okay, Jenny, maybe you are right about that part; yes, I did wake up one morning, realized I had feelings for George, but it's only been since that first morning in the hospital that I knew he cared for me too. I always knew, but a woman wants to know that the man wants her too, more. Now I am just a bag of emotions, daydreams, wet panties," she said, blushing and then giggling, surprised she was sharing such intimate details with Jenny.

"Sarah, I know what you mean because if Ned didn't ask me to marry him soon, I was going to stop seeing him alone; it was getting too hard to behave if you know what I mean, and I don't want to," said Jenny giggling at her clever innuendo towards Ned's manhood. She could not stop smiling because she was enjoying her first, completely open conversation with Sarah. "Sarah, I don't even know what I feel because I've never felt it before; it's all new to me, but one thing I can say is that I'm looking forward even more to our wedding night," she said shocking Sarah, even herself.

They burst out laughing, understanding perfectly well that their anticipation was part of the excitement in their minds; that is wrapped up in emotional investment, time spent getting to know their man; in Jenny's case, a lifetime.

"Hi, ladies, want to share? Ned asks, walking into the kitchen with another stack of dishes; he put them on the counter nearest the sink.

"Thanks, honey, it's just girl talk," she said, enjoying the freedom to express her love for Ned in words, not be on guard like she was keeping some clandestine secret; she felt relieved, excited.

"Do you know about how many more dishes out there, Ned? Jenny asked, trying to track time.

"We have quite a few more stacks," he stopped, laid out another series of towels, and then went for more plates. Ned returned a few moments later and started drying, repacking the dishes back into the storage crates. He did all the stacks, went for more dirty dishes; he was a speed demon.

"Jenny, Ned is a wonderful man; I'm happy for you. When's the wedding?" She asked, placing another stack of dishes on the towels.

"We haven't even talked about that; it happened so quickly, besides it's Francine, Herman's day, so we wanted nothing to interfere with that; we'll have our day too," Jenny said, draining the sink, refilling it again; Sarah did the same.

Ned brought in two more stacks, went to find the mosquito net for the bassinette for baby Sasha, took it to Kelly; the bassinette was placed on a small table beside Kelly's chair.

He came back, dried more dishes, and stacked them neatly on the kitchen corner counter.

It seemed they were slowly outgrowing the kitchen, may have to expand a wall before they had the restaurant finished; but that would be more work for Mr. Hedley he did not need right now, Jenny thought as she watched Ned trying to find space.

"Hey ladies, the business is growing faster than we have space to put all this stuff," he said, filling in the last space on that wall.

"I was thinking the same thing," Jenny said.

"Me too, wow; it's funny it didn't look this much when they first started coming in, but now," said Sarah looking around the kitchen at several stacks of clean, dirty dishes on the counter and tables. She did not see any of the dozen or so trays she knew they had put out or the twelve glass jugs but saw about twenty dirty glasses waiting for them on the other table; it seemed no one reused their glasses. It was going to be a long night, she thought, long day, she had never had such a wonderful day in her life; she smiled at the chaos that she now loved.

"Oh, Ned, leave out about twenty plates, bowls, dessert plates, etc., for people to have more food later. We still have soup, beef stew, fried chicken, and more roast beef, ham, rice, and peas, leftover keeping warm. We want to give everyone something more to eat because we ate so early in the day; this might go on for quite a while still," Jenny said, finishing that stack of plates draining the sink, refilled it; she wiped her hand, took off her apron. "I'm going to go see how much food is still on the trays outside, maybe bring some in to wash; we've got to clean as we go, or tonight we'll be heartbroken about the giant mess. I'll be back, Sarah; thanks," Jenny said.

"Congratulations, Ned, I'm happy for you, Jenny; she a whirlwind of energy, Ned. I hope you're ready," Sarah said and broke out into giggles.

"Thanks, Sarah. I am not sure about a whirlwind, a Tsunami, maybe. That woman is a Tsunami like Mabel," Ned said, stacking more plates. "And I'm happy for you, George...." She interrupted him.

"He's been talking to you about me. What did he say....no, I do not want to know," she said, confusing even herself.

"It's okay Sarah, George loves you very much; just give him some time, you'll see. Sometimes we men big, strong as we seem we have questions about ourselves too you know.

We question ourselves all the time. Are we good enough? Can we provide a good life for our wife, family? How are we going to do that? We are more critical of ourselves than women in general, at least the men in this house anyway. The only thing that matters, Sarah is that George loves you, the children," he said, hugging her when she started crying. "Where is George, anyway, haven't seen him for a minute?"

"I took him to have a nap; he was hurting a little," Sarah said, draining the sink again, gave it a good clean down, and then filled it.

Jenny came back with three trays stacked on each other, followed by Jake and Mona, and put them on the table.

Ned wiped her tears, released her from another hug, and went over to hug Jenny.

Mona, Jake came into the kitchen; he ran over to his mama. "Mama, are you okay?" he asked, suddenly concerned; he never liked seeing his mother cry; it brought back bad memories.

"I'm fine, Jake; these are tears of joy," she said, hugging her son tight; she let him go, resumed rinsing dishes.

Jake looked at Mona puzzled, but Mona already guessed the conversation was about George; she had that look on her face; that happy, crying snot was running down your nose, smiling in love face that women get.

Jenny released Ned from his hug and asked, "Mona, Jake should we start taking down the bamboo stakes outside so we can start putting away some of the decorations? I do not want us to take a chance on it raining. What you think, remember the children will be asleep or too tired or having too much fun to want to help," she said

"It's okay; we'll wait till almost everyone is gone before we start taking them down. The stakes we can wash off the bottoms lay them carefully in the living room; untie the decorations tomorrow if we are too tired. The lamps we can put in the ground under the roof by the Barn; they won't get wet, but we'll pack up everything before going to bed," Mona said; Jake nodded his head in agreement.

"We can go take the decorations off Mr. Kimberley, Ms. Henderson cars, around the house now," Jake said, looking from Jenny to Mona, who nodded her agreement; they were off.

"Let us do one more round of washing, then let us go outside; have some fun too, ladies. You know what they say about all work, no play," Ned said, looking at his wife-to-be.

"What do they say about all work, no play Ned?" Jenny asked, clearly teasing him.

"It makes a dull Ned that what they say, Jenny. It makes a very dull Ned" He finished wiping, stacking the last of the plate, took up ten small dessert plates, forks, etc., took them outside, put them on the small table. Then he went around, collected all their empty plates, trays from the tables.

Mona, Jake walked to the front of the house, went over to the cars with the box for the decorations.

"This is one of the best days I've ever had in my life," Mona said, turning to Jake. "And working with you all day, yesterday was the most fun of all," she said, started taking down the paper balls, angels, and the heart and folding them and put them away.

"It been amazing for me too, Mona; I've had the best time working with you; I'm proud of what we did. Plus, Mrs. Cooker says she is going to pay us for our work; this will be our job; that will be nice," Jake said, carefully rolling up the streamers, placing them in the box.

"We can pay Margaret, Thomas them too," Mona said, excited that they had their first paying job. "Hey Jake, did you finish that picture for their wedding gift?" she asked, plucking the last of the paper decorations off the car.

"Yes, I did; it's on the table covered up; I hope they like it; I've never done a portrait of two people before. Thanks for helping with the eyes; your eyes always look so real, lifelike; it's kind of creepy but cool," he said, rolling another streamer. Then he said, "I almost didn't get it done; it was crazy this week, but thanks to your help." They moved to the wagon, finished that, returned to the backyard, did the stakes closest to the house, on the periphery; they left the box at the side of the house.

"Come on, let's go dance Mona, I like that song; it's not the same as on the radio, but they're pretty good," Jake said, pulling Mona with him to the dance floor; he was that excited.

Mona liked this side of Jake; he was coming out of his shell, looking happy for the first time since they had come to Mrs. Cookers' all those years ago.

Jake dragged her right into the middle of the dance floor where all the children were dancing; as a matter of fact, everyone was dancing, smiling, talking altogether, and enjoying themselves.

Jenny, Kelly, and Sarah got the older men onto the dance floor. Mr. Spillman said, "I don't dance," but then he reluctantly went on the dance floor and had a ball.

George awoke from his rest, looking refreshed. He rejoined the party. Ned and Carlton went to get the women; even old Mrs. Lindsay was on the dance floor with her cane shaking her old legs. The older folks had a different way of dancing that made Mona laugh and even dance like them.

Ms. Henderson took off on a visit to the lady's room and stayed for ten minutes. George carried her onto the dance floor; there would be no sitting around. George got her dancing with Steven, who had also verbally declined their invitation to the dance floor. But liquor, music, food, family, friends, the safety of feeling at home plied with more alcohol had a way loosening up even the most conservative of souls. Steven, Heather was no different; before long, they talked, laughing, spinning, twirling, dipping, and dancing close along with the music, everyone else.

They looked comfortable, at ease with each other, which was a huge bonus considering they both went silent around the opposite sex unless they worked with you. They were painfully shy but had bonded over a few of Steven's unique concoctions; Steven, Heather had entirely relaxed by the time they had hit the dance floor.

An hour later, the band took a break so everyone could have a rest, more food, or something cool to drink after the long musical set; they were all sweating, thirsty. Some women had more liquor as Steven poured generously of what he had donated for the wedding party.

302

Finally, Gabriel came and went straight to the bride and groom to apologize and congratulate them, briefly explaining his absence was due to an emergency he had to deal with in Maple Lane. He had to help with the transport of a group of criminals Federal Marshall Courtney Campbell had to take across several State lines before being transported to the next Marshall. These men had their gang attack another Marshall in a few towns south of here, he had explained.

"Not to worry, Gabriel, we knew there was a good reason you weren't here; now go have a drink, eat something; I want a dance later," Francine said, tapping his hands. He hugged her, shook Herman's hand congratulated them again; he walked over to Steven, Calvin, who were standing together talking.

"Gentlemen, I use the term loosely," he said, using a phrase he used since their teenage mischief, rampages together.

Steven hugged him, handed him a drink, and said, "Good to see you, old man; what criminal activity held you up this time." Steven did not want an answer; Gabriel always had some of the most outlandish stories to tell, including some of their adventures.

"How is it going Gabriel, you look a little tired old man; you, okay? Calvin said, concerned about his old friend; they were three of the four Musketeers of their youth; he knew Gabriel had taken on a lot covering three towns as the lead Sheriff.

"Same ole crap different day; you know the spiel," he said, taking a long drink of Steven's concoction. Then he said, "This is delicious, but I want to know now; will anyone here be able to walk or drive home after a few of these, Steven? He asked, finishing the glass, holding it out for more.

"I hope not," he said, refilling Gabriel's glass again, his own, and Calvin's.

They did not notice Jenny, who had walked up with food on a tray. "Okay, gentlemen, you can't be plying Sheriff Gilmore with liquor on an empty stomach. Mr. Spillman, please take the jug with you to the table; he's got to eat first; he looks like he hasn't had a good meal in days," Jenny walked towards the table, which was set for the old friends to sit together. On her tray was soup, salad, an assortment of meats, rice with peas.

"Thank you, Jenny. You are right. I haven't eaten a proper meal in two or three days," Gabriel took his seat at the table.

"You two want anything else to eat; I can make you both 'the works plate.' It contains a little bit of everything. Mr. Spillman, I have your favorite beef stew, Mr. Kimberley, your favorite stuffed Cornish hens," Jenny smiling at the men who looked like they had had too many drinks already.

"Thank you, Jenny," Steven said; he was in his happy zone.

"The Cornish hen would be great with the works." Mr. Kimberley said.

Jenny, you look lovely. And the decorations in this place are beautiful; This is amazing." Gabriel said.

"Mona and Jake are the lead decorators; the other children, George and Ned, helped; they did a great job," Jenny said. She left the men alone to continue their conversation about decorations.

Sarah, Kelly, Ned, and George, who looked refreshed after his nap, were in the kitchen, fixing food plates.

The children had gone out to find Jake's rooster Monster and Mona's chicken, Chickpea. They enjoyed the game of chicken, chasing children around the yard, and pecking at their heels. The game, though fulfilled, was over when the evening turned into night.

The big celebration ended. Everyone was well fed, liquored up, and ready to disperse to their places of abode.

Jake and Mona offered to help with cleaning up.

"No, Jake, you two have done enough; go get some rest," Jenny said, walking back to the sink to finish the stack of dishes while Sarah, Kelly, George, and Ned collected all the remaining food, trays, serving bowl, jugs, glasses, cutlery from outside.

Jake hugged Mona at her room door "Night Mona," he said, quickly kissed her on the cheek; he smiled shyly and walked away.

"Night, Jake," she said and went into her room; that was the second time he had kissed her on the cheek; she was happy. Mona reached her room, took off her clothing, got on her nightgown; she said her prayers, thanked God and her mama for blessing the day. She fell asleep happy that everything had gone so well. Her mama was waiting for her in her dreams.

TWENTY-FOUR

Love Leads the Way

Mona looked around in amazement; her eyes filled with joyful tears. She had been dreaming about the launch of Ms. Mabel's & Mrs. Cooker's Family Restaurant Bakery; the day arrived.

Love permeated the atmosphere, and Fanfare was all around.

Business would open for lunch hour service for the first time; all Mona could do was turn around in slow circles and looked at everything—the handy work of Mr. Hedley, his men, Mr. Zimmerman, and everyone. It was incredible, splendid, superb, overwhelming, breathtaking, grand, very humbling; those were just some of the words she could think of off the top of her head.

Mr. Hedley, his men, had built two large windows at the front that let in lots of natural light; the bottom of the building was done with all yellow bricks, which we never expected, another surprise from him. The upper part of the building was made of horizontally placed planks of wood painted white, positively affecting yellow bricks and white walls.

Inside, he created three wood and glass showcases, one standing six feet tall with glass, wood doors that opened, and layers of wood shelves lining it. The two others lined two of the walls closest to the original kitchen exit. He had built enough space from the walls

A G ELLIOTT

so they could move around quickly, stack, serve from behind the showcases. He had used quality highly polished wood that caught the sun's beams; reflected more light into the place.

He had worked with Mr. Zimmerman to build four bench booths that seated eight people comfortably at each. Then they worked out the number of tables distributed throughout the space; came up with ten large tables able to seat six to eight; ten small tables able to place two to four comfortably. They also added a few more tables in Mr. Spillman's Bar, installed two new booths, refurbished his tables, chairs. Mr. Hedley had created a proper kitchen that held three of Mr. Cooper's stoves now, plus two of mama's old stoves. We could not let them go.

Jake, I had decorated each table with fresh flowers in a small vase with red, white ribbons tied into bows. The tables were set with cutlery, glasses, a white cloth napkin for each person, and a water jug. All the showcases were filling with various kinds of cakes, loaves of bread, pastries, biscuits, potpies, etc.; everyone was running around trying to put the last of the things in their place; Mona just stood there in the middle of everything, mesmerized by it all.

"Mona, what else do we need to do? Mona, are you okay?" Jake asked again because Mona seemed a million miles away.

"Yeah, Jake, I am okay; I am just a little overwhelmed about mama's dream coming through, that's all; it's more beautiful than I imagined. Mr. Hedley, Mr. Zimmerman; their men are amazing, wow," she said, turning to Jake, who was just standing there watching her spin around and around.

"It does look amazing, Mona; everyone's excited too. It is almost time, Mona. What else do we need to do?" No answer. "I think we're done; what you think?" Jake saw that Mona was still in la-la land, so he started putting away the boxed decorations in the back himself.

"Mona, you go stand around looking all pretty turning around in a circle looking at the place Chile," Mrs. Cooker-Hedley said as she

307

brought out a large tray of Jenny's bacon biscuits, put it on the top shelve of the showcase.

"Sorry, Mrs. Cooker, sorry I still have to get used to Cooker-Hedley; it's a mouth full. I can't believe it; it finally here; it's beautiful," Mona said, still spinning around.

"It's beautiful, Mona, Herman and, Mr. Zimmerman did a wonderful job for us," she said, stopping to take another look herself. "Your mama must be very proud; I can feel her everywhere in this place" she looked around again. "Mona, Jenny wants to talk to all of us before we open, so please go get everyone together in here," Francine said.

"Yes, mam," Mona said as she went through the second door Mr. Hedley had built leading to the storage room. It was lined with shelves all along all four walls, sectioned off by supplies; cutlery, glass, dishes, decoration, etc.; you get the idea. Four long tables were built in front of each shelving section to allow us to organize, prepare.

Jenny had hired two young men 'Peter Manley on days, Fredrick 'Freddie' Smith on nights' to help with the dishes, two young women 'Simone Grant on days, Rebecca Cole on nights' to wash napkins, tablecloths, iron them; their duties also included the aprons, dishcloths, kitchen towels to help Mrs. Baker.

Ned was helping two new hires, 'Oscar Finely and Norman Newton, to help with clearing and re-setting tables the way he had trained them.

"Uncle Ned, Aunt Jenny wants to meet with everyone before we open," Mona said, poking in her head.

She went to the other side of the room where Jake, Thomas, Margaret, and Marie were putting away the last of the decorations. "Come on, guys, Aunt Jenny wants to talk to everybody in the main room," said Mona as they finished up their packing, trailed out behind Jake.

Herman had put more shelves in the storage room at the back of Mr. Spillman's Bar. "Mr. Spillman, Aunt Jenny would like to see everyone for a meeting before we open," she said, walking outside.

"Okay, Mona, I'll be right there," Steven called out from behind a pile of boxes stacked on a shelf.

"Hi Uncle George, Aunt Jenny wants us to meet now," she said as she passed him on her way outside.

Outside she turned right, entered the door to the cleaning room, which was large, well ventilated; it was the dishwashing, tablecloth, napkin washing, cleaning area that had been set up with its small stove to boil water for the washing tubs.

"Mrs. Baker Aunt Jenny would like to have a meeting with everyone before we start," Mona said, walked through the inner door to the kitchen where Jenny, Kelly, Sarah, Mrs. Cooker was checking all the pots; watching the last of the loaves of bread bake before they set them out to cool on the racks.

The smell of fresh bread permeated the kitchen even with all the windows open and the two side doors. They took out the loaves of bread, put in the second large roast, ten more chickens to bake; they would be cooking all day, hoping to keep up with the crowds.

Jenny looked around one more time, said "Mrs. Morgan, if we're not back in twenty minutes, take out the chickens, don't forget to rotate the metal plate in ten minutes, so the chickens brown evenly. Oh, please keep one eye on the grits...." Jenny was saying when Mrs. Morgan interrupted her.

"Jenny, don't worry, everything will be fine; it's okay," she said, taking her by the hand, hugging her. Mrs. Morgan would stay in the kitchen; watch the food while Jenny held the final meeting before they opened.

"Let's go get this meeting going," Francine said, ushering Jenny, the rest of us through the kitchen door into the main building.

The children were seated at the table by the kitchen door that also doubled as the staff table, which was partially hidden behind a partition with built-in small shelves for sugar, salt, pepper shakers; on top slots were made for the menus, pens, and small paper pads to write each order. The four new waiters, two young women 'Pebbles Porter, Tiffany Victor, two young men Marlon Senior, Albert Green, would all rotate between days, evenings; however, today, they would all work all day.

Everyone stood waiting for Jenny to start, impatient to get back to what they were doing; they had less than an hour before the door would be opened.

"Hi everybody, I just wanted to thank everyone for all their hard work helping to make this dream a reality. Marlon, Pebbles, I want you to stay in the Bar, serve the customers there; Tiffany, Albert worked in the restaurant but helped each other when you see the need. All the orders are written down, posted in the kitchen; when your order is ready to be served, keep track of everything on one bill, and collect it at the end of the meal.

Francine, you, and Kelly will be in the bakery, Mona and Jake can help you both today, but they can float; help whoever needs more help at the time.

George will help Mr. Spillman in the Bar until Frank comes in later; all alcohol will be sold, paid for separately; that's okay, right, Steven?" she asked.

"I think we should keep the Bar separate, so there are no mistakes or mix-ups," he said, nodding.

"Ned will float, help wherever he is needed; everyone else knows what they are doing.

Francine, would you like to say something, maybe a prayer?" Jenny asked and then reached for Sarah's hand, held it; she held Kelly's until they were all holding hands.

"Dear heavenly father, we want to thank you for the blessing you have given us to bring us this far in our celebration of the love, life of Mabel Johnson. Thank you for your continued blessing as we start this next stage of her dream; bless everyone here who has decided to work with us, keep us safe, ask your blessing for this day, and many more. Amen," she said; everyone said, "Amen."

"I think the only thing left to do is to tie the ribbon across the door for us to cut to do the official opening. Mona, are you ready with the scissor to cut the ribbon?" she asked, but she saw the piece of ribbon, scissors sitting on the table near the front door. "Any questions?" she asked, turning to look at everyone; they were all shaking their heads to indicate no. "Okay, everyone, thanks, you know what you have to do. Thank you," she said, started for the kitchen.

Jake went outside, tied the ribbon across the entrance, and came back inside.

"Thank you, Jake," Mona said, looking out the window because people were beginning to gather, mainly women, their children.

"No problem, Mona; you ready?" Jake asked because she looked a little nervous, a first for Mona.

"I'm just so excited Jake, hope everything goes perfect," Mona said with a look of excitement, dread.

"Even if everything doesn't go perfect, Mona, it'll be okay; it's our first day; so, don't worry so much; besides, there's nothing we can do when the thing is going to go bad; it's how we handle it when it does go bad Mona," Jake said with wisdom beyond his years.

"You're right, Jake," Mona said, sat down at the table looking around while everyone buzzed about them.

Jake sat beside her, looked around too to see if they had forgotten anything, but everything looked in place, ready, even the ribbons they had tied to the planters at the front door.

More people were gathering outside; they looked like they had dressed up to come out to lunch. We hoped the local newspaper would come but hired a local photographer anyway to document the moment.

Mrs. Cooker had matching black skirts; pants made for the men, women; they all wore white shirts, a small black apron around

SHADOWS OF THE PAST: TURNING POINT

their waist. The business name was embroidered on their shirts, with small name tags.

"Besides Mrs. Cooker, Jenny, Mr. Spillman will be outside cutting the ribbon with you; that's lots of company," Jake said, watching his brothers over at the other table, looking like they were ready to start running around and play.

They still had about half an hour, so he decided to take them for a walk around the yard out back; they could sit outside by Mr. Spillman's flower garden. He turned to Mona. "Hey, Mona, want to go sit by Mr. Spillman's garden with us. They look bored; Thomas is twitching, that means trouble," he said, taking her hand, leading her towards their table. "Come on, let's go out back, but you can't get dirty, okay; you have to promise," he said, reaching their table; they nodded, followed him, Mona out.

"Hello children, where are you all going? Mr. Hedley asked, coming in from the back with a large vat of homemade beeswax polish with some Bari Olive oil dropped in it. He had explained to me that their olive oil made everything shine like a brand-new penny. He had been using it on all the wood in the restaurant, had those young men we hired polishing every inch of wooden walls twice. The first time was to polish, let it sit on the wood for an hour or two, and then go back and polish again, doubling the shine. He had the young women doing the same to all the tables, counter area. They were learning right from the get-go that everyone was responsible for cleaning, keeping the place Spic & Span at all times, no matter your position.

He even had Mr. Spillman, Ned, George polishing the entire Bar area; it was a complete overhaul of the place. As he said in the meeting, there was no way he would create this beautiful restaurant without giving the place that started it all a revamp. He insisted he had all the supplies he needed to cover the Bar, but Steven still insisted on contributing to the upgrades.

They agreed with a two-hundred-dollar handshake; Steven would keep his workers happy at the end of the day with drinks or two.

The women always fed the staff, set a budget in their operations cost for just that because everyone should walk away with their paycheck; it was our, we are good to you, you are good to us policy.

"Just taking them out back for a couple of minutes, Mr. Hedley, they are getting antsy just sitting around waiting; that's trouble waiting to break out. We're just going to sit by Mr. Spillman's flower garden," Jake said as they passed him in the small hallway.

"Okay, but don't get your mama's upset by getting dirty now but have fun. We'll be ready in half an hour to open; everyone excited?" he asked, stopping momentarily to double-check his old Waltham pocket watch. He said it was passed on to him from his great-grandfather; it was over a hundred years old; it still worked like a charm; Mona had never seen him without it once, ever. He said with all that he had aside from us, his family; it was his most important possession, he would one day pass it on to Ned because he did not have any children of his own; Ned had been like a son to him.

Mona never told Ned any of this because after Ned's father had died, Mr. Hedley was the only fatherly male role model that had been consistent in his life all his life.

"We won't, Mr. Hedley; we know we'd get licks today, right guys," Mona said with authority as Margaret, Thomas, and Marie nodded their heads that they knew.

"Have you all eaten? Eat now because you know once that door is opened, it will be a crazy house. Jake, why don't you and Mona get some sandwiches and drinks. I'm sure you all are hungry by now," Mr. Hedley said, which they hadn't even thought about while running around finishing up. But now that he said it, Mona became aware of her stomach.

"Come to think of it, Mr. Hedley, I am hungry; anybody else needs food?" Jake asked. They nodded.

"Then sit outside; Mona and I will serve you," Jake said, walking off so Mona would follow.

"Mama, can we bring our food outback?" Jake asked.

"Oh my, we plum forgot to feed these children in all the madness, rush, I'm a little hungry myself come to think of it," Francine said, getting a tray, started to place a variety of sandwiches. "Mona, go get some chips; come on, Jake, help yourselves, now. I'll take care of the men, Kelly; you take care of the women".

Mona and Jake went off with trays of food and drinks.

Jenny did not budge. She ate her sandwich while she stirred, tasted, turned, poked, and prodded the food she had been preparing.

Francine watched Jenny from the prep table in the kitchen, where everyone, including her, sat. "Jenny, you remind me of Mabel; remember, she always kept working when everyone else sat down to eat. Come, sit down, digest your food properly, Chile," she said, looking at Jenny and seeing Mabel standing in front of her.

"I will in a minute Mrs. Cook...Francine, but time is running out," she said, remembering that she wanted her to call her Francine now; because Mona was right, Cooker-Hedley was a mouth full to keep on repeating.

"We're right on time, my darling; everything is ready; come on, sit down, eat something," Ned said, coming into the kitchen; he had a half-eaten sandwich in his hand. He kissed Jenny on the cheek, took her hand, and led her to the table with the other women. She sat down reluctantly. "Okay, just for a few minutes," Jenny said, still watching the pots; the oven.

"Jenny, we're fine stop stressing," said Ned taking the last bite of his sandwich. "I'm going to make sure the children are okay" he walked out the back to find them in the garden.

"Later, ladies," Herman said, walking into the kitchen; he went over to kiss his wife.

"You ready to go out front, Francine? Steven is ready; Ned's going to get Mona" Herman took her hand; she had just washed them; took off her apron.

"Okay, I guess it's time," Francine said, taking Herman's hand; they walked out of the kitchen together into the main room where Mona, Steven stood waiting for them.

They walked out the Bar entrance and walked over to the restaurant entrance; there were about fifty women with their children; a few men waited to enter.

"Ladies, gentlemen, thank you for coming out to the grand opening of Ms. Mabel & Mrs. Cooker's Family Restaurant Bakery, the re-opening of Spillman's Bar. We honor the memory, life of Mabel Johnson, who started this dream, her daughter Mona who inspired us to continue her dream, will cut the ribbon to open our new restaurant," Francine said, moving away from the door so Mona could cut the ribbon. Steven just stood there beaming like a Christmas light.

Mona cut the ribbon, opened the door, and stepped aside to allow everyone to walk in. People were visibly taken aback by the beauty inside the restaurant; Jake, Margaret, Marie, all four waiters started seating everyone as they came in, distributing them throughout the restaurant. It was divided into six sections with numbered tables; each waiter had their area to serve.

Mona, Steven, Francine walked through the doors themselves after everyone had entered, been seated; they could tell already that if more people came, they would quickly run out of space. The Kimberley's, other workers would also be there for their regular lunch; Mr. Hedley had wisely put in two long tables, ten stools on two sides of the Bar to provide for single diners.

Francine held hers, Mr. Spillman's hand, said, "I'm so very proud of both of you; look around, see what love made happen" she walked them further into the restaurant; she had tears in her eyes.

"This is what love made," she said again as Steven took out a handkerchief; handed it to her.

"No more tears Francine, this is supposed to be a joyful day; let's have more smiles than tears," Steven said, hugged her then Mona. He was getting emotional too, so he said, "I'm going to go help

George, the team at the Bar" Steven walked away before tears started to fall from his eyes.

He went straight to the back room to compose himself, scolding himself for being so emotional at his age; he was dropping tears like a little girl of late, something he has never done before.

"How you are feeling, Mona," Francine asked, wiping away some tears; she hugged her again.

"I'm thrilled, Mrs. Cooker; it's all because of you, Jenny, Ned, Mr. Hedley, Mr. Spillman, everyone else working to help mama's dream become a reality. I'm grateful, thankful for all that everyone has done," Mona said, choked up with emotions.

Francine dabbed Mona's eyes, repeated Steven's words, "No more tears; this is a celebration. Come on, let us go help the others" she walked over to the entrance of the kitchen, Mona went, stood in the bakery section as children stared at all the delicious baked goods in the showcase.

The restaurant's noise was cheerful; people complimented staff on a job well done; everyone was smiling, eating, talking, and having a good time.

Mona picked up one of the sample trays that had small pieces of Jenny's bacon biscuits, proceeded to walk around so everyone could taste a sample. She gave the children at the counter some first; then, she moved on to the tables. They were going to push sales with a small selection of some of their products every day; it was an instant hit; they had to make 20 more batches just to keep up.

Orders were moving fast; waiters were rushing to fill orders before the real lunch crowd came. The regulars were the men from the mills, factories who helped build the business from the ground up, Mabel's loyal customers. Most of them would still sit in the Bar section for their meals because they wanted to have a pint with their meals. They were now ordering from tables instead of the table at the back entrance to the new kitchen.

"Mona, this is wonderful; what' is it called?" Mrs. Beecham asked after tasting the bacon biscuit. "And the restaurant is so beautiful your mother would be so proud; she must be smiling down from heaven."

"Thank you, mam, she would be proud; this was her dream, we are all proud, these are called bacon, veggie biscuits; they're new. You can order them with your meal or take some home from the bakery," Mona said.

"Thank you, Mona; I will have some to eat now and purchase some to take home; they are divine."

Mona finished passing out that tray, went to get another for the Bar customers, which was not much yet; only a few of the older men in town sat there. But she could see off in the distance the men coming for their lunch; you could see the chatter, excitement, even from a distance. Mona finished up and put the tray back on the bakery counter in front of the sign that said samples.

Jenny was in the kitchen yelling orders one after the other as they came in; Herman had put up a long string that the waiters would place their orders on clothing pins as they came in.

On the Bar side, Mrs. Baker unpinned them, brought them to the kitchen, yelled out orders "Two roast beef with gravy, mashed potatoes, coleslaw on the side, one fried chicken with fries, gravy, two ginger beer, one lemonade. One baked, two fried chicken, all with mashed potatoes, gravy. When the orders were ready, she would yell orders from table one to twenty and yelled out more orders.

Once customers had eaten, paid, the recipe was returned to the kitchen along with the cash; paid was written on it; cash was placed in the sales box set up in the corner. Mrs. Cooker would collect the money, put it in a separate bag tucked in a secure corner when the cash started to overflow the box.

Mona heard when the Bar doors opened, and the men came in; they stopped dead in their tracks when they saw the changes; created a bottleneck at the door. Mona called out, "The lunch crowd is here," as a warning to the kitchen that they were about to get way busier.

The waiters brought out the last of their orders; they were ready to serve the workers.

Ned, George, Jake helped take orders for the men because they had to get back to work within the hour. Jenny, the women, had started preparing for the rush by lining up plates with various sandwiches, salad, would only have to put their ordered side on the plates, which included fries and gravy, chips, mashed potatoes, etc., their drinks.

They also lined up lemonade glasses, ginger beer because they had an idea of what they would order. But they were never entirely sure because their orders always depended on how hungry they were; how much they had to spend. Everyone was served within thirty minutes of arriving, which was excellent timing by any standard.

The new business launch went like clockwork; by the end of the first day, everyone was tired but happy with the results. They had sold out all the food; it seems the entire town came out to support their efforts. Uncle Ned, George hardly had time to talk to their friends, mothers; Samuel, Jack, Daniel, who came from Maple Lane to have a meal; celebrate with them.

They had finished cleaning and preparing for the next day by eight-thirty; the children had been sent home with Kelly, Sarah, by six-o-clock, it had been a full day for them; along with Mrs. Baker, Mrs. Lindsay, the other older women.

Mrs. Cooker and Jenny thanked everyone for making the first day of the business a great success. By nine-o-clock, they all left for home; Steven Spillman was beyond happy about the day; the Bar was packed when they left. They made sure to leave plenty of chips, biscuits, and potpies to feed the hungry customers throughout the night.

Back home, Francine and Herman gathered everyone in the kitchen, brought out several bottles of Champaign, sparkling cider for us to celebrate; Herman poured everyone a glass.

Then Francine said, "Today, we celebrate a dream becoming a reality; I want to thank each of you for your hard work; commitment to Mabel's dream. It was a successful day with many more to come; thank you so much. Jenny, you are a marvel; Kelly, Sarah, I appreciate you so much, dearest daughters. Children, you were amazing, Jake, Ned, George, Herman; your contribution has been priceless. And Mona, for a ten-year-old child, you sure got some nerve," everyone laughed. "From the moment you went over to the house, took all your mama's things to want to make your mama's dream a reality, it has just been one rollercoaster ride. I thank you, everyone, here at this table. Mabel is here with us celebrating" we clicked glasses and drank.

"Thank you, everyone, for loving my mama enough to follow this dream. Love made this all happen," Mona said with tears in her eyes; she had been crying the entire day on, off, was now emotionally drained.

The group hugged each other, sat around talking about the day they had until the children started yawing, went off to bed, including Mona, Jake. Then Kelly, then Sarah, George, Jenny, Ned stayed to clean up.

Francine, Herman went back to his house; she had moved into his home after their wedding. Herman gave his horse and wagon to George and bought a deep cherry red 1947 Plymouth Deluxe car as a wedding gift for him and his new bride to travel together.

Ned and Jenny cleaned up and went to their separate rooms; even though they were engaged, they wanted to wait. Jenny had given Ned an unexpected taste of the sweet fruit; now, they were tingling all over with excitement and anticipation.

They kissed passionately; Jenny said, "Two more weeks, Mr. Cooker, two more weeks," she kissed him again, went into her room to her bed. They went to bed exhausted but happy; tomorrow was another long day of many more to come.

Jenny, Ned, Sarah, George all decided to have their weddings together; they had decided to kill two birds with one stone because time was now of the essence that they had a striving business. They did not think they would be able to take two Saturday's offs without disappointing their now growing customer base that looked forward to having lunch, dinner five days a week at Mabel's.

They had also been requesting a breakfast service, but the family was reluctant to start one so soon after the launch; they just did not have the strength of the trained staff to support that part of the business. But they were thinking about it.

This time the wedding took place in Pastor Hayles church, the reception was back at the house, the entire family worked overtime to make another fantasy fairy tale wedding for the two couples.

Francine, Kelly, the business staff worked tirelessly to do all the cooking and preparations. Sarah, Jenny had nothing to do except looking beautiful on their wedding day, the men handsome.

Herman booked their honeymoon suite in Maple Lane for three nights; gave them five hundred dollars each additional gift.

The morning of the wedding, the women were sent off to Mrs. Nelson for hair, makeup, and dressing, and the men to Herman's for dressing before the church service.

Ms. Henderson would take Jenny, Sarah, to the church in her car; Calvin would take George, Ned in his. Everything was ready for another family wedding to throw down.

At the church during the wedding Ned, George each made up their vows for their new wives, and they were so touching it had everyone crying.

Ned said, "Jenny, I have loved you my entire life; I have watched you grow into a beautiful woman; loving, caring, strong, strong-headed, focused, smart, fearless, daring. I love these wonderful things about you. I feel grateful that you are a part of my life; I look forward to being your husband."

Then Jenny said her vows, "Ned, I have loved you all my life. I love your strength, tenderness, kind heart, the man that you have become. I will cherish our love and life together; most of all, I look forward to building our lives. I love you, Ned Cooker,' she said.

Then George said his vows, "Sarah, the moment I first saw you at Mrs. Cooker's, I was smitten by your love, kindness, and your giving heart. You impressed me with your quiet strength, your fortitude to give your children a better life. Every time I see your smile, my heart skips a beat; I hope that I can be the man that will make all your dreams come through. I promise to love, honor, protect you; our children for the rest of my life," he said, very emotional now.

Sarah's vows went like this "George, when we met, my heart didn't feel anything because it was so broken, battered; I never saw love as a possibility for me anymore. But over time, you became my friend, my children's playmate, my confidence; we all grew to love you; actually, it crept up on me before I even knew it. I love you with all my heart; I promise to love you, take care of you; our family" Sarah had tears streaming down her face.

It was a cry fest for sure.

Pastor Hayles asked for the rings; they were pronounced husbands, wives, left the church in a hail of rice, confetti for the reception at the house, followed by a line of cars, wagons that passed through town with plenty of onlookers.

Dinner, liquor, and music greeted them when they arrived as Francine, Sarah, Mona, even Carlton, and everyone else went into high gear to treat them to a royal wedding experience.

Jake, Mona; children had decorated the backyard again, even more, elaborate this time; after all, it was two weddings in one. They had two head tables for the brides, grooms, more tables, candles, and more paper streamers; the dance floor was larger, surrounded by lit kerosene stakes and tall standing candles on miniature bases.

Carlton had finally started courting Kelly; it looked like another wedding could be in the plans before long, so he became part of the family gatherings, activities.

By eleven, two separate taxis had arrived to take them off to their honeymoon suites in Maple Lane.

"How are you feeling, my love?" Ned asked Jenny, kissing her one more time; he held her hand.

"I am perfect, Ned, just perfect," Jenny said, leaning on his shoulder, holding him tighter.

"Mr. Cooker, we are almost there. Do you have any special request, or would you like to make a stop anywhere?" the driver asked, watching the couple in his back seat.

"No, thanks, Charlie; we have everything that we need," Ned said because the family had two baskets for both couples that would sustain them for at least two days. They could see George, Sarah taxi ahead of theirs.

"Very good, Mr. Cooker," said Charlie as the hotel came into view; Maple Lane was full of people milling around even at eleven-o-clock.

He pulled up in front of the hotel, got out, opened their door, they got out. He then went to the back, got their bags, and the picnic baskets as the hotel staff came to retrieve them. They met George, Sarah at the lobby check-in desk; they were escorted to their rooms two doors down from each other.

Once the hotel staff had placed their belongings into the rooms, Ned and George scooped up their wives; took them across the threshold into their honeymoon suites.

Ned placed Jenny gently on the floor near the bed, kissed her on the nose; she turned around in the room to take a better look. He went to lock the door.

She was nervous now that they were alone. This would be their official night together; Kelly, Sarah had told her the first time would be painful if Ned were not gentle, but pleasure would follow; she knew. She sat down on the bed, wondering if she would please him if he would pleasure her; they had both never been with anyone to compare.

322

Ned saw her nervousness, took her hand in his, said, "Jenny, I know you're nervous, I'm nervous too. We can take as much time as we like. Let us have a drink."

"Thank you; I think it will help; I am a little nervous," Jenny said, taking off her sweater to be more comfortable.

Ned poured two Champaign glasses, brought one to Jenny.

"To us, a lifetime of love," Ned said, clicking her glass. He drank slowly.

"To us, I love you, Ned Cooker," she said, drinking her glass far too quickly. She had had quite a few drinks throughout dinner, and she had stretched her champagne glass out too often during the reception

"You sure you want another so quickly, honey; this thing will creep up on you like a thief, knock you clean off your feet," he said, filling her glass, his again.

"I'll be okay, I think," she said, not sure because she was already feeling a little dizzy. She drank only half of the second glass; put it on the end table by the bed. She got up, wobbled slightly, giggling because the alcohol had fully relaxed her, made her feel less nervous.

She got to her bag, took out her wedding gift from Kelly, Sarah, a sexy red nightgown made of lace, silk with a robe with soft fur around the collar, down the front, it also came with little slippers that matched. She excused herself, went to the bathroom, which had the largest bathtub she had ever seen in her life. She took a bath to refresh herself, put on her new nightgown, left the bathroom tentatively; she was even more nervous now.

"Oh Jenny, you look so beautiful, sexy," Ned said, kissing her deeply; he had an erection already.

She went, sat on the bed, and finished her Champaign but had no more, and her head was spinning; she lay back on the bed.

Ned went into the bathroom next, changed out of his suit, bath, put on a sleeping pant, undershirt; his muscles popped out of the shirt.

Jenny felt herself pulsating at the thought of them further consummating their marriage, love; they had waited since that night.

He went over to the bottle, poured himself another drink; he was nervous too; he sat on the bed beside her. "Jenny... I'm a little nervous; this time is different....," she interrupted him with a kiss.

"Ned, we'll be learning together," she said, taking off her robe to reveal her sassy little nightgown.

"Should I turn off the lights?" he asked, removing his undershirt to reveal a solid and broad chest and muscular arms.

"No, Ned; I want to see your eyes, your body. I want you to see me when you touch me," she said; the Champaign was taking hold of her, she laughed again.

"Okay," he pulled his pants down.

Jenny saw his full erection. She gasped at the size of his manhood.

Ned traced his lips down her neck and shoulders, gently sliding down her nightgown. He had waited a long time to see her without clothes; Jenny's skin felt like creamy, dark chocolate; she was trim and yet muscular; her breasts were firm. He nibbled each one and pleasured her slowly; his excitement stood at attention between his legs. An eruption shoots through Jenny's body in response to Ned's pull on her breasts.

"I love you, Jenny Slater; I have always loved you. I waited for this moment because you have always had my heart. You are my everything," Ned whispered as he nibbled on her ears, sending her into total ecstasy. Then he took her, and she let out a suppressed scream; it was over. They fell asleep in each other arms.

George carried Sarah across the threshold, placed her on the bed, he had kicked the door closed behind him, but now he went back to lock it.

Sarah was nervous, hoping it would not show too much, but she was slightly overwhelmed by all the past two months' events, the day. It had been years since her wretched husband last touched her; the times he did bring her no pleasurable memories. Only with the conception of the beautiful sons made the ordeal of sleeping with him bearable; what was it maybe a dozen times.

Maybe three or four times between each pregnancy; it was horrible; she had no good memories of their experience as man, wife.

She almost cried when she remembered her sad past, but she thought about George and the joyful memories she intends to make with him. She tingled at the thought.

George took a bottle of Champaign and two glasses. He poured her a drink.

"Are you okay, Sarah? What's wrong?" George asked, noticing her mood had changed; something was wrong; she had tears glimmering at the corner of her eyes.

"It's nothing, George," she said, wiping the tear that had formed; she took a long drink from her glass.

George watched her as she tried to compose, reinforce herself with the Champaign; she sighed. "You're not okay, Sarah; please talk to me," he said, putting down his glass; he reached out, hugged her, held her tight. Whatever was bothering her, he just wanted to make her feel safe; that is what a man does for a woman, a wife, mother, a sister; he protected her.

"It's just past bad memories trying to creep into these good memories before we make them more," she said, looking into his eyes where she saw love, compassion. Sarah knew she had to put old painful memories in the past, but sometimes it was like an infection that never went away but flared up expectantly every now, then.

"Mrs. Morgan, I want you to know that whatever troubles you trouble me. I love you, Sarah, so whatever still haunts you from your past, I hope I can share a lifetime making the rest of your memories erase those," he said, kissing her gently on the lips, but with urgency, he had never felt before.

"I know George. I love you," Sarah said, kissing him back but stopped herself, him, because she wanted to go freshen up, change; it had been a long day. "George, I want to go freshen up, change," she said, hugging him before she got off the bed, walked over to the table to grab her nightgown, she went to the bathroom.

George finished his Champaign and put on his sleeping pants; without the matching shirt, he hoped Sarah would want him to be comfortable, laying next to her. He knew it would be hard for him to be in bed with Sarah and not have her fully.

He was staring out the window when the door behind him open; Sarah stepped out in a beautiful red lace nightdress trimmed with fluffy fur and matching robe and slippers. She was stunning.

George exhaled.

"Sarah, you are beautiful."

"You like it?

"You have excellent taste," George said, moving closer to her. "Red is beautiful on you; I'll remember that" he kissed her deeply, pulled her gently into the bedroom, and kicked the door shut.

The old radio on the windowsill was playing; *I Love You for Sentimental Reasons*; the lights were dim.

"You want to dance? Sarah asked.

They dance until the song ended. Sarah was tingling with anticipation. George scooped her up and placed her gently on the bed; he could no longer contain his desire; his masculinity stood up to ensure her full attention. Sarah parted her legs to welcome George, and he entered without hesitation.

They climaxed together in sounds and movements and fell asleep intertwined in each other's arms.

TWENTY-FIVE

New Love Friends & Old Enemies

Mona looked at the beautiful gold leaf plated picture frame of her, her husband Maxwell Alexander Malcolm; she picked it up, looking at the happy couple they were when they had first married. It was the wedding of the decade; no expense was spared by his family, as the only child of Mr. & Mrs. Marcus and Elizabeth Malcolm, whom they loved and cherished. It was a magical time for them; they were in passionate love; they connected. They would conquer the world together. She put the picture back in place and sighed; she hoped she had not lost him forever.

She faded back into her memories.

Time moved on rapidly after the three weddings: Kelly's making the fourth in the Cooker's household. Within a year, there were three more children born to add to our growing family. Ned, Jenny had a son called Samuel, Sarah, George had a son too; they called him Oscar; Kelly finally had a son after four daughters for Carlton Spencer.

They rotated, taking care of each other's children to ensure the business's operation ran smoothly; they hired Pamela Sue to take care of them the other times. They were happily married couples, created a special bond through family, work.

Unfortunately, Mrs. Nelson died six months later; her children came to bury her, wanted to sell her home. Mr. Hedley bought it and gave it to the family; he also built a bigger house on Mona's mama property, Mrs. Nelson. He and Mrs. Cooker turned it into a bed and breakfast hotel.

Mrs. Lindsay died a month after Mrs. Nelson; the family buried her because she had no living family; she had willed her home to the family. Her home was refurbished into a fancy dress shop, with Cindy Kimberley advising them on the latest fashions taking the big European cities by storm. It was smack dab in the middle of town; Mr. Beatly helped because he saw it as a good opportunity for the growing town.

Cindy eventually convinced Calvin Kimberley to leave town; travel with her to Europe and other destinations. He was going to leave the care of the house in the hands of Ned and Mr. Hedley, who would make sure it was well maintained while they were away. Calvin looked pleased like he had found peace. However, the secrets, lies they never told each other lurked just below the surface of their seemingly happy new life together. Still, they both looked comfortable for the first time in their lives; no one wanted to disturb that. Not yet anyway.

Mr. Spillman started courting Ms. Henderson; they seemed happier than anyone had ever seen them; the family was rooting for them because they needed each other. Steven was smiling all the time now; the Bar was growing quickly along with the restaurant's addition. The business was growing so much that they had to hire five more people to manage the day-to-day operations. They had more business out of town than Maple Lane; they had Ned, George; now Carlton delivered products daily; it was a crazy exciting time; they finally invested in two 1949 Ford trucks.

The children were growing swiftly, participated in every special occasion the business was hired to do; they were paid for their work that provided extra incentive to their happy tasks.

The older children tried to help more once their baby brothers were born; they were proud to be the older sisters or brothers.

Mona and Jake continued to paint, were looking forward to going to school when they were older to become artists; they also studied hard with Ms. Henderson, excelled. Mona, Jake developed a deep affection for each other; it grew over the years before college. Mona also took an active role in developing the business, bringing new ideas to offer services along the way.

The years passed quickly with busy hands; they would be off to school soon in some big city far away. Ms. Henderson had been getting information on various art schools around the country, helping them master their newfound love, passion, and painting.

As promised, Mr. Beatly continued to support Mona, Jake with their artistic endeavors, so did Mr. Kimberley, Mr. Spillman, who competed to outdo each other. They were Fairbanks' pride; Steven commissioned several pieces for the Bar and restaurant, which he paid handsomely.

Mertel had shacked up with a new man who she had no use for other than to get a comfortable roof over her head and a free meal. She thought sleeping with him was a small price to pay for a comfortable home, somewhere to hide until she planned her next move. She was vexed with Mrs. Cooker and that little bitch, Mona Johnson, who had embarrassed her in front of everyone in Fairbanks. They were the source of all her problems; she was bitter and angry; she never faulted herself for her mishaps.

Mertel would often travel north to Fairbanks; she crept into town in the shadows. She was still in pursuit of her worthless father; she had plans for him, for them. He owed her, owed her big; he was going to pay; he would help her take revenge on those people in Fairbanks.

She was mad, fuming mad when she saw the new restaurant bakery; she thought that was her money they were using to make it successful, though deep down, she knew the reality was different. She was beating a dead horse there; she knew it; she was just jealous. Worst that she heard that old bag Mrs. Cooker got married again, how Herman had given her all those expensive pieces of jewellery; she was green. So, she plotted, plan when next they would see her ... when she was ready.

Michael McIntyre looked out the window again; he had tried to be happy with the life he now had with Leila, but he could not help missing the life he had left behind. Now he struggled to find space in the small three-bedroom house they had purchased in the small town of Dorset just north of the border of Kentucky, to just be by himself; and think.

Leila was always up his ass complaining about this and that; he was exhausted. He had grown bored of her, her nagging; complaining; she could not cook, could not clean; she expected him to hire people to cook, clean, wash for them.

He was not happy; he saw his money quickly depleting at a faster rate than it had taken to accumulate it.

The only thing that kept him going was that he was planning his revenge on Calvin Kimberley; he would have to find a way to strip Mona Johnson of the fortune he had willed to her; his corrupt mind would not allow him to think of anything else but revenge. That was his only thought; how to get back at them; somehow, he had to find his daughter Mertel. She would know things that he was interested in finding out. She would become his ace in the hole, he knew she would want something from him, but he was okay with that. He would go looking for her; he knew he would find her; they had the same goal to destroy them; take everything from them.

Michael knew he would have to get rid of Leila to move on securely; he did not trust her anymore. She was just too unhappy to be trusted now; even with all that he gave her, she would never be happy, not with this lifestyle. So, he planned, waited....it would be soon, very soon.

Sheriff Gilmore settled into his routine after his promotion with more staff and responsibilities. His focus was to find Michael, Leila, Sam, Mertel; arrest them. The fallout of Michael's theft had impacted more people in town than they had first expected, with many losing everything; they called for blood. Mertel and Sam were personal because of his love, respect for Mabel, Mrs. Cooker, little Mona. He had taken out the files often; left them constantly on the top of every pile of files that sat on his desk as a constant reminder.

Gabriel heard the whispers that Mertel came back to town on a few occasions, lurked in the darkened corners of town unseen by anyone but her few associates, who denied being her friend until when pressed for more answers or possible jail time. They told him she was still enquiring about Mona; the rest of the family cursed them upon hearing any good news about their lives. Then she was gone; they never knew when she was coming but appeared like a ghost when they least expected. Some said she creeped them out because sometimes they felt like she was watching them without their knowledge whenever she appeared. Plus, she knew their darkest secrets; they always felt like her hostage because of that fact. So, they spilled whatever beans she asked about so their bacon would not be fried when she lit her fire. Gabriel understood their fear. The more he learned about Mertel, her past, the more dangerous she became. Even six foot seven Sam Cumberland ran in fear to get away from her. He signed. Gabriel grabbed his hat, stood, walked to the door, turned off the light, left for the Bar; he was hungry, tired, needed some company.

Mr. Hedley had spoken to Gabriel on several occasions about Mertel, the various crimes she had committed against his family, worried it was not over. The content of that letter still disturbed Herman, so he, Calvin, Gabriel, and Francine made a collective decree not to tell Mona or the rest of the family about its subject matter, especially about what happened to her father. Mona would be even more devastated, angry. It became their shared secret; he finally understood the burden Francine carried her entire life, bearing other people's secrets. Herman finally understood her pain, dilemma, and sacrifice, wondered how she hadn't gone mad yet, and kept a smile on her face. The little that he knew always bothered his mind; he found himself looking over his shoulders a few too many times over the past year or so for his satisfaction; rattled by the depth of depravity of Mertel Fletcher's mind. Herman worried about protecting those he loved but recognized he was no spring chicken anymore; agile as he was for his age, time was ticking on, he had more years behind him than in front. He scolded himself once more about his inactions over the years, fear to show his love to Francine, but concluded each time nothing happened before it is time. Now he would spend the rest of his life doing all he could to protect Francine, the rest of the family from Mertel, history.

Calvin looked around at all the people as they milled past him; Cindy, they would be finally off on their first trip together, seemed happy on the surface. Yet he worried about all the secrets that still lurked between them, acting as a barrier to real intimacy, freedom to speak what was in one's mind, heart. And he worried about the secret left behind in Fairbanks that he knew could not stay buried forever. And when Calvin decided to burn all the boxes of files that had sat in his living room that would give him Cindy a clean slate to start their life together without any old baggage, he found her files.

Yes, he burned the documents but felt the weight of the content submerge his very being into its filth. He did not feel clean, even though he had changed his ways, stopped drinking, yet a drink was never far from his mind on those days of the distress of his soul. It was like the memories wanted to pull him back into the bottom of a bottle; this time, he knew he would be lost forever. He also knew there would be a reckoning when all those buried secrets he left behind were dug up for all to see; would he be forgiven; he only had desperate hope for the latter. He took Cindy's hand in his, put on a smile to hide his pain, carried on; because he knew him, Cindy had a few demons haunting them; they were perfect companions.

Cindy squeezed Calvin's hand when he reached for hers, almost to reassure him and herself that this was the right thing to do, even as she too worried about all the secrets that bubbled between them as they started a new life together. She wondered still if he had read the file as guilt washed over her like an ice bath; she shivered, held his hand tighter. Cindy realized there was no turning back now, was fully engulfed in the continued deception, lies, and secrets that marked their lives together; now, they carried their secrets close to their heart, hoping there was still space for them to love each other. She was convinced that there was but would there be room for forgiveness once all was said and done; she pulled her coat closer to her body to ward off the chill she felt on the still-warm day, walked off into an uncertain future with the love of her life.

Then Calvin stopped, as his bags were about to be packed unto the boat said, "I cannot do this, Cindy; I cannot leave Fairbanks, not like this; not with all the.... You know this is a lie, right, Cindy. I love you, but this is a lie; it would be unfair to try and live it now. I'm so sorry, Cindy please; forgive me, forgive me, I forgive you, and understand, I want you to go live your life, forget Fairbanks, forget me," Calvin said suddenly frantic, looking into her eyes, then around; to escape.

Cindy reached out to him, but the look in his eyes told her that it was over. "I'm sorry, Calvin. I'm so sorry," Cindy kept saying over, over again; she knew he was right, as much as she wanted to flee with him, she must move on.

Calvin hugged Cindy tightly and began to weep; he was ready to let her go, let go of the past, guilt, shame, hate, and go quietly into the night. She deserved to be free and happy.

"Please go, Cindy; I will always love you and be thankful for your love and our son," Calvin said, looking deep into her eyes as tears streamed down his face faster than he could wipe them away.

Cindy was too stunned to speak, so she just nodded, kissed him on the cheek, then lips; their tears mingled. Calvin handed her a handkerchief. Cindy left, never returned to Fairbanks; she died at a ripe old age of ninety-two, alone with her secrets, lies, memories, and regrets, never remarried or had any more children or love in her life.

Calvin had wept when he found out what his father tried to do to Cindy. He lamented that she took the deal; he wept at the cards, presents she sent for Thomas that was never delivered; he wept at the snide, disrespectful notes, jokes, and comments Michael, his father wrote over the years they handled the file. He cried himself into a new stupor and wept he had sent Cindy away without her knowledge of what he knew, though he knew Cindy suspected.

Calvin Kimberley returned home but never unpacked; he drank himself into a final stupor, feeling he had no right to live a life with any joy. In his last act of redemption, he lit the family's house on fire, thinking that it was fair payment for all the pain it had brought to everyone that lived in it; finally, he freed all the ghosts that lived there. He thought he heard them screaming their condemnations as the flames filled its four walls. He left the house on foot, walked to his destination, killed himself using his father's favorite gun at the exact spot Monica Johnson had died all those years ago, coming full circle.

Calvin's suicide stunned everyone, as they had seen him leave with Cindy that morning, saying their goodbyes, for now, happy for him and Cindy. It was like an ice-cold blanket over the recent joy they had experienced, wished for him. He left a final confession letter for Mrs. Cooker and Mona; they buried him in the Kimberley's plot with all the other Kimberley's, their ghosts, secrets, and lies.

Francine looked out the window one more time as a cold wind blew in from the mountain ridge lashing at the yard's trees. She looked at Herman sleeping peacefully beside her; she felt grateful, brought the blanket closer around her to ward off the sudden cold she felt; it was not just from the wind. Her mind was not at ease as it should be after many beautiful things happening around her; the marriages including her own, the births, the business, all the old, new love blossoming around her. She should be doing cartwheels, okay, maybe not at her age, but she should be happy, but the past still lurked in the corners of her life, her heart, and she fought to be happy.

Gabriel updated them on the activities of Mertel's secret visits into town; he wondered if any of them would ever be safe from Mertel Fletcher and Michael McIntyre. Sam was running for his life; jail, wanted no part in Mertel scheming.

Francine's mind was tired, Herman in the middle of it; she looked at him, blissfully asleep. Something she wished for herself but could not achieve. She snuggled down into the bed, curled up closer to Herman, closed her eyes, and hoped that sleep would come, finally.

Soon after Mona's sixteenth birthday, Mrs. Cooker was on her death bed after a long bout of pneumonia that not even Dr. Tailor, modern medicine, or any of her concoctions could cure and seemed ready to go now. She had been slowly gathering each of us for that final, personal talk, set her affairs in order. Herman fussed about her tirelessly caring for her full-time as we tried to make both as comfortable as possible; they both showing their age now. Francine had deteriorated even faster after Calvin's suicide and letter, now news of Mertel's surprise encounter with Mona six months earlier that had Mona asking new questions.

Mona remembered a big storm hit Fairbanks that night; the winds howled outside the windows of Herman's house like a wolf wanting to blow it down or break in. It was like heaven was angry as lightning and thunder competed for the most attention as if arguing with each other. Francine had spoken to everyone, even Ned, Jenny; now Herman sat beside her, holding her hands. Shoring up her strength and courage, he looked worried, sad, hurt, and a little angry, yet he kept a smile on his face every time she called his name, ready to do her will. Mona had forgotten how old they both are; now, looking closer at them, they looked tired.

Mona knocked on the door, went in when she heard Herman say, "Come in, Mona."

"Do you want me to stay or go, Francine?" Herman asked, ready to leave.

"Herman, I think I have to do this one alone, thank you," Francine said, trying to pull herself higher on the pillow.

"Let me help you, Francine," Herman said, rushing to her side, fluffing pillows and all.

"Thank you, Herman, you make too much fuss," Francine said, kissing him warmly; they hugged, he left.

Francine called Mona over, hugged, kissed her, said, "What I'm about to tell you goes back before I was born; what my mama told me, and what I know now after a lifetime of helping people keep their joys, burdens, secrets, lies. I have lived with the guilt my entire life; most importantly, I have had to learn to forgive myself, others to find peace; that is not easy to do, baby, especially when people's lives depend on you. I had hoped I would never have to tell you any of this, to shelter you always from the cruel truths of our world. Sometimes, I wish I could go back and change everything, but I cannot and have lived with that. Please forgive me, Mona, for everything," told me everything about the Johnson family history and the Kimberley's; answered all Mona's questions she could while hot tears ran freely down both our faces; we wiped them away together.

"I forgive you, Mrs. Cooker, I love you, and thank you for telling me," Mona's said, reverting to her former title. They held each other crying until Herman knocked on the door when Pastor Hayles, Dr. Morgan, came to the house; death was calling Francine to her maker; she had made her peace with him and everyone.

The entire family gathered around her bed after Pastor Hayles, Dr. Morgan spent their time; soon after, Francine Cooker- Hedley died at age eighty-five years old, quietly surrounded by family and love. We buried her beside her three other husbands with room for her current, who was the first to outlive her. Herman died quickly, quietly a year later; he was never the same after Francine's death; he let everything to Ned, especially his grandfather, father's watch, the family.

Mona pushed her diary to the side. She was famished. The scent that came from Mrs. Hamilton's good cooking invaded her senses when she lifted the cover from the dinner plate.

"Mrs. Malcolm, you must eat; you haven't eaten the meals I brought you today. I made your favorite; Roast beef, mash potatoes, gravy, and a salad, just like you taught me."

Mona raised the lid of her dinner plate

"Please, Mrs. Malcolm, eat some; Mr. Malcolm will blame me if you wither away from starvation."

"Yes, you are right, thank you, Mrs. Hamilton; I'm starving," Mona said and moved to the small table and ate.

Memories of having a meal with her mama Mabel, Mrs. Cooker, and the others came in like a tsunami. Tears flowed down Mona's cheeks. She is awash in sadness.

ABOUT THE AUTHOR

Angelita Grace (AG) Elliott was born in Kingston, Jamaica, moved to Canada before her tenth birthday, and now lives in Toronto, Ontario, Canada. Ms. Elliott is the mother of four beautiful children: Kwamiebena (Kwame), Kieoni, Kievonie, Karema, two grandchildren Zion and Jerimiah. She is also a business owner (Visions in Green), a cultural events management company, the curator of BAM (Black African Museum), International Children's Inventors Museum, and Indigenous featuring African Diaspora, Children, and Indigenous inventors, inventions, and contributions to the world and S.T.E.M (Science Technology Engineering & Mathematics). Ms. Elliott also has an African Art & Fabric museum and exhibition. Ms. Elliott partnered with the Jamaican Canadian Association of Ontario to launch the BAM STEM Scholarship in June 2021. Ms. Elliott started writing in high school, continued writing; this is the second book of the trilogy Mona's Secret Diaries shadows of the Past with Book One, The Chronicle (2020), Book Two Turning Point (2021) .

Praise for MONA'S SECRET DIARIES
Shadows of the Past: Turning point

Book two, of the trilogy offers some answers and creates an atmosphere of anticipation. Will Mabel's dream restaurant be successful? What happened to Ned / Jenny? Did Mona find love in Fairbanks? I can't wait for the answers. Grab your copy of book 2 and join me on this journey!
—**Rose Allen-Gordon, Brampton, Ontario**

The complex relationships between the characters; draw in the reader and create a seamless, intimate connection. The reader is held spellbound as secrets after secrets are revealed. "He remembered Monica. It was Déjà vu. "More secrets; Mona thought, as she watched the interaction between three of the most influential people in her life that she loves."
—**Colin St. Hill, North York, Ontario**

I had the honor of purchasing my book directly from the author. If you're looking for something fresh and new, then this is the book. This author will take your mind away from your daily life and put you in a new world that will keep you captivated for hours.
—**G Q Henderson, Mississauga, Ontario**

COMING SOON!

MONA'S SECRET DIARIES
BOOK THREE

SHADOWS OF THE PAST:
THE RECKONING

Mona Amanda Johnson was finally leaving Fairbanks for her trip on the River Grand of Life. She was ready to start the next phase of her life in a new city, had been accepted by all the historically black art colleges, universities she had applied to, but she wanted to stay close to home. Mona chooses Meadowview School of Excellence (1821), one of the oldest schools of its kind in South Carolina, because the programs were excellent, produced some of the top painters of the day, launching their careers into the world. She had meticulously prepared for her next adventure in life but was unsure of what the world outside of Fairbanks held for her; she did not want to leave Fairbanks for a big city where she would become lost in its melee of people, cars as they became more and more popular. Mona wanted to ease herself into the outside world, while Jake was excited, anxious to leave for the big city, any big city; he wanted to disappear into its melee; quietly do his own thing. They would see each other on holidays, special occasions now, but still stayed close.

Mona opened her eyes, she could see him in her mind's eyes, and she picked up, looked at the old picture of Jake that she had in a classic silver picture frame; it was the only picture she had let of him, he was smiling, his eyes sparkling with excitement. It was the day before he left for school. He looked so happy; Monster, his rooster, was still pecking at his feet. That bird knew something was about to change in its life, so he was trying to get Jake's attention. Mona drifted further into her memories of Jake, her best childhood friend that could have become more, if only. Monster, the rooster, had pecked at his

340

feet until he picked him up.

"What is it, Monster? He is one crazy bird, but I love him," Jake said, stroking him tenderly. "Remember that day when we chased him and Chickpea around the yard, and how Monster hid in the bushes?"

"Yes, I remember; the others were very disappointed when he disappeared into that bush after all that chasing," Mona said, laughing.

"Yes, but I did not think it was amusing at the time; looking back now, it was funny as hell, wasn't it?" I was too angry back then to fully appreciate the fun."

"Let us take some pictures of you and Monster. These will be great memories." She kept a picture of Jake by himself.

Jake let Monster down; Monster stayed at Jake's feet, satisfied, looking strangely proud. Still, he was a rooter, but this one had an attitude from day one; it never changed. It was all about him when he wanted you; otherwise, he paid you no mind. Monster was one of a kind; the other roosters in the yard knew it too and gave him space.

Made in the USA
Monee, IL
18 June 2021

71652579R00204